“I must hide.” Jane rushed to the large wardrobe in the corner, then stopped.

She glanced back and forth between Jasper and the door. “If Philip catches me in here, he might force us to wed.”

Jasper stopped tucking in his shirt. She didn’t know her brother very well if she thought he would force her into a marriage, even after finding her in a compromising situation, but he couldn’t take the chance. He strode up to her, pulled the shirt over his head and flung it away. “I think not.”

He took her by the arm and pulled her against him. She let out a startled squeak as she hit his chest.

“What are you doing?” Her fingertips pressed into his flesh, jarring him as much as her.

“Jane, open this door at once,” her brother demanded, and the brass knob began to turn.

“Making sure he sees me as an unsuitable suitor.” He pressed his lips to hers as the door swung open.

Author Note

When I wrote *A Debt Paid in Marriage*, I had a lot of fun creating Jane. In many ways she is as serious and severe as her brother, Philip Rathbone, but with a naive confidence and rebellious streak. They are wonderful characteristics that both help her and, at other times, create a number of difficulties. I enjoyed exploring how her old friend, and new husband, Jasper, allows her to develop and overcome both of these aspects of her personality.

Jane was a familiar character to me but Jasper was a new surprise. This is the first friends-to-lovers, marriage-of-convenience story that I have written. It was a treat to create Jasper and Jane's close childhood friendship, to explore the pain and troubles of their eight-year separation and discover how, despite the passing of time, they still remained close. Jasper sees Jane in a way she cannot view herself, and she does the same for him. Through their relationship, they both get a second chance not only at love but at life. I hope you enjoy this return to the characters in *A Debt Paid in Marriage*, and if you are new to the Rathbone family, I hope you enjoy this story and get a chance to read where it all began.

GEORGIE LEE

The Secret Marriage Pact

ISBN-13: 978-0-373-29929-4

The Secret Marriage Pact

This edition published by arrangement with Harlequin Books S.A.

For questions and comments about the quality of this book, please contact us at CustomerService@Harlequin.com.

Printed in U.S.A.

A lifelong history buff, **Georgie Lee** hasn't given up hope that she will one day inherit a title and a manor house. Until then, she fulfills her dreams of lords, ladies and a Season in London through her stories. When not writing, she can be found reading nonfiction history or watching any film with a costume and an accent. Please visit georgie-lee.com to learn more about Georgie and her books.

Books by Georgie Lee

Harlequin Historical

The Business of Marriage

A Debt Paid in Marriage
A Too Convenient Marriage
The Secret Marriage Pact

The Governess Tales

The Cinderella Governess

Scandal and Disgrace

Rescued from Ruin
Miss Marianne's Disgrace

Stand-Alone Novels

Engagement of Convenience
The Courtesan's Book of Secrets
The Captain's Frozen Dream

Visit the Author Profile page at Harlequin.com.

For Nicola Caws in thanks for valuable guidance and insight into my stories.

Chapter One

London—1825

The rat! What's he doing here? Jane Rathbone balled her hands into tight fists at her sides. She stared across the auction house at her one-time fiancé, Milton Charton. Camille, his plain and meek wife, was nowhere to be seen.

'The bidding for the Fleet Street building, a former tobacconist's shop and residence, will now commence,' the auctioneer announced. 'Do I have an opening bid?'

Milton raised his hand.

Revenge curled inside Jane. If he wanted the building, she'd make sure he didn't get it. She flung her hand in the air, upping the price and drawing the entire room's attention, including Milton's. The businessmen narrowed their eyes at her in disapproval, but Milton's eyes opened wide before his gaze shifted, she hoped guiltily, back to the auctioneer.

'What are you doing?' Justin Connor whispered from beside her, more amused than censorious. He was here with Jane's brother, Philip Rathbone, who intended to obtain a warehouse near the Thames. Jane had accompanied them because she'd had nothing better to do.

'I'm bidding on a building,' she answered as if she were purchasing a new bonnet. Thankfully, Philip had gone off to speak with an associate, preventing him from interfering with her spontaneous plan. Since she'd reached her majority last year, he no longer controlled her inheritance but it didn't mean he couldn't interfere in her management of it. With him occupied, she could spend her money how she pleased and she pleased to spend it on a building.

'I assume your sudden interest in acquiring property has nothing to do with Milton Charton,' Justin observed with a wry smile.

'It has everything to do with him.' She didn't care if she was buying a house of ill repute or what Philip thought about her little venture when he finally returned. Milton would not win the auction.

'Then by all means, don't let me stop you.' Justin waved toward the wiry man with the pince-nez perched on his nose who called for a higher price. Across the room, Milton raised his hand again and Jane was quick to follow, driving up the bid and making her old beau purse his lips in frustration. She'd once found the gesture endearing. It disgusted her today.

Milton's hand went up again and Jane responded in

kind, pretending to be oblivious to the disapproving looks of the other male bidders. She ignored them, as she did their sons when they sneered at her bold opinions, or when their wives and daughters had whispered about her after Milton's surprise marriage to Camille Moseley.

The auctioneer continued to call for bids until the other interested parties dropped off, leaving only her and Milton. Except this time Milton hesitated before he raised his hand.

I almost have him. Jane suppressed a smile of triumph as she raised her hand without hesitation. Milton didn't have the means to compete with her, or his father's astute investment sense. Thanks to her inheritance, she possessed the money, and with her business acumen she'd find a way to profit from the building. It was a pity people were against the idea of a single young lady doing it. If they weren't, she might become a force to be reckoned with in the Fleet like her brother. As it was, she was simply a spinster aunt. Oh, how she despised Milton.

Jane raised the bid three more times as Milton became less sure about the price he was willing to pay to acquire it until he finally failed to counter her.

'Going once,' the auctioneer called.

Milton tugged at his limp cravat and shifted in his cheap boots, but he didn't answer.

I've won.

'Going twice.'

Milton frowned at her, but she held her head up high in triumph. He deserved to be embarrassed in front of his associates just as he'd humiliated her in front of all their friends.

'Sold, to Miss Rathbone.' The gavel came down, sending a shockwave of critical rumbles through the gentleman before they turned their attention to the next item on the block. They respected Philip too much to say anything openly to her, but it wouldn't stop them from thinking her odd. She no longer cared. With no husband or house of her own, the building would give her some much-needed purpose and a future.

Justin tipped his hat to her. 'Congratulations on your victory. Shall we go and collect your prize?' He motioned to the payment table. They would have to pass Milton to reach it.

'Yes, let's.'

She allowed her brother's old friend to escort her across the room, not only to rub Milton's nose in her victory, but to secure the property before Philip returned. She didn't want him to find a way to stop the purchase from going through. He wouldn't approve of an expenditure based solely on revenge. He preferred rationally motivated investments. So did Jane, except for today.

She fixed on Milton as she approached him, daring him to meet her gaze, and he didn't answer it until she was nearly on top of him. Better sense advised her to continue past him, but she wanted to dig the knife in a little deeper.

'Thank you for the rousing bidding war, Mr Charton.' She was determined he experience some of the humiliation she'd endured when he'd all but left her at the altar two years ago. 'I hadn't intended to buy a former tobacconist's shop today, but I'm quite delighted now I have it and you don't.'

Milton's dough-faced shock changed to one of gloating she wanted to smack from his full cheeks. 'The building wasn't for me. It was for Jasper.'

'Jasper?' Her heart began to race with an elation she hadn't experienced in years. 'But he's in America.'

He'd left, like so many other people in her life. He wasn't supposed to return.

'Not any more.'

'Did we get it?' The voice from her childhood drifted over her shoulder, bringing with it memories she'd long forgotten. She was gripped by the thrill of running with Jasper through the Fleet when they were children, of turning pennies into pounds with their schemes and eavesdropping on his older sisters at parties. With the memories came the hope in every wish she'd made for him to come back or to send her word he'd changed his mind about their future together. The letter had never come.

Jane fingered the beading on her reticule, ready to walk away instead of facing Jasper and having her cherished memories of him ruined the way Milton had crushed his. A long time ago, the three of them had been so close. Heaven knew what Jasper must think of her now, especially if Milton had been filling his ears with stories. She didn't want to see the same oily regard in Milton's eyes echoed in Jasper's.

No, Jasper is nothing like Milton, she tried to tell herself before the old fears blotted out her reason. *Then why did he never write to me? Because I scared him off the way I've scared off every other man since.*

Stop it, she commanded herself. She wouldn't allow either the Charton brothers or her own awkwardness to get the better of her; she would be sensible, as always. *It was only a childish infatuation anyway.*

Jane took a deep breath and turned, determined to face her past, all of it, except it wasn't the past smiling down at her, but the present. The lanky fifteen-year-old she'd parted from nine years ago was a man, and taller and sturdier than his brother Milton, who was one year older. During the time he'd spent in America learning the cotton trade from his uncle, his jaw had widened, carving out the angles of his cheeks and filling in the awkward gangliness she used to tease him about. He'd grown so tall she had to step back to see his face and the light brown hair mixed with blonde streaks. He wore a well-tailored coat of fine, dark wool with subtle black-velvet accents on the collar and cuffs. It was offset by the deep blue waistcoat hugging his trim middle. Savannah had added elegance to his masculine frame.

'Mr Charton, welcome home. I never thought you'd return.' She struggled to hold her voice steady despite the excitement making her want to bounce on her feet.

'Neither did I.' He took off his fine beaver hat to bow to her, revealing the slight wave of his hair across his forehead and the genuine delight illuminating his hazel eyes. Whatever Milton had told him, it hadn't poisoned Jasper against her. 'It's wonderful to see you. I've been looking forward to it. I didn't expect it to be here.'

He wanted to see me again. It was a far cry from the boy who'd told her not to wait for him after she'd finally summoned up the nerve to admit she craved more than friendship. She flicked a bead on her reticule before she eased her tight grip on the silk. Despite the awkwardness of their last meeting, he was here, as inviting as when he used to fetch her for another adventure. *Perhaps I did mean something to him.*

She moved to speak when Milton's bitter words interrupted them like clattering cutlery at a party.

'She bought the building.'

Jane struggled to hold her smile while Jasper's tightened about the edges. It sucked the thrill out of Jane's triumph and their unexpected reunion. She flicked the bead so hard it cracked, cursing Milton and her misguided impetuousness. It was Milton she'd wanted to hurt, not Jasper.

'Congratulations on your acquisition,' Jasper graciously conceded. 'You've always had your brother's talent for transactions. I'm sure you'll put the building to good use.'

'I'm sure I will.' She buttressed her confidence against the shame undermining her as powerfully now as the morning Mr and Mrs Charton had told her of Milton's elopement and apologised for their eldest son's behaviour. 'If you'll excuse me, I must settle my account.'

'Of course.' Jasper tipped his hat to her and stepped aside. 'I look forward to seeing you again, Jane.'

Her name on his lips sounded as natural as rain on a roof. She raised her eyes to his, catching the old mischief brightening the dark irises. It brought an impish smile to her lips. *This* was the Jasper she'd cherished, and he blotted out all memory of the one who'd forgotten her after he'd sailed away.

'I look forward to seeing you again too, Jasper.' When she did, it wouldn't involve scampering in the Rathbone garden, but she was sure, and she couldn't say why, it would be fun.

The heady scent of Jane's gardenia perfume continued to surround Jasper as she walked away with Mr Connor. Jasper had expected a great many things today, but seeing Jane hadn't been one of them. It was almost worth losing the building to hear her speak, the faint lisp she'd had as a child gone, her voice a tone closer to smooth velvet. Her posture had changed too, the stiffness of her movements having gained a more graceful and fluid charm. He'd caught the spark of pride lifting her chin when he'd complimented her on her business sense. In the brief exchange, it was as if nine years hadn't passed, but it had, turning her from a young lady into a woman who commanded his attention even from across the room.

'You lost the building to that arrogant chit because you weren't here,' Milton spat.

Jasper's elation snapped like dry hay. 'I was held up.' He'd slept later than intended, exhausted from another long night and the effort of maintaining the façade necessary to hide his nocturnal activities from his family. 'And watch how you speak of her. You were the one who betrayed her like a coward. No wonder she bid against you.'

'You always did side with her against me.' Milton curled his lip in irritation, not having the decency to be ashamed of what he'd done.

Jasper frowned. It wasn't only Jane who'd changed while he'd been gone. He'd looked forward to his reunion with Milton when he'd disembarked at Portsmouth, eager to unburden himself of the anguish and torment he'd experienced in Savannah during the yellow fever epidemic, but Milton wasn't fit to be a confidant. If he told his brother the truth about Savannah, and London, Milton would use it against him when it served his purposes, or simply out of spite. He wouldn't keep Jasper's secrets the way he had when they were young, the shared knowledge binding them together as much as the closeness of their ages. Jasper didn't know what he'd done to earn his elder brother's dislike and he barely recognised the one person he'd been closest to as a child, with the exception of Jane.

He spied her across the room where she bent over the payment table to sign the purchase register. He couldn't see her face, only the elegant curve of her hand on the pen and the fall of her red cotton dress over the roundness of her buttocks. For a moment he regretted never having written to her while he was away. He could have used her friendship, especially after Uncle Patrick had accused Jasper of driving him to his deathbed while Yellow Jack had stormed through Savannah.

Jasper studied the flimsy printed auction list, shoving the guilt aside as he searched for another available property to fit his needs. There was nothing. *Damn.* The building Milton had lost was perfectly situated on Fleet Street and would have been Jasper's best chance for creating a more respectable establishment than his current one.

'If she were a proper lady she wouldn't even be here.' Milton flicked a piece of fluff off the arm of his poorly tailored wool coat. 'And if she'd acted more like a proper lady I might have married her.'

Jasper crushed the thin catalogue between his hands, wanting to thrash his brother with it. 'You're a fool, Milton, and growing older has only made it worse.'

'What's it done for you except bring you back with some tat you've been fortunate enough to sell despite the smell of plague clinging to it?'

Jasper stepped toe to toe with his brother. 'Shut your mouth before I knock your teeth out.'

Milton's smugness drooped like his backbone. Jasper threw the catalogue at his feet and strode off, done with him and the auction. His day and all his plans lay in tatters because of his brother and Jasper's own stupid mistakes.

He strode to the wide entrance door where men

continued to stream in and out to examine the auction items. He paused on the threshold to take in the street, the stench of dust and filth making him cough. An open-topped caleche passed by filled with ladies smiling and laughing together, their lives like everyone else's carrying on in the bright sunlight illuminating the street. He should be glad for the activity after the deathly silence of Savannah and heartened to see not every world had collapsed, but after so much death it was difficult to do. Few here understood what he'd been through. Milton certainly didn't.

How dare he sneer at the epidemic. The pampered prat didn't know what it was like to be stalked by death, to have all his money mean nothing because no amount of it could buy food to stave off the gnawing hunger or save those you loved from being carried off. No one around him did, except those unlucky enough to have witnessed it in other places, or those poor souls confined to the deepest slums of St Giles and Seven Dials.

A dark mood threatened to consume him when a flash of red caught his eye. The Rathbone landau rolled past the auction house, the hood open to take advantage of the fine day. Jane sat across from her brother, her profile sharp as she spoke with him, hands moving with her agitation. The dark brown curls beneath the red ribbon that held the bonnet in place bounced in time to the carriage's pace. It mesmerised him as much as her full lips. She didn't notice Jasper, but he couldn't pull his attention away from her. Seeing her again had been like stepping though the door of his parents' house after nine years in America and inhaling the familiar scent of cinnamon and brandy, the smell of his childhood.

He watched her until the vehicle rolled down the street and was finally lost in the crush of traffic. Isolation swathed him when she vanished from sight. Gone was the young girl who used to scamper with him and Milton, her surety in herself and her ideas eternally exasperating her brother and Jasper's parents. Gone, too, was the boy Jasper had been. An ocean of experience and deception separated him from everyone he'd ever known. Yet in his brief moment with Jane, he'd touched something of the innocent young man he'd once been. He wondered, if he sat with her a while, could he be carefree and blameless again? It wasn't possible. He couldn't weigh her down with the awfulness of his past or his present deceits.

He started down the auction-house steps and made for the jeweller across the street, ready to pay a pound or two for a fine walking stick or something equally expensive. His soul might be in the gutter. It didn't mean the rest of him needed to wallow there too. He'd escaped death. Now he'd make sure he enjoyed life again.

'Mrs Townsend and I trained you to handle your affairs better than this, Jane.' Philip chided from across the landau before he turned to Justin. 'You should've stopped her.'

'She's not my sister.' Justin threw up his hands in

protest. 'Besides, she'd old enough to decide what to do with her money.'

'On that point, we disagree.'

'He's right. It's my inheritance and I'll spend it as I see fit,' Jane insisted.

Philip didn't answer, refusing to be baited into the fight Jane was aching for. Despite gaining control over her money there'd been little she'd been able to do with it except pay the milliner's bill. Seeing Jasper today had reminded her of the few clever transactions she and the Charton boys had hustled as children. The experiences had given her a taste for commerce, but as her dresses had become longer her world had reduced in size until it nearly choked her. Jasper's world had expanded and, judging by his fine clothes, he'd done well for himself in America. It made her wonder why he'd decided to return. 'You knew Jasper Charton was home, didn't you?'

Philip's jaw tightened, almost imperceptibly, but she caught it. It was one of his few tells. To her surprise, he didn't deny her accusation. 'Yes.'

'Why didn't you or the Chartons tell me?' It wasn't like the Chartons not to fête a family member, especially one who'd been gone for so long and endured so much.

'Mr Charton asked me not to. Jasper had a difficult time in Savannah and needed a chance to recover. He was very ill when he came home.'

'I'm sure he was.' Mrs Charton had shared news of the yellow fever which had ravaged the port city. Jane had worried along with her over Jasper, as eager as his mother was for the letter telling them things were all right. She might not have heard from Jasper for nine years, but it didn't mean she'd stopped caring about him. Waiting with Mrs Charton had felt too much like when she was six and her own mother had been stricken with the fever. The long days had passed as she'd prayed, hoped and bargained with the Almighty to make her mother better. He hadn't listened and her mother had passed, and it'd been all her fault. 'Why did Jasper come back?'

'His cotton-trading business collapsed after the epidemic. He plans to use the money his uncle left him, and the capital he raised from the sale of his Savannah properties and goods, to establish a new business in London. Jasper needs the Fleet Street building you purchased and the opportunity it offers. Since you don't, we'll visit the Chartons tomorrow and you'll offer to sell it to him.'

'I'll do no such thing. I'll start my own endeavour with it.'

Philip flexed his fingers over the handle of his walking stick. 'Be sensible, Jane.'

'I am being sensible. I need something more to do than tend the rose garden and listen to my niece and nephews tear through the house.'

'And I've given you ample opportunities to do so.'

'Yes, always behind you and your reputation, never out in the open where everyone can see it's me successfully managing things.'

'As well as the merchants of the Fleet regard our family, they won't countenance a single young woman in trade. It would damage both your reputation and mine and hinder all our future dealings.'

She twisted her reticule between her hands, the deed to the building crinkling inside, before she let go. Philip was right. Customers and other merchants would recoil from her if she began openly to oversee some venture of her own. Jane dropped back against the squabs, cursing her unmarried state once again. 'I hate it when you're practical.'

'It's nothing but a headache when you aren't.'

The landau carried them past the building she now owned in the middle of Fleet Street. The staid façade with its small Ionic columns reaching up to the first floor sat squat between two taller ones. A round outline of dirt above the front door indicated where the sign from the now-defunct tobacconist's used to hang. She rested her arm on the landau's edge and tapped the wood. The building was hers and, despite what Philip said, she would not relinquish it; she would use it to make something of her life and escape from this limbo of being an adult while being treated like a mindless child. She needed activity, industry of her own, or she would run mad. Now she needed to decide what she'd do, and how she'd do it, without drawing attention to herself or needing Philip's help. Her brother might have her best interests at heart, but it didn't mean she wanted him or anyone else deciding her path.

She glanced across the landau at Justin who chatted with Philip. Perhaps he could be her secret front. He might help her, if only because he thought it a lark, but with his wine business and the demands of his wife and family, she doubted he had time to dabble in any endeavour of hers.

There must be some man willing to be the front for a business. She continued to trill her fingers on the trim, mulling through the people she knew and not finding one likely to support her admittedly odd idea. No one had ever gone along with her schemes except at one time Milton, and Jasper.

Jasper.

Jane stilled her fingers. She could become a silent partner with him in whatever plans he had for the building. It would be a perfect arrangement—except for her having to hide her involvement from everyone, including Philip. However, being a silent partner was better than nothing at all, and she would only have to be silent in public.

Unless I can find a husband, and quickly.

She rolled her eyes at her own ridiculousness, wondering if she was going mad from boredom and how long it would be until she began collecting small dogs and refusing to leave the house. If landing a gentleman was as simple as selecting a stock, she'd be a wife by now. Besides, all her friends and acquaintances had taken every man worth having in the Fleet, except for Jasper.

'Philip, did Jasper return with a wife?' Jane asked, interrupting his and Justin's conversation.

'No. Why?'

She shrugged. 'I was curious.'

Philip narrowed his eyes in scrutiny before Justin drew him back into conversation.

So Jasper isn't married. She rested her elbow on the landau's edge again and tapped her fingers against her chin. The vehicle vibrated beneath her arm as it crossed over the cobblestones. *And he needs money and a building, and I have both. I wonder if he'd like a wife in the bargain, too.*

She and Jasper had been friends once and friendship was an excellent basis for a marriage. After all, she'd tried affection with Milton and look where it had landed her. There was no reason not to try something more practical with Jasper. He might have rebuffed her advances nine years ago, but this wasn't about romance. It was business. She could present her proposal in rational terms, appeal to his good sense and make him see how perfectly logical, reasonable and completely insane the idea was.

She dropped her forehead into her palm. *I should buy a dog and be done with all pretence to sanity.*

Even if she was foolhardy enough to approach Jasper with such an outlandish plan, he wasn't likely to go along with it this time any more than he had before. Nor was she thrilled by the prospect of leaving Philip's influence to surrender her fortune and all legal responsibility to a husband. However, she doubted Jasper would be difficult about it, especially if they came to an agreement beforehand on how she'd manage her affairs. She was certain they could, assuming their discussions even reached the negotiating stage and he didn't turn her down outright. He probably would and she didn't relish another Charton rejection. Two was quite enough.

The landau turned off noisy Fleet Street and on to quiet St Bride's Lane. The steeple from St Bride's Church cast a thick shadow over the houses facing it. Behind the high wall encircling the churchyard lay the graves of her parents. Failure whipped around her like the breeze. She'd failed her parents years ago, now she was failing them, and herself, again.

I won't be a spinster.

Another rejection wasn't an appealing prospect, but neither was the future stretching out in front of her like a dusty dirt road. With each passing year her prospects for making her own life were diminishing. Yes, Jasper might ridicule her for proposing this scheme, but if he accepted…

She sat up straight and tried not to shift in the seat. She'd have her freedom and a life, home and business of her own at last. It might not be the loving marriage like the one Philip and Laura enjoyed, or the grand passion she used to dream about while reading the scandalous books Mrs Townsend, her sister-in-law's mother and Jane's old mentor, tutor and confidant, used to slip her, but one could never be disappointed by something one had never expected. Besides, she didn't need Jasper's heart, only his hand in marriage.

Chapter Two

'You're undressed! Why are you not up already? It's past noon!' Jane waved her hand from the top of Jasper's head to the rippled and exposed stomach, and the dark line of hair leading her gaze even lower. She was already out of breath from running up the Chartons' massive front stairs, but catching Jasper in his bedroom without his shirt was suffocating. His toned chest tinged with a honey hint of a tan nearly knocked her away from the closed door. She'd known Jasper Charton and his family her entire life. But she never thought she'd see quite this much of him.

'I wasn't expecting company.' Jasper wiped the last of the very musky and, if she was not mistaken by the scent, expensive shaving soap from his face and haphazardly hung the towel on the washstand bar. He made no move to take up the rumpled shirt sagging over the foot of the bed, and perched one fist on his hip as though it was every day an unmarried young lady burst into his bedroom unannounced. 'What are you doing up here?'

'We must speak about the building.' She fiddled with the key in the lock of the door but her shaking hand wouldn't co-operate and she gave up.

Concentrate! This was no time to be distracted. With her brother and Mr Charton downstairs, and Mrs Charton distracted by one of her grandchildren, Jane had precious little time alone with Jasper. 'I have a plan for it, but I need your help, as a friend. We're still friends, aren't we?'

His eyebrows rose in surprise. 'Even after what Milton did to you?'

'You had nothing to do with it, and he isn't pertinent to the matter I wish to discuss today.' Actually, proving to everyone, including herself, she could catch a husband was very much a part of this, but he didn't need to know it.

He cocked one eyebrow. 'You want to talk business, in my room, alone?'

She picked up one of the pair of diamond cufflinks in the dish on the table beside her, then put it down. It did seem foolish when he pointed it out, but speaking here was better than trying to whisper downstairs and risking someone overhearing their negotiations. For this to work, everyone, including Philip, must believe they were marrying for the right reason. 'Of course. We have privacy.'

'Which makes me wonder if business is really all you want?' With a wicked smile he slipped the top button of his fall through its hole. He was teasing her as he used to do and the easy familiarity of their old friendship slid between them. It was more potent than the pulling of her pigtails and she adjusted the top of her spencer, breathless once more as she stared at his long fingers on the button, waiting to see what he might reveal. Offering him her innocence wasn't an unpleasant bargaining chip, especially since she was dying to finally experience the deed she'd heard Jasper's sister whispering about at so many parties. If she got with child it would certainly force the matter.

When the fall slightly opened she snapped out of her stupor. This wasn't how this was supposed to go. He wasn't supposed to undress or suggest more than business, even if what she was about to propose involved exactly that. 'Yes! Well, sort of.'

'Sort of?' He let go of the button, but failed to fasten the one he'd already undone. It revealed more of the dark hair leading from his navel to places unknown.

'I have a building and you need one for your new enterprise. We can become…partners in your endeavour.'

The word 'marriage' twisted her tongue. She still couldn't believe she was doing this. One would think she'd learned her lesson nine years ago. Apparently, she hadn't.

'Your brother won't be happy about you wading so openly into business. Or being up here.'

'I don't care what Philip thinks and I wouldn't be single when I share in the trade.' Jane took a deep breath, the portion of the negotiation she'd spent the better part of the night and this morning contemplating, and dreading at last upon her. 'I would be your wife.'

Jasper's smug amusement dropped like the towel off the rail of his washstand. 'My wife?'

'It's perfect, don't you see?' She hurried up to him, drawing close enough to feel the heat radiating off his skin. She took a cautious step back, acutely aware of how much taller and wider he'd grown since he'd left. She tried not to be distracted by the more intimate terms of marriage, but with the sunlight caressing the angles and sinew of his shoulders it was difficult. 'You want the building and I want my freedom. There's only one way for us to get both. We'll get married.'

'Married?'

'We'll work together to build up your whatever-it-is.'

'A club for merchants.'

'Excellent.' She had no idea what that meant, but they could discuss the details later. 'You've been gone from London for so long, you lack connections. My connections through Philip, combined with my keen managerial sense, the property I purchased—the one you wanted—along with your particular expertise in this kind of venture will make us quite a force. And you know how good I am with negotiation.'

He smothered a laugh. 'Yes, I remember.'

But he wasn't rushing to agree. The same tightness in the pit of her stomach as when she was thirteen and begging him to offer her some promise of a future together knotted her insides again. Anger began to creep along the edges of her confidence. 'You remember what good friends we were, though you never troubled to write me a single letter the entire time you were in Savannah. Do you know how much I could've used your friendship, even from across the ocean?' She winced at this slip. What in Heaven's name was she thinking saying such a thing?

'I do.' Regret flickered in his eyes and he raised his hand as if to graze her cheek, the ruby on his small finger glinting in the sun before he lowered it again. 'But marriage is different from children scampering through the Fleet in search of a shilling or eavesdropping on the adults.'

'You sound like my brother.' She crossed her arms in front of her. 'And I'm perfectly aware of the seriousness of a union, which is why I think one based on friendship is the best kind. Don't you agree?'

'No.' He didn't even hesitate in his answer. 'As much as I respect and admire you…'

'Don't.' She held up one hand, humiliation clipping her words. 'That's the drivel your brother tried to placate me with when he returned from Scotland with his simpering wife. I expect better from you, Jasper.'

'All right, you'll have it.' He dropped the lothario act and spoke to her as he had when he'd told her there could be nothing between them once he left for Georgia. 'There are extenuating circumstances preventing me from marrying anyone, even an old and valuable friend.'

'You're already married?' It wouldn't surprise her.

Everyone appeared capable of finding someone except her.

'No.'

Well, this was a small relief. 'Betrothed?'

'No.'

'Keeping a mistress?'

'Of course not. Where did you get such an idea?'

She tilted her head in pride. 'I'm not a complete innocent. I read novels and the newspapers.'

He stroked his smooth chin with one large hand. 'And yet you are, aren't you?'

'If we married, I wouldn't be, now would I?'

His eyes flashed the same way they had when she'd turned around to greet him yesterday. 'No, I don't suppose you would be.'

'It'd be quite an honour for you.' She lowered her head and peered up through her lashes at him, imitating the young ladies she usually scoffed at during parties. She felt like a fool doing it, but she was willing to try anything to persuade him, even the promise of something more carnal.

'That's one way to put it,' he choked out through a laugh.

'Then why are you objecting?' She dropped the dewy-eyed pose, having expected him to respond with something other than humour. She was losing him as much now as when he'd set sail and she couldn't. She was tired of being a failure and she wouldn't fail at this. 'You need me and you know it.'

'Yes. I always have.' A loss greater than their mere time together, one she'd experienced the day her mother had died, and in the many years since, filled his words. Whatever had happened in Savannah, it'd scarred him like her parents' passing had damaged her. He did need her the way she needed him and for more than just a club.

'Then why are you refusing me?' she asked in a softer tone. It made no sense.

Voices from downstairs filtered up through the floorboards. He should insist she return to her brother, but he hesitated. She was offering him the building, her help in establishing a legitimate venture, and something his fifteen-year-old self would have sold his soul to acquire. But a wife? He was struggling to keep everyone out of his affairs, not searching for ways to draw someone deeper into them. Except this was Jane. If anyone could help him make a go of his club it was her, but he couldn't ask her to share his secret and to deceive her family the way he was deceiving his. Nor could he risk her realising the terrible man he'd become in Savannah, not when she viewed him as an old friend still worthy of her affection.

The time ticked by on the ornate dolphin clock perched on the excessively gilded bedside table while he racked his brain for a delicate path out of this indelicate situation. He needed a reason why he was refusing her, one she wouldn't try to logic her way around or hate him for saying.

'Be honest with me, the way you used to be,' she demanded.

I can't be, with you or anyone. Nor could he wilfully hurt her. She'd taken a risk by approaching him and he admired her too much to treat her as poorly as his brother had. Despite his not having written to her while he was gone, she'd still believed in him and their mutual past enough to ask him for his future. If he told her even one of the real reasons behind his refusal, it would put her off him and this idea, and he wasn't ready to pull himself down in her eyes.

There was a more subtle and less hurtful way to make her abandon this notion of marriage.

He stepped closer, affecting the smile he used to employ with agitated gamblers in Savannah, smooth, charming and convincing. 'Because I'm not sure you could handle the level of honesty I'm prepared to offer you.'

'What do you mean?' She didn't step back and he inhaled her flowery scent. It was lighter and more alluring than the cloying mixture she'd fancied at thirteen, the one which used to remind him of her whenever he inhaled it on a passing woman in Georgia. He might not have written to her after he'd sailed away, but she'd never really been far from his thoughts.

'Your brother wouldn't approve of the match.'

'I'm past the age of needing his permission to marry.' She waved her hand in dismissal, her fingertips grazing his chest before she pulled them back. Her faint touch raked him like a pitchfork. She must have felt it, too, because she clasped one hand in the other and nervousness softened the crease of irritation between her eyes.

'You shouldn't approve of me either.' He pressed his palm against the wall behind her, all the while ignoring the curves indicating her maturity. He must convince her to forget him by giving her a reason to run from him, no matter how much he wanted to slip his arm around her waist and pull her closer. 'You see, I don't want to marry. I want to enter into a less formal arrangement.'

Her gaze slid along the firmness of his bicep beside her ear, then traced the line of it to his face. She frowned at him. 'You want me for a mistress?'

Jasper swallowed hard to keep from laughing. Jane was nothing if not blunt and practical. She always had been, as well as headstrong and impetuous. It was a delightful combination of traits he still enjoyed and hated to drive away. 'You could say that.'

He allowed the suggestion to linger between them as if it had been hers and not his. Jane's lips parted in uncertainty, her full breasts hugged by the fitted yellow spencer rising as she drew in a long breath. He pressed his fingertip tighter into the wall, glad he hadn't removed his breeches for fear he might embarrass himself as he imagined her agreeing to his idea. It'd be a disappointment to them both if she did. He'd done a lot of dishonourable things, but he would never ruin Jane by following through on his suggestion. However, the temptation in her blue eyes, the faint brush of her breath across his naked chest almost made him relent. He could lean down and claim her lips and at last learn what they tasted like, after considering it so many times when they'd both been young, curious, and for the first time aware of one another as more than friends. He moved his head a touch lower, wondering if the old curiosity, as opposed to a desire for a business, had really brought her here. Whatever her motives, it was time for her to leave before someone discovered she was up here.

'Jane, are you in there?' Mr Rathbone's voice carried in from the hallway.

Jasper's fingers stiffened against the wall. *Too late.*

'How did Philip figure out I was in here?' Jane ducked under his arm and began to pace in the centre of the room, revealing how much she did care about her brother's opinion.

Jasper picked up his shirt and tugged it on. 'The new maid must have seen you. The woman is a busybody.'

Jasper had been forced to slip past her to leave the house late at night numerous times. What she was doing up at those hours he'd never discovered, but he suspected it had something to do with his father's brandy and if he could he would soon see the woman dismissed.

'Jane. Are you in there?' Mr Rathbone punctuated his question by pounding on the door.

'I must hide.' Jane rushed to the large wardrobe in the corner, then stopped. She glanced back and forth between Jasper and the door, the plotting narrowing of her eyes both familiar, and terrifying. 'If Philip catches me in here, he might insist we wed.'

Jasper stopped tucking in his shirt. She didn't know her brother very well if she thought he'd force her into a marriage, even after finding her in a compromising situation, but he couldn't take the chance. He strode up to her, tugged the shirt over his head and flung it away. 'I think not.'

He took her by the arm and pulled her against him. She let out a startled squeak as she hit his chest.

'What are you doing?' Her fingertips pressed into his flesh, jarring him as much as her.

'Jane, open this door at once,' Mr Rathbone demanded, and the brass knob began to turn.

'Making sure he sees me as an unsuitable suitor.' He pressed his lips to hers as the door swung open.

Jane barely heard her brother's angry breaths or Justin Connor's howl of laughter from the hallway. Jasper's warm mouth on hers consumed her entire attention. It made her knees weak and she shivered as Jasper slid his tongue out to tease hers, his large hand against her back pressing her firmly into his bare chest. There could be an entire crowd watching them and she wouldn't notice, all she wanted was for him to lay her on the bed, slide up her skirts and satisfy the ache making her almost moan. He didn't so much as move a hand down to grasp her bottom, but broke from the kiss and leaned back. A shock as powerful as the one he'd sent hurtling through her coloured his own hazel eyes.

This was definitely not how she'd imagined this plan unfolding.

'What the devil were you doing?' Philip's voice was so even it made Jane cringe. He hadn't said a word to her during the entire carriage ride home. Not even Justin, who leaned against the French doors of Philip's office watching them as if they were a theatrical performance, had dared to break the icy chill. Philip hadn't spoken until they were settled in his office with Laura and all their past quarrels and disagreements beside him. Jane preferred the silence. It was less lethal.

'I was trying to reach an agreement with Jasper about the building.' She straightened the tortoiseshell comb in her hair, attempting to remain calm and level-headed, but with Jasper's sandalwood scent still clinging to her spencer it was difficult. 'He didn't agree to my terms.'

'It didn't look like it when we stumbled in on you,' Justin observed through a restrained laugh.

'Don't you have a wine shop to see to?'

'This is much more fascinating.'

'Justin, please.' Philip rubbed his temples with his fingers, addressing Jane once again. 'You decided to discuss the matter with Mr Charton alone, in his room, while he was undressed?'

'It wasn't my intention when I first went upstairs, at least not the portion where he was undressed.'

'You shouldn't have been up there at all.' Philip dug his fingers harder into his temples while Laura and Justin exchanged amused looks. Not so Philip. He dropped his hands to the blotter and pinned her with a seriousness to still her heart. 'You risked ruining your reputation and our relationship with the Chartons, and for what?'

My freedom, she wanted to cry, but she bit it back.

He was right, again. With her ridiculous plan, she'd risked more than minor humiliation or the disapproving tsking of merchants and their wives. The Chartons were good enough friends to be discreet about the matter, but they weren't a family renowned for keeping secrets. There were too many of them. It would only be a matter of time before someone heard of this and it would end whatever slim chance remained of her some day finding a husband.

'Ever since Mrs Townsend married Dr Hale, you've been stubborn and wilful,' Philip stated.

'She hasn't been so bad since my mother left,' Laura said, trying to soothe him. Given Laura and Philip's past, and the way she'd snared Philip by surprising him in his bath with a pistol when she and her mother had been on the verge of ruin nine years ago, she was the last to pass judgement on Jane's behaviour.

'No, she's been worse than usual.' Justin chortled.

Philip glanced at Justin who took the none-too-subtle hint for him to leave.

He winked encouragingly at Jane as he passed, but she couldn't muster so much as a tight smile to reward his optimism. He would go home to his wife and children. When this was over, Jane would still be alone.

Laura remained behind, the pity in her eyes adding to Jane's disquiet. She didn't want to be pitied by anyone, for any reason. There'd been enough of that in the weeks after Milton's betrayal and years ago after she'd lost her parents.

Philip rose and came around the desk to face her,

his anger fading to brotherly concern. 'What's wrong, Jane? Tell me the truth and we'll find a way to deal with it.'

She stared at the portrait of their parents hanging behind Philip's desk, too ashamed to look at him. He'd guessed her plan today had involved more than a desire to be wilful, but she couldn't explain to him the guilt and aching loneliness carving out her insides, and how it always grew stronger around the anniversary of their parents' deaths. He would try to banish it with logic and reason. Jane had learned long ago certain notions couldn't be dislodged with either. 'I told you, I want industry of my own.'

'But that's not all of it, is it?'

In his tender voice there lingered the memory of him holding her the morning their mother had died only a week after their father had passed. She'd cried against his chest and followed him around for the next month, clinging to him because she'd been afraid he'd die, too. He'd never pushed her away, but had kept her by his side until the day she'd finally been brave enough to let him out of her sight and go play with Jasper. Even when she'd been thirteen and doing all she could to disobey him, he'd never failed to love her. He was the only one, and she was at last succeeding in driving him away, too.

She screwed her eyes shut and forced back the tears. Everyone she'd ever cared for—her father, her mother, Jasper, Milton, even Mrs Townsend—had all abandoned her and it was her fault. She hadn't done enough to keep their affection, like she hadn't behaved well enough to keep her mother from going away.

'Perhaps we can discuss it,' Laura offered.

Jane opened her eyes and took in the two of them standing side by side. It was meant to be a show of compassion, an attempt to reach out to her, but it only pushed Jane further inside herself. Their happy union drove home her growing isolation and how far down in importance she was to everyone.

'There's nothing to discuss.' It would sound childish spoken aloud. There were many people who loved her, but each of them had their own lives while she hovered on the periphery, watching theirs unfold while hers was stuck like a coach in the mud. 'I'd like to be alone now.'

If they didn't leave, then all sorts of immature things might tumble out of her, along with tears.

Philip nodded, took Laura's arm and escorted her from the room.

Jane stared out the French doors to the blooming roses in the garden, her mother's roses. She struggled hard to remember her mother tending them, her old dress dusted with dark soil, oversized gloves covering her hands. If Jane closed her eyes she could just catch the faint scent of her mother's lilac perfume above the wet earth, hear her melodious voice calling for Jane to bring her the spade. It was the only clear memory she had of her mother and she wasn't sure if it was real or something she'd created, like the image of a happy life with Milton.

How much enjoyment will he derive from this little

incident? It'd taken her ages to face everyone again after he'd eloped with Camille Moseley two weeks before their wedding. She didn't relish having to endure more ridicule or proving to everyone he'd been smart to do it because she was nothing more than an obstinate hoyden. Philip was right—instead of making things better for herself, she'd once again made them worse.

Jane marched to the doors, threw them open and stepped outside. She stopped on the shaded portico to take in the sun-drenched garden. At the back was a high wall broken by a metal gate, separating the Rathbone garden from the alley and mews behind it. There'd been many family gatherings here, parties and celebrations, quiet moments, and one or two daring ones. It wasn't a comforting sight, but a confining one.

No, this won't be the extent of my life.

She stepped into the sunlight and allowed its warmth to spread across her face. Today might have been a disaster, but it was one of the first times in nine years that she'd been adventurous, and alive, and it was all due to Jasper. She craved more of what she'd experienced today, not the guilt and humiliation in Philip's office, but the heady delight in Jasper's embrace and the pleasure it'd ignited inside her. She stared at the pink rose bobbing on a bush in front of her. This was dangerous. Emotions weren't supposed to play any part in this plan, yet they'd slipped in between them the way his tongue had between her lips.

She touched her mouth, remembering his wide-eyed amazement when they'd parted from the kiss, and his more pressing reaction lower down. Perhaps it was good he'd tried to dissuade her from the union by acting the rake. It'd stopped her from making more of a fool of herself with him, as she had at thirteen.

She flung her hands down to her side. No, this wasn't about some silly girlish infatuation; it was about seizing a future and she must make him see it. Hurrying in to her brother's desk, she snatched up the pen and set a blank sheet on the blotter. In swift strokes she told Jasper Philip was considering forcing him to make her an honourable woman and they must discuss it before he took action. She didn't like lying to him, but it was the only way she could think of to tempt him here so she could overcome his objections. After all, he'd said he needed her and he did, as much as she needed him.

'What the hell were you two doing?' Jasper's father blustered while his mother sat embroidering, as sensible and calm as her husband was agitated.

'Discussing business,' Jasper answered in all seriousness. He slipped his hand inside his coat pocket and fingered the letter which had been delivered a short time ago. He had to admire Jane's tenacity; she was determined when she set her mind to something and she'd set her mind on him. With the firm imprint of Jane's breasts against his chest sharper than a shot of brandy, the thought of allowing things to play out as Jane had written held a certain appeal. After the kiss, she could have asked him to rob a mail coach with her and he would have gone along. It had taken him hours to come to his senses.

His father dropped the crystal stopper of the decanter on the table beside it. 'In your room?'

'I didn't invite her there. She appeared all on her own.'

'Preposterous. It's not something a lady of her breeding would even consider.' His father shook his head. 'Next you'll tell me she gambles and I detest gambling. Men default on my loans because they're throwing their money away at the tables while leaving their children to starve and their businesses to founder. Why, I had a cheesemonger's son in here the other day trying to beg money from me because he's wasting everything while his father slaves away. The man made me sick.'

This wasn't the first time Jasper had heard this sort of thing. He'd grown up having the evils of gambling drilled into him. He should have listened to his father.

'I think this little incident sounds exactly like something Jane would do. She's always been a bit wild.' His mother drew a long thread through her embroidery hoop, amused rather than disgusted by Jane's more than usually outlandish behaviour. 'You remember the time she dressed up as a boy to visit the coaching inn with you and Milton.'

'Or the time she went with us to buy tobacco at the auction, thinking she could sell it at a higher price by the docks.' It was one of Jasper's fondest memories of Jane.

'She made quite a profit from that little endeavour, didn't she?'

'So did I. It was Milton who lost money because he wouldn't listen to her and buy a pouch.'

'Well, there's your brother for you.' His mother loved her children, but wasn't blind to their faults, not even Jasper's. If she ever learned the true extent of them, she'd throw Jasper out of the house. She was a patient and tolerant lady, but even she had her limits. If his father ever found out where Jasper's money really came from he'd exile him from the family for good.

Jasper took a deep breath, pushing back his worries. He'd make sure his father never discovered the true source of his income or his inheritance.

'What the devil has got into the two of you?' His father frowned. Mr Rathbone had informed Jasper's parents of the incident, to his surprise leaving out the part about the kiss. It was a good thing he had. With so many Charton siblings, there were few secrets anyone in the family could keep. At times, Jasper was amazed he'd been able to hold on to his for so long. 'Miss Rathbone isn't a child any more, but a grown woman who should know better than to act like a wh—'

'Henry, mind your tongue,' Jasper's mother warned.

'Don't get me wrong, I love the girl like she was my own and she has an admirable head for investments, but all this nonsense today does make one wonder.' He took a hearty drink.

'She's stubborn, like her mother, God rest her

soul.' Jane's mother had been Jasper's mother's best friend.

'You're lucky Philip didn't march you two up the aisle.' His father poured himself more brandy, stopped by a stern look from his wife from filling up the glass. 'Maybe I should. Man like you establishing himself in London after being gone so long doesn't need Philip Rathbone working against you. You need him with you.'

Being so intimately connected to Mr Rathbone was the last thing Jasper needed. If anyone could ferret out Jasper's secret it was Philip. Jasper had caught the scrutiny her brother had lodged at him the moment he'd broken from Jane in his bedroom. It was the look he remembered from when they were kids and the man could guess at once exactly where they'd been and what they'd been up to. He had the elder Mr Rathbone's gift for sizing people up in an instant.

Jasper fingered the letter again, wondering if her note was to be believed and if Philip was indeed planning to haul Jasper and Jane to the altar. If so, he'd have to find a way to turn Philip down and it wouldn't be any easier than refusing Jane. He admired him and his father was right, he couldn't afford to make an enemy of the man. The best he could hope for was Philip turning his attention elsewhere and having no reason to pry into Jasper's affairs by insisting on a wedding.

'Whatever happens, you can't let it distract you from establishing your club. The money from the sale of your American goods won't support you for ever,' Jasper's father continued. 'I'm still amazed what you brought back from Savannah garnered as much as it did.'

'It appears there's a better market here for old Louis XIV than in America. So much for superior English taste.' Jasper forced himself to laugh, pretending like always to be light-hearted. It was the only way to hide the lies weighing him down.

'You'll run through the money if you keep spending it like a drunk earl,' his father blustered and Jasper pressed his lips tight together to hold back a retort. Like the rest of his family, his father failed to understand why Jasper indulged in a few fine things. Death had brushed up against him in Savannah and he was determined to embrace life in London. Besides, it wasn't only himself he spent money on, but on the footmen and dealers who needed it more than he did.

'I don't know what you learned about managing your affairs from your Uncle Patrick. Heaven knows he…' A warning look from Jasper's mother made his father abandon whatever line of reasoning he'd embarked on concerning his mother's favourite brother. 'Either way, you're here now, not in America. You must be swift and decisive and stop missing out on opportunities like the Fleet Street building.'

Jasper nodded as his father continued to lecture him about how to handle his affairs, but Jasper's thoughts wandered from his future and his past to fix instead on Jane. He touched the letter again, the paper smooth like her lips beneath his. He'd meant for the kiss to put her off him. Instead of dissuading her, he'd given her even more reason to pursue him and for him to accept. In her soft sigh he'd heard her whispering for him to follow her out of the shadows of his lies and into respectability.

He wondered if he could.

He plucked a glass paperweight with a wasp suspended inside it off the table beside his mother, the glass cool and smooth against his palm. At one time he would have followed Jane's intuition and believed, like she did, in everything working out as planned. After the things he'd seen in Georgia he no longer could, and he couldn't corrupt her the way his uncle had corrupted him.

However, if anyone could help him establish his club, it was Jane. She'd always had a knack for making money.

He rolled the glass between his palms, amazed to find himself considering her offer. A partnership with Jane might have advantages, but it held so many risks. Living as one man during the day and another at night was wearing on him, and not having complete privacy in his parents' house while his Gough Square town house was being repaired further complicated things. He'd inherited the residence from Uncle Patrick and had intended to move there in the weeks after he'd came home. Then he'd got a good look at the place. It hadn't been well maintained in the thirty years since Uncle Patrick had left it. Jasper had been forced to employ a builder to see to the much-needed repairs before he could hope to move in. They were almost finished and he would at last have complete privacy, one he didn't wish to impede with a marriage.

He couldn't continue the deceit inside the intimate bonds of a marriage, but as a friend, she might understand. He could confide in her the way he hadn't been able to do with Milton or anyone else, and trust her to keep his secret the way she'd trusted him enough to be alone in his room and take his nakedness in her stride, confident he'd do nothing against her will. He was certain of it, even if it risked making her recoil from him.

His hand stilled, trapping the paperweight between his palms before he set it down. He hated to lose her regard so soon after he'd returned, but he must reveal a little of the ugliness ruling him in order to make her understand why they could not marry.

Chapter Three

Jane trudged upstairs after a tense and uncomfortable dinner. Philip's anger had vanished, but there'd been no mistaking his weariness over her behaviour and his constant need to correct it. If her niece and nephews hadn't chattered throughout the entire meal, masking the adults' silence, she would have been able to hear herself chew.

The lively conversation she used to enjoy at meals before Mrs Townsend had left to marry Dr Hale no longer existed. Instead, all discussion seemed to focus on Thomas, Natalie and William's lessons or antics. Jane loved her niece and nephews, but she missed Laura's mother and the long hours they used to spend discussing the latest gossip or news. Mrs Townsend, or Mrs Hale as she was now, might not be far away, but Dr Hale's busy medical practice commanded her time, leaving her little freedom to linger over tea with Jane.

She stopped at the top of the stairs, wishing she

could speak with Mrs Townsend the way she used to, especially to discuss Jasper's unexpected kiss. She had no idea what to make of it, or how to stop thinking about it. With one finger she traced the curve of the polished wood banister. The potent memory of his tongue caressing hers made her heart skip a beat and his silence all the more irritating. He hadn't rushed to answer her note.

I should've listened to Philip and simply sold Jasper the building. Her plan had only succeeded in making her appear like a desperate fool. How many times did Jasper have to tell her he wanted nothing more from her than friendship before she'd listen?

Friendship was the only thing I was offering. He was the one who wanted more. And she should have pushed him away and upbraided him for his forwardness and salvaged something of her pride. If she hadn't enjoyed the kiss so much she would have.

I can't believe I was so weak. She slapped the top of the rail and strode down the hall to her room. Inside, with the door closed, she undid the front flap of her dress and shrugged out of the garment. Laying it aside, she breathed deeply against the soft boning of her stays and made her way to the washstand. She poured some water into the bowl, dipped her hands in and was about to splash her face when her eyes met Jasper's.

'Good evening, Jane.'

She jumped back with a stifled yelp, sending the water in her hands spilling down over her neck and chest, and rolling under her stays. The cold liquid made the fabric of her garments stick to her skin. 'How did you get in here?'

Jasper stepped out of the shadow between the washstand and the armoire, took the towel from the rail and handed it to her. 'The way you taught me to when we were children.'

Except Jasper was no longer a boy; he was a man, as his semi-nakedness had proven today. She snatched the linen out of his outstretched hand, careful not to brush against him. He dropped down on the bench at the foot of her bed and watched her dry her face. Together with Milton, they had spent many nights huddled there, whispering their plots for surprising the housekeeper with frogs and getting a peek at the shops, at least until the day the adults had made it clear there were to be no more night-time games between them.

'Is there some reason you decided to sneak past Philip's men to come see me?' She should speak to Philip about his men failing to guard the house, but she was more flattered than perturbed. Milton had never been so bold.

'Yes, I received your note.'

Jane twisted the towel between her hands. 'And?'

He shook his head. 'You have to give up on the idea of us, Jane.'

She tossed the damp towel on the washstand. 'As you did when I was thirteen and I told you I'd wait for you?'

'This isn't a child's game.'

'Then why bother with all these theatrics? Send a note and be done with the matter.'

'I can't.' Jasper came to stand over her. He smelled of night-air-dampened wool with a hint of spicy snuff. It was a heady mixture which enticed her to draw up on her toes and inhale, but she kept her feet firmly on the floor. If she was going to be rejected, again, it wouldn't be while sniffing him. 'I know you, Jane. Once you decide on something it's difficult to talk you out of it, but I must.'

She took a step back, ready to tease him with some of the same heat he'd tried to singe her with today. He wasn't the only one who could play the game of wiles. 'Are you sure that's the only reason you're here?'

He slid his gaze down to her chemise and the tight breasts beneath it. She wasn't sure what he could see through the wet cotton, but she hoped it was a great deal and made him at least regret his rejecting her. He took his time admiring her and she shifted on her feet, trying to ease the tension creeping through her. She was seized by the desire to fall on him and do all the things she'd imagined while she'd stared at his half-naked body in his room. There was no Philip to stop her. If Jasper took her in his arms and fulfilled the offer in the press of his lips against hers this afternoon, she wouldn't put up much of a resistance.

The low rumble of a suppressed laugh rippled out of his throat. 'You think you know something of the world and men, but you don't.'

She raised her chin in defiance. 'I know enough.'

He leaned back against the bedpost and pinned

her with the same wicked smile as he had right before he'd kissed her, his confidence as annoying as it was seductive. 'You don't know anything. Not about me or about life.'

He was right and it chafed as much as the wet chemise sticking to her stomach. She'd seen nothing of the world and, except for this afternoon and a rather dull few minutes in the dark part of the garden with Milton, she had very little experience with men. 'You think you're the one to teach me?'

'Yes, and I'll prove it.' He slid her dress off the chair where she'd tossed it and held it out to her. 'I'm going to show you something no one else in London knows about me.'

She tilted her head at him, puzzled by his sudden seriousness. Whatever he had planned clearly didn't involve more of his naked body against hers. Too bad. 'You have the French pox?'

He jerked back. 'No!'

Well, at least this finally struck a blow. 'Then simply have out with it and save us both the bother.'

He shook the dress at her. 'It's better if you see it.'

'I can't. If I sneak out with you and Philip discovers me gone, he'll commit me to a convent.' She'd wounded her brother enough today with her silly scheme. She didn't want to worry him if he came in and found her gone.

'You have to be Catholic to become a nun.'

'Not with Philip's contacts.' Her brother knew someone everywhere and could always get exactly what he wanted when he wanted it. She wished she were so abundantly influential.

'Well, before you're cloistered, come with me. You'll understand why we can't marry after you see it and how the fault is with me, not you.'

The pain edging his entreaty made her heart ache. She wanted to pull him out of his darkness, not because she was plotting to ensnare his hand, but because she didn't want her old friend to suffer alone the way she did. 'I don't care about your faults.'

He lowered the dress, his expression filled with the same anguish as the night he'd told her about his parents' plans to send him to apprentice with his uncle. She held her breath, silently urging him to confide in her once more, but as fast as the old Jasper appeared he was gone, covered by the smooth gallant who'd embraced her this afternoon. 'Come on, the Jane I used to know wouldn't have shied away from an adventure.'

He was right. She'd always been the one to drag the Charton brothers into mischief. How things had changed. Milton had turned out to be a bigger rat than the ones shuffling along the garden wall, Jasper had gone off to find his life and Jane was still waiting for hers. Tonight she would have it. 'All right, I'll go with you.'

She took the garment, her fingers brushing his before she pulled back. It was as fleeting a touch as a raindrop, but it doused any remaining reservations she might have about going with him. This was dangerous, not in a get-with-child way, but in a lose-your-head-and-be-hurt-again sort of way. However, while they were together tonight there was still a chance to change his mind.

She snapped out the dress then lowered it to step inside, very aware of how bending over revealed the tops of her full breasts above the stays and how keenly he watched her. She hid her sly smile by focusing on doing up the tapes. Let him be tempted and then try to tell her he wanted none of it. She didn't believe him or the salaciousness of his secret. They were rarely as interesting or as awful as people painted them.

When she was done dressing and had donned a sturdy pelisse, he held out his hand to her, his fingers long and his palm wide. 'Are you ready?'

Her heart raced as the old memories collided with the coming thrill of a new adventure. She hadn't felt this excited or daring in ages. She slipped her hand in his, drawing in a sharp breath as his fingers closed around hers. 'Yes.'

'You can't marry me because of a warehouse?' Jane stared up at the squat building, the mouldy stench of the nearby Thames River making her wrinkle her nose. 'These don't frighten me. Philip owns a few.'

'It's not the warehouse, it's what's inside.' He fiddled with a small iron ring, making the keys hanging off it clatter together.

'Unless you have bodies for the anatomists stacked in there, I very much doubt it. Even then, I could probably do something with them.'

'I don't doubt you could.' He shot her an appreciative smile as he unlocked the door and pushed it open. 'But I'm not a resurrectionist.'

'Good, it's a rather smelly business.' She strode through the small door set beside the larger one used to load and unload freight.

He joined her in the darkness of the warehouse, drawing the door closed behind them. Slivers of moonlight fell in through the high windows at the top and the few cracks in the wooden walls, illuminating the dust kicked up by their entrance. The warehouse was nearly empty except for a few paintings in large, gilded frames leaning against a far wall. They were kept company by an overly ornate set of bergère chairs, a few crates and a wide but dismantled four-poster bed. 'Shouldn't there be more here? It seems a waste to pay rent to store so little.'

'They're the last of what I brought back from America. I sold the rest. Besides, storage isn't the only thing I use this building for, as you're about to see. Come along.' He led her through a narrow door at the far end, past empty crates without their lids and bits of straw littering the floor around them.

Beneath the steady cadence of his boots, Jane caught the dim sound of laughter and footsteps from somewhere overhead. She thought she was imagining it until Jasper opened another door to reveal a narrow staircase. More laughter and voices drifted down from upstairs. 'Are you having a gathering in a warehouse?'

'You could say that.' He avoided her eyes as he slid the keys back in his pocket.

'Jasper Charton, are you running a house of ill repute?'

His head jerked up. 'No, at least not the kind you're imagining. Even if I was, don't appear so excited. It isn't right for you to be so thrilled at the idea.'

'It isn't right for me to be in a warehouse with a single man in the middle of the night either…' she threw open her arms '…and yet here I am.'

'Yes, here you are.' He pulled his lips to one side in displeasure, as if his plan wasn't unfolding quite as he'd imagined. Good. It'd be a welcome change to have someone else's plans go awry instead of hers.

'Well, are you going to show me?'

'I'm debating it.'

'The time for that has passed.'

'I suppose it has. Come on then.' Jasper took her hand, his fingers tight around hers as he started up the stairs. She held on to him, the pressure of his skin against hers making her a touch dizzy as they climbed to the first floor. Her curiosity increased with each step as she tried to guess what he'd brought her here to see. She hoped it wasn't just warehousemen relaxing over cards after a long day. She was tired of disappointments. There'd been too many of them lately.

They stepped into the hall and stopped before a closed door. Light slipped out from under it along with muffled conversation and the faint aroma of pipe smoke. She studied the light beneath the wood, noting how it dimmed and brightened as someone on the other side passed between the source and the door. She waited anxiously for him to open it and reveal what was on the other side, but instead he led her past it to the far end of the hall. She could see the dark recess of an opening and the top of another, much wider, staircase leading back down to the ground floor and the front of the building. It was quiet here, the sounds drifting out of the other room muffled more than they should be in an old place like this. There was also nothing here except a lantern on a metal hook breaking up the endless line of knotted planked wall. She wondered if he meant to lead her back into the warehouse when he reached up and pushed aside the wide plate connecting the metal base to the lamp. It exposed a brass ring hidden behind it.

Now he really had her attention.

He pulled the ring and a portion of the planked wall popped open, revealing a door concealed by the wood and the darkness.

'Impressive,' Jane conceded, jealous. As children, they'd dreamed of having a secret room of their own. The empty space beneath the stairs in the Charton house was the closest they'd come, but every adult had known about it, along with every servant who used to check there first whenever they couldn't find them.

'Don't compliment me yet.' He unlocked the door and led her into an office far more opulent than Philip's. Gilt-framed paintings adorned the far wall and an elaborate peacock inkwell punctuated the lustrous blotter. Sumptuous leather furniture complemented the narrow-legged burled-wood desk and added to the gaudy wealth of the decor.

'Are you sure you're not running a house of ill repute because your office is decorated like one.'

'This came from my uncle's house in Savannah. He had a penchant for gaudy furniture. I sold the worst of it a while back.'

She hated to think what the rest of it looked like if this was the most conservative. She was about to say so when he faced her, as serious as a bailiff. 'Promise me, no matter what happens between us, you won't reveal to anyone what I'm about to show you.'

She didn't share his sense of gravitas. 'Your accounting books?'

He ignored her humour and took her hands. His eyes bored into hers with a severity she'd only seen the morning they'd laid her parents to rest. It turned her as serious as him. 'I brought you here because I can trust you, I always could, and I need someone to confide in. I thought I could do it with Milton, but he's proven himself unworthy.' A stricken look crossed his face, reminiscent of the one Philip had worn the morning Arabella, his first wife, had died after giving birth to their son Thomas. 'Promise me.'

She imagined the loss of his closeness with Milton might be to blame for the darkness colouring his eyes, yet deep down she suspected it wasn't. 'I promise.'

He let go of her and went to a painting of a large house with tall columns hanging on the wall. He swung it aside to reveal a peephole. 'Come look.'

* * *

Jasper held his breath as Jane rose on her tiptoes and pressed her face to the hole. The light spilling out of the room beyond spread over her fine nose and high cheeks, and he caught something of the mischievous imp he'd begun to love before his parents had sent him to America. Except it wasn't their past captivating him tonight, it was the present. She was so stunning and innocent and he longed to draw her close instead of pushing her away. He couldn't because she deserved better than a damaged and deceitful man, and it was already too late. There was no stopping Jane from being disgusted by what he was showing her and no way of preventing her from telling everyone if she decided to betray him.

She won't. It was the old bond they'd shared in childhood when they used to sneak away from lessons with the bird-like tutor to go and play. It continued to connect them, despite the years they'd spent apart. 'This is how I make my living.'

'You're running a gambling hell.' She pressed her hands against the wall and leaned in closer to the hole.

He rested her painting on a small hook, then slid aside the portrait of a dog beside hers to view the tables full of men playing cards across the green baize. The cut-crystal lamps hanging over each table cast circles of light to surround them. Men recruited from the nearby slums who'd demonstrated even a modicum of manners moved between the guests to refill brandy glasses and light cigars, and, most importantly, extend credit. 'Not only do I own the Company Gaming Room, I'm the house bank. The players bet against me and most of the time they lose.'

A loud cheer went up from across the room as Mr Portland, a rotund man with a long face, threw up his hands in victory. 'Sometimes, they win.'

Mr Bronson, a lanky gentleman in a fine suit and a bright red waistcoat, Jasper's partner in this affair, approached the winner to offer congratulations and payment.

Jane studied him, but he continued to observe the room, bracing himself for the sneer of disgust he was sure was coming. They'd both been raised to detest gambling as man after man had approached their fathers and brothers for money to cover their debts and save the businesses they were throwing away with the dice. Jasper was contributing to the very thing which had ruined so many, including him.

'Why, Jasper Charton, I never thought you had it in you to be a rogue.' He turned to face her, stunned to discover her blue eyes, illuminated by the candlelight concentrated through the hole, open wide in amazement.

'You're not supposed to be impressed.' He set the dog painting over the hole and then reached past her face to return the house painting back to its original position.

'I admit it's a bit shady, but it doesn't mean I can't appreciate what you've done and how much you've accomplished in a matter of months.'

'It's a gambling hell, not a cotton-import business.' He pressed his knuckles into his hips. This wasn't the reaction he'd expected and yet he couldn't help but smile. This was exactly like something she would do. 'I thought your brother raised you to detest gambling?'

'I thought your father did the same. It seems it didn't stick for either of us.' She cocked her thumb at the wall. 'I assume he doesn't know about this.'

'No one in the family does. Can I trust you not to tell them or use this against me in your matrimonial pursuit?'

'Of course. I'm not low enough to blackmail a person.' Jane crossed her arms beneath her round breasts. 'But I don't see how you'll keep it from them for ever. Isn't this illegal?'

'No, but it's not entirely legal either, rather a grey area, which is why I don't draw much attention to it.'

'And no one around here has noticed so much coming and going at night?'

'Drunks are the only people in this area after dark and a dram here and there keeps them quiet. It, and the front and back entrances, are why I chose this building.'

'Impressive.' Despite himself, he basked in her compliment before her next questions dissolved it. 'Did you do this in Savannah?'

Guilt struck him as hard as shame. 'I did.'

'What did your uncle think of it?'

He strode to the fireplace, debating whether or not to take her deeper into his confidence, but the freedom to finally speak about this part of his life muted his usual caution. He'd brought Jane this far, there was little harm in taking her a touch further. 'He's the one who taught me to do it.'

'He was a gambler, too?' She rushed to join him at the ornately carved marble mantel.

'He never gambled and neither do I. It isn't wise.'

'Well, he certainly wasn't a cotton merchant, was he?'

'Maybe when he first went to America, but he couldn't tell the difference between Egyptian cotton and South Carolina cotton by the time I joined him. I was as stunned as you are when I learned of his true trade.' Stunned and in awe. To a young man of fifteen who'd thought he'd been banished from his family and consigned to a colonial backwater, the vice-filled rooms and the income they gave him had been a scintillating temptation. He'd embraced the life, even when its darkness had shown itself in the haggard faces of losers at the Hazard table. 'Pretending to my mother to be a cotton merchant was Uncle Patrick's way of explaining the source of his wealth without offending anyone's sensibilities.'

'And your mother never suspected the truth?'

'She's quick, but Savannah is a long way from London.' The distance was the most enticing aspect of coming home, but not even an entire ocean could separate him from his past failures. 'She loved her brother, but my father wasn't as enamoured of him. Father would've despised him if he'd known the real source of his income.'

'And he wouldn't have sent you to him.'

A sense of lost days flitted between them. He

wished he'd never left, then all the horror he'd witnessed, and all the sins he'd committed, might not have happened and he'd be worthy of accepting Jane's hand. 'Uncle Patrick built a fortune on merchants, sea captains with prize money, cotton traders and tobacco planters looking for more respectable entertainment than the seedy dives by the docks, a way to fill the time between when they saw their wares off and when they returned to their rural homes or ruined themselves at our tables.'

'If they were stupid enough to gamble, then they got what they deserved,' Jane pronounced.

'I used to think so, too.' *Until Mr Robillard.* He stared into the fire, watching the flames dance the way they had in the biers scattered throughout Savannah to try to drive off the miasma sickening the city. It hadn't worked. 'I've learned a little more compassion since then and I have rules about limits. The men who play here know I won't allow them to end up drunk and broke in the gutter.'

It was a lesson he'd learned the hard way, one his uncle certainly hadn't taught him. If he'd learned it sooner, many men and their families might have been saved from destitution. Try as Jasper might to atone for his sins in London, he couldn't make up for the many he'd committed in Georgia.

'How do you keep this a secret? I recognise most of the men in there from their dealings with Philip. They must recognise you.'

'They've never seen me in there. The man in the red waistcoat who spoke to the winner is Mr Bronson. He was Uncle Patrick's long-time employee in Savannah. After my uncle died…' Jasper took a deep breath, forcing back the memories '…I offered him the chance to be more than a servant and to share in a good amount of the profits. He's the face of the Company Gaming Room, the one clients approach with troubles and concerns, then he comes to me. It hides my involvement in the club.' It was one of the many façades he'd adopted since coming home. 'My clients are merchants, businessmen, or foreigners with a taste for English gambling who'd never be admitted to one of the more fashionable clubs.'

'You don't cater to toffs? They'd be more lucrative.'

'And troublesome. Their titled fathers would wreak havoc if their progeny lost the family estate to a mere merchant. The toffs also find my wager limits repugnant. They can afford to throw away their fortunes. Most merchants can't.'

'Then why is Captain Christiansen in there?' She pointed to the wall, beyond which sat a lanky gentleman with his long fingers tight on a fan of cards, who Jasper knew sat at his usual table with more empty drink glasses than chips in front of him.

'He's a second son and he's losing the money he earns from captured ships, not his father's wealth, otherwise Lord Fenton would be in here putting a stop to it at once.' Jasper motioned for her to sit on the leather sofa behind her. He took a box of fine sweets off the corner of his desk and held them out to her. 'I also allow him to play here because he offers the other patrons information about oversees interests and ports they can't obtain elsewhere.'

'A wise decision.' She selected one round confection dusted with sugar, pausing to look up at him through her thick lashes. 'If this is the source of your income, then why did you want a building in the heart of the Fleet? It'd be hard for you to hide your activities there.'

She bit into the treat, as perceptive and tempting as ever. He tossed the box on his desk, then sat on the leather chair across from hers. 'Many men come here for more than cards; they want to discuss contracts, stocks and markets in a space more conducive to sensitive deals than a coffee house. It's the edge my establishment offers, the one I wish to cultivate and turn into a respectable business. The building would've been the perfect place for it.'

'You could have the Fleet Street building if you agree to my terms.' Her tongue slid over her bottom lip to lick off a bit of confectioner's sugar clinging there. The gesture almost made Jasper slide across the gap and take care of the sweetness for her. Instead, he threw his hands up over the back of the leather's curving edge. Not only should she not be here, but he shouldn't be reacting to her like this. It wasn't right and still he couldn't dampen the heat rising inside him.

'You know I can't.' It was time to think with his mind and not parts lower down. 'I'm not an honest merchant like Milton or my sisters' husbands.'

'Good, I'm glad.'

'Don't be.' He'd been naive about the dangers and temptations which could rob a man of his worth. He was too familiar with them now and didn't want to visit them on her. 'It isn't easy being up all night, sleeping in the day, and lying to everyone about everything.'

She leaned forward with the same determination she'd used to approach him this afternoon. 'Then let me help you become respectable again. We can establish the club together, secure more patrons and devise many means of making money off them, either through wine and cigars or expensive baubles for their wives sold at inflated prices.'

Jasper rubbed his eyes with his fingers. 'Jane, be sensible.'

'I am being sensible. A busy man must placate his wife and jewellery is an excellent way to do it. By selling ready-made pieces at the club we can save merchants a trip to the jewellers.'

Jasper peered at her through his fingers. 'I hadn't thought of that.'

'Fine stationary for their contracts would also be good and the services of a private solicitor to keep things confidential.'

Jasper rubbed his chin. 'Property agents might not be a bad idea, either, and we could take a cut of their sales.'

She laid her hands smugly on her knees. 'See, I can help you.'

He snapped out of his interest. He was supposed

to be putting her off him, not being drawn into a potential partnership. 'No, you can't.'

'I can and you'll see it and change your mind.'

He leaned forward, one elbow on his knee. 'I promise you, I won't.'

She matched his position, bringing her face close to his. 'I promise you, you will.'

They stared at one another in challenge, so close together he could see each curling lash rimming her eyes. The temptation to kiss her again gripped him and he was certain she would allow it, but he held firm against the desire to lean in and claim her lips. He was here to discourage her, not trifle with her. The rattle of dice and conversation from the adjacent room drifted in despite the thick padding he'd paid builders to add to the walls. Her small breaths glided over the back of his hand where it hung between his knees, the need to resist her beginning to lose its urgency. He'd expected her to loathe him, not go along with him as if he'd invited her to a box at Drury Lane Theatre. Maybe allying himself with her wouldn't be as dangerous as he'd first believed. She could help him and in deeper ways than mere negotiations and sales.

He sat back, putting distance between her and temptation. Revealing his involvement in a gambling hell was one thing, but he wouldn't entice her into this life the way his uncle had enticed him. 'I think it's time to get you home.'

'But we haven't resolved anything.'

'We'll discuss the rest in the carriage.' He checked the glass peephole hidden in a knot in the door to make sure the hallway was clear, then tugged it open. 'We don't want your brother to discover you missing and make you Sister Mary Saint Jane.'

She wagged one finger at him. 'Don't think you'll put me off so easily.'

She strode past him and into the hallway, her confidence as alluring as her perfume.

Jane allowed Jasper to lead her out the way they'd come in and to hand her into the waiting carriage. The night chill made her shiver as she settled against the fine leather seats. She could pull the rug up over her knees, but the bracing air kept her on guard to continue her fight. Warmth might lull her into cosiness and make her forget what she needed to do on the ride home, her last real chance to change Jasper's mind. She'd seen his determination waver when she'd made the suggestion about the jewellery and the solicitor, and again when they'd faced one another. He might outwardly protest, but inside he was weakening.

He settled across from her and with a knock on the roof set the conveyance in motion. They rode in silence as the carriage came around the building and passed the front entrance of the hell where a few vehicles waited for their riders while another pulled up to the front door to let off a new arrival. Then the building faded into the distance and the warehouses gave way to narrow streets and dark, ramshackle buildings. After a street or two, Jasper covered a large yawn with the back of his hand.

'If you allowed me to handle things, you'd hardly

have to do any work,' she offered. 'You could sleep in until noon as much as you like. Unlike some wives, I wouldn't mind.'

'I appreciate your offer, but I won't have you lying to your family the way I've had to lie to mine.'

'It wouldn't be a lie, just an omission of certain details, which I have no issue with. After all, Philip and Laura don't consult me on their affairs and decisions. There's no reason why I should worry about their thoughts on mine.'

'It isn't so easy. It's been hard misleading my mother about my exhaustion or lying to my father about why I can't make morning appointments. If taking up residence in other lodgings while my town house is being repaired wouldn't invite more questions from them I would. As it is, they think I'm tired all the time because I'm still recovering from Savannah and the crossing. Do you know how many times my mother has threatened to summon Dr Hale? They trust me and I'm deceiving them and it eats at me.'

'What eats at me is continued failure and disappointment.' She took a deep breath, working to settle herself. He was flustering her and she would lose the debate if she allowed her emotions to run roughshod over her reason. 'I've managed the weight of those for the last few years, I think I can manage the bother of a few harmless fibs.'

'I don't doubt you can,' he explained softly, 'but I won't let you.'

Her chest constricted. Those were the same words he'd used the night of his farewell party when they'd stood in his father's study and said goodbye. She'd blurted out how she'd grown to care for him as more than a friend and would wait for him to come back. He'd been touched by her offer, but had refused to allow it, sure he wouldn't return.

Except he had.

She stared out the window misted with dew. A few fat drops slid down the glass, catching others as they went before dripping off. This wasn't about an old infatuation she'd put behind her ages ago, this was about establishing her future with him. Despite all his protestations against her, he was here with her alone in his carriage with enough faith in her to reveal his greatest secret. It was a more honest response than all his excuses against their marriage and it gave her hope she could still win his co-operation, if not to-night, then perhaps in the near future.

'I'm sorry I didn't keep in touch with you after I left,' he offered. 'More than once I wondered what you were up to here in London.'

'Not very much.' She smoothed her skirt with her hands, touched by his apology. It eased a great number of old disappointments. 'There were dances and picnics, shopping and dinners, and the weddings of all my friends. No one took a fancy to me, at least no one who didn't bolt.'

'I'm sorry for what Milton did.'

'Don't be. I wasn't in love with him as much as I was in love with the idea of my old friend being my husband.' The possibility still held more appeal to her than waiting for some future romance. She didn't need love, not if she had Jasper, her friend, for a husband.

'I'm surprised Philip allowed the engagement. He of all people should have recognised Milton's weakness.'

'He did, but I didn't listen.' She'd ignored every warning thrown in her path until the morning Milton had left her. 'I wish I had. It would've spared me a great deal of embarrassment.'

'You're better off without him.'

'I am and his eloping spared me from having to wear the thin little ring he purchased. His poor wife has it now.'

'Milton always was miserly.' Jasper grinned and so did she, glad to find some humour in her misfortune.

'What about you? Did you impress the ladies in Savannah?'

He reached up to grab the strap above the window. 'I had my share of amusements.'

'Did you now?' She was as curious as she was jealous.

A spark of mirth lit up his eyes. 'There was one tobacco merchant's daughter I tried to court, but she rebuffed me the moment she discovered I wasn't a lord but from the same solid merchant stock as her father.'

'Did she ever get her title?'

'No, she died in the epidemic.' The mischievous Jasper faded into one much older than his twenty-four years. He turned to stare out the coach window at the dimly lit streets, a darkness coming into his eyes which made her shiver. 'You have no idea the things I lived through in Savannah.'

He spoke with a weariness she understood. It was the one she'd experienced during the two weeks of her parents' illness and which swathed her around this time every year. Jane leaned across the carriage and clasped his fingers tight. 'It's over now.'

The pressure of her touch seemed to startle Jasper, but he didn't recoil from her. Instead he turned his hand over to hold hers. 'No, it's not. It's still with me and sometimes as real as you sitting there.'

He let go of her and sat back, rubbing his thumb across the tops of his knuckles as he fisted his hand and brought it to his lips. A long moment passed and the clatter of the equipage settled in the quiet. Then he lowered his fist to his knee, tapping it in time to the rocking of the coach. 'When the epidemic first began no one really thought anything of it. Every summer there were incidents of yellow fever—even I had a mild bout of it the summer before. It'd claim a few people and then disappear when the weather turned cold. It was clear something was different that year.'

'But you didn't know what.'

'Not until it was upon us.' He continued to stare out the window, his attention fixed on something not outside, but in the past and across an ocean. 'Those who could fled to their plantations, but death followed them. I was one of the thousands caught in the city after the quarantine.'

'How awful it must have been.' She longed to embrace him and drive away the sadness in his eyes, to comfort him the way he'd done for her so many times around the anniversary of her parents' death, but she didn't move. It was clear by the stoic set of his jaw he didn't want her pity any more than she ever wanted anyone else's.

'It wasn't so bad at first, with people flocking to our hell to enjoy themselves before death snatched them away. I enjoyed life with them; you see, once you've had Yellow Jack, you can't catch it again, but it doesn't mean you can't suffer or be afraid. We stayed open until the authorities closed all the public places. By then everything was falling apart, and even if you weren't sick, you were starving. No amount of money or influence could buy you food. It was the first time I've ever experienced what it was like to be without and unable to provide for those I care for.'

'Your uncle?'

He nodded. 'There was nothing I could do to save him and I could barely feed him either. It's the reason I started the hell when I came home. Yellow Jack may not be here, but I've seen what happens to people who fall into poverty. I don't ever want to be unable to provide for those I care about again.' He offered her a sad and apologetic smile. 'Unfortunately, gambling is the only trade I know.'

'I understand. I'm not supposed to want a business, but without a husband, in the end, it might be the only thing to keep me should something ever happen to my inheritance. I don't want to be spinster, but I certainly don't wish to be a poor one.'

'You won't be. You're too clever.'

She wished she shared his high opinion, but she didn't. He had his hell and would some day have his club. She would still be alone and growing older. However, nothing she had suffered or endured compared to what Jasper had gone through. She admired his strength and vowed to be more like him. He hadn't given up in the face of death and sickness. She couldn't crumble beneath a few setbacks.

The carriage rocked to a halt at the entryway to the alley behind the Rathbone house, the one which led to the garden. The mist had thickened during their ride, but the faint outline of the garden gate was visible. It'd been a lifetime since Jane had last viewed it from this angle, when she and Jasper and Milton had returned from an outing, with her dressed in Philip's old clothes and a soft hat covering her hair. Back then, she used to creep through the shadows and in the garden gate, steal past Philip's room and slide into bed as if she'd been there the entire night. Tonight, she'd do it again once more.

Jasper stepped out of the coach and held out his hand to help her down. She gripped it as she joined him on the pavement, reluctant to let go. She didn't want to leave him to ride home alone with the memories of all the awful things he'd seen accompanying him. To her surprise he didn't release her hand, but covered it with the other one. 'Thank you for not judging me too harshly for what I do.'

'I could never judge you harshly, not even for refusing me.'

'It's why I trusted you.'

She wrapped her arms around his neck and pulled him close. 'If you need someone to talk to, don't be afraid to come to me. I'll listen and keep anything else you want to tell me a secret.'

She squeezed him tight and then, before he could refuse this offer, hurried across the short distance to the garden gate, conscious of him watching her the way he used to do to make sure she was home safe. At the gate she stopped. The moisture collecting on the wrought iron wet her fingers while she slowly pulled it open to keep the old hinges from squeaking.

Jane threw Jasper one last look. He touched his hat to her, the faint grey of it just visible in the silver light of the half-obscured moon. She slipped into the garden, past the fragrant flowers and the dew-moistened stepping stones, her regret at having to leave him as strong as the scent of the roses.

The mist grew thicker and colder the moment Jane disappeared from sight. It wasn't like the air in Savannah which could drown a man with its heat, but lighter and more mysterious, like Jane. He opened and closed his hand at his side, the warm pressure of Jane's fingers against his still lingering, along with her concern.

He took hold of the carriage-door handle to keep from chasing after her and changing his mind. It'd been a relief to speak with her instead of trying to hold back his memories, and the truth of his income, as he did with his family. When they'd spoken of Savannah, she hadn't hugged him in pity like his mother had when he'd first come home, the spaces under his jaws hollowed out, the depths of his suffering hidden like the banknotes tucked inside his trunks. Instead, Jane had merely listened, her presence stopping the spectre of the past from rising up from the shadows to consume him.

He stepped inside the carriage and rapped his knuckles against the top to tell the driver to move on. Each turn of the wheels carrying him away from St Bride's Lane, and Jane, made him more agitated. So many mornings he rode home from the hell before dawn, yearning for someone to speak with about the night's challenges or simply to view him in a better light than he viewed himself. With his family, he had to pretend his troubles were not what they really were and allow lies and falsehoods to separate and isolate him from the people who'd welcomed him home.

The carriage made the turn towards the warehouse and rolled past the cluttered windows of the shops locked tight for the evening. Soon, the shops gave way to the square, shapeless buildings lining the river. Weariness began to smother him the closer they drew to the hell. He was exhausted by the deceit and the walls it created around him, except there wasn't one between him and Jane. Tonight, she'd listened. The concern in her blue eyes calling to him, the hints of yellow near the irises reminding him of the sky during the many sunrises he'd been glad to meet during the awful weeks of the epidemic. The flicker of her pulse against his fingertips had been a potent reminder of how alive and good the world could still be and how he might be a part of it again.

The warehouse came into view and the carriage slowed to a stop. He hopped down, his determination not to marry Jane weakening with each step as he approached the rear door. It would be risky having someone so close, but she might be the one person who could keep him from sliding further into the darkness. He'd seen what years of loneliness and dissipation had done to Uncle Patrick. Uncle Patrick had spent his life surrounded by others, fêted and admired, and in the end all his money couldn't buy their loyalty or their help when he'd been at his weakest. Jasper didn't want to become like him. He'd thought to pull himself out of his old life by his own bootstraps. Maybe it was a more feminine hand he needed for the final steps.

He took the key ring out of his pocket and swung it on one finger, imagining the two of them working together and rising in prominence like her brother, or wielding the kind of influence his father enjoyed. It would be like his first few years in Savannah when he used to mingle with influential men or host parties in his Franklin Square house. For a time tonight, with her, he'd been free to be his old self and not have to lie. It was the life he'd imagined when he'd gone to the auction, the one he'd thought he'd lost until Jane had appeared and made him realise it could still be his.

He clutched the keys in his palm, stilling their spinning. It was one thing for Jane to know about his hell, it was another for her to be involved in it. He couldn't corrupt her the way his uncle had corrupted him or risk leaving her to wrestle with even a small measure of the guilt and blame he endured because of the affair with Mr Robillard. Except it wasn't a part of the hell she wanted, it was a part of him and his club. He could give her the club, and himself, and keep back the hell and the ugliness of Savannah. She needn't be involved in the tempting of players, but she could share in the freedom it offered to enjoy the finer aspects of London, the ones denied to her by her current situation. She'd come to him with a proposal for a partnership, to help him build a reputable professional life with the added benefit of more enticing nocturnal pursuits. It was an opportunity he could no longer resist. His time with her had always been an adventure. It would be again.

Chapter Four

'Miss Rathbone, good morning,' young Chester Stilton greeted Jane as she came downstairs for breakfast. Despite having been up most of the night, she'd awakened at her usual time just after sunrise. Force of habit was stronger than fatigue.

'Mr Stilton, it's a pleasure to see you here so early.' It wasn't, but she had to be polite to Philip's clients. After the last day and night, she'd had her fill of young men and was in no mood to entertain any more. All she wanted was to continue on to the dining room and the large pot of coffee sure to be waiting there.

'I certainly didn't ask to come at this ungodly hour, but my father insisted.' Mr Stilton's thin upper lip pulled back in displeasure, revealing teeth as yellow as a wheel of cheese. Rumour was he rarely rose before noon, long after his industrious, and poorly named, cheesemonger of a father had gone to work to support his family and pay off his wastrel son's large tailor bill. She wondered how long it would be until Chester Stilton began to seek loans to support his spending habits, assuming he hadn't already done so to maintain his supply of the gaudily striped waistcoats, white hats and bright blue coats. 'My father is here to pay off the loan your brother extended him last year. He wanted me to join in the discussion and learn a little something about money, as if I should take lesson like that from a man like your brother.'

Jane stiffened. 'With all the credit the tailor extends you, one would think you possessed ample experience handling money, and debts. How proud your father must be of your ability to spend his hard-earned money on your clothes.'

'As proud as your brother must be of paying his spinster sister's milliner bills. You couldn't even land staid Milton Charton of all people.'

'I'm holding out for better prospects than the limited ones before me.' How dare a man whose waistcoats were of more use to his father than he was pass judgement on her or Philip's worth. She made a motion to leave, but he stepped in front of her.

'As much as I don't care for your brother or his moneylending ilk, for the right price I'd gladly take you off his hands.' He swept her with a lascivious gaze which would have made a lesser woman blush.

She didn't so much as twitch, but stared him down the way she would a slug crawling on one of the rose bushes. 'What an honour to be added to the long list of other wealthy women in the Fleet who've spurned you.'

His lip dropped down to cover his yellow teeth. Before he could answer with what she imagined would be a less than witty response, the door to Philip's office opened and the elder Mr Stilton, sharing his son's long face and displaced front tooth, emerged smiling from inside. 'Thankfully the better sort are hungering for my particular brand of cheddar, otherwise I don't know where we'd be. Thank you again for your assistance, Mr Rathbone.'

Mr Stilton grabbed Philip's hand and shook it vigorously before coming down the hallway to stand beside his son. 'Miss Rathbone, how wonderful to see you this morning. I hope my son wasn't being too cheeky with you, although if he was I wouldn't mind. Chester, you couldn't do better than to have an interest in Miss Rathbone. The girl is as sensible as she is pretty. What do you say, Miss Rathbone, any interest in my boy?' He clapped Chester on the back, failing to notice the chill between Jane and his son.

From over the elder Mr Stilton's shoulder Philip shook his head ever so slightly. Jane hardly needed the warning. Chester might feel he'd finally hit the bottom of the matrimonial barrel, but she wasn't so desperate, yet.

'Thank you for your kind offer, Mr Stilton, but I'm afraid my interests lie elsewhere.'

'More's the pity.' Mr Stilton shook his head, then turned to Philip.

Jane didn't hear what he said as she strode off to the dining room, doing her best to appear dignified. Once out of view, she stormed inside and up to the sideboard, immediately garnering Laura's attention.

'Jane, what's wrong?'

'Nothing, except for the yellow-toothed wastrel of a cheesemonger who decided to insult me this morning.' She scooped out a hearty helping of eggs and smacked them down on her plate, wishing the china was Chester's face and the spoon something more substantial. Jane marched to her place at the table beside Laura and tossed down her plate, causing some of the egg to spill over the side and on to the polished surface. She dropped into the chair the footman held out, her one comfort being the cup of black coffee he set beside her plate. She stared at the dark liquid, wondering if she could slip some brandy into it without anyone noticing. It would take the edge off her anger and the disappointment in herself.

There'd been a grain of truth in Chester's insult. She was a spinster and time was not improving her situation or her prospects. When she'd held Jasper's hand last night, she'd wondered if her fate was about to change, but it hadn't. Despite his insistence, and her gut feeling, a morning like this one made it hard for her to believe the fault was with Jasper and not her.

'Don't let him get to you.' Laura laid a calming hand on Jane's arm. 'You're a wonderful young lady and some day the right man will come for you. You'll see.'

'When?' Jane demanded, poking the eggs with her fork.

'I don't know, but we'll put our minds to it and find you someone, or at the very least, something to entertain you. Perhaps you could stay with my mother for a while? She might introduce you to some of the new surgeons Dr Hale is training.'

'You mean men who haven't heard about my being thrown over?' She shouldn't be sulky with Laura. It wasn't her sister-in-law's fault she was on the shelf. If she weren't so bold with her opinions and insistent on having her way, she might not be in this situation. She could only imagine how many young men who'd been trounced by her during debates on stocks must be gloating at this comeuppance.

'That's not what I mean,' Laura clarified, more understanding than annoyed. 'But you could help her. It might take your mind off—'

Thomas, William and Natalie came barrelling into the room, talking at the tops of their voices. Judging by the dirt on Natalie's dress and the dust on the boys' shoes they'd been playing in the garden.

'Mama, Mama, Thomas pulled Natalie's pigtails,' William, the youngest boy, lisped over the noise of his brother and sister trying to get their mother's attention. The bedraggled young governess sagged against the doorjamb to the dining room before she recovered herself and entered, keeping to the rear, knowing Laura preferred to be involved in most of the children's issues. Unlike many mothers, Laura didn't relegate the children to the second-floor nursery not to be heard from until it was time to be presented to their parents. Instead, they ran openly through the house like whirlwinds, as Jane, Milton and Jasper used to do.

'No, I didn't,' Thomas insisted, with all the seriousness of Philip and Jane. His hair was lighter like his mother's, while his younger half-sister and -brother had the darkness of Laura's.

'William started it,' Natalie accused.

'No, I didn't.' The little boy took a swing at his sister and the two of them were back to squabbling.

Jane tried not to sigh while she waited for the row to die down, but the children were insistent in their quarrel. Laura threw Jane an apologetic look which begged her to be patient, but Jane was tired of waiting. With a half-understanding smile, she left her coffee behind and fled the chaos of the dining room for the quiet of the hallway. In the past she and Mrs Hale would have crept off to the garden to discuss the matter. There was no one to speak with now. She wandered past her brother's office to the back door leading to the garden. The Stiltons were gone and Philip sat behind his desk, speaking with his warehouse manager about some goods he'd been forced to seize from a client who'd defaulted on a loan. If Philip had been alone, she might have at last talked to him. She needed to speak with someone, to believe there might be one person who'd listen and give some attention and priority to her concerns. The truth was, there was no one.

Jane wandered out into the garden. She stopped at the edge of the portico and took in the sun falling across the white and red roses bouncing on their stems in the light spring breeze. The sight of the flowers didn't calm her as it usually did, it only added to her frustration. If her mother were here, she would listen and make Jane a priority as she had when she was six. But her mother and father were gone and it was her fault they'd left.

Stop it. She sat on a bench in the centre of the garden. Frustration, anger and loneliness welled inside her until she wanted to walk through the gardens and knock each bright rose from its stem. She closed her eyes until it passed, but the disquiet accompanying it failed to ease. She wanted a place and life of her own and she had no idea how to find one.

'Good morning, Jane.' Jasper's voice carried over the birds and the distant noise of the streets.

She rose and turned so fast, the garden swam, but Jasper remained stable in the centre of it. 'What are you doing here?' She wasn't sure if she was delighted or distressed by his unexpected arrival.

'I came to see you.'

'Well, I'm not sure I wish to see you.' She crossed her arms over her chest, flattered and irritated all at once. 'I've had enough of condescending gentlemen this morning.' *No matter how impeccably dressed they might be.* Jasper, like young Mr Stilton, was no stranger to his tailor, but there was a muted elegance to his dress the gaudy young cheesemonger lacked.

'Tell me who's ruffled your feathers and I'll pummel him for you.' He said it with a smile, but she caught a hint of seriousness in the slight narrowing of his eyes. If only she could set him on Mr Stilton. The cheesemonger's son deserved a beating.

'He isn't worth bruising your knuckles.' A little hope fluttered in her chest. He'd risen rather early this morning to seek her out and she suspected it had something to do with last night. 'I assume you're here to discuss more than my morning's conversations.'

'I am.' He motioned to the bench.

She dropped down on the stone, the coolness of it seeping through her morning dress. He sat down beside her, the heat of his body noticeable against the chill of the spring morning. 'Well? What brought you here?'

Unlike most people, he didn't flinch or scowl at her directness.

'I've given a great deal of thought to what we discussed last night and I've realised you're right.' He stretched out his legs. His boots covered his calves before stopping just below his knees and the polish reflected the grey of the house. 'I need your skills and talents, your knowledge of the Fleet and business. And what more could a man ask for then a friend for a wife?'

Her heart raced so fast she thought she might have to run around the garden to calm it. *He wants to marry me, to have me help him with his club.*

She smoothed the front of her dress with the air of aloof uninterest Philip had taught her to assume when haggling with difficult merchants. She might have proposed first, but she wasn't going to jump at his offer like some desperate spinster, or allow her desire to prove people like Chester Stilton wrong lead her into another mistake. 'So you now believe we'd be good partners?'

'Yes.' He clutched the edge of the bench with his

gloved hands and flexed his fingers over the stone. 'When I told you my secret, you didn't hate me for it or threaten to reveal it. Instead, you understood and wanted to help. You have no idea what that means to me.'

'Yes, I do.' She'd held back from telling Philip and Laura so many truths because she didn't want them to laugh or scoff at her. Jasper wouldn't laugh. He never had, not even when she'd blurted out how much she'd cared for him nine years ago. He could have been cruel and taunting, but instead he'd been tender and honest, saying he didn't feel the same way. She was glad for that now. It meant he couldn't play on her emotions as his brother had. But his honesty didn't extend to everyone—Jasper was willing to deceive his family about who he really was and what he did for a living. He could easily deceive her, too, about the depths of his affinity for her and his reasons for changing his mind.

'With your brother's connections we can secure a common licence and be married by the end of the week and you could start work on the Fleet Street club at once.' He leaned closer to her and lowered his voice. It flowed over her like a warm breeze. 'Besides, I got a little taste of you the other day and I liked what I sampled. Marry me and there will be more of that, much more.'

A chill raced along her arm and it sparked her curiosity about the more intimate aspects of a union. The idea this *could* become something deeper than two friends making a bargain hovered between them.

It almost made her forget about her objections. Almost. 'Be serious.'

'I am serious.' Jasper didn't sit back, but rested one elbow on his knee, remaining tantalisingly close. 'I thought you were, too, after your outlandish proposal which, if I know your brother, got you nothing except some bother.'

'I was serious.' She was also scared.

'Then why resist now?'

She took a deep breath, not wanting to be so vulnerable, but this was no time to hold back. Her entire future rested on this one proposal, and her getting it right this time. 'I don't want you to marry me out of some temporary convenience or because I'm an easy solution to your present problems. I don't want to be forgotten or overlooked the moment you no longer need me and I don't want you to conceal things from me the way you've concealed them from your family. I was embarrassed enough by your brother's secret when it came out. I don't want to be surprised by any of yours. I want you to be my friend, my true, real and forthright friend, like you used to be.'

He stared down at the ground, his mirth fading.

'You can't do it, can you?' she challenged, the prickliness she'd first greeted him with returning.

'No, I can't talk about everything I experienced in Savannah. Surely you understand.'

She studied him and how the sun and the shadow from his hat darkened the circles under his eyes. Philip had taught her long ago to read people, but she'd never been as talented at it as he was. However, there was no mistaking the depth of Jasper's pain, one she understood all too well. Like her, there were things he couldn't talk about either. 'I do.'

She glanced over her shoulder at the spire of St Bride's Church rising up over the house and the churchyard where her parents lay.

'The anniversary was last week, wasn't it?' he asked, following her gaze.

She turned back to him, her grief softening. 'I'm surprised you remember.'

'How could I forget?' He had accompanied her every year to lay flowers on her parents' graves and sat beside her in the churchyard while she'd grieved.

Jasper studied Jane, wanting to drive away the strife clouding her eyes. He'd never seen her so weak or vulnerable but, like him, their time apart had changed her. She'd been cast aside by his brother, humiliated in front of everyone, then left to linger as a spinster. He wouldn't treat her so shabbily, but she'd asked for an openness he couldn't bestow, all the while having no idea what she was asking for. He couldn't tell her about Mr and Mrs Robillard and risk her recoiling from him. Nor could he embroil her in the business of the hell and make her as dirty as him.

'Well, Jasper?' she prodded.

He might not be able to tell her everything about the hell or his past, but he could share his current situation with her—if not the worst parts of it, then certainly the best. He could help her to enjoy life the way he intended to after so much death and find a way to make sure the darkness never touched either of them again. He took her hand and met her steady gaze. 'I don't want you for mere convenience. I want you because you are my closest friend. I promise I will respect you as you deserve and be as open and honest with you as I can be.'

A hope he hadn't seen in anyone, including himself, since well before the epidemic brightened her face. It lightened some of Jasper's strain. In her innocence, she believed all would be well. With her beside him, perhaps it would be. 'We must speak to Philip at once so he can make arrangements. I'm sure he won't object.'

'I do not give my consent.'

Jane stared at her brother, dumbfounded. Laura peered back and forth between the couple and her husband, as shocked as Jane. Jasper stood casually beside her, hands crossed in front of him, hat dangling from his fingers as if their future together wasn't at risk. It irritated her more than it comforted her, adding to her annoyance at Philip's answer.

'What do you mean you don't consent?'

Philip folded his hands over the blotter. 'I have reason to doubt the veracity of Mr Charton's interest in you.'

'The veracity of his interest?' She forced herself not to shift on her feet and to face him as she would a difficult butcher trying to overcharge her for poor-quality meat. She recognised this look; it was the one he used to give her whenever she'd ask to go to the milliner's for a new dress. He'd always suspected her of choosing something much too adult for her young years, and he'd been right. At thirteen, almost everything she'd done had been to test him, to prove to everyone she was no longer a child but a young woman capable of making her own decisions. It had taken Mrs Hale's gentle guidance to make her realise she was not yet an adult and there was no reason to look older simply to spite the world. However, she was an adult now and she wouldn't cave under his scrutiny.

'He did his best to dissuade you from a union yesterday and now he wishes for your hand. I want to know why,' Philip explained to her, not Jasper.

'He wasn't against it. He was merely surprised by the way I went about discussing the matter. Even you said it was ill-advised.' Her conceding the point didn't ease the stern set of her brother's jaw. 'Since he's had some time to consider it, he's come to realise, as I have, we're still good friends and it would be a perfect union. Don't you agree?' She took Jasper's hand, demonstrating some affection, but careful not to overdo it. If she told Philip the two of them were madly in love, it would make him even more sceptical.

'I do.' The lightness in Jasper's answer made her wonder if he realised how in danger of having their plans thwarted they stood. She might be over the legal age to marry, but they needed Philip to obtain a common licence and arrange the church, and anyway, she wanted his consent. She was going to have to lie about the true source of Jasper's income, she didn't wish also to sneak behind her brother's back to the altar.

Philip eyed Jasper with hard scrutiny. 'I'd like to speak with Mr Charton, alone.'

Jane threw Jasper a wary look, but he didn't appear ruffled by the requested interview. Instead, he nodded to let her know all would be well. She hoped so. The idea of having yet another one of her plans fail irked her.

'I can't believe Philip is being so difficult,' Jane complained to a sympathetic Laura when they were alone together in the front sitting room.

'He's doing what he believes best for you,' Laura explained, despite the perplexed crease between her brows. Evidently, Philip's behaviour baffled her, too. 'He always has.'

'I've decided what's best for me and it's Jasper.' Jane dropped on to the sofa near the window.

Laura didn't argue with her and Jane was almost disappointed. She craved a little vigorous debate. It wasn't just Laura and Philip who were sceptical. She had her own doubts and they'd been nagging at her since they'd left the garden to speak with her brother. She wondered if there was anything about Jasper she should be concerned with. If there was, Philip was sure to sniff it out. Oh, how he irritated her; she wanted to rely on her own intuition and judgement and stop being dependent on his.

'Mr Charton strikes me as a very charming and persuasive gentleman. I'm sure he'll bring your brother around.' Laura sat down beside her. 'Though I do wonder how you two arranged all this in so short an amount of time.'

Jane stopped fiddling with the tassel on a pillow and stared at her sister-in-law. *Do she and Philip know I slipped out with Jasper last night?* No, it wasn't possible. Philip's men might be very astute and loyal to him, but they weren't infallible, as Laura had proven when she'd crept in here. She hadn't even had the advantage of Jane telling her the best way to do it. Since then, she'd won Philip's heart and had helped him to move past the grief which had left him distant and closed off from everyone including, at times, her.

She wondered if she and Jasper might ever come to have a relationship like Philip and Laura's. Love hadn't been a part of their negotiations. Good. It was better if she never expected it as then she'd never be disappointed. Besides, she was too old to fantasise about romantic nonsense. Compatibility was more valuable than a passion, even if it dampened instead of ignited her heart. She'd believed in love once and maybe some small part of her still did. It didn't matter. This was an excellent arrangement. She hoped Philip realised it, too. In the meantime, there was Laura's scrutiny to address.

'I chanced to meet Jasper while leaving Mrs Fairley's yesterday afternoon. We had a very long discussion on the matter.' It was a shady version of the truth, omitting the more scandalous details of his having slipped into her bedroom to spirit her away to a gambling hell in the middle of the night. She wondered if she should mention at least the leaving with him in the middle of the night part to force Philip's hand. However, if he hadn't marched her and Jasper up the aisle after the incident at the Chartons', she doubted he'd insist on a marriage because of some late-night escapade. Philip was much too level-headed to act out of emotion, which further worried her about his conversation with Jasper. She hoped Jasper was managing well.

'And what did you discuss with Mr Charton?' Laura leaned forward in the same manner Mrs Hale used to do when she and Jane shared gossip. It was almost enough for Jane to drop her voice and tell her the truth, the way she used to with Laura's mother. She missed the old intimacy, connection and friendship. It'd never come easy to Jane except with Mrs Hale, and Jasper, but not even they knew the darkest guilt she carried about her parents' death, nor could she tell them about the hell. Jasper had sworn her to silence and she would be worthy of his faith in her.

'We discussed his business and how I could help him with it.' If Jasper was working to win Philip over, then Jane must do the same with Laura.

'You two discussed business?' Laura tilted her head in disbelief.

'Your mother and Philip went to a great deal of time and trouble to teach me accounts, contracts and negotiations so I could some day help a husband manage his affairs. It's time I finally put those skills to use instead of trimming roses and telling the housekeeper how to make sure the grocer doesn't short-change us. I'm tired of being useless.'

This was as close to the truth of her and Jasper's discussion as Jane was willing to venture.

'I understand.' Laura took Jane's hand. 'When my uncle sold my father's draper shop and I was left with nothing to do every day, I almost went crazy. I was so accustomed to working, I couldn't sit idle. I can only imagine how it's been for you. I'm sorry I didn't see it before or do more to help you.'

'It isn't your fault, it's no one's, except perhaps mine.' Jane unclenched her fingers, wondering if she should have made an effort to speak with Laura sooner, but there were some things Jane couldn't share with anyone. 'Somehow, I've managed to drive good gentlemen, and one very bad one, away.'

Laura squeezed her hand. 'Not at all. You're simply discerning, like your brother, and you've been waiting for the right one. I think Mr Charton is perfect for you and I believe Philip will see it, too.'

Jane wasn't as convinced of her desirability as Laura, nor of having been waiting for the right gentleman. If she had, it hadn't been out of choice.

Footsteps in the hallway made them both rise and face the door. Philip entered first and Jane studied his face, searching for signs of an answer. The lines at the sides of his mouth were softer and the suspicious scrutiny previously hardening his blue eyes was gone.

Jasper convinced him!

Jasper strode in behind him as if his gambling house had received a massive win. He winked at her and Jane had to resist throwing her arms around his neck in congratulations. Instead, she returned the wink, blaming the racing of her heart on the thrill of them having succeeded. Though he would be her husband, she refused to view him as anything but a friend with more intimate benefits.

'I give you both my consent to marry.' Philip kissed her forehead in congratulation, as he used to when she was young and did well at her maths lessons, before she'd grown older and begun to rebel against him for reasons she still didn't entirely understand. When he straightened, he took her hand and gave it to Jasper. 'Mr Charton and I will speak tomorrow about drawing up the marriage contract and securing the common licence. You can wed as soon as the required seven days are past.'

Jane wondered what Jasper had said to convince Philip of the need for a quick marriage. With Milton, he'd insisted on a long engagement, giving Milton time to live up to Philip's low expectations. Perhaps Philip now allowed the wedding to hurry because he was tired of looking after her and exhausted at having to talk sense into her. He was giving her to another man and relieving himself of the burden.

No, I shouldn't be so uncharitable. Whatever her brother's motives, there was no mistaking his tender expression, much like the one the elder Mr Charton sported whenever he mentioned his grandchildren. It eased a measure of her fears, as did Laura's excitement.

'Wonderful!' Laura embraced Jane in congratulations. 'You two will be very happy.'

Jane returned the hug and over Laura's shoulder she caught Jasper's eye. A strange awkwardness stiffened his movements as he shook Philip's hand. She stepped away from Laura and Jasper let go of Philip. Jane and Jasper faced each other but his attention darted around the room with a tinge of uncertainty before he fixed on her. It was then the reason for his unease struck her. He might trust her with the secret of his gambling house, but there was another, darker one directly behind it, something to do with the things he couldn't tell her about Savannah. It reminded her too much of Milton and how he'd managed to conceal his relationship with Miss Moseley. Worry dampened her enthusiasm. Once the parson's mousetrap was sprung, they'd be stuck with one another for better or for worse. In her haste to change her situation, she wondered if she'd inadvertently made it worse.

Jasper sat at his desk in the warehouse office, dealing with an order for wine, but the memory of Jane continued to dominate his thoughts. Perceptive as always, she'd realised at once that they were going to be man and wife. She'd also caught his momentary doubt while he'd shaken Mr Rathbone's hand. It had caused her to retreat into a reserve making her resemble her brother. He'd wanted to tell her his concerns had nothing to do with her and everything to do with him, but there hadn't been a chance.

He slipped the ruby ring off his finger and turned

it over and over. In Savannah, he'd spent years collecting money, property and influence, and in the end it had been worthless. In London it was different and yet it wasn't. Money made the difference between having a proper life or doing without. All he needed to do was look at his footmen and dealers to see how wages had lifted them out of poverty and given them and their families the chance to thrive instead of merely subsist. Once Jasper had wed Jane, she would become his responsibility. If Jasper lost everything to some extremely lucky gambler, or if their families learned of the hell and turned their backs on them, it would be like Savannah all over again. Except, this time, there'd be no family or inheritance or collected goods to help him start over. They'd be ruined and he'd be the cause of it.

'A right lucrative night last night, Mr Charton,' Mr Bronson greeted Jasper as he entered the secret warehouse office. The older man drew out his vowels in the lazy way people from Savannah did. Jasper had found it amusing during his first year in the bustling port city, the easy manner of speech slipping into his own so that a few years into his apprenticeship his accent had become too garbled for anyone to guess where he was really from. It'd given him an air of mystery in Savannah, charming the ladies during garden parties at the big plantations. It had made him stand out here, too, as his seventeen-year-old twin brothers Giles and Jacob enjoyed teasing him about during family dinners. He'd struggled to lose the languid manner of speaking, but now he was snapping his vowels in place as day by day he left his time in the southern state behind. He wished his past and his concerns were so easily set aside. 'What about Captain Christiansen. How did he do?'

'Lost another five hundred pounds before we sent him home.' Mr Bronson handed over the man's signed debt, then dabbed his forehead with his red handkerchief, the warm room making him perspire.

Jasper slipped the ruby ring back on his finger as he examined Captain Christiansen's name scrawled at the bottom of the paper. 'Seems like more than a man who hasn't taken a prize ship in a while can afford to lose.'

Mr Bronson strode to the window and slid up the sash. The cooler air laced with warmth from the coming summer spilled into the room. 'Didn't go quietly this time either, complained loudly about having a right to spend what he wants.'

'Not in my establishment, especially if he's going to make a scene. Scenes aren't good for business.' Jasper stared out the open window and the early morning sky dotted with thick clouds. The fresh air wasn't refreshing so much as unsettling. 'If he returns tonight, keep an eye on him. Hopefully, his current losses will encourage him to be more cautious with his play.'

'And if they don't?'

'We may have to find a discreet way to bar him from the club. We don't need Lord Fenton coming in here trying to redeem his son.'

Mr Bronson hooked his thumbs in his waistcoat pockets. 'Don't get y'all scraping to those sallow-faced men. Be better if you'd chucked them out like we Americans did.'

'Some days I agree with you, but old habits are difficult to break.' Jasper dusted his signature, then blew it off and handed Mr Bronson the papers.

'Yes, they are.' Mr Bronson rolled the debts in his hands. 'How many old habits are you going to give up when you have a wife nosing about?'

'None. She'll simply accompany me to the jeweller's and the theatre and help me enjoy my fine wine and food while working with me to establish the club.' Jasper leaned back in his chair, far less cavalier than he appeared. Jasper had told his partner about his plans before he'd approached Jane and now silently agreed with him. Once Jasper and Jane were living together as man and wife, he'd have to balance what he told her about the hell with what he held back, giving her just enough to satisfy her interest while keeping her ignorant of all the goings on. It would mean more deception, but it was necessary. He couldn't stand to have Jane spit on him like Mrs Robillard had when Jasper had approached her with his condolences. 'Better to be a married man than risk becoming a recluse.'

'You don't need a wife to avoid that.' Mr Bronson chuckled. 'You have a cook and a housekeeper and more willing company in other corners to see after your needs.'

'True, but how many of those paid people stayed around to help Uncle Patrick after he fell ill?'

'We don't have to worry about that here in London.'

Jasper touched the edge of the bills of mortality tucked beneath his blotter. 'I hope not, but there are other tragedies capable of befalling a man and leaving him in need of someone with more interest in his affairs than payment to step in and handle them.'

'I thought that's what you had me for.' Mr Bronson laughed. He removed a pouch of tobacco from his waistcoat pocket along with a clay pipe and began to pack the bowl with the fragrant weed.

'I do, but relations are sometimes more reliable.' Jasper wouldn't fail Jane the way Mr Robillard had failed his wife. 'I also know you Yanks. You'll want your own establishment sooner rather than later, to make something of yourself, to be your own man.'

'You are right, Mr Charton.' Mr Bronson pointed the stem of the pipe at him before setting it between his teeth. 'I'll have to strike out before you expect me to take a missus.'

'I wouldn't dare temper your excursions into the West End by suggesting such a thing.' Jasper waved his hand in the air to indicate the future. 'At least not yet.'

Mr Bronson took a deep drag on his pipe, then let the smoke out of the side of his mouth. 'Have you told her about Mrs Robillard?'

'No.' A breeze rustled the curtain, carrying into the room the faint scent of summer. Jasper rounded the desk and slammed the sash closed. 'You're not to tell her.'

'You can trust me to keep silent. I've been where you are, what with my father, God rest him, being a preacher and railing on about the ills of drink and cards. He'd have starved before taking my money if he'd learned how I really earned it.' Mr Bronson fingered the watch chain hanging in an arch from his pocket to where his father's timepiece hung from a button. 'No reason a lady has to hear about such ugliness.'

Mr Bronson touched the rolled debts to his forehead in a kind of salute, then turned on the heels of his fancy boots, the best his money could buy in London, and strode out of the room.

Jasper rested his hands on the back of one of the pair of shield-backed chairs near the window and took in the room. He should return to work. There was a great deal to be done now the Fleet Street building would be available, and Jane had given him new ideas, but he couldn't. He stared at the fire burning in the grate. Summer was slowly descending on the city, bringing with it unknown threats. His hands were tight on the carved wood and the edge of the fancy decoration bit into his palms. Yellow Jack couldn't touch him or anyone here, but it didn't mean some other pestilence might not come in with the summer wind and snatch away what remained of his peace of mind. Except it wasn't really disease he feared here as much as his own failings.

He left his office and entered the quiet of the gaming room. The smell of tobacco smoke, stale wine, sweat, hope and desperation hung thick in the air along with the dust motes. Everything had been set to rights, the chips stacked neatly at the tables, the packs of cards beside them fresh and ready to be opened by the dealers tonight. The Hazard wheel sat silent, too, the white balls lined up and waiting to click into place as men cheered and spent their money.

Jasper picked up a Hazard ball and rolled it between his fingers. He pitied many of the players, especially those like Captain Christiansen who rushed into forgetfulness through the cards. Jasper wondered what horrors Captain Christiansen had seen during his time at sea and if those memories drove him to recklessness the way they'd driven Jasper to return to this life.

He gripped the Hazard ball tight, his sins pressing down on him. There'd been many times before the epidemic when he'd begun to question this profession, but he'd ignored his doubts. Wealth, influence, standing, his uncle's pride and his own had drowned out the voice of his conscience. Mr Robillard's pistol shot had silenced the gaiety and left his conscience screaming. It still did and yet he'd come crawling back to this life the moment he'd set foot in England.

He set the ball down beside the others and, winding his way through the tables, left the gaming room, avoiding his reflection in the gilded mirror across the room. He didn't have the stomach to face the real Jasper, the one he hid from Jane and everyone, the ugly crooked thing his uncle had made him and he'd willingly become.

He locked up the upstairs rooms and left through the main warehouse. In the cavernous space, employees he paid well to keep quiet among their dockworker brethren unloaded shipments of wines, cards, food and other goods for tonight. The activity made his establishment appear like all the others crawling with carts and horses, with drivers and men calling to one another to shift about the various merchandise coming and going. Outside, the rising sun just touched the peaked tops of the buildings. Soon it would be higher and cast light into the deep shadows between the warehouses, further tanning the already ruddy faces of the men streaming in and out of the district as they went about their morning work.

Usually the bustling activity invigorated Jasper, but not this morning. He was pulling Jane into the mire by asking her to keep this secret the way Uncle Patrick had asked him to keep his. How long until he corrupted her the way he'd been corrupted?

No, I won't let that happen. They'd work hard on the club during the day, and he'd see to it they enjoyed themselves at night, both in town and in bed. She would remain ignorant of the true business of the hell until he could finally part with it.

'You there, you scoundrel,' a woman's voice rang out, silencing a few of the workmen stomping past Jasper, their backs bent under the weight of the casks they carried. 'I'll have a word with you.'

Jasper faced the woman barrelling down on him the way Mrs Robillard had approached him once. Her clothes were too worn to make her a merchant's wife, but the reticule weighed down by something heavy swinging by her thick hips set him on edge.

'If you think I'm going to allow you to ruin my son

the way my husband ruined himself, you are wrong.' She jerked up the reticule and stuffed her hand inside. The memory of Mrs Sullivan pulling a gun on him the night she'd lost her prized diamond at a dice game rocked him. Mrs Sullivan had missed.

He didn't wait to see if this woman's aim was any better, but closed the distance between them. 'How can I help you, madam?'

He offered her a hearty smile, the one he once employed with planters and their wives as he placed his hand on her wrist to stop her from removing whatever weighed down her reticule.

'Let go of me, you wicked man.' She jerked free of him and her hand came out of the bag empty. She was oblivious to the many workers taking an interest in the conversation. Jasper needed to quiet her and quickly. He didn't possess enough money to silence them all.

'Please, step inside my warehouse and we can speak.'

'We can speak here. You think I don't know what you're getting up to in this place?' she screeched. 'I've seen the money Adam comes home with and I know there's only one way he be can be earning it.'

At last he understood who the woman was and how to deal with her. He stepped closer and dropped his voice, painfully aware of the men around him leaning against crates while they pretended not to listen. 'Adam is my employee, not a client, and a very well-paid one because I trust him to remain quiet about my business, as I'm sure I can trust you, too.'

He reached into his pocket and plucked out a banknote. He didn't look to see the value before he took her hand and pressed it into her palm. She closed her fingers on the note and tugged it out of his grip. Then she opened the crumpled paper and her light eyebrows rose with surprise. Everything about her demeanour changed as she shoved the money inside her bodice.

'I understand completely, sir. I'm so sorry if I misunderstood, only his father was a gambler, and a drinker, and all but ruined us, forcing us from our home and into the filth of St Giles.' Tears filled her eyes and she wiped them away with the sleeve of her faded dress. 'When Adam started going out at night and coming home with money, I worried he was turning out like his father. I followed him here last night, heard the men talking about their wagers and I thought for sure I'd lost him.'

'Your son is one of my best footmen.' Jasper wrapped his arm around her thin shoulders. 'But if the wrong people find out about this place and shut it down, he'll lose his good wages.'

She peered up at him with round and worried eyes before her gaze darted to the watching men as she realised her mistake. 'I won't tell anyone. You can count on me. His wages keep me and his sisters from starving and allowed us to move out of St Giles. I assure you, I wouldn't knowingly do anything to jeopardise this place, Mr…?'

'Patrick,' he lied. She knew too much already.

'Mr Patrick. Thank you for all you've done for

him. I'm so sorry for thinking so little of you.' She kissed the back of his hand, grateful in a way he didn't deserve. He smiled and accepted it despite the urge to climb in the carriage and be alone with his shame. When at last she took her leave, hurrying off even faster than she'd approached, Jasper strolled to his carriage to appear to all as if nothing was amiss and give no one a reason to consider the matter.

The men went back to their work and Jasper stepped into his carriage. Once inside, the vehicle set off and he sagged against the squabs, breathing for what seemed like the first time in days. 'It's all right.'

Except it wasn't. There'd been a moment when he'd feared her accusations would rise and the woman would announce to the entire wharf what took place above stairs at night. If too many people learned of it, then it would only be a matter of time before word spread and he could no longer keep this place a secret from his family. They'd already put him on a ship once and sent him off believing they'd never see him again. To be in London and banished from their circle would be worse, especially if he dragged Jane down with him.

The carriage rocked to a stop in front of the Charton house. Jasper climbed out and jogged up to the front door, hoping no one was about. He needed peace to think and cursed again the repairs to the town house. When he'd first arrived home, the noise of his nieces and nephews, the talk of his parents and the continued comings and goings of his sibling had been a welcome relief after the deathly still of Savannah. Today, they would be an annoyance.

'Is everything all right, sir?' Alton, the butler, asked when he pulled open the front door. The thin man with the wide nose had been with the family since Jasper was a little boy. He knew Jasper as well as his old nurse, forcing Jasper to lie to him the way he lied to everyone else.

'Yes, thank you.' He made for the stairs, eager to reach the solitude of his room before anyone else noticed he was home. He didn't make it.

His mother came out of the front sitting room, concern furrowing her brow at the sight of him. 'Jasper, you seem troubled. Is anything wrong? Perhaps something you'd like to discuss with me about your evenings?'

She studied him the way she had when he was a boy and she used to summon him to her dressing room to interrogate him about what he'd been up to in the street. The vague notion she might know about the hell drifted through his mind before he dismissed it. If she had learned of it, she'd never be this coy in approaching him about it.

'No, nothing.' Jasper flashed the widest smile he could muster, feeling like a fool and a charlatan. But they were the ones who'd sent him away to learn his uncle's trade, even if they'd been ignorant of what it'd really involved. With all the subtlety and finesse of a fifteen-year-old, he'd railed at them for their decision and done everything he could to make them change their minds. They'd remained firm in spite of their own doubts and love for him, believing Uncle Patrick would provide their second son with the best opportunity to make something of himself.

His tension softened as he took in his mother's concerned face. They hadn't known the truth and they still didn't. If they ever learned about it, their guilt would be as great as his. They'd done what they'd thought best for him. Now, he would do what he thought best for them by allowing them to remain ignorant of the real consequences of their decisions and his. 'I'm fine. I had trouble sleeping again last night.'

'The dreams again?'

'Yes.' It was the reason he'd been giving for weeks to explain his long nights out. There had truly been nightmares when he'd first come home, but now they'd faded. Sadly, his need to use the excuse had not. 'After I woke up, I went to the theatre, and then to Mr Bronson's. I needed to be around people and I didn't want to disturb anyone here.'

'Of course,' his mother agreed with some hesitation. Then she reached up and took him by the chin, turning his face side to side to examine him. 'You look like you did when you first came home.'

He knew exactly what she meant. It was the reason they'd given him three months of peace before announcing his return. 'I haven't been sleeping well.'

His mother removed her hands from his face and clasped them in front of her. 'I think Jane will be good for you. She'll help you to deal with many things and perhaps forget some of your old experiences.'

Jane. He glanced at the side table in the entrance hall and the blue German glass pitcher the same deep azure as her eyes. It wasn't only the risk of discovery he'd faced today, but the very real threat of violence. If Adam's mother had had the chance to remove the pistol weighing down her bag, and Jasper and Jane had already wed, Jane might be a widow and left to deal with the revelations about Jasper and his club. He had too much honour to foist his embarrassments and troubles off on someone else the way Mr Robillard had done. 'I must see her this morning. There are matters we need to discuss.'

'Of course.' His mother patted his hand. 'Be good to her, Jasper. She deserves it and you deserve her care.'

'Yes, she deserves the best.' Sadly, it wasn't him.

Jasper removed his hand from hers and made for outside, refusing to hail a hack or summon the carriage again. He needed the brisk walk as he made for St Bride's Lane.

The surety with which he'd pledged himself to Jane began to dim in the bright daylight. He'd had doubts once about what he did in Savannah and he'd ignored them, blithely carrying on until they had destroyed people. *That* had garnered his attention. He'd had reservations about bringing Jane into this sphere, but he'd ignored them, too, insisting the best course of action was to link her life with his. This morning's encounter made him doubt his decision. It was one thing to burden her conscience with a few of his secrets. It was another to place her in real danger or set her up for potential embarrassment the way Milton had done. He couldn't allow Jane to be hurt.

It wasn't long before Jasper reached the junction of St Bride's Lane and Fleet Street. He stopped at the opening of the lane. It was calm compared to the bustle of the main thoroughfare. He should keep walking, go to his town house and make sure all was on course with the repair work to welcome them after the wedding, but his feet wouldn't move. With the practised skill of a man always betting against others, he weighed his risks against the odds. Leaving her now would certainly hurt her and turn her against him for good. The risks of his lifestyle were less clear, but potentially more deadly. He didn't want to deliberately hurt her, but he didn't want to see her wounded because of his more illicit life. Perhaps, if she understood something of the danger, at least as much as he was capable of telling her, she might help him decide. It was a gamble he didn't wish to take, but he couldn't ignore his intuition this time.

A sick feeling swam in the pit of Jane's stomach as she faced Jasper. Until this moment, his unexpected appearance had been a welcome distraction from drawing up guest lists, breakfast menus and packing her things. He hadn't smiled once since he'd arrived, nor cracked a joke or made light of anything. It was eerily similar to the way Milton had approached her the morning before he'd eloped.

'What exactly are you trying to say?' Fear tightened her throat. *He's going to call it off. No, if he'd changed his mind he would have sent a note instead of coming here himself.* It was slim comfort. There was a reason he was standing here viewing her as if he'd already lost her.

'I want to make sure you understand fully what we're about to do, including the potential dangers. It's something we may have overlooked in our rush to wed.' He glanced past her to make sure no one was eavesdropping. Then he shifted closer and dropped his voice. 'Not every player loses. There's a very real chance someone could win and bankrupt us, or a cheater I unmask might lash out at me or you. You must be sure this is the kind of life you want.'

He's trying to get me to cry off. She certainly would not. If she had to club him over the head and drag him up the aisle to ensure he said his vows, she would. She wouldn't be humiliated in front of the Fleet Street community again. 'After a lifetime of living here, having been in the house the night Laura's uncle tried to kill her, I'm well aware of the risks involved in dealing with money and people.'

'I don't doubt you can handle any challenge our life together might create.' His words were light, but there was no missing the deep furrow marring his brow, or his insistence in pressing on. She might not be willing to end things, but it didn't mean he wouldn't. 'But we can't be so lax about it or the realities of our situations.'

'Which are?'

He hesitated before he answered. 'The danger aligning yourself with me might put you in.'

She waited, bracing herself in anticipation of the words she expected to follow and end everything. Outside, her niece's and nephews' high voices rang out, tensing Jane's already tight nerves, but still Jasper didn't speak.

Don't do it, please, don't turn away from me. Her cheeks burned with her silent shame until she was sure they were the same red as her velvet dress. She didn't want to beg or to be this weak in front of him, but his pulling back cut deeper than when Mrs Hale had moved away. He'd promised to create a life, home and business with her. They weren't even married and he was already reneging on his word.

'What's really wrong, Jasper, please tell me?'

Jane studied Jasper with the same pleading look as the men who approached Mr Bronson in search of more credit. Her desperation cut him because he'd caused it. Instead of waiting and better thinking things through, he'd come here in a panic and created a doubt which hadn't existed before and it had hurt her.

Down the hall, the back door leading from the garden squeaked opened. The Rathbone children's footsteps rang through the house, accompanied by their high voices as they called to one another. It echoed with the sound of his childhood when he and Milton used to tear through the same door and race upstairs to find Jane and bring her out to play. He especially remembered the months after her parents' deaths when he'd come here to fetch her, eager to see his heartbroken friend smile again. Those days were gone, but Jane was here with him, as beautiful and trusting as back then. He couldn't throw her over the way his brother had. If she'd set her mind to facing all challenges with him—and Heaven knew after living with Philip Rathbone she was the best woman to do it—he couldn't push her away. He would find a way to keep her safe.

He pulled her to him and clutched her tight against his chest. Resting his chin on her smooth hair, he inhaled her gardenia scent and allowed it to soothe his concerns. 'Forgive me. I didn't mean to startle you with my visit. I just wanted to make sure you were completely aware of what marrying me means.'

She relaxed against him with a sigh of relief and slid her arms around his waist. 'Of course I'm aware of it. Despite it all, I still want to be your wife and work with you.'

'And you will.'

She leaned back but didn't pull away, her usual exuberance colouring her cheeks with a pink more alluring than the shameful red he'd brought to them a few minutes before, the weight of her as natural in his arms as his coat on his shoulders. 'Philip spoke to Reverend Claire this morning. It's all set for Friday at eleven o'clock, the soonest we could do it given the seven-day wait. The Reverend was stunned when he found out I'm marrying you. I'm surprised he didn't look up the rules of consanguinity to make sure it's all right for a woman to marry her former fiancé's brother.'

Jasper laughed, the first genuine one he'd enjoyed in ages. This was how it had always been between them and this was how it would continue. He'd make sure of it. 'I don't think he's so medieval.'

'I hope not for I have no desire to appeal to the Archbishop for a dispensation.'

He softly cuffed her under her chin. 'We could always elope and stun a few more people.'

'And deny everyone in the Fleet the chance to come and gawk? Heavens, no. I want them to be there when we see this betrothal through. And we will.' Her warning was clear. She would make him live up to his promise.

'Yes, we will.' He took her hand and brought it to rest over his heart. Her pulse flickered in each fingertip against his as he drank in her wide blue eyes and the full lips which were parted in anticipation. She wasn't just his greatest friend; she was about to be his wife. At fifteen, he'd longed for this, but he'd hesitated to tell her for fear she'd laugh at him. Then the night of his farewell party, with the single candle in the study making her eyes sparkle, she'd vowed to wait for his return. The missed opportunity had crushed him. It wasn't only his family he'd been exiled from, but a future with her. It was why he'd denied any feelings other than friendship and why he hadn't written despite dreaming of her. He'd been too angry over the chances stolen from him.

But they hadn't been stolen, only delayed.

The old bitterness faded under the soft pressure of her fingertips on the back of his neck and her stomach against his as he leaned down to press his lips to hers. A charge of passion arched between them, driving away his exhaustion and worry, and invigorating him like nothing since before the dreaded summer in Savannah. In her arms, the future surrounded him and he wanted to embrace it as he did her. With her help, he'd build a new life and at last bury the old one. He'd finally leave Savannah behind and Jane would be there to help him do it.

Chapter Five

'Are you sure you want to wear this dress?' Mrs Fairley, the blonde modiste, asked as she laid the silk creation across the back of the *chaise* in her fitting room. The modiste had sewn this dress for Jane's wedding to Milton, making it the only one she could have ready before Friday. Jane had insisted Mrs Fairley keep it, determined to wear it to the next Charton party and give Milton a taste of what he'd rejected. When the opportunity had finally arisen, Mrs Fairley had talked her out of her revenge, making Jane realise she'd only embarrass herself.

'Yes, I'm going to wear it.' After Jasper's visit this morning, Jane didn't want to waste money on a new gown she might not use. If this one didn't make it to the altar she'd sell it in Petticoat Lane herself instead of allowing it to moulder here like some shed skin. Then she'd use the money to buy a dog.

'Let's see it on you.' Mrs Fairley helped her pull on the dress, then ushered her up on to the stool. The cream-silk skirt brushed the tops of Jane's stocking-clad feet, the intricate embroidery of the interlaced diamonds decorating the hem and weighing it down. Blue-and-silver embroidered flowers coloured the bodice and set off her blue eyes. The dress was stunning, despite its past, and she craved the chance to wear it, at last to be a bride instead of a cast-off spinster—assuming Jasper intended to go through with the wedding.

'Are you excited about the marriage?' Mrs Fairley asked as she knelt to examine the hem.

'Yes.'

'But?'

Jane fingered a bit of lace. After this morning, she needed to speak with someone, and Mrs Fairley had always been discreet, even back when Philip had been the one paying her bills. 'I'm worried about Jasper. He was acting strange this morning.'

She explained about Jasper's visit and how sure she'd been that he would break the betrothal. What she didn't say was how, while she'd waited for him to do it, it had reminded her of sitting beside her mother's bed when she was six and begging for her to forgive her for being naughty, begging her not to leave. Jane bit her tongue, refusing to cry. She'd made so many promises during her parents' illnesses, vowing never again to disobey them and apologising over and over for slipping off to the fair against their wishes and bringing the fever into the house. In the end, her promises hadn't made a difference, neither had Milton's. There was nothing to make Jasper honour his.

'Do you think there is another woman?' Mrs Fairley asked as she slipped a pin in the hem.

Jane took a deep breath, the silk sliding up and over her chest before settling back into place. 'I don't think so, but it seems I'm the last to realise when a man takes a paramour. Besides, he hasn't been back in London long enough and there's nothing stopping him from marrying whoever he wants.'

'He wants to marry you.'

Jane touched her lips with the tips of her fingers. His kiss this morning had surprised her as much as the one in his bedroom. Despite having seen it coming, she hadn't expected the force of it. She'd leaned in to Jasper, savouring the tender pressure of his mouth against hers. In the salty taste of him there had lingered more than a deal or mere friendship and convenience; there had been the tantalising hint of a deeper connection. When he'd pulled back, she thought she'd seen the same realisation in his eyes but his smile and quick wit had covered it, making her wonder if she'd imagined it. Jane took another deep breath, almost afraid to say the next words aloud but they'd been boiling inside her since he'd left. 'I'm no longer sure he does.'

'I assume your brother approved the marriage?' Mrs Fairley knew Philip well. He'd loaned her the money to establish her shop after her husband had been wounded in France. She'd done a great deal of business with his family and friends ever since.

'He did.'

'Then take his consent as proof of your good judgement.'

'What if he's wrong this time?' Buying a building on a whim was one thing, but a marriage was entirely different. Once they were wed, Jasper, as her husband, would control her money, property and everything else. She doubted he'd act like a tyrant, but the darkness in his eyes when he'd first arrived at her house made her uneasy. She didn't want to marry him only to find out he wasn't the carefree friend she adored but someone else, a stranger she knew nothing about. 'What if I'm rushing into something I can't undo?'

'You wouldn't be the first Rathbone to do so, would you?' Mrs Fairley teased.

Philip and Laura had hurried to the altar and in the end found love. Jane wasn't convinced her haste would be rewarded nor was she willing to hope for such a happy outcome. Love had not been a part of their negotiations. 'Maybe Philip approved the match because he thinks it's his last chance to get rid of me?' The idea Philip had finally lost faith in her made her tremble.

Mrs Fairley stood. 'Mr Rathbone would never do anything not in your best interest. He loves you too much.'

Jane tried to believe it, but after having so many people leave her it was difficult to think her brother wouldn't do it, too, some day.

Mrs Fairley laid her hands on Jane's shoulders, squeezing them to ease the tension. 'Maybe it's not you Mr Charton doubts, but himself. Maybe he doesn't believe he's worthy of you.'

If so, he'd certainly be the first. 'Not Jasper. He's always been so sure of himself.'

'You think you know him, but I imagine, given your time apart, there's still a great deal for you to learn.' Mrs Fairley said it as though the discovery would be a grand adventure.

Jane wasn't so sure. Mrs Fairley was right, she didn't know Jasper as well as she believed, and she was making decisions based on nostalgia and desperation instead of reality. She didn't want another engagement to end, but marriage was the most binding of contracts. If she got it wrong, it might ruin her life more than it helped it. She twisted her hands in front of her, hating this uncertainty. There was only one way to face it. She must see Jasper again and put her doubts and his to rest.

'I hear you had a bit of an odd encounter with Adam's mother today,' Mr Bronson observed as he touched a burning reed to the bowl of his pipe and inhaled.

Jasper signed a paper, then set it aside to study his partner. 'Who told you about it?'

'He did, apologising the entire time. Thought I'd talk to you about what you want to do about it. Can't have her getting hysterical in public again.'

'There's nothing to be done. Tell him we spoke and make it clear he needs to ensure her silence. Then we forget the matter.' He wouldn't see Adam's siblings suffer from the loss of their brother's wages because of his mother any more than he could have abandoned Jane this morning. He set his pen in the elaborate holder, still cursing his foolishness. In the future, he'd have to be more careful about keeping his concerns regarding the hell to himself. 'Is Captain Christiansen here?'

'He is, but he isn't playing too deep, at least not yet. He's only had one or two drinks and the night is still young. However, there's the son of a cheesemonger in there with a fever to his play I don't like.'

'Yes, I saw the man's debts from last night. Cut him off when you go back inside and tell him he's banned from the club. Let him ruin himself elsewhere.' The Captain he would tolerate, but not the cheesemonger's son. The man didn't possess enough business knowledge to make his presence here of any value.

'You really going to give this up?' Mr Bronson waved at the office.

'When it's feasible. I'll turn ownership over to you and retain a percentage of the profits.' He picked up the wine order and added a few bottles of Spanish wine to it. Mr Portland, who owned a good many stocks, was more willing to speak to others about them after a few glasses of the tart liquor.

'Ah, so the answer is yes, and no.' Mr Bronson circled his pipe stem in the air.

'I can't afford to lose the income, not with a wife to support.' And the money he needed to send to Mrs Robillard and pay for his workers' wages.

'Probably children, too, they have a way of coming along.'

'I won't see them go without if the club isn't as lucrative as I hoped.' Rapacious hunger, and the filth and horror of disease had seized him once. He'd vowed never to become poor and end up in Seven Dials with the twin evils plaguing him or those he cared for again.

'Does your wife-to-be know this?' He set the pipe between his teeth.

'Not yet.' With her accounting skills, he knew he couldn't keep this detail from her or hide the transactions regarding Mrs Robillard for ever.

'Don't see why you need to tell her at all. A woman shouldn't be involved in a man's business.'

'I don't agree.' Except he did. Jane would have as large a hand as she wanted in the club and his life, but he would not allow her to be entangled in the business of the hell, or his past.

'For a man with so much to do you certainly sleep late.' The melodious female voice carried over the quiet of Jasper's bedroom, drawing him out of a deep sleep.

He opened his eyes, straining to see through the darkness cast by the heavy curtains covering the windows.

A little light sparked and then met the wick of a candle. It illuminated Jane's round face while she carried it from the hearth and set it on the table beside his bed.

'What are you doing in here?' He picked up the ornate dolphin clock next to the candle and peered at the hands. One-thirty. He didn't usually sleep this late. It explained the fatigue sticking to him like mud.

'I came to fetch you to visit the building on Fleet Street. I didn't expect to find you still in bed.' She stood over him like his mother used to do, more tempting than scolding with the glint of mischief in her azure eyes.

Jasper pushed himself up and leaned back against the stuffed pillows, trying to shake off his weariness. 'How did you sneak past my parents?'

'I didn't sneak. I came in through the front door. Your mother was the one who sent me up. Since we're betrothed and a date is set it seems she is no longer scandalised by the idea of my seeing you déshabillé.'

'So I see.' His mother possessed a practical sense of things.

'Even if she hadn't told me to come in here, your father's security is so lax it's a wonder the thieves of London aren't parading through the sitting room every day helping themselves to their things, and yours, though I'm not sure who'd want *your* things.' She picked up the clock, wrinkling her nose at the overly ornate gilding on the case before she set it back down. 'Your decor will have to change once we're married.'

'I look forward to it.' And to more intimate time in the bedroom with her. The memory of her lips beneath his made him trill his fingers on the cool sheets, eager to touch her silken hair and a few other soft and enticing places. He crossed his hands on his stomach. Temptation was dangerous, as he'd discovered in Savannah, but he'd be a liar if he said he'd never been tempted by Jane. At fifteen, despite their long friendship, salacious thoughts of her had cost him many a goodnight's sleep. He could imagine what his fifteen-year-old self would say if he knew he was days away from experiencing one of the many fantasies he'd concocted about her in the middle of the night.

'So, what, or should I say who, kept you up so late last night?' she asked in a crisp voice. There was no missing the jealousy flavouring her question or the true intention of this visit. *She's here to make sure I uphold my end of the contract.* Her brother had taught her well.

'I was quite free of female company if that's what you're getting at.' He ran his hands through his hair, determined to prove himself and make her forget yesterday's misstep. 'But if you'd like to keep me awake tonight, I wouldn't protest.'

Her eyes dropped to his chest, then lower down to another muscle hidden beneath the coverlet. 'I'm keeping you awake right now.'

'Indeed, you are.' He laced his fingers behind his head. 'Anything in particular you'd like to do about it?'

'Not this morning.' The faint hint of pink colouring her cheeks undermined her courage. It increased his desire to pull her into bed and teach her something, but he didn't. He doubted his mother was so open-minded when it came to their betrothal.

It was time to get down to less pleasurable business. 'What about the Fleet Street building do you wish to discuss?'

She rose, plucked his discarded Jermyn Street shirt off the foot of the bed and flung it at him. 'Get up and we will visit it together and I'll tell you.'

'I've given a great deal of thought to the food we'll offer here,' Jane announced while they stood in the entry hall of the musty building. It had been closed up for weeks and the remnants of tobacco and shattered clay pipes lay scattered across the unpolished floor.

'Shouldn't we consider the condition first?' He wiped a line of dust off the dull banister. In the midst of their dirty surroundings, Jane dazzled in her fitted blue pelisse with the stiff collar brushing the slant of her delicate chin. The hint of the cream dress beneath, and the smooth skin of her chest visible at the open V, made concentrating on work a challenge.

'I did, right after I purchased it. My builder assures me it's sound and, with little more than some cleaning and paint, we can open as soon as everything else is in place. Tell me which rooms you intend to use for what activities and I'll start gathering the necessary items.'

He motioned with his hat to the front window overlooking Fleet Street, determined to think about the club and not the subtle hint of her curving hips beneath her long skirt. 'We'll offer cigars and wine in there. The back room will be a lounge.'

'And upstairs?'

'Private rooms for men to conduct confidential business.'

She crossed her arms under her full breasts. 'What kind of confidential business?'

'The business kind of business.' He took her hand and slid his other around her waist. Her eyes widened when he snapped her close, her chest catching like his before his wink drew out her smile. Then he waltzed her into the dining room before spinning her out so her skirts flared around her ankles. He let go of her, sending her whirling gracefully across the empty room. 'Do you think we should offer dancing?'

'Certainly not. We don't want to distract men from spending money.' She pressed one hand to her chest and struggled to speak through her giggles. The collusion making her eyes flash reminded him of when they used to sneak out to Club Row Market to feed the puppies for sale before their owners caught them. 'But we'll serve better fare than what they're used to and give them a reason to bring clients here instead of dining at home.'

'Good idea. I'll leave it to you to choose the chef and the menu since you're more acquainted with London tastes than I am.' He spun his hat between his hands, picturing the room full of tables covered with white linen and fine port and beef with men discussing contracts and trade. Jasper would stand proud among them instead of skulking in the shadows of night. His only ties to the hell would be the money which would continue to come in and protect them from the prospect of poverty.

'I already have an idea for a special cheese, a delicacy to tempt them. We must also choose the decor. This must look like a respectable place of business, not a colonial bordello.' She slid him a teasing look before turning her attention to the dining room. 'You can close the hell at once and sell its contents to pay for what we need here.'

Jasper tightened his grip on his hat, denting the brim before he released it. 'I can't.'

She whirled to face him, shoulders set for a fight. 'Why not? I thought you wanted to leave it behind.'

'I do, but I owe it to Mr Bronson to offer it to him before I depart. I can't do it as a gutted shell.'

She narrowed her eyes at him as if wanting to say she didn't entirely believe his intention to give it to a friend instead of closing it outright. 'Have you spoken to him to see if he even wants it?'

'I have and he does.' At least this was the truth.

'And will you be keeping a share of its profits?'

Damn, she was too intuitive. He wasn't ready to have this conversation, but there was no avoiding it now. 'Yes.'

'You can't expect to clear your conscience with a toe in each world.'

'I can't risk us going broke if the club fails either.' He wouldn't have them burning through his money and hers in an effort to stay out of debtors' prison.

'It won't fail. We won't let it, especially if our livelihoods depend on it.'

He didn't share her confidence, not after all the

times he'd seen men go from wealthy to broke with one turn of the cards. His silence dimmed her optimism.

'We will be able to attract enough patrons to support the club and us, won't we?' Jane picked at the button on her glove in a rare moment of self-doubt and it struck Jasper hard. It wasn't like her to question her plans.

'We will. Mr Bronson will spread the word among our guests, especially the more influential ones. We'll offer them a special membership, entice them into joining and others will follow. It always worked in Savannah.'

'Did it now?'

'Attracting patrons is the one other skill Uncle Patrick taught me that I excelled at. How do you think I drew men to the Company Gaming Room so fast?' The sense of accomplishment he used to experience on nights when every chair at every table was filled and a crowd two or three deep stood behind them gripped him. He should be ashamed, not proud. The one consolation was realising he'd soon put some of what he'd learned to reputable use.

'Then I have no doubt we'll be successful in London.'

Her faith in him was touching if not disconcerting. His uncle had believed in him and he'd let him down. He wondered how long it would be until she and all the others, both here and in America, who relied on him, suffered the same disappointment.

'Hello?' Mr Bronson called out, breaking the quiet between Jasper and Jane. 'Anyone here?'

'In the dining room.' Jasper turned as his associate strolled into the dining room. 'We were just talking about you. I was telling Miss Rathbone what an excellent partner you are.'

'So exceptional, I brought you last night's take.' He handed Jasper a leather folder full of banknotes.

'Thank you, but how did you find me here?'

'I went by your house and they told me you were here.' This wasn't the first time Mr Bronson had gone searching for him at the Charton house. He'd met Jasper's family shortly after their return and during the many times he'd collected Jasper on the pretext of other business while they'd been establishing the Company Gaming Rooms.

Jasper tucked the folio under his arm and drew Jane to his side. 'Miss Rathbone, allow me to introduce my associate, Mr Gabriel Bronson.'

'A pleasure to meet you.' Mr Bronson swept off his hat and folded into a deep bow.

Jane curtsied, then rose with an impish smile. 'Quite an angelic name for a gambler?'

'My father was a preacher.' Mr Bronson set his hat on his head and hooked his thumbs in his waistcoat pocket. 'Tried to redeem me before I was even a man. Didn't realise I was already lost.'

'And what about Jasper, how lost was he in Savannah? He's told me so little of it. I want to know what he was like there.'

Mr Bronson exchanged a wary glance with Jasper. 'There isn't really much to tell. It's not so different here than it was there. He still enjoyed the finer things like clothes, and wines, but he had to come to London to find the finest fiancée.'

To Jasper's amazement, Jane blushed. 'I don't believe you. There must have been something different about him there.'

Mr Bronson took his tobacco pouch out of his pocket and swung it in a small circle in front of him. 'Well, Jasper did attend the theatre more and of course there was the gaming room.' He described to Jane the gaming room in all its glittering and gaudy splendour and Jasper's and Uncle Patrick's place in it, trips to the theatre and parties at the finest Savannah homes with the mayor and other influential men. Jasper could barely recall the lively and carefree man he used to be before the epidemic, the one he could be again with Jane by his side.

'I didn't realise Jasper was so influential in Savannah, or how wide a swathe he cut through high society,' Jane remarked with amusement when Mr Bronson finished his tale.

Jasper shook his head. 'It wasn't as impressive as he's making it sound.'

'Or you're being modest.'

'He's right Miss Rathbone, I might have embellished a little, but I want you to think well of your husband-to-be.'

'Will you be at the wedding, Mr Bronson?' Jane asked.

'No. I don't fancy formal events, but I wish you all the best, Miss Rathbone. You've found a fine man in Jasper.' He slapped Jasper on the back. 'Now, if you'll excuse me, my bed is calling.'

With another imperial bow he took his leave.

'For a rake he's a charming man. I see why you chose him to be the face of your gaming room,' Jane observed once he was gone. 'And you're right. It wouldn't be fair to sell it out from under him. I'll use my money to purchase the necessary furniture and accoutrements.'

'No, I have ample funds for it. I'll advance them to you and you can purchase what you need with them. I'll also give you free rein on contracts and spending once we're married, sooner if you'd like. We can visit my solicitor, Mr Steed, tomorrow and make all the necessary arrangements.'

'Yes, I want everything to be in place so I can begin at once and, while the hell is still yours, make sure the two of you promote the benefits of our club,' Jane added.

'We've already begun. I can also sell what's still in the warehouse since I'm sure you have no desire to see it installed in our house.' He came up to her and placed his arms around her waist, holding her as naturally as he breathed.

'You're right. I have no desire to decorate like the Sun King.'

'Too bad, the bed in the warehouse is quite sturdy.' He pulled her tighter against him.

She laid her hands on his shoulder and playfully peered up at him. 'Is it, now?'

He brought his mouth so close to her ear, his lips brushed the lobe as he whispered, 'Very.'

She shivered and he closed his eyes, nearly groaning at the sweetness of her response.

'Then perhaps we can keep the one piece.' She ran her finger along the lapel of his coat, the gesture as tempting as it was subtle.

He was about to accept the silent invitation in her eyes and touch his lips to hers when the bells of St Bride's Church rang out and Jane jerked back. 'Oh, we have another appointment.'

He brushed her neck with his lips. 'Are you sure you want to go?'

She pushed him out to arm's length, the businesswoman in her winning out over the vixen. 'We aren't married yet and there's a cheesemonger expecting us.'

A half-hour later they stood in Mr Stilton's shop, sampling a variety of cheddar like none they'd ever tasted before. It was difficult for Jane to concentrate on the tang of the cheese with the taste of Jasper still so sharp. He wore a fawn-coloured coat over a dark waistcoat. Both were tailored to fit his firm chest and offer a hint of what she'd seen the other morning. In the carriage on the way here, she'd considered tempting him into another peek, but had refrained. She'd been audacious enough in her proposal, she didn't wish to appear like a harlot or ruin the delights of the wedding night with her impatience.

'What do you think?' She licked a crumb off her

lip, subtle in her teasing, aware of Mr Stilton watching them.

'It's a true temptation to the palate.' The potency in Jasper's eyes stole any suggestive responses from her tongue. Flirting didn't come naturally to her, except when she was with him.

'I sell this variety to some of the most important men in London.' Mr Stilton rocked on his heels in pride, his soft chin raised.

'An excellent angle for marketing it to our clients, at a mark-up, of course,' Jane suggested to Jasper.

'Of course.'

Jane fell silent while Jasper spoke to Mr Stilton about how much they would need and a possible date for delivery. She calculated the price, as she had with everything else connected with establishing the club, and it was substantial. If Jasper harboured doubts about the solvency of their venture then she couldn't fault or chide him for hanging on to part of the hell. Not even her inheritance would be enough to save them if the losses proved too large. She'd seen enough men come to Philip for loans for shops and ventures only to have a fire, flood or sunken ship send them spiralling into insolvency. Even Philip had once come close to losing everything. In the months after they'd lost their parents, while he was caring for her and taking over their father's business, he'd extended a sizeable loan to a silversmith who'd defaulted. It had almost ruined his entire business. Mr Charton, having been a good friend of their father's, had stepped in to help stop Philip from being ruined. She'd been a child then, but in her grief she'd caught the strain in Philip's face and overheard enough conversations to realise the severity of what was going on. Philip had worried with Mr Charton over not being able to provide for Jane or being forced by his losses to leave her with the Chartons and it had terrified her. She'd been a burden he hadn't needed at a time when everything had been falling on his shoulders and there'd been nothing she could do to help him. She wondered what burden she now placed on Jasper and if this was why he'd hesitated about the wedding yesterday.

Jane stepped a touch closer to Jasper. She'd wrangled him into marrying her. It made her wonder whether he offered wanton kisses, suggestions and compliments because he really wanted to or because, having made his decision after yesterday's doubts, he must now convince them both it was the right one.

'Thank you, Mr Stilton, for everything.' Jasper shook the cheesemonger's hand, then guided Jane towards the entrance of the shop, his arm solid on hers.

She placed her hand over his as they stepped outside on to the pavement. She was no longer a helpless child, she was a grown woman who would not be a burden to him; she would be a partner in their success. It was how much of a partner he intended to be that she still worried about.

They left the shop and were not three feet from the entrance when Chester Stilton staggered out of a hack, his usually pristine clothes as rumpled as the skin beneath his eyes. With her doubts trailing her, he was one of the last people she wished to encounter and she tugged on Jasper's arm, hoping to hurry past before he noticed them. They were not fast enough.

'Miss Rathbone, here to change your mind about my offer?' Chester called out, forcing her and Jasper to face the man.

'I see your credit with your tailor has run out.' She motioned to the patched tear on his lapel.

He reddened with shame at being caught looking less than impeccable. Then he leaned in close to her, his eyes as bloodshot as his breath was foul. 'Come to sneer at me, spinster?'

'Mind how you address her,' Jasper warned from beside her.

Mr Stilton curled one lip at him, revealing his yellow teeth. 'Who are you?'

'Jasper Charton.' Jasper took Jane's hand. 'Her fiancé.'

'Picking up your brother's leftovers, I see,' Mr Stilton sneered before turning to Jane. 'What did you do to get him? Purchase him like you couldn't purchase his brother?'

Jasper slid in between Jane and the cheesemonger's son. He stood a good head taller than Chester and leaned so close to him, he was forced to bend back to avoid being nose to nose with Jasper. 'Speak to her like that again and I'll see to it your debts are called in. I don't mean your debt at the tailor, I mean the gambling ones you've run up at the Company Gaming Room.'

Jane stifled a squeak of surprise while struggling

to hold her look of disdain. *Mr Stilton gambles at Jasper's hell.*

Mr Stilton's lips dropped down over his teeth and the blood drained out of his flushed face. 'How do you know about those? I've never seen you there.'

'I'm a well-connected man. If you don't wish to be strung up by your debts, or have your father inadvertently learn of them, you'll keep your opinions about Miss Rathbone to yourself. Do I make myself clear?'

Mr Stilton flicked a nervous glance at Jane before nodding in agreement.

'Good, then we've settled the matter.' Jasper straightened, turned to Jane and offered her his arm. She took it, jutting her chin out in defiance of Mr Stilton when they stepped around him. 'Good day, Mr Stilton.'

Jane didn't dare speak until they were down the street and well away from the cheesemonger. 'Why did you threaten him with his club debts?'

His arm beneath her hand stiffened. 'Because he deserved it for insulting you.'

'But you risked him finding out about your involvement in the hell. If he had, he's weasel enough to have used it against you.'

'I've seen him gamble. He isn't smart enough to make the connection.' Jasper stopped and faced her. 'Besides, you're worth the risk.'

Jane's back stiffened. She'd waited years for someone to value her like this, someone not related to her by blood or marriage. The fact it was Jasper seemed right, but the old doubts refused to be silenced. 'No, I'm not.'

He brushed her cheek with his fingers. 'Despite what you believe, you're an exceptional woman worthy of respect and admiration. I'm the one who doesn't deserve you.'

'Of course you do.' People shuffled by on the narrow pavement, silently scolding them for blocking traffic. Jane was barely conscious of their censure as Jasper caressed her cheek with his thumb. He'd been willing to risk having his respectability challenged to defend her, and it was obvious he didn't regret it. This more than his words—his offer to turn over his affairs at once, or his kisses, spoke to how much he valued her and their coming union.

Mrs Fairley was right. Jane hadn't made a mistake.

Chapter Six

'In case you're unfamiliar with what will take place tonight, allow me to explain,' Mrs Hale offered while Laura did up the buttons on the back of Jane's wedding dress. With her straight nose and auburn hair tinged with grey, Mrs Hale resembled Laura, except her eyes were pale brown while Laura's were hazel. 'When a gentleman and a lady are alone together…'

'Yes, I'm well aware of what will transpire.' Jane had eavesdropped on Jasper's sister enough times when she was younger to learn the full extent of things. However, having an understanding of how the deed worked and experiencing it were two very different things. Jane took such a deep breath, she feared the buttons might pop off their threads. If what was to come with Jasper was anything like his kisses, she wasn't sure how she'd make it through tonight without melting into a puddle.

'Too bad, I was looking forward to describing it in more flowery language than I usually hear in Dr

Hale's practice.' Mrs Hale laughed from her place on the sofa. It was the first time the three women had been together in months and her presence helped calm Jane. She'd been like a mother to her, helping her grow from a young girl to a woman and calming her on more than one occasion when Jane had been fuming over some slight or one of Philip's decisions. In Mrs Hale's smile and the delighted way she spun her cane as she held it in front of her, Jane could almost imagine her own mother here.

She would be here if it hadn't been for me. Jane tried to smile while the other ladies continued to joke and tease, but her lips were as tight as her nerves.

'If you have any questions after the deed, you know where to find me.' Mrs Hale clapped with the same restrained exuberance she'd shown when Laura had made her a grandmother. Then she rose and came to stand beside her, fingering the fine embroidered lace cascading from the shoulders of the dress to brush the hem of the skirt. 'I'm glad you'll finally be able to attach a good memory to this bit of silk. You deserve to be happy.'

Her eyes misted with tears as she took Jane by the shoulders and turned her to face the mirror. Any reservations Jane might have had about the dress vanished as the thirteen-year-old girl who'd spent days in this room mourning the departure of her friend, and praying he might some day return, rose up inside her. He had come back to her. He was the first.

Philip rapped on the door and then entered. He wore his best morning suit, as handsome today as when he'd married Laura. He stopped at the sight of his sister, and his eyes shone with pride. 'You're lovely.'

He came forward and pressed a tender kiss to her forehead. Tears blurred her vision, but she brushed them off with her gloved fingertips, not wanting to meet Jasper with red eyes. Philip was almost the only parent she'd ever known, and for all her wanting to have a home of her own, she was at last leaving his. Every argument they'd ever had and each disagreement meant nothing compared to the affection in his smile.

'Thank you.' *For everything.* He'd always been a loving brother, doing his best to raise her. She'd miss his steady presence, despite all of their butting heads.

'Are you ready?'

The day she never thought would come was here at last. She would finally be a bride. It was time to go and claim her life with Jasper. 'I am.'

Jasper stood at the altar, Reverend Claire beside him, his younger brother Giles serving as Jasper's best man while Jacob sulked in the pew at not having been chosen. A few years ago it would have been Milton beside him, but he was the only Charton not in attendance. He and his wife had elected to stay away from the church, but at his father's insistence he'd grudgingly agreed to bring his wife to the wedding breakfast at the Rathbones'.

Jasper's three elder sisters and their husbands and children sat in the first few pews. While his numerous nieces and nephews whispered and giggled with the Rathbone children, his sisters and his mother sniffed into their handkerchiefs. A few months ago they'd been worried he'd die in Savannah. They were overjoyed to see him now on his wedding day.

He rubbed the back of his neck and the slight perspiration beneath his collar. They cared for him and he was deceiving them all. They'd despise him if they ever found out about the hell and shun him just as surely as they embraced him today. He'd have no one to blame but himself if they did. If the day ever came, he hoped they showed Jane as much tolerance as they'd extended to Milton. He couldn't bear to have her cast out of her family for his mistakes.

'You're not nervous, are you?' Giles ribbed, pulling Jasper out of his worries.

'No.' He exchanged a hearty smile with his younger brother. 'Just eager.'

And he was. The day he'd left London with Jane's willingness to wait for him still fresh in his mind, he'd believed every hope he'd ever harboured of being with his closest friend was finished. He'd make sure she never suffered because of him, or viewed him with the same disgust he'd come to see his uncle with. She would remain innocent where he'd been corrupted and he would do everything he could to make sure she never wanted for anything.

The organ struck up, drawing Jasper and the entire church's attention to the back. Jane appeared at the top of the aisle, resplendent in an ivory-silk dress with a train of lace, walking with dignity beside her brother in time to the organ music. Her cobalt-coloured eyes fixed on his, so alight with joy it took his breath away. He'd thought luck had deserted him in Savannah, then he'd come home and met her again. She knew more about him than anyone in this church and still she was willing to bind her life to his. He didn't deserve her admiration, but he'd find a way to be worthy of her.

At last, Jane reached him and, after a few words from the Reverend Claire, Philip offered Jasper his sister's hand and her future. Jasper couldn't stop the smile from spreading across his lips and Jane answered it with a playful one of her own. It echoed with the memories of them laughing together at his eldest sister Olivia's wedding. At the reception, they'd played the game of what if, taking turns imagining who their future partner would be. Secretly, he'd hoped it would be her. Today, it was. It wasn't desperation that had guided her up the aisle to him, but a connection they'd shared for years, one which hadn't been broken by time or distance or all his sins.

At Reverend Claire's instruction, they faced him. While the Reverend spoke, Jasper was aware of nothing but Jane beside him, her fingers solid against his and her light perfume brushing his senses. She was as gorgeous, trusting and innocent as he was dark, experienced and dishonest, but if she believed in him then it was time to start believing in himself.

When Reverend Claire asked if there was anyone

who objected to the marriage, Jasper didn't flinch or peer over his shoulder to see if someone came forward. No one, not even his previous doubts, spoke up.

Reverend Claire drew out the silence as though he expected some objection, if not from the audience then from the groom. Jane studied Jasper out of the corner of her eye, wondering if he held any of the second thoughts he'd expressed to her the other day. But they were nowhere to be seen as he drew his lips to one side in a playful grin she matched.

Hearing no objections, Reverend Claire continued until it was time to exchange vows. With a seriousness to put her brother to shame, she faced Jasper, delighted to see him bring the same gravity to the solemn words. He'd already made one promise to her in private—to always honour her. Today, he'd make a few more for everyone to hear.

Then it was her turn. So many times Jane had been selfish in her wants, but it was no longer about her any more. Jasper needed her as much as she needed him, not only to build his business but to rebuild the part of himself Savannah and the fever had damaged. She raised her eyes to his, determined he see how seriously she took her vows to him, too. He gently caressed one of her fingers with his as if hearing her silent promise.

Then Reverend Claire called for the rings. Giles handed Jasper a small box and Jane shifted on her feet, eager to see what he'd selected for her. She gasped when he opened it to reveal a diamond larger than the one in his cravat pin set in a thick gold band. He slipped it out of its case and on to her finger, the weight of it making her eye him with a sly smile.

He cocked a self-satisfied eyebrow at her and from the corner of her eyes she noticed all the women in the pews shifting to get a better look. She tried not to smile too wide in delight. Vanity was a sin, but she didn't care. She was wearing the biggest diamond in the church. Without waiting for Reverend Claire to tell her, she threw her arms around his neck and pulled him into their first married kiss.

Jasper escorted his new bride, who beamed like the morning sun, back to the Rathbone house and the wedding breakfast. A parade of revellers and well-wishers followed the new couple across the street and inside. Even Milton and his wife were there although they refrained from joining the receiving line.

Once the formalities were through, everyone went to the garden and the tables of food arranged among the rose bushes. A harpist played in the shade of the portico while hired footmen wove through the guests, offering champagne and headier spirits for the gentlemen. Jane was happily showing her ring to Justin and his wife Susanna when the clink of a spoon against a glass drew everyone's attention.

'To my son and his lovely wife.' Jasper's father's deep voice carried over the garden from where he stood on the portico with Giles and Jacob. His nose was red, his eyes heavy. Despite it being the middle of the day, he'd indulged in a generous amount of Mr

Rathbone's fine Madeira. Jasper joined Jane as the entire crowd turned to admire them. 'I can't say I'm surprised to see you married, you two were as thick as thieves as children. One time, I caught them sneaking out of our house with a rope, threepence and a bottle of my best wine...'

'Henry, I'm sure no one wants to hear such stories today,' his wife gently reminded him, stopping him from finishing his tale of the morning he'd caught Jasper and Jane plotting to sell the wine and buy the pony Philip had refused to purchase for Jane.

'I suppose you're right.' Jasper's father rubbed his chin before he seemed to recall why he'd begun to speak. 'What I mean to say is, you two were meant to be together and I can't tell you how happy I am to see it happen at last. We worried about you, Jasper, when you were gone, feared you'd never make it home again, but you returned to us and to Jane.' He raised his glass to them. 'We love you both and wish you the greatest happiness.'

The guests raised their glasses in agreement. Jasper swept Jane's lips with a sweet kiss and the guests applauded.

'Well done, Jasper and Jane, well done.' His father clapped before hurrying to chase down a footman with a full tray of wine.

Jane entwined her arm with Jasper's. 'He's quite the orator, isn't he?'

'Indeed he is.' The speech reminded Jasper of the many his father had given during family dinners and Christmas mornings as a boy, the ones he'd missed while he'd been away. Across the garden, his father spoke with some associates, confident and sure of himself despite his having imbibed a little too much. If he ever learned what exactly Jasper had made of himself in Savannah, and London, he'd never toast him again.

Beneath the clear blue sky hanging over the garden, and with the guests laughing and chatting, it was difficult to take his worries seriously. With Jane working alongside him, they'd have the club founded in a matter of weeks and he could stop living two separate lives. He might retain a percentage of the hell, but he'd have nothing more to do with its nightly activities, no extending of credit or having a hand in how any of the clients decided to waste their livelihoods. His father would never find out exactly what he'd sent his son to and what kind of man it had made him.

'Jane, come with me.' Olivia, Jasper's eldest sister by ten years, hurried up to Jane and took her by the arm. 'Lily, Alice and I have some advice we're dying to give you.' She led Jane off to join his other two sisters near the fountain along the back wall, welcoming Jane into the circle of married ladies. Olivia, with their mother's fair complexion and lithe frame, talked the most, taking her role as eldest sister and potential marital mentor very seriously.

'Olivia wasn't so welcoming of Camille and Father wasn't so effusive with his congratulations at my wedding dinner.' Milton appeared at Jasper's side, intent on bringing shade to the sunny day. He'd always been the most serious of the three of them, fretting over the consequences of their plotted adventures. He'd become even more morose as an adult. 'But then you always did get the better deal.'

Jasper took a sip of his champagne to bite back the remark about it being his and his wife's own fault they hadn't received a warm wedding reception. This was not the time to start an argument. 'I think you got the better end of the deal. I've seen horrors you can't even imagine.'

A shadow seemed to pass over the garden until Jasper caught Jane's eye. She flashed him a proud smile to drive back the darkness encroaching on him and he raised his glass to her.

'There can't always have been death and disease. There must've been something more thrilling to have kept you there for so long.' It was the first sentence Milton had uttered to Jasper without each word dripping with condescension or jealousy.

Jasper studied Milton, seeing a hint of the brother he'd left and not the rival he'd become. 'There was at one time, but nothing, and especially no one, there who can compare to here.'

None of the women he'd been with in Savannah, not the jaded widows who gambled as hard as the men, nor the bored planters' wives who were eager to educate a man new to intimate nights, could match Jane. Her beauty was like deep water, not flashy or overdone, but steady, enhanced by her curves and the smooth fit of her dress. Her innocence called to him, as did her sharp wit and head for business.

'Of course, I haven't done too poorly.' The brief moment of fraternity vanished as Milton puffed out his chest in pride and lifted his champagne glass to his wife who stood in the corner. 'I've done well with Father, increasing his profits on more than one occasion, and I have a fine wife.'

Camille responded with a small smile before peering longingly at Jane and Jasper's sisters while they continued to talk. It gave Jasper a better understanding of why Milton had chosen her over Jane. His wife held back where Jane strode forward and she wasn't likely to show Milton up or reveal his weakness in business by exercising her strength. Milton might have avoided the challenges of a strong wife, but Jasper would welcome them, especially tonight. 'If you'll excuse me.'

Jasper wove his way through the guests to reach Jane, who stood now with Mr and Mrs Rathbone. Once beside her, he took her hand. He caught the slight intake of breath as he caressed her palm with his thumb.

'Tell me about your cotton-trading business in Savannah, Mr Charton,' Mrs Rathbone pressed. 'My father was a draper, and I used to help him in his shop. I once knew a great deal about southern cotton. I'm curious to see how much I remember.'

Jasper's thumbed stilled on Jane's palm and her fingers tightened around his. He knew as much about cotton as Uncle Patrick had, which was nothing. He hadn't expected Mrs Rathbone to be an expert. He racked his brain, trying to remember any of the conversations he used to overhear while pouring libations or slipping notes for more credit beneath the cotton-growers' pens. Nothing came to him.

'Don't pester him with work, Laura.' Jane batted her free hand at her sister-in-law. 'We're here to celebrate, not to be serious.'

'Marriage has changed you already, Jane. You rarely ever pass up a chance to discuss business.' Mr Rathbone regarded Jasper and Jane the way he used to when they were children and he caught them entering the house after being up to no good. Thankfully, Jasper's mother approached and drew the host and hostess away.

Jane brushed her forehead with the back of her hand. 'I see what you mean about lying to everyone.'

'Why didn't you tell me your sister-in-law knew about cotton?'

'Because I haven't heard her speak of it in years. I didn't think she'd bring it up today.'

'I might have to read up on the subject before our first family dinner,' he joked, working to set her, and himself, at ease.

Jane tried to share in Jasper's humour, but the brief interlude with Laura and Philip had left her shaken. Jane might have put Laura off the subject, but she'd noticed Philip scrutinising her and her husband.

My husband.

She stepped closer to him. Let Philip scrutinise them. She was a married woman now and he no longer had a say in her affairs.

* * *

It was dusk when the merry guests saw Jane and Jasper off in his landau. She could barely sit still beside him as the vehicle carried them from St Bride's Lane to Jasper's town house in Gough Square. In the privacy of the conveyance, she considered starting their marital relations early, but she didn't want to shock the driver when they arrived at their destination.

Instead, she enjoyed the weight of his arm on her shoulders and the solid muscle of his thigh beneath her palm while they laughed about Mr Jones having tried to outdrink Mr Charton and failing.

Once they reached his house, he introduced her to his few servants, then showed her around the recently painted and repaired narrow rooms filled with the same gaudy furniture as his office. Like the furniture in the warehouse, it had belonged to his uncle and had come with the house. They poked into this room and that, discussing the minor details of housekeeping while avoiding the most important one waiting for them above stairs. They'd been friends for years and shared some of the most private events of their lives. None of those would compare to what was about to pass between them.

At last, with darkness settling over the house, they lit the candles and followed the housekeeper, Mrs Hodgkin, upstairs. Jane's things were settled and away in Jasper's room, her life at last completely one with his, leaving only the melding of their bodies to accomplish. At thirteen, she'd dreamed of this night, but as she'd watched him from the back of Philip's landau as it pulled away from the Charton house, leaving him to his family and the ship that would carry him away, she'd never believed it possible. She held up her hand and the large diamond in her wedding band sparkled in the candlelight. He was hers and she was his.

'Do you like it?' he asked.

'I do. It's as overdone as the rest of your things.' She motioned to the large, gilded four-poster bed from the warehouse, all but engulfing the room. It had been assembled and cleaned with a large mattress affixed to its sturdy frame.

'Redo the rest of the decor if you like, but I assure you, by tomorrow you will not want to part with this piece.' He slapped the post of the bed and it barely shivered, unlike her.

'You're so sure.' She swallowed hard, suddenly nervous.

'Incredibly so.' He slipped his arms about her waist and the room constricted even more.

'I hope you're right. After hearing so much about the deed, I'd hate to be disappointed.'

'You won't be.' He entangled his fingers in her hair, dislodging her curls from their pins as he brought his lips down to cover hers.

She gripped his shoulders and her knees began to fail. This was it, the moment they would at last become more than friends, but man and wife. She followed his lead, trying to match his moves as though they were engaged in a game of chess, but she soon gave up. All she could do was feel his breath against her cheeks, his hands gliding up her back and the anticipation engulfing her insides when he began to undo the buttons of her dress. Button by button he freed the silk from her shoulders until it dropped down over her hips to pool at her feet.

He leaned back to take in the curve of her waist beneath the stays and her breasts taut against the confining boning. Her skin tingled with the expectation of his touch, but instead he shrugged out of his coat and waistcoat before pulling his shirt over his head to reveal his captivating chest. He was all hers now and she was free to do anything with him. She touched his stomach lightly while he slid his hand up along the satin around her waist before reaching behind it to undo the laces of her stays. While he worked, he pressed light kisses to the tops of each breast, making her breath quicken before she inhaled sharply as her stays came loose and dropped to the floor.

The chemise billowed out around her as she stepped forward to caress the line of him, as curious about him as he was of her. Beneath his breeches she saw the evidence of his need and wanted to see more. She undid one button of his fall, waiting for him to stop her, but he watched with a crooked grin, his pupils as wide and dark as the next button she undid. At last the fall gaped open and she hooked her fingers inside the waist of his breeches. His chest expanded as her fingers brushed the smooth skin beneath while she pushed the buckskin down over his hips.

She followed them lower, coming face to face with

his desire and wondering how she'd accommodate such a thing. She stood up fast, embarrassed for the first time this evening. He didn't leave her to suffer, but gripped the sides of her chemise and pulled it over her head. She stood before him naked, her breasts heavy beneath his admiring gaze, but she made no move to cover herself. She trusted him to guide her tonight.

He caught her by the waist and pulled her to him again. Her breasts flattened against his chest while his member pressed hot and full against her stomach. He clasped her buttocks as he brought his mouth down against hers, raw and hungry in his need. With small circles he traced the line of her neck. She arched back while he dipped lower and lower until his lips took in the tender point of her breast. She cried out, digging her hands into his hair as she braced herself against the sensation his caressing tongue created deep inside of her.

Aware of the ache he'd raised, he slid his fingers down her hips, trailed them across her stomach and then slipped them between her legs.

None of the books ever described this! She rose up on her toes, his caresses pushing her toward something just out of her reach. Then he withdrew and she moaned in frustration as she lowered herself, but he didn't allow it to last. He gathered her into his arms and carried her to the bed, continuing to tease her tongue with his.

The sheets were cold as he laid her on them and then covered her body with his. He gently nudged her legs apart with his knees and settled between them. She gasped as he pressed against her and she opened herself wider to him, ready to take him in. He didn't push forward but lingered there, painfully close and yet holding back.

She shifted her hips toward his, trying to draw him in, but he moved away again.

They'd been apart for too long, across too many years and so much sadness. She wanted to be one with him, to claim all of him as he was claiming all of her. She brought her lips to his ears. 'Please, don't draw away.'

He stilled in her arms. His heart beat against her chest and he rested his cheek against hers so she couldn't see his face. She didn't move, wondering if she'd made some mistake and if he'd slide off and leave her with the terrible, aching need in her body and her heart.

At last he rose up on his elbows. Sweat glistened on his forehead. 'Are you sure you truly want me?'

'I always have.'

He claimed her mouth with urgency, as if he could kiss her deep enough to erase their time apart. Then he brought his hips forward and in one smooth motion joined with her at last.

Jasper muffled her mouth with his, taking in her cries of pleasure as she took him into herself. He wrapped his arms tight around her, groaning as he claimed her innocence, selfish in his desire to have it and her. This was how it should have been years ago, with nothing between them, not her experiences or his, their lives intermingling in a way no one could interrupt. Her fingernails dug into his back as he stroked deeper into her, wanting to bring them so close they might never be apart. In the sweet entwining of her legs with his, he could feel her pulling him into her. She wanted all of him and he would find a way to give it to her, to be the man he'd promised he would be.

With her breath fast in his ear, her whimpers vibrating through his chest, he drove them toward a release greater than their bodies until at last their pleasure crested and they cried out together.

'Was it all you expected?' Jasper asked as she lay beside him, her hair spilling across the pillow and over her shoulder to cover the pink tips of her breasts.

'It was more divine than I could have imagined.' She stretched like a cat on her back beside him, making her full breasts arch and stoking the fire which still smouldered inside him. 'I probably shouldn't tell you so. It'll make you arrogant.'

He turned on his side to face her and laid a hot hand on her stomach, making small circles around her navel. 'Good, I take pride in my skills.'

The dolphin clock chimed ten times. Each knock of the tiny hammer against the bell stilled his hand and stole some of the calm he'd experienced during their lovemaking. In her arms he'd forgotten about the hell by the Thames and all the steps that had led him to it and everything it meant.

'What's wrong?' Jane asked.

'Nothing. I'm not used to being home at night. I'm usually at the hell.' It was a half-truth.

She rolled on her side and pressed her supple body against his, bringing her lips tantalisingly close to his. 'I'm sure Mr Bronson can do without you for one evening.'

'I'm sure he can.'

Chapter Seven

'Are you certain this is where the auction is being held?' Jasper asked as they ascended the stone stairs into the building in Somers Town.

'The paper was quite clear on the matter.' To Jane's amazement, he'd been incredibly solicitous in accompanying her here, despite her having woken him from a deep sleep this morning. Over the last two weeks, Jane and Jasper's lives had settled into a quiet routine. They spent afternoons and evenings in preparation for the opening of the club, then dined together before retiring upstairs for more intimate discussions. Afterwards, Jasper would go to the gaming room and remain there until dawn when he returned home to sleep while Jane rose.

'From what I remember of London, this seems an odd place for a lady of, what did the advert say?'

'Fine breeding fallen on hard times.' Jane read from the cut-out advertisement for the auction to sell the goods of a genteel lady who'd recently died without heirs. Despite the very questionable neighbourhood, the quality things being sold to clear the deceased woman's debts included a fine set of china Jane hoped to purchase for the club. As a married woman with her husband by her side, she was free to travel here and to bid on anything she liked. It was a welcome change from the last auction she'd attended.

From an open upstairs window, the knock of the gavel against the wood and the auctioneer's booming voice announcing 'Sold' carried out over the noise of the street.

'Hurry, before we miss the best items.' She took Jasper's arm and pulled him inside, eager to reach the auction and get him away from the gaudily dressed woman across the street trying to catch his attention.

'I'm coming.' He bounded up the stairs past her, pulling her along. At the top, he tugged hard enough to make her skip over the last tread and land with a bounce in front of him on the landing. He caught her other hand and pulled her against him and away from the drop. The rumble of his laughter rose up to meet hers, the joy they'd taken in one another over the last weeks increasing. Whatever doubts she'd entertained about Jasper before the ceremony had long been destroyed by his constant humour and the hours they'd spent together. He wanted to be with her and they were revelling in their newfound freedom.

A balding businessman in a light coat mumbled his apologies while he passed them on his way out. His presence forced Jasper and Jane to assume a more professional air before they entered the room. It was a large one in the old house, a ballroom maybe, converted like the rest into a private apartment. True to its past it was embellished with chipped wainscoting, scrolled doors, tall windows hung with thick curtains and an abundance of gilt furnishings and knick-knacks.

'It looks like your office,' Jane whispered as they slipped behind the gathered crowd and gawked at the massive amount of baroque mirrors.

Jasper lowered his head to hers. 'Maybe this is who purchased all of my old things.'

'If you recognise anything, don't buy it back.'

'Why not? Aren't you eager to own a sofa with this much red brocade?' His breath tickled her ear while he motioned to the sofa behind them. 'Think how it would go with our bed and what we could do on it.'

'We could be quite wicked.' Jane slid him an enticing sideways look, almost ready to abandon the auction for home and more carnal pursuits when the auctioneer announced the next item.

'A large lot of French china in a classical pattern.' A man held up a plate and bowl. The china was the only thing of style and taste in the entire room.

'The set is perfect for the club and enough to get us started in the dining room.'

'Are you sure you want something from here?' Jasper fingered the tag of a very strange statue on the table beside them. The bronze couple was locked in an embrace worthy of the red sofa.

'I do.' The auction began, and only when she'd

made the opening bid did she wonder at Jasper's question. 'Why shouldn't I?'

His eyes danced with mirth. 'No reason. Continue on.'

With the auction in progress, she couldn't pause to interrogate him. Winning the china proved easier than securing the Fleet Street property and it didn't come with a parcel of censorious looks from the other gentlemen crowded into the apartment. Whatever had enticed the other attendees here it didn't include a sizeable set of French porcelain. In a few bids, she'd won the lot at a price she couldn't wait to boast about the next time she dined with Philip.

'Congratulations, my dear. You've made quite an acquisition.' Jasper raised her hand to his lips and brushed it with a kiss. It sent a tingle down her arm and into places deeper down before the tight press of a restrained smile made her cock her head at him. He knew something she didn't and it was amusing him to no end.

'What are you thinking?'

'About the allure we'll offer to our clients. They can brag to their friends about eating beef off the notorious Mrs Greenwell's china.'

All Jane's plans to brag to Philip about her splendid purchase vanished. 'What?'

He pointed at the portrait of an almost-naked woman hanging on the wall behind them and surrounded by a number of other works to make her blush. Then it struck her why the address seemed so familiar. At one time, Jane and Mrs Hale had followed the famous courtesan's exploits in the papers, sniggering together at her boldness and quick to hide the stories whenever Laura or Philip had entered the room. It had been years since the woman's name had appeared in the gossip columns, but there was no forgetting her antics, including a dip in the Vauxhall Gardens lake in nothing but her chemise.

She whirled on Jasper, who continued to smile like a sly fox. 'Why didn't you say something sooner, or stop me?'

'Because I enjoyed watching you bid. You have a flare for auctions.'

'But think of the money we've wasted. If anyone finds out where we got the service they'll be horrified.'

'Or intrigued.' Jasper nudged her with his elbow. 'The china is the closest most men will ever come to a famous courtesan and we'll offer it to them. It'll make our club the talk of the Fleet.'

No, this was not at all as she'd imagined. It was better. 'You think so?'

'I do.'

'Then let's purchase the couch and really give them something to discuss.'

Jasper sat at his desk in the gambling hell, signing off on letters of credit. Through the wall behind him, a great cheer went up. *Someone must be doing well at the Hazard table.* He returned his pen to the gilded holder of a peacock with full plumage and reached for an equally ornate duster. He didn't wish the winner ill despite what it meant for the night's takings. After his day with Jane, it was difficult to be in a bad mood. Jane's joy at the auction, and the zeal with which she'd acquired a few more of the scandalous old woman's things, had been a delight to see. Afterwards, they'd spent the rest of the afternoon writing adverts for the club, the work drawing them closer together and hinting at a far better future than the one he'd imagined more than a week ago. With regret he'd left her to come here, eager to return to his bed and her arms come the sunrise.

A series of loud groans from the night's boisterous crowd began to puncture the quiet of Jasper's sanctuary. *The player's luck must have given out.*

Jasper reached for the grocer's bill when raised voices and an argument made him halt.

'Damn you, man, I'll do as I like. Spin the wheel.'

'Sir, please, listen to reason,' came a dealer's voice.

'Spin, you bastard.'

Mr Bronson rushed into the office. 'Captain Christiansen is playing too deep and losing and he isn't happy about it. I tried denying him credit, hoping it would be enough to discourage him, but he has his own money tonight, more than I've ever seen him bring here.'

'Where did he get it? He hasn't been to sea in months,' Jasper asked, rising from the desk.

'Don't know, but he won't have much of it if he keeps playing the way he is.'

Jasper traced the edge of the brass peacock's fan. 'All right, cut him off. Take Adam with you and escort Captain Christiansen downstairs as discreetly as possible.'

'That'll be hard. He's likely to make a fuss.'

'Then try to appeal to his gentlemanly sense of embarrassment and do what you can. I'll wait down there for you and tell him he's banned from playing here.'

'You sure you want to make yourself known?'

Jasper twisted his wedding band on his finger. 'This place will soon be yours. Better he have a grudge against me than you.' It would be Jasper's first steps out of the shadows, one of the many he'd have to take to leave this life behind.

Mr Bronson headed back into the game room to orchestrate the delicate removal of Captain Christiansen while Jasper made his way downstairs. He waited in the dim light of the warehouse. The scratch of a rat scurrying through the few crates stacked along the wall was barely audible over the laughter and voices drifting down through the ceiling. As much as he hated these encounters they were necessary. If he'd stepped in and taken similar action with Mr Robillard, and heaven knew how many others, so many things might be different now, including his view of himself.

He didn't need to wonder if Captain Christiansen was being disagreeable. His loud protests as Mr Bronson and Adam, the bulky footman, escorted Captain Christiansen to the ground floor were proof enough.

'How dare you treat me like a pickpocket?' Captain Christiansen wrenched out of Adam's firm grip. 'Do you know who I am?'

'The second son of Lord Fenton,' Jasper announced, stepping into the lantern light near the back door to meet the men.

'And who are you?' Captain Christiansen demanded. He was tall and round faced like his father the Earl, but with a higher forehead and more hair. His skin was tanned from his years at sea and would never lighten to a more aristocratically preferred pallid white.

'Mr Patrick, the owner of this establishment.' It was one thing for Captain Christiansen to meet him, but he wasn't ready for the man to spread his identity all over London. Jasper might be working to leave this life, but he still couldn't risk his family learning of it. 'I thank you for your patronage, but it cannot continue.'

'You think I don't have enough to play in your rotten room, but I have more money than you can imagine.' He poked one finger in the air at Jasper.

'I'm sure you do.' Jasper allowed the man his dignity in an effort to make him more compliant. 'But I don't permit men to ruin themselves here. I must insist you no longer frequent this establishment.'

'You can't ruin me. My brother is sick, the wasting disease.' He seemed to relish his brother's impending demise.

'I'm sorry for his ill health.' Even with the lingering estrangement between Jasper and Milton, he'd never wish death on him, even if it meant Jasper and not Milton would inherit his parents' wealth and business. It made the need to be rid of Captain Christiansen all the stronger.

'My almighty father settled a great deal on me to make me resign my commission. I'm suddenly precious to him when before he didn't think twice about throwing me to the horrors of the Navy at thirteen.'

Jasper exchanged a wary look with Mr Bronson. Captain Christiansen hadn't been playing with his money, assuming he had any left, but his father's. In the last few days, Jasper had heard disturbing rumours about the Fenton family's mounting debts. He had no idea how much of Lord Fenton's already diminished wealth this man had lost.

Captain Christiansen mistook the silence. 'Already regretting kicking a future earl out of your filthy gaming room?' The captain was reaching far into the future and his lineage to try to assert dominance over Jasper—it didn't work. He'd lost his respect for nobility in America.

'I'm safeguarding the legacy your father has settled on you, the one you'll some day pass on to your son.' The Charton family might not have a manor house or a title, but his parents had always valued family and the business Milton would one day inherit, the one his father had inherited from Jasper's grandfather.

'There's your legacy.' Captain Christiansen spat at Jasper's feet. 'I could crush you and your little hell if I wanted to and I might just.'

He stormed past Jasper and out of the warehouse door into the thick fog blanketing the neighbourhood.

'I think that went well,' Mr Bronson said, his voice echoing in the dark room.

'As well as can be expected. Adam, please return to the gaming room.'

The footman hurried back upstairs.

Mr Bronson took his pipe and tobacco pouch out of his pocket, but did nothing with either. 'He can't ruin us. What we're doing isn't illegal.'

'I never thought you a legal scholar,' Jasper joked, trying to shake off the tight worry in his shoulders and Mr Bronson's words.

'I'm not, but I've been doing things like this long enough to make a habit out of knowing the local laws. Captain Christiansen can't do anything more than bluster.'

'No, but Lord Fenton could make things difficult for us, perhaps even see us closed. Earls have a way of wielding influence. Let's hope he doesn't take an interest in his son's evening activities.'

'How long do you think the son's been playing with his father's money?'

'I have no idea, but I'll have to find out.' He wasn't sure how he'd do so. He didn't know anyone in the Admiralty who could tell him when the captain had resigned his commission. Mr Rathbone might be on good terms with someone there, given his vast network of connections, but it would mean telling him about the club. Perhaps Jane could assist him, but he refused to drag her into the mire of his gambling affairs. He'd have to find a way to discover it on his own. 'How much did Captain Christiansen lose before you cut him off?'

'Two thousand. I was distracted by another matter and the Hazard man is new and didn't know to tell me.'

'Two thousand might be enough to catch an earl's attention.' He rubbed his eyes with his fingers. As pleasurable as his mornings with Jane were, he was tired from missing a great deal of his usual sleep since the wedding. 'Uncle Patrick wouldn't have been this sloppy about managing clients.'

'He didn't exactly manage them as much as he fleeced them,' Mr Bronson snorted.

'You shouldn't speak ill of the dead.'

'I know.' He shoved the tobacco pouch back in his pocket and tapped the pipe bowl against his palm. 'What are we going to do about Captain Christiansen?'

'Nothing tonight.'

'Then go home and get some sleep.' Mr Bronson clapped him on the shoulder. 'You look like hell.'

Mr Bronson headed back upstairs, leaving Jasper alone in the warehouse. He didn't make for his carriage, but stared at the emptiness around him, broken only by the gaudy furniture in the corner. The furniture was some of the last tangible remnants of his life in Savannah, except for his uncle's ring on his finger, the one he'd won from a tobacco merchant. Jasper had no idea how much of the man's other goods and wealth his uncle had taken from him or how much of what Jasper had inherited had come from a similar source.

He twisted the ring on his finger. Jasper might have stopped Captain Christiansen from ruining himself, but he couldn't say how many other men had thrown their livelihoods away in Savannah without his knowing.

They chose to throw it away.

Even if he left the business it wouldn't stop men from chasing luck or betting on cards. Better they do it under the eye of a man who intervened rather than the many in London who'd bleed them dry. These were the tales Jasper had told himself, the ones he hoped Jane never discovered.

Chapter Eight

The Covent Garden Theatre glittered with the thousands of candles in the chandeliers hanging over the audience. Jane could barely sit still or concentrate on the performance on stage. She was too busy watching the audience from her place in the box Jasper had rented for the evening. She and Mrs Hale used to read about performances when she was younger, but Philip had deemed them improper for her to attend. Now she was a married woman, she could come here as much as she pleased and no one could disapprove or look askance at her because of it.

This was exactly how she'd expected married life to be.

'Are you enjoying yourself?' Jasper approved the bottle of champagne the footman held out to him and sent the man on his way.

'I could get used to doing this every night.' She sat back from the edge of the box where she'd been perched to watch the King carrying on with his mistress, Marchioness Conyngham, in a box across the way. Jane and Mrs Hale used to read about the woman in the papers. She never thought she'd be watching her and His Highness together before her and everyone. Between this spectacle and the glow of the last few nights of lovemaking, she felt very wicked and wanton. Philip was right to have kept her away from here.

'It can't be every night.' He wrapped a linen towel around the bottle and worked out the cork with a muffled pop. Then he poured some of the straw-coloured liquid into the two glasses on the narrow table between their chairs. Each turn of the bottle as he poured to avoiding spilling a drop whispered with his experience. This wasn't his first theatrical performance. 'I must work if I'm to keep you in style.'

Jasper took a deep drink of the champagne, barely tasting it as he examined his wife. She wore a rich purple gown embellished by a thin line of lace along the bodice where the tempting mounds of her breasts rose above the silk. Maturity and poise hung in every elegant curl tucked in the combs at the back of her head, but her wide-eyed amazement and the ease of manner between them were just as alluring. Around her there was no pretending he was someone else, no lies about slipping out to his hell. They simply enjoyed their marriage and all the delights it offered.

'Do you like your new earrings?' He caressed the curve of her ear, following the delicate skin down to where the gold-and-diamond bauble shimmered with each of her movements.

She laughed as she pulled back, her joy as effervescent as the champagne. 'I love them, but you mustn't keep buying me things I don't really need.' She twirled a gold bracelet on her arm, another of his lavish gifts.

'It's the reason I bought them for you.' And why he sent funds to Mrs Robillard. Spending money on them was the single penance he could do to make up for his failings. 'You're too sensible to spend my money so shamelessly.'

'You should be, too.'

'I don't buy anything I can't pay cash for right away. You won't find a bill clinging to me.'

'Not even if I looked very, very, hard, over every inch of you?' She traced the line of his jaw with one gloved finger while balancing her champagne glass in the other hand.

He caught her fingers with his. 'Not even then.'

She bit one lip with her teeth with the same anticipation tightening his insides. 'We'll see tonight.'

The audience laughed and Jane whipped her attention back to the theatre. Jasper held her hand, enjoying her delight as she watched the spectacle in the audience as well as the one on stage. Her excitement reminded him of the thrill of seeing Savannah when he'd disembarked after the crossing and the morning his uncle had revealed his secret. It was the first time he'd thought well of the city and his years there instead of cursing it, and it was all thanks to Jane. It was hard to be around her and not view potential and possibility in everything instead of ruin.

I should have allowed her to wait for me, written to her and continued what she'd tried to start during our last night together. When she was old enough, she could have gone to him in Savannah, perhaps helped him see the pitfalls of his life and leave it, or at least been there with him through the darkest days.

She laughed with the rest of the audience, her eyes sparkling with her amusement, and he was glad she hadn't come to him. It would have killed him to see the hollowed-out disbelief mar her expression as it had everyone else's during the awful summer. He rested one ankle on his knee and settled back in his chair to enjoy the performance. He'd been at the hell the last few nights, but tonight he'd be home in bed with her. He squeezed her hand and she flashed him a smile to chase off his concerns.

Then Jasper glanced across the theatre. A few boxes below the King's he noticed Lady Fenton seated near the edge of her box with her noticeably wan eldest son. Jasper withdrew his hand from Jane's and took up his champagne flute to enjoy a bracing sip. There'd been no inkling Lord Fenton intended to involve himself in Captain Christiansen's debt, but it didn't mean either the Earl or his son weren't planning something. He wouldn't know until they sprung it on him. Until then he continued to search for someone in the Admiralty who could tell him when the captain had resigned his commission, but he'd found no one. It undermined the peace he found with Jane tonight, one to both settle and scare him. He'd been content in his life once before and Mr Robillard had stolen it. He wondered who might take it from him this time.

The curtain rustled behind him and the footman appeared again.

'Sir, this arrived for you.' He handed Jasper a note.

Jasper took the note, his enthusiasm for the evening dropping. It was from Mr Bronson telling him to come to the hell at once.

'What's wrong?' Jane asked.

He folded the paper and tucked it in his pocket. 'Mr Bronson needs me.'

'He can't handle whatever it is?'

'If he's asked me to intervene, it must be bad. I'll be home as soon as I can.' He rose and kissed her on the forehead, irritated to be pulled away, but the hell paid for every aspect of this evening and their life. No matter how much he wanted to stay here with Jane, he couldn't ignore business.

Lord Fenton stood across from Jasper in the warehouse. Mr Bronson had insisted he wait here instead of upstairs and Jasper was glad. The less Lord Fenton knew about the Company Gaming Room, the better.

'To what do I owe the honour of this visit, Lord Fenton?' Jasper asked, even though he could guess.

'I wish to discuss my son's debts. I understand he lost a considerable sum here.'

'Not as much as he would have if I hadn't asked him to leave.'

'A gambling-hell owner with a heart, how quaint.' The aristocrat sniffed.

'A father coming to discuss his grown son's debts, what filial love,' Jasper shot back.

'Mind how you address me,' Lord Fenton sneered. 'The very existence of this lowly club hangs on my good graces. With a few words placed in the right ears I could see this establishment closed for good.'

Mr Bronson shot Jasper a wary look over the Earl's shoulders.

'With a few equally well-placed bribes I'm sure I could keep catering to a clientele far below the notice and interest of a lord. After all, I wouldn't want you to sully your hands dealing with mere merchants.' He might be preparing to leave the club, but he wouldn't see it closed and Mr Bronson and all the employees left without wages or employment. Let the man mortgage some property or do an honest day's work to meet his commitments.

'I won't have the Fenton name sullied by allowing some third-rate hell to take a substantial part of my son's settlement. I want the two thousand pounds he lost to you returned at once.'

Jasper imagined Lord Fenton wouldn't dare to march into a club in St James's and demand the return of money, but he had no compunction about doing it here.

'He understood the rules of wagers as well as you do, my lord, and he paid his debt like a true gentleman.'

'It wasn't his money to gamble with,' Lord Fenton continued as if it made a difference.

'That is a matter for you and him to discuss, I have no part in it.'

'You will give me back the money.' Lord Fenton banged his walking stick against the floor as if sheer will could move Jasper. It couldn't.

'Our discussion is now at an end. Good evening, Lord Fenton.'

Lord Fenton clasped the handle of his walking stick so hard Jasper thought he heard the wood crack. 'You will regret this.'

The man turned on the heel of his polished shoe and stormed out of the warehouse.

'What charm these lords have.' Mr Bronson pulled out his red handkerchief and wiped his brow.

'And an aversion to scandal and having their debts made public, especially when they have a wastrel son to marry off. It may keep him from troubling us further.'

'Seems a slim string to hang our peace of mind on.'

'It is, but it's the only one we've got.' Overhead, footsteps made the rafters rattle. Jasper looked up into the darkness. Everyone above him seemed so sure of their lives, but he understood how fast everything could fail. Disease wouldn't undo him in London, but his own mistakes and weaknesses might. He'd already lived through complete ruin once. He couldn't bear to endure it again.

The click of the bedroom door closing pulled Jane out of a deep sleep. She rolled over, confused about where she was until the gilding of the four-poster bed glimmering in the light from the grate caught her attention. With a contented sigh she turned to tempt Jasper into the exertion they'd been denied by his being summoned away from the theatre, but he wasn't beside her.

He stood by the window, staring out at the darkness just beyond it. The languid man who'd poured champagne was gone, replaced by the serious one who'd told her of Savannah in the carriage the other night.

She sat up. 'Jasper? Is everything all right?'

He turned his back to her as he undid his cravat. 'Yes, it's fine.'

'You don't appear as if everything is fine.'

'There were some things I had to deal with at the club.'

'What things?'

'Nothing you need to worry about.'

'Of course I worry about it, especially after you leave me at the theatre and then come home looking like the devil.'

He jerked the linen from around his beck. 'If I say it's nothing, then it is.'

She drew back a touch on the bed, wide-eyed with shock. He'd never snapped at her before.

He flung the linen over the back of a chair and scraped his hand through his hair, more contrite than irritated. 'I'm sorry, it was a difficult night. I had to deal with some issues I failed to face sooner because I've been distracted.'

By me. Once again she'd brought problems into a

house, except this time it wasn't her parents', but her own. She wished she hadn't pestered him. It was another testament to how stubborn she could be when she wanted her way and the trouble it could cause. 'Then come to bed and let me help you forget about it.' She shrugged a little to make her chemise slide down over her shoulder to reveal the top of one full breast, wanting to be close to him and settle the unease inside her and him.

It didn't tempt him. Instead he turned his back to her to shrug out of his coat and waistcoat. 'It has been a long night. I need some sleep.'

Jane tugged the chemise back up to cover herself, as baffled as she was wounded. He hadn't hesitated to tell her about the Company Gaming Room, even treating his secret as though he'd killed a man, not backed a few card games. Tonight he was tight lipped about his troubles. It wasn't right, she wanted him to confide in her, but she couldn't force him to do it. Insisting had never made her reveal anything. She doubted it would work with Jasper.

She settled back down in the bed while he continued to undress, the whisper of his clothes the only conversation between them. She was tired and so was he. The last few nights had been pleasurable but long. They both needed rest and afterwards he might be more willing to talk to her.

At last, he slid into bed beside her, but didn't reach out to hold her or laugh with her like he normally did when he returned early in the morning from his hell.

'Goodnight.' He kissed her on the forehead, not

with affection but with dismissal before rolling on his side, his back to her.

She turned on her side, too, careful to stay as far away from him as she could. How dare he dismiss her like some maid! She had no idea why he'd done it. The new earrings lying in a crystal dish on the table beside the bed caught her eye and a bolt of fear made her stiffen.

Maybe it's me. Maybe he regrets our marriage. The old nagging feeling she wasn't worthy of affection covered her like the early morning darkness before she pushed it back. Nothing in what he'd said or done since the ceremony had hinted at such a thing, until he'd all but shoved her away tonight.

She stared at the far wall turned orange by the smouldering coals, determined to be sensible and not fall prey to late-night worries, but it was difficult. Eventually, he was sure to explain, but patience wasn't one of her stronger virtues.

She closed her eyes, ignoring how cold the bed was when he didn't hold her. The uneasy sense this wouldn't be the last time Jasper might not turn to her for comfort continued to nag until the rising sun lit up the room and, unable to remain still any longer, she rose to begin her day.

Chapter Nine

Jane sat at the burled-wood-and-gilded writing desk in the sitting room to review receipts and the correspondence she'd collected in regards to the building. The new furniture would be delivered in a few days, an elegant and sizeable amount commissioned by a London merchant who had been sunk by the sudden drop in coffee prices. Jane had snatched up the unpaid goods at a splendid price and they would soon be installed at the club.

Jasper had yet to rise and, if it hadn't been for Mrs Hodgkin interrupting her more than once to discuss the dinner menus, she would have been quite alone this morning. After the delight of the theatre, this wasn't exactly how she'd pictured spending today.

Johnson, the butler, entered with a few letters. 'Would you like me to leave these here or take them up to Mr Charton?'

'You can leave them here. They're enquiries into services. We needn't bother Mr Charton with them.'

Johnson placed the letters on the table beside her then left, his wan face not betraying whatever he thought about his employer sleeping so late. Jasper had mostly been at his parents' house since coming home and all the servants in this one were new. They knew as much about his affairs as they did about his gaming hell, which was nothing. They were kept in the dark about it to make sure they didn't inadvertently mention it in front of his family. They thought he went to a club for gentlemen merchants every night.

Jane set down her pen and rose. She wandered to the window and pushed aside a curtain to take in Gough Square. A nurse and her young charges were out in the centre, enjoying their daily walk, and there was no one else to be seen. The clerks and shop owners who filled the houses in the square were up and hard at work, including her, while her husband slept.

She turned away from the window and leaned against it, biting the nail of her thumb. Jasper couldn't have built a successful gaming hell if he was a layabout.

Maybe I should be glad he's still in bed. Once he was up they'd have to face each other and the lingering questions and awkwardness of last night. He hadn't been pleased to see her then—she wasn't sure he'd be any more excited by her presence now.

It left a sour taste in her mouth as she sat down to read a note from the painters about progress on the Fleet Street property's walls and she tried her best to forget it. Hopefully, his distance and reluctance to talk to her was nothing more than a fluke. Years ago, there'd been times when Philip, after seizing collateral in the middle of the night to keep a debtor from making off with it, had been up, too agitated to sleep. She'd come downstairs to sit with him and talk. Unlike Jasper, Philip had welcomed her company.

Enough of this. It had taken a while for Laura and Philip to come together nine years ago. It hadn't been easy and they'd struggled during their first few months of marriage to become acquainted with one another after wedding as strangers. Jane had the advantage of a long history with Jasper and their entire lives together, but it didn't mean the adjustment to their new situation wouldn't be difficult. This was only a setback and setbacks were to be expected. She would be sensible about this and not act like a flustered lover or dwell on the incident and make it worse.

She began a reply to the painters when the sound of the front knocker made her pause. It was loud and she hoped it didn't wake Jasper. She twisted the new gold bracelet on her arm as she listened to the butler open the door. She expected to hear the butcher she'd summoned to give her a price on his goods. Instead, a gaggle of female voices filled the house.

Jasper's sisters.

Before the butler could announce them, they spilled into the sitting room in a wave of chatter and greetings.

'I hope you don't mind us intruding.' Olivia tossed her reticule in a chair to announce she didn't care whether she was intruding or not, she intended to stay.

'We were shopping nearby and wanted to see how you were getting on,' Alice added.

'Oh, I adore the way you've rearranged the furniture.' Lily peered about the room, adjusting her dark curls after removing her bonnet. She flung it down on top of the pile of reticules and pelisses rapidly mounting on the chair.

'I assume Jasper is at the club today?' Alice asked while she removed her gloves.

'Yes, he's usually there during the day. I sometimes go with him, but I had to stay behind to see to some other matters.' Jane glanced out of the sitting-room door and at the empty stairway just beyond it. She hoped Jasper didn't wake up and come downstairs. If he did, he should hear his sisters and know better than to reveal his presence. She was sure neither of them wanted to make excuses for why he was home or for his sisters to think he didn't work as hard as their husbands, or that there was some reason Jane had lied to them about where he'd been. She didn't like lying, but it was necessary. He did work as hard as their husbands, but not at a business they would approve of, at least not yet. It almost made her wish the sisters would leave so she could return to the organising of the club. The sooner it opened, the sooner Jasper might leave the hell and whatever had made him so aloof this morning.

'Make sure he doesn't work too hard,' Lily admonished as she sat down at the small tea table near the window. 'He always comes to Mother and Father's appearing exhausted. I've seen smaller bags at the coaching inn than beneath Jasper's eyes.'

'Perhaps it isn't work keeping him up…' Olivia suggested.

The sisters threw back their heads in laughter. Jane smiled, not as amused. In the past, with them being so much older than her, they'd rarely paid her much mind. Today, they treated her like their equal, not a young naive girl to be instructed or ignored, and she was repaying their respect with fibs and falsehoods. Jasper was right, it wasn't easy deceiving everyone they knew.

'Johnson, tea,' Olivia called as she joined her sisters at the tea table. 'Oh, I'm sorry, Jane. Forgive me for forgetting my place, this is your home now.'

'I don't mind.' But she did mind them calling unannounced. It would be difficult to hide Jasper sleeping in the mornings if his sisters decided to make a regular habit of it.

'When will Jasper be back? I want to chide him for making you work at all,' Lily enquired. They'd always chipped at each other more than the other siblings, because she, being closest in age to Jasper, had felt it her place to boss him around. It appeared she still did.

'I don't know,' Jane mumbled as she took hold of the back of the chair to pull it out and sit down. She didn't want to give them a time and have them lingering here waiting for him to return and then catch him coming from upstairs.

Alice grabbed Jane's wrist and held it up, letting

out a long whistle as she admired the new gold bracelet. 'How beautiful. Did Jasper give it to you?'

'He did.'

'Tristan never gives me such elaborate gifts,' Alice complained as she took the chair beside Jane's.

Lily eyed the bracelet with her mother's scrutiny. 'Uncle Patrick must have left Jasper more money than he told us about for him to be able to afford such things.'

'Yes, he did.' Thank goodness she wasn't wearing the earrings. She didn't need to raise any additional questions about Jasper's income, ones she had no intention of answering.

'Oh, Lily, stop being so practical and allow them to enjoy themselves,' Olivia scolded before turning to Jane. 'Is all going well with the club? We expect it will open soon?'

They all leaned in to hear Jane's answer.

'Soon.' Jane smiled a little too wide, not liking this topic any better than the one about money or Jasper's whereabouts. 'There's no end of details to deal with.'

'Oh, don't we know.' They all shook their heads in agreement, each of them active in their respective husbands' businesses, as well as minding the children and running the households. The reminder of their own responsibilities turned the conversation from Jane and Jasper's affairs to the sisters' second-favourite topic besides gossip: family. All during tea they discussed their husbands and children, sparing Jane from any more awkward questions, but not relieving her worry Jasper might appear and raise more. If he did, she hoped he had a good reason for why he was upstairs when Jane had said he was out, for she didn't.

After an hour of tea and conversation, the Charton sisters rose to take their leave.

Olivia dug into her reticule and withdrew a note for Jane. 'I almost forgot. Mother and Father have decided to hold their first dinner for you the evening after next. Say you can make it.'

'We can.' Jane fingered the invitation, pretending once again to be elated. She'd spent the better part of the morning deceiving the sisters about her and Jasper's income and habits. She didn't relish further sullying her conscience by making up more tales during an entire evening with Jasper's parents, except there was no avoiding it.

'I remember my first dinner after Daniel and I married,' Lily mused, then pursed her lips in displeasure. 'Jacob drank so much he made himself sick.'

'If Alice hadn't smuggled him so many glasses of port it never would have happened.' Olivia laughed, too much like their father to mind.

'I did no such thing,' Alice protested as the sisters made their way out of the house and to their waiting carriage.

Johnson closed the door behind the chatting sisters, then held out a letter to Jane. 'Mrs Charton, this arrived while you were with the ladies.'

Jane took the missive, turning the cheap and wrinkled paper over to read Jasper's name and address written in a round and flowing hand, a woman's hand.

Jane swallowed hard until she noticed the postmark. Savannah. Whoever this was, she was safely on the other side of the ocean.

And still writing to Jasper.

Jane turned the letter over a few times, wondering if she should open it. She wasn't a jealous person, but the strange way he'd behaved this morning, and the distance between them as they'd lain together in bed, gripped her. She wondered if this woman had something to do with his change in attitude.

His business being hers, she saw no reason to leave it sealed except for fear. Inside the tattered missive might be a truth about Jasper she didn't wish to discover. She wasn't sure she could bear the humiliation of learning she didn't have Jasper's real affection and never would.

Stop this! She didn't want to cower beneath her fears and worries.

'I'll take it up to him.' She might keep their business from his sisters, but she would not countenance secrets between them. Whatever this was, she would face it and deal with it.

Jane marched upstairs and into Jasper's room. She threw open the curtains and a wash of sunlight lit up the bed.

'What are you doing?' Jasper grumbled from where he lay in a tangle of white sheets and pillows. He sat up, blinking at her, his hair mussed, a slight stubble along his jaw. In the open collar of his shirt she caught the sheen of perspiration. Her interest in the mysterious letter began to ebb at the sight of him and she fingered the curtain, her skin warmed by more than the sun on her back. She longed to linger with him in bed, but it wasn't her habit to be so wanton during the day, especially when there were issues to address.

'It's time for you to get up.' She let go of the curtain and perched beside him on the bed, flicking the letter with the edge of one nail, reluctant to bring it up despite her former determination. 'Your sisters were here. They said you need more sleep.'

'Do they now?' Like all younger brothers he didn't think much of their wisdom. 'Apparently, you don't agree with them.'

She ignored his comment. 'And they want more nieces and nephews.'

'It'll be difficult to do both at the same time, but I'm certainly willing to try.' He took her arm and pulled her against his chest, the merriment of the theatre enveloping them again. The strange man from before dawn was gone and her old friend was with her once more. He was warm against her bare arms, his skin moist from the spring air filling the room. It contrasted with the coolness of the sheets in the part of the bed where he hadn't been lying. She slid closer to him, allowing his kiss to make her forget all the worries and concerns of this morning and the letter.

He laid her down against the sheets, covering her body with the delicious weight of his. She hooked one leg around his, her dress sliding up to reveal her thigh, and he clasped it with one hot hand, meeting her urgency. He slid his hand beneath the muslin of her skirt and traced the line of the ribbon holding up the top of her silk stockings.

The letter in her hand crinkled, reminding her why she'd come up here. She flung it away and surrendered to his need and hers. He was her Jasper again, tender and attentive, his body as familiar to her as her own. He belonged to her, despite his past and hers, and the distance between them from before dawn was forgotten as they melded together.

Jasper lay against the sweat-dampened sheets, the anxiety of last night and this morning driven off by Jane's sweet caresses. He smoothed her hair and she turned to look up at him, her chin on his chest and her firm breasts pressed against his stomach. A wariness their lovemaking had banished returned to draw her lips tight. It was the same look she'd greeted him with when she'd first marched in here. It unsettled him and he reached for her to drive away her censure or uncertainty with his caresses.

He tucked one slender lock behind her ear, then cupped her cheek with his hand. He shouldn't have pushed her away this morning. He should have confided in her, told her about Lord Fenton's threat and allowed her sweet voice and curving arms to soothe him. But there was no reason to undermine her peace of mind by suggesting the hell and the money he made from it might be in danger. Without his income, her dream of the club and a fine life beside him, the one she'd envisioned when she'd first proposed they marry, would end. Let her be a happy wife for as long as possible, the two of them enjoying each other and the pleasures of life, not mired in all its troubles and confusions. Jasper had tasted enough bitterness in Savannah. He didn't need it here. 'What's wrong?'

'A letter arrived while you were sleeping.'

'Not bad news, I hope?'

'I don't know. I didn't open it. It's for you.' She leaned over and snatched it off the floor, curving her back and tempting him with the roundness of her bare buttocks. Before he could do more than caress the firm flesh, she sat up, her hair falling down her shoulders to cover her breasts, the delight in her eyes dimming as she held out the paper. 'It's from Savannah.'

All his passion crashed to the floor.

He took the envelope. The weeks it had taken for the letter to cross the Atlantic in the musty hold of a ship had left it watermarked and wrinkled along the corners, but it hadn't obscured the handwriting. He recognised it at once.

'Who's it from?' she asked.

The distance he'd kept from her this morning returned to slap him again. He sat up and swung his legs over the side of the bed. Moments ago, they'd been open and vulnerable with one another—now he intended to close off a part of himself again. 'Maybe a land developer or merchant needs me to sign a paper. In the rush to settle my affairs, I probably forgot something.'

'It's in a woman's hand.'

'With so many dead, often widows are the only

ones left to do business with.' It was a partial truth and the best he could offer her.

'I see.' Her shoulders eased, but not the anxiety making her bite her bottom lip.

He slipped his hand behind her neck and drew her to him. 'Don't worry, there's no woman in my life except you, not in London or anywhere else.'

'You promise?'

'I do.' He swept her lips with an honest and tender kiss, then rose, despising himself and all his lies. 'Now, I must dress. There's a solicitor I plan to visit, one recommended by Mr Steed, who might be interested in our offer of retaining his services for our clients.'

'Good.' There was no enthusiasm in her word, just suspicion and wariness and it faded the glow from their lovemaking.

He tugged one finely pressed and folded shirt out of the wardrobe and pulled it on. 'I thought we might visit the Royal Theatre tomorrow night since we've already seen Drury Lane. I've never been there. Would you like that?'

'Yes, it would be grand.' She didn't sound elated.

He turned to his mirror to tie his cravat, aware of her watching him, the room shrinking and tightening under her scrutiny and his own unease. He couldn't open the letter in front of her. There would be too many questions and answers he refused to give. He wished he had a private space of his own. With the exception of his office at the hell there wasn't one so he endured the present tension. He had no choice.

He shrugged on his coat, eager to be free of her questioning glances and the hesitation marring her natural spontaneity. It was too much like the way his parents used to regard him whenever he left the house after dinner while tossing lies at them about where he was going. He hadn't expected or wanted it to be like this with Jane and it hadn't been, until today. He sat down to pull on his boots, struggling to remain cheerful and light under the weight of her presence. 'I saw a necklace at the jeweller's yesterday. It would go well with your earrings. Would you like it?'

'If you want to buy it for me.' She shrugged, her breasts rising and falling to tempt him to stay, to take her in his arms and touch the connection they'd enjoyed when they'd come together, but he didn't. The letter and everything it meant was a wall between them and at this moment he could not overcome it. 'Lily already thinks you're being too extravagant and your inheritance must be larger than you've told everyone. I said it was. I misled them about a number of things this morning.'

'I told you it wouldn't be easy.' Jasper brushed her cheek with the back of his fingers, leaving his hand to linger by her face, wanting to drive away the strife clouding her eyes, but he couldn't.

He was causing her distress, but he refused to discuss his concerns about Captain Christiansen or the reason for the letter from Savannah. It pained him to keep so many things from her, but she'd already been forced to lie to her brother and sister-in-law at the wedding breakfast, and to his sisters, and he'd noticed the anxiety it caused her. He couldn't ask her to carry any more of his secrets than he already had.

'And I accepted it so I have no one to blame but myself,' she replied with a bravery her sad eyes betrayed. She did blame him because she'd guessed he wasn't telling her everything, especially about the letter.

He tucked the missive in his coat pocket, hiding it away like he hid the story behind it. Every day they were together, he danced closer and closer to telling her the truth. He was deceiving her like he was everyone else and it hurt more than any of the other times he'd done it. He'd vowed to make her the most important person in his life and he could keep the promise. However, he hadn't vowed to reveal his whole self to her, both the good and the dark so tortured he shuddered to think of it. He wouldn't have her spit on him the way Mrs Robillard had. 'It'll change soon.'

'Will it?' It was the first hint of doubt since before the wedding and it increased his own.

'Of course. Now I must go before I lose what's left of the day.'

Jane watched Jasper all but sprint from the room, and her. They'd been so close when they'd made love. Then she'd shown him the letter. He might have smiled and chatted as though all were well, but it wasn't and once again he'd balked at telling her why. All she could surmise was that it had to do with the hell, and Savannah, and it wasn't as simple as a forgotten signature or missed transaction.

She picked up her discarded clothes and began to dress, at a loss for what to do. It wasn't in her nature not to insist on having her way, but she couldn't chase Jasper down and demand he speak with her. She didn't want to drive him off more than she already had and risk losing the warmth of his touch or the joy of his company. Assuming it wasn't fading already, or perhaps something she'd never really possessed.

She clutched her chemise to her chest, Mrs Fairley's words about her not really knowing him coming back to her. The modiste was right—after nine years apart, there were aspects of Jasper still hidden from her, including his full life in Savannah. He might have come home, but it didn't mean his heart wasn't with someone there. He'd done nothing before to make her suspect another woman, but catching cheaters wasn't her strength.

She shimmied into her stays, reached around behind her and began to lace them up, pulling so hard on the laces she feared they might snap. She refused to be left alone and forgotten by the one man who'd pledged before their family and friends to cherish her, but if his heart lay elsewhere, there was little she could do to secure it. If she pestered him too much for affection and confidences he didn't want to give, then one day she might awake to discover him gone, the way his brother had disappeared to Scotland.

She let go of the laces and slumped down on the edge of the bed. They might be married, but it didn't mean he couldn't leave her. Not even a ring or a ceremony could bind him to her if he didn't want to be bound. He must still have friends in America. He could go back and make a new life for himself while leaving her here to wonder when and if he might ever return. Being abandoned would be a bigger embarrassment than never having married.

She rose and jerked on her dress. *Let him leave me.* The marriage gave her the freedom to engage in trade without censure. Except it was no longer an occupation she wanted without Jasper. He did care about her, he always had. His kiss had been as honest as his caresses, but something had changed between them over the last couple of days and she wasn't sure what it was or why.

Sadly, she had no idea how to cross this new barrier or bring out the man she'd met at the altar, and there was no one she could discuss it with. He'd sworn her to secrecy about their life together so she could hardly have tea with Laura and ask for advice. She'd have to figure this out on her own. She rose to finish dressing, trying to keep her chin and her spirits up. She would be sensible about this. They were married and would be together every day. She'd find a way to pry his troubles from him and banish them so they never came between them again, despite the sickening feeling this was darker and deeper than she was prepared to face. Give her contracts or loans any day. She could handle those, but things like emotions and marital relations left her baffled.

Hearty laughter drifted in from the gaming room, making Jasper look up from signing debts. Jasper couldn't share in his clients' joy, not with his missteps with Jane and the unopened letter staring at him. After he'd left her, he'd paid a call on the solicitor, treating the man to a fine dinner while enticing him to work for the club. When Jasper had ordered a second bottle of wine, he'd tried to convince himself it was to woo the man, but it wasn't the real reason he'd chosen to dine out. It was to avoid Jane.

Facing her before dawn after Lord Fenton's visit had been difficult. He hadn't meant to be short with her, but he'd needed peace and a chance to ponder things. It was difficult to do with her so close and insistent on asking him what was wrong. Better she remain ignorant of the workings of the hell in case real trouble descended on them.

Then, when all had been well this afternoon, and he'd held her in his arms thinking their early morning troubles were over, the letter had reared its ugly head. He should've been more cordial in addressing her concerns, but his mind had turn to brick when she'd handed him the letter. The more sleep he lost, the harder it was for him to maintain control, the way it had been impossible for Uncle Patrick to remain calm when Jasper had demanded he do right by Mr Robillard.

Jasper closed his eyes, still able to see Uncle Patrick standing across from him in the old Savannah gaming room, his full face as red as his ruby ring.

'You're choosing that spineless planter over me after everything I've done for you?'

'What you're doing isn't right and you know it.'

'Now you're the moralist? You didn't mind taking his money before and spending it on your fancy house and fine things, did you?'

The anguish of facing the man he'd once admired, his image of him warped like a bad mirror by his experiences, still burned. Everything he'd believed and cultivated about himself and his life in Savannah had died in that moment.

He opened his eyes. The letter sat before him on the blotter. He couldn't ignore it any longer.

He tore it open and unfolded the paper to read Mrs Robillard's words.

Dear Mr Charton,

I am writing to inform you my eldest son, Jackson, has decided to apprentice with a doctor in Boston. As you might imagine, the cost is beyond what I am able to afford.

I am grateful for the assistance you continue to provide to me and my children. I appeal to you to forward these additional funds to allow Jackson to set himself up in the world, as you are the one who helped pull his father down. I have included the amount and where it should be sent.

I look forward to your prompt reply.

Mrs Robillard

Jasper set the missive on the blotter. Despite everything Jasper had done for her and her children, her hate showed in every word. Unlike his uncle, he recognised how much he deserved it.

He wrote a note to Mr Steed to send the requested money and a little more for Jackson's living expenses. It was the right thing to do, even if no amount could ever undo the damage he and Uncle Patrick had wrought or the way it still haunted him.

Mr Bronson knocked once, then entered, less jovial than usual. 'Not a very lucrative night for us.'

Jasper's pen stilled over the paper. He glanced at the paintings adorning the walls. They weren't reproductions, his uncle having acquired most of them in payment for debts. They were a safeguard against too many losses. Most men might come here for business connections instead of cards, but it didn't mean Jasper's fortunes couldn't change the same way Mr Robillard's had. He'd made rules against how much a client could lose, but not the amount they could win. 'Anything I should be concerned about?'

'No, just Mr Portland enjoying a good run of luck. They never last. I don't expect his to.'

'Let's hope not.' Jasper sealed the note to his solicitor, not as cavalier about Mr Portland's winning streak as Mr Bronson, especially when a cheer rattled the paintings behind him. Part of him hoped Mr Portland's good fortune held. If he won enough to bankrupt this place it might be a godsend, forcing Jasper out of this life and all contact with it for good. Except without the income from the hell he couldn't pay for Jackson Robillard's future, his employees' or Jane's.

'Something wrong?' Mr Bronson asked.

'I received a letter from Mrs Robillard.'

Mr Bronson nodded, needing no explanation. He'd been there and seen everything.

Jasper sat back and laced his hands over his stomach. 'Tell me, if the quarantine hadn't been imposed and Uncle Patrick hadn't fallen ill, could I have convinced him to return Mr Robillard's plantation?'

Mr Bronson took his pipe out of his pocket and tapped the bowl against his palm. 'I like to think regaining your good opinion meant more to him than being king of the manor, but it's hard to say. He could be a good man to those he cared about, but he had a nasty streak, too. He tried to keep it from you because he used to say if someone like you admired him then he couldn't be all bad, then Mr Robillard came along. It was the first time you got a glimpse of what a grasping bastard Patrick could be. It's why he got mad at you. Realised he couldn't fool you any longer.'

This wasn't anything Jasper hadn't mulled over during the countless hours alone in his house in Savannah during the quarantine while he'd listened to the cannons being fired to clean the air, his body hollowed out with hunger and the stench of death all around him. There'd been warnings before Mr Robillard: a debtor beaten up here, a man thrown out there, furniture and goods appearing in the middle of the night with no explanation asked and none offered. Jasper had chosen to ignore these, too enamoured of Uncle Patrick to see the truth until Mr Robillard had forced it on him.

He twisted the ruby ring on his finger, his uncle's

ring, the one he'd removed from his hand before the men had come to take his body away. Jasper hid the truth about his past from Jane, the way Uncle Patrick had hidden his from Jasper. It wasn't right, but if he snatched away her illusions the way Mr Robillard had stolen his, she might despise him as much as Jasper had his uncle. He couldn't bear to see her admiration for him turn to disgust. Without her, he might never be more than the damaged and deceitful man who climbed the warehouse stairs each night. He wanted to be more, even if he wasn't sure if it was possible. He would do all he could to shield Jane from the destruction of her dreams, but the letter's arrival reminded him of how many things were out of his control.

Jasper rose and handed Mr Bronson the signed debts, returning to business. Things had happened and no amount of 'what ifs' could undo them. He must move forward, no matter how much the past still hung on him. Too many people relied on him for him to succumb to his doubts, though they seemed to increase every day.

Chapter Ten

'I can't wait for you to see what I've done.' Jane's voice carried over the clack of the horses' hooves as the carriage carried them towards the building on Fleet Street.

Jasper had awakened out of a deep sleep at noon to find Jane standing over him and he'd braced himself for another round of questions. They hadn't spoken since he'd left her yesterday, but instead of pressing him about the letter and the hell, she'd pulled him from bed, explaining her ideas for the club in rapid sentences and excited words, pretending, like him, all was well between them.

She continued to speak and Jasper watched her more than he listened. This was what he wanted her to be, a thrilled young wife instead of a strained worried one, the woman who still believed in him and their future. 'I'm sure your improvements are brilliant,' he complimented.

She touched her finger to her chin and looked up

at the carriage roof. 'There is a noticeable lack of cherubs in the new decor so you may not care for it.'

'Then I insist on one or two gilded pieces, for nostalgia's sake. The dolphin clock from our bedroom, perhaps?'

'I'd indulge your request except I don't want prospective clients clasping their cravats in horror.'

Jasper threw back his head and laughed, the lightness he'd always enjoyed with her returning. 'No, I don't want to drive our clients away.'

The carriage came to a halt in front of the Fleet Street club.

'We're here.' The carriage door banged against the side as she flung it open and dashed out. The ribbons of her blue bonnet fluttered behind her as she weaved through the people cluttering the pavement. At the door to the building she stopped and waved one fawn-coloured glove at him to follow, her smile bright like the sun off the windows.

He slowly approached her, admiring the dark lustre of her hair and the joy she found in his company. She was like a flower growing through the cracks of the pavement, something beautiful in the midst of the ugliness of his life. When he was with Jane, he could believe he wasn't so awful or beyond saving. He wondered who would arise to make Jane see the truth about him, to make her despise him as much as he'd come to despise Uncle Patrick.

He jerked to a halt at the foot of the three stairs leading into the building, his heart racing in panic. *I can't lose her.*

'Come on, what are you waiting for? You must see it.' She grabbed his hand and tugged him through the doorway.

'What do you think?' She threw out her arms where she stood in the centre of the entry.

Jasper turned slowly, taking it all in. Before, it had been difficult to imagine the building as more than a former tobacconist's shop and house. Legitimacy and respectability whispered in the green-and-red paint on the walls in various rooms and the furniture with simple lines decorating them. In one, comfortable chairs were arranged in sets of twos and threes in corners, near the window and in front of the fireplace, encouraging men to come in, sit down and discuss trade and contracts. Under Jane's guidance, it had been transformed into something he'd dreamed about since coming home and maybe even before. 'Amazing.'

'As you can see, I found a place for our purchase.' She pointed to the red couch in the high-ceilinged entrance hall, stately against the far wall, its gaudiness muted by the staid surroundings. 'It's the first thing men will see when they enter.' She stepped closer to him and slid him a saucy glance, making the curls by her temples whisper against her cheeks. 'If you could let it slip where it came from, and embellish the story to say this was where Mrs Greenwood entertained the King, it'll draw more men in here.'

'Too bad we didn't buy the painting of Mrs Greenwood to hang over it.'

Her full lips formed into a plotting, and enticing O. 'I wonder if we could still get it.'

'We could make some discreet enquiries.' He trailed his fingers across her shoulder to tickle her neck, her enthusiasm as irresistible as her soft skin.

She playfully batted his hand away. 'No enquiry into a famous courtesan's portrait can be discreet. Besides, I don't want to be too obvious about our efforts to attract patrons.' She sauntered to the staircase to inspect the repairs to the banister.

He strode into the dining room where tables of various sizes stood with tasteful dining chairs encircling them. The newly acquired china sat in neat sets at each place ready to be marvelled at by clients. He ran his hand along the flat line of the back of a chair. In the daylight it was stunning, in contrast to the Company Gaming Room which showed its tired tackiness in the sunlight. This establishment breathed potential. The very real possibility he might at last break with his disreputable life and remake himself, to be able to walk into his parents' house and face them and Jane with a clear conscience, to stride down the streets with his head held high, openly greeting the men who gathered here, filled him with hope.

The heels of Jane's boots clicked across the wood floor as she came to join him. 'Isn't it wonderful?'

'It is.' He wrapped his arms around her waist and held her tight, more grateful than passionate. He'd been fighting alone for so long, thinking it was up to him to heave himself out of the muck. All the while she'd been working and striving to help him. Perhaps he should tell her everything. Maybe she'd find a way to free him from his past and present troubles the same way she had worked so hard to free him from the hell. It tempted him as much as her hand sliding beneath his waistcoat and her fingers twining in his hair to bring his mouth down to hers.

He was about to take her to the couch and add another story to its lore when a cough made him stop. They let go of one another, straightening their clothes as a lanky youth entered the dining room from the hallway leading to the back of the building. 'Miss Rathbone—I mean Mrs Charton. I didn't expect you today.'

'Good morning, Mark.' Jane shifted effortlessly between seductive wife and practical businesswoman. 'Jasper, Mark is the son of one of Philip's men who guard the warehouse. I hired him to keep an eye on things when the workers aren't here. We don't need thieves pinching our new furnishings.' She turned to the young man, wagging a finger at him like a schoolmarm. 'However, if we were thieves we could've been out of here with half the fixtures before you came in on us.'

The boy lowered his bushy red head. 'I'm sorry, Mrs Charton, I was in the back seeing to a delivery from the draper.'

'Good, the new curtains have arrived. Did the plasterer call again?'

'No, but another man came here this morning. Says he knows Mr Charton and wished to see him.'

The entire building shifted around Jasper before he forced it to still. 'Who was it?'

'Wouldn't give his name, but he was thin with nice clothes, if a bit tattered about the edges.'

It didn't sound like anyone Jasper knew, but it didn't mean Lord Fenton or Captain Christiansen hadn't learned who he really was and sent someone to harass him. Whether they meant to do more than threaten to shut down the club he didn't know. He'd seen bankrupt gamblers in Savannah take out their frustration on dealers and hell owners in dark alleys. It wasn't difficult to imagine it happening here, though somehow an earl would remain blameless while Jasper and Jane suffered. 'If he calls again, inform me immediately. I want to meet him.'

'Should I send him to your house, sir?'

'No!' Jasper coughed, aware of the surprise in Jane and Mark's wide eyes. He cleared his throat and spoke again, careful to keep his voice as even as if he were giving instruction for the baker. 'Tell him to wait for me here, then summon me at once.'

'Yes, sir.'

'That will be all, Mark,' Jane dismissed him and the boy shuffled back to wherever he'd been before they'd arrived.

She turned to Jasper, a wrinkle of concern marring her forehead. 'Who do you think the stranger is? Someone from Savannah who might out us?'

'There aren't enough people left in Savannah to out us.' Her willingness to include herself in the fraud of the Company Gaming Room touched him, except it wasn't right. He was the one with secrets, not her, and the desire to be alone gripped him once more. He wanted space to think without having to pretend he wasn't troubled, but he wouldn't have it while she stood here watching him. 'Most likely someone I used to know. Father told everyone I was back once the moratorium was lifted.'

She eyed him like her brother used to, but much less subtle in her suspicions. 'Then why the need to keep him from our house?'

Tell her. She had a right to know the potential danger the stranger represented, but still he held back. Each night she went to bed believing she was safe. He couldn't shatter her peace of mind, especially over something that might turn out to be nothing. The man could be anyone, maybe an old acquaintance or even the former owner of the shop. There was no reason to frighten her. 'I'm sure your brother taught you it doesn't hurt to be cautious.'

'He did.'

'Good, then let's not worry about it unless we must. There are, after all, other more pleasurable matters to dwell on.' He pulled her into a kiss. It whispered with a deeper affection, one he was hesitant to name or bring out into the light. It wasn't fair to allow her to believe he was a strong man of integrity, but he couldn't endure losing the faith in her blue eyes. She still believed in good and bad and the strength of love. He didn't wish to steal these things from her the way they'd been ripped from him. He needed her belief in him and their future to help support his. He allowed the tender kiss to come to a sweet end and drew back to study her beautiful face. In her embrace he was Jasper Charton again, not the wounded man who'd returned in his place. 'Shall we try the couch or should we venture home?'

'As the curtains are not hung and Mark is still about, I think we should go home.'

Jane clung to Jasper during the carriage ride home, made weak by the play of his fingers beneath her skirts, the heaviness of his hands on her breasts through her bodice, and the raking of his teeth against her neck. The demands of his desire and hers muted the noise of the streets but not her suspicions about the stranger, or Jasper. Her decision to ignore the events of yesterday and continue on had made things well between them for a while, but the moment Mark had mentioned the stranger, she'd felt Jasper pulling away from her. Even now when he held her, it wasn't only to make love but to distract them both. Again, something was wrong and he refused to tell her what.

Their spirited sprint up the front stairs of the house once they reached home didn't contain the lightness of the auction in Somers Town or their night at the theatre. Even once they were in bed with her skirt hiked up about her waist and his jacket discarded on the floor, his mind was somewhere not even her caresses could touch. The hesitation which had settled over him didn't come off as easily as his waistcoat, despite how hard he worked to make her believe otherwise. Even while she undid the knot of his cravat and traced the hollow of his neck beneath with her tongue, the quickness of his kisses and the steady pace of his fingers were almost mechanical. He was here, yet he wasn't as free with her as he'd been before. She considered holding back a part of herself, too, but she couldn't. Whatever was bothering him, he was, in his own way, turning to her instead of pushing her away and she cared too much about him to deny him the comfort of her embrace. She fumbled with the buttons of his waistcoat, wanting nothing to come between his body and hers. Despite her suspicions about him, in his arms, she felt beautiful, and special and loved.

Love.

She pulled back, her hands stilling on his shirt, unsure if it was really love. She hadn't bargained for anything but friendship when they'd negotiated their betrothal and she hesitated to assume there might be more. At times, their shared humour drove away his brief flashes of darkness, and his confidence in her abilities kept her doubts about herself at bay. He was so much more to her than a friend and the fire in his eyes tempted her to defy her fear and say it aloud, but she couldn't. She wasn't sure he'd say it back or appreciate her trying to drag him into affection he wasn't willing or prepared to give. She took his face in her hands and kissed him hard, meeting his furious passion with her own, wanting, like him, to lose herself in their coming together, to forget her worries and simply be one with him.

* * *

They lay together hours after the sun had set and the trays of dinner brought to their room had been discarded on a table near the door. Jasper held Jane while she slept, his body content from their lovemaking, if not his mind. In the Fleet Street building today, he'd begun to believe he could finally leave the gambling life. Like Mrs Robillard's letter, the stranger had reminded him how tight a hold it still had over him.

He pressed a kiss to Jane's temple and inhaled her sweet perfume, searching for the calm she offered, but he failed to find it. During their first few minutes in bed when her eyes had held his, more than friendship had passed between them. Remorse had stopped him from reaching out to seize it. If he'd never gone to America, if he'd rejected Uncle Peter's vices instead of embracing them, then he'd be worthy of Jane's heart.

He closed his eyes and tried to sleep, but the clock beside him chimed twelve times and exhaustion made his thoughts spin faster. She was doing everything she could to free him of this life while he was clinging to it, and risking her peace of mind and her safety in the process. He took a deep breath, concentrating on Jane's steady breaths and the softness of her cheek against his arm to try to settle himself. In his mind he pictured her beneath him, crying out in pleasure at his touch, laughing with him at jokes and sharing his troubles. It settled him for a while, but the later it grew, the more the agitation inside him continued to build. He should stay here tonight with her, but he wanted to go to the hell. If Lord Fenton or Captain Christiansen had connected him to the club, then they might confront him tonight, allowing him to deal with them instead of worrying about what they might do.

Jasper slid his arm out from underneath her. She murmured in her sleep and he paused, waiting to see if she would awaken, but she rolled over and went back to sleep. He lingered bedside the bed and watched her sleep, a peace he craved decorating her pretty face. He wanted to caress her soft cheek, to crawl in beside her and hold her, to see if she could push back the shadows tonight like she had in the carriage, but the demons were too strong. With regret, he took his clothes off the back of a nearby chair and left the room.

'Jasper Charton, I've been waiting for you.' Chester Stilton stepped out from the shadows near the warehouse door, his cravat as dishevelled as his hair.

Jasper paused beside his carriage, careful to keep his panic under control. 'What are you doing skulking about warehouse doorways in the middle of the night?'

'I went to your building in Fleet Street, but you weren't there. I'm glad you decided to come here tonight to play. I must speak with you.'

So Chester was the one Mark spoke to. What he wanted remained to be seen, but as long as Chester believed Jasper was another gambler, it lessened the risk of him seeing him here. Jasper could think up a thousand ways to explain his presence to his parents if need be, more lies, more deceit. It came too easily to him, even if it still stung his heart like a punch. 'There's no reason for us to speak. We aren't associates or friends.'

'I know we've had our differences, but I need your help.'

'You insulted my fiancée.'

Chester shrugged, trying to appear humble, but it further distorted his already rodent-like appearance. 'A lapse in judgement on my part, but you didn't catch me at my best. I must play tonight. You said you were connected here. Perhaps you can speak with the owner. I need to win before my creditors force me abroad.'

The fever lighting up his small eyes made Jasper take a step back. He'd seen this look in a hundred other men's eyes before they'd lost everything. That moment was when Jasper should have stepped in to stop them, to save them from being consumed by their habits. As much as he disliked Chester, he wouldn't give him the chance to ruin himself.

'No, I won't help you. Go home and speak with your father about work, tell him about your debts and find an honourable way to pay them before it's too late.' He was a desperate man which explained why he'd approached him. Desperate men were capable of anything, except walking away from the cards.

Chester's greed turned to hate and he clutched Jasper by the lapel. 'You think you can look down on me because your father refused to give me a loan?'

Jasper knocked his hands away and pushed him

back, ready to pummel the man if it drove him from here and saved him for the mistakes so many, including Mr Robillard, had made. 'I don't care who my father extends money to or not. His business isn't mine and if you're smart, you won't rely on luck to save you. Only hard work and legitimate effort can do that.'

Chester pulled back in disgust as if Jasper had suggested he accept the King's shilling and enlist to escape his debts.

Then the door to the warehouse opened and Mr Bronson stepped through it, a number of credit notes in one hand. He failed to notice Chester. 'Jasper, good you're here. I need you to sign for Mr Portland's credit. He isn't so lucky tonight.'

Jasper flicked his glance to Chester and Mr Bronson caught his mistake too late.

Chester was all triumphant smiles while he glanced back and forth between the two men. It made Jasper wish he had struck him.

'No wonder you knew about my debts,' Chester hissed with gloating realisation. 'This is your place, isn't it? It certainly explains the clientele and all the expensive things you can afford.' He jerked his thumb at Jasper's carriage.

'What are you doing here? You were told not to come back,' Mr Bronson growled with an authority to help cover his mistake, but both he and Jasper were acutely aware of it.

The cheesemonger's son tugged at his collar before he regained his nerve. He turned his beady eyes on

Jasper. 'I'm glad I did. It seems tonight will be more lucrative than I originally imagined. What will you pay to keep me from telling everyone what you're up to here, especially your sanctimonious father? Imagine how he'll feel when he learns his progeny runs a gambling hell, especially after giving me a lecture on the evils of cards? He'll be the laughingstock of the Fleet.'

'I won't give you a farthing.' This wasn't the first time someone had tried to blackmail him. He'd learned from Uncle Patrick long ago never to give in. If he did, Chester would own him and every night it would be a new and larger demand until he ruined him, then eventually told his secret anyway. He was already a slave to the hell, his past and all his lies. He wouldn't become one to this fool. 'Say what you like to who you like, it makes no difference to me.'

Chester's smug smile dropped like his jaw. Jasper brushed past him, Mr Bronson falling in step beside him as they headed inside.

'You'll regret not paying me,' Chester yelled after them before the door swung shut, leaving him outside in the mist.

Jasper stopped in the darkness, pressed his fists to his hips and took a deep breath.

'I'm sorry,' Mr Bronson offered, his voice as tense as Jasper's insides.

'It's not your fault.' *It's mine.* Try as he might to avoid complications, they seemed to be seeking him out.

'What are you going to do about him?'

'I don't know. With any luck, he'll flee abroad before his desire for revenge outpaces his good sense.'

'We could handle it the way Patrick used to,' Mr Branson suggested.

'No.' He was too much like his uncle already without sinking to the level of common street thug. 'We'll leave it be for now.'

Jasper rubbed his chin, his many mistakes piling up on him, along with those of his uncle. Uncle Patrick no longer had to face them, but Jasper did, every day. He had a sickening sense that his carefully constructed world was about to come crashing down around him. There was nowhere else for him to go if things fell apart here and this time so many more people would suffer.

The bark of a dog on the street outside startled Jane out of sleep. Her back was cold and she turned over to find Jasper missing, again.

He must have gone to the gambling room. She pulled the coverlet up to her chin and snuggled into the soft mattress, but the sound of a bird outside announcing the coming dawn, and the front door opening and closing downstairs, made her sit up. She listened for the fall of Jasper's boots on the stairs, but heard nothing except a slight noise in the sitting room beneath their bedroom. It wasn't like him to linger downstairs when he came home.

She twisted the sheets between her fingers, wondering if she should go down or leave him alone. He hadn't come up for a reason and she feared her questions would revive the awkwardness of their previous early morning encounter. However, if he was suffering she didn't want to leave him alone. In the weeks after Philip's first wife had died, Jane had caught Philip up at night many times. The helplessness Philip had experienced over his wife's death had haunted him and robbed him of sleep. He hadn't been any more forthcoming about his reasons for being up than Jasper had been the other morning, but she'd guessed. Then Laura had come into Philip's life and helped him to open his heart and leave the tragedy of his wife's death behind. It had brought them closer together and uncovered the love developing beneath their marriage of convenience. Jane wanted to do the same for Jasper and be to him what Laura was to Philip.

Unless it wasn't Savannah keeping him up, but guilt. She turned the diamond wedding ring on her finger, hesitant to risk rejection again, but she didn't want to sit here in the darkness with so many questions about the letter and his sudden reserve torturing her either.

She rose, tugged on her robe and left the room.

The wood of the stairs was cold against her bare feet. Outside, a few voices of men making their way along the street carried in through the closed windows. In another hour or so light would fill the sky and more people would join them to begin their long day.

Once downstairs, she crept up on the sitting room, pausing outside to listen to the steady fall of Jasper's feet as he paced inside, her courage wavering. It was clear he craved solitude and she didn't relish another fight, but she couldn't leave him in pain either. Jane braced herself and stepped into the room. 'Jasper, what's wrong?'

He whirled on her, his pale skin reddening at the interruption. Embarrassment brought a faint flush to his cheeks before it vanished, replaced by the testy irritation of a lack of sleep combined with being startled.

'Nothing, go back to bed.' He flicked his hand at her.

'No.' He was mistaken if he thought he could dismiss her like a child.

'Don't be so stubborn.'

His accusation rattled her more than it should have. Milton used to call her stubborn, so did Philip, Justin and, on a few occasions, Mrs Hale. It had turned people off her so many times, but she had never thought it would happen with Jasper. It bit into her determination, but still she continued on. 'I want to know what's wrong and don't lie to me about it not concerning our venture or some other such nonsense. I want the truth about whatever is going on at the hell and the letter you received today.'

His eyes flashed with irritation. 'I needn't explain myself to you or anyone.'

Jane stepped back, stunned but not cowed. 'If you think you can hide things from me, you're mistaken.'

'I'm not hiding anything.'

'You wouldn't behave like this if you weren't. Tell me what it is.'

'I said there's nothing.' The tightening of the lines at the corners of his eyes betrayed him. She'd cornered him, but it was a hollow victory.

'Liar.'

'Don't chastise me like you've never had troubles you've kept from everyone.'

The image of her mother's sickroom and her on her knees beside the bed almost startled the argument out of her. She hadn't told him about her guilt. She'd never told anyone. With him all but scoffing at her, she wasn't about to reveal her greatest failing. 'This isn't about me. I've seen how this kind of thing eats at people and the damage it can do. Philip worked so hard to hold back from Laura, even after her uncle tried to kill her. It changed him and almost drove a wedge between them until Laura overcame it.' *With love,* she wanted to say, but this wasn't the time to say it and put him off the idea for good.

Jasper studied her with a sadness to make her ache. 'You must accept there are things you can't know about me.'

Like who the woman who wrote the letter is. Fear began to overwhelm her but she held it at bay. If she allowed it to engulf her, she'd lose this argument for sure. 'So you say, but what happens when there are children? With the way we've been carrying on there are sure to be. Will you be there for them at night like your parents were for you or will you be too busy handling your private affairs to care about their welfare or mine?'

'You wouldn't say such things if you had any idea what I'm dealing with to ensure your and our future children's welfare.'

She marched up to him. 'Then tell me everything you're facing, no matter what it is, and we'll find a way to deal with and overcome it together.'

His expression went blank and she held her breath, thinking he might at last confide in her. A coal popped in the grate and outside two men called to one another before their voices faded off down the street. 'I don't need your help. I need my privacy.'

'Fine. Pace a hole in the floorboards for all I care, but don't wake me when you finally decide to come to bed.'

Jane fled the room, her hands shaking at her sides. This wasn't the Jasper who'd kissed her so tenderly and laughed with her during the day. He was a stranger she loathed and she didn't know what had brought about the change.

Perhaps Mr Bronson knows what's wrong. She considered paying a visit to the hell and asking him, but she hated to garner information about Jasper in such an underhanded way. She didn't know how he would react if she did and he discovered it.

She paused in the upstairs hallway, catching the faint reflection of herself in the black-speckled mirror. She was no longer sure this was a fluke and not some indication of how their future together might be. Jasper, her oldest friend, her husband, was, like everyone else, pulling away from her. In the darkness, the image of her six-year-old self being chased out of her mother's sickroom by the cranky old nurse reflected back at her.

'You've done enough damage already, child, now get out.'

'But I want to see my mother. I need to see her and say I'm sorry.'

'Your apologies won't help her. You should have listened when she told you not to sneak out to the fair instead of insisting on having your way, you naughty child.'

Jane screwed her eyes shut against the image and the stinging tears. The nurse had had no right to be so cruel and dismissive, and neither had Jasper. *I was only trying to help him, like I wanted to help Mother.*

Her father and mother had been the first ones to leave her.

He won't leave me. He can't. He needs me. She dashed into their room and slammed the door shut. She snatched up the poker and knocked the coals with it, trying to elicit some warmth from the fading fire and making the flue ring with the racket. Without her, Jasper would never have his club, assuming he really wanted it. She'd heard nothing more about any plans to turn the hell over to Mr Bronson but she also hadn't asked. After tonight, she wondered if she'd be able to question him about anything without it getting his hackles up.

She dropped down on the hearthrug, tossed the poker aside and pulled her knees to her chest, barely touched by the warmth emanating from the grate. The chill creeping through her was too severe and it made her teeth chatter. She wondered if the man she'd faced tonight was the real Jasper, the one she'd caught more than once hovering in the shadows just behind the carefree man. Perhaps she hadn't noticed it before because she'd been too eager to marry to see the truth.

Tears slid down her cheeks. She'd wanted a life for herself and in marrying Jasper she'd thought she'd achieved it. She'd also wanted to be the most important person to someone and she wasn't. Whatever he was hiding or trying to accomplish by keeping their spheres so separate was the most important thing to him. She came in a distant second and it stabbed at her because for all her hesitations about saying the word while they'd been intimate yesterday, she did love him. She always had and it hadn't stopped during their time apart. She'd tried to convince herself she didn't need his heart and could exist in a marriage without love, but like so many other aspects of her present situation it was a lie. She wanted him as much now as the night she'd tried to secure his heart nine years ago, to be his true wife in a real marriage, and he was pushing her away this morning like he had then. It made the sting of it even more severe.

This wasn't at all how she'd expected marriage to be.

Jasper slouched in the chair with a view of the window. He stared at the brightening sky and the single star visible over the building across the way. He needed sleep, but he didn't go upstairs. Jane had left him an hour ago and other than the clank of a poker echoing through the chimney, he hadn't heard anything from the floor above since. If she was asleep, he could slip in beside her and rest. If she was awake, he wasn't sure he could endure another spat. If she did rail at him, then he deserved it. She'd come down to find him because she cared and he'd shoved her away, as careless of her feelings as Uncle Patrick had been of Mrs Robillard's plight. He hadn't meant to be short with her, but during the day it was easy to be close to Jane, to laugh and tease with her. Not even her tender touch could drive back the ghosts at night.

He tapped the arm of the leather chair. The charade required to maintain his life was starting to crack around the edges and he wondered how much longer he could hold it together before something slipped and he revealed more than he was willing to explain. The effort of having to conceal his troubles, to sneak past her and then add more lies to the ones he already maintained when caught made it more difficult to control. He needed space to wrestle his past into submission and there was only one way to achieve it. She wouldn't like it, but it must be done if he hoped to find a way to defeat his demons and be the kind of husband Jane deserved.

Chapter Eleven

Jane climbed the stairs to their room in search of Jasper, her feet dragging with her exhaustion. It had taken ages to fall asleep after the row with him this morning. When she had, it'd been a light sleep only. Near sunrise he'd climbed in beside her, careful not to touch her. She'd pretended to be asleep to avoid another argument, but she'd remained wide awake, sure he did, too. Around six, when he'd at last fallen into a deep sleep, she'd risen, unable to lie there any longer.

She'd gone downstairs and thrown herself into business for the club before paying a visit to the furniture maker to arrange for the sale of the remaining things in the warehouse and to purchase more sedate items for the private conversation rooms. She was back home now and there was no more avoiding him today, not when she needed to discuss the transfer of goods from the warehouse to the furniture maker. Jasper had granted her a free hand to make contracts or buy and sell items, but some matters still required his assistance.

The sight in their bedroom stopped her short.

Mrs Hodgkin and the scullery maid were carrying Jasper's things out of their room and into the adjoining one.

Fear slammed into her chest. *He doesn't want to be with me any more.*

'What are you doing?' she asked the housekeeper, hating the way her voice shook.

Mrs Hodgkin stopped, surprised by the question. 'Setting his things in the other room as Mr Charton requested.'

'But *this* is his room.'

'I thought you'd be more comfortable if you had this one to yourself.' Jasper's voice carried from behind Jane. Mrs Hodgkin and the scullery maid slipped away to finish their task as Jane faced her husband. 'I don't want to disturb you as I come and go at night, nor can I be disturbed when I'm sleeping in the mornings.'

He made it seem as if it was for her benefit when in reality it was for his. She refused to allow it to stand. 'And you thought to inform the servants before you told me?'

'You've been gone for some time,' he stated as if it was reason enough to take action behind her back. It made her wonder what else he was doing and not telling her about, like the letter and the woman who'd written it.

'And you were so eager to be out of my room you couldn't wait?' She might not have wanted to hurt him at the auction, but she wouldn't mind doing so now.

All she could see was her having to face Philip, her friends, all of the Fleet while they sneered at her for not having been able to keep a husband. 'How long until you decide to leave this house as well?'

He had the nerve to balk at the question. 'Never.'

'Then am I to go?'

He hesitated before answering in a measured voice, 'Jane, this changes nothing between us except where I sleep. Most married couples don't share a room and it will only be until I give up the hell and return to normal hours.'

'And when will that be? Have you spoken to Mr Bronson about it, made any arrangement, or were you too busy packing up your things to see to your own affairs?'

He pressed his lips tightly together and she knew she was right. It terrified her because it meant she might be right about his leaving, too. It was the man from the sitting room this morning appearing again. It frightened her as much as seeing his things piled on the bed in the adjoining room.

'This isn't right, Jasper, and you know it, and nothing you say will convince me otherwise.'

His face softened, as if he sensed his decision had hurt her and he wanted to soothe the sting. He slipped his arm around her waist and tried to pull her close. 'Having separate rooms doesn't mean you'll always be sleeping alone.'

She went stiff in his arms, waiting for him to apologise to her and explain what had happened last night at the hell and promise her things between them would be fine again, but he didn't. Instead he brushed her cheek and temple with his lips.

The stubborn woman inside her wanted to push him away, but the one who craved his affection made her languid in his arms. Maybe this was his way of apologising and making things right between them, the way last night had been his means of seeking comfort. He made a trail of kisses across her cheek and down to her jaw and caressed the hollow of her neck with his tongue.

She tilted back her head and closed her eyes, savouring the sweep of moisture and the sweet tickle of his breath. She forgot all of her arguments for or against the plan as he began to undo the small laces at the back of her dress. It wasn't an attempt to keep them apart. He wanted her—it was apparent in the quickness of his breath in her ear and the eagerness of his fingers against her skin. She was his wife and this arrangement wouldn't be for ever.

Then she turned her head and noticed his things laid out on the bed in the adjoining room. It was no coincidence Jasper had thought of this arrangement after she'd confronted him and refused to leave him be. With his kisses he was trying to pretend everything from this morning hadn't happened and all was resolved between them, but it wasn't.

She wrested out of his embrace. 'Don't try to placate me. The next time you attempt to make love to me, be sure it's because you want me, not because you want your way.'

She stormed out of the room and down the hall,

refusing to be humoured like a child or made to come or go according to his whims. She'd hold out on him until he finally told her something or decided he wanted separate rooms to become separate lives.

She came to a halt at the top of the stairs, all her early morning worries rushing back to her. *I should march in there and confront him, refuse to allow whatever it is he is trying to do,* but her usual stubbornness failed her and she didn't move. She was wary of what else he might do if she did insist on them sharing a room. She didn't want to make demands, drive him away, or lose the warmth of his touch or the joy of his company. *Maybe I was too fast to anger and walk out.* If she'd held him tighter, been more complacent instead of haranguing, she wondered if she might have changed his mind.

She went downstairs to the sitting room and began to pace, confused and lost about what to do. His embrace last night before their fight, and their time at the club, had contradicted everything he was saying and doing today, but he was withdrawing from her and she must stop it, even if she didn't know how. She wished there was someone she could speak with, but if she dared broach the subject with one of Jasper's sisters, the story would spread through the family like a fire and probably jump to the Rathbone household. Heaven knew what Philip would say. It eliminated Laura as a confidant, too, especially since Laura and Philip had no secrets between them. Though he kept his business separate from his family, he was at home in his office during the day, taking as much interest in Laura's life as she did in his. She could speak with Mrs Fairley, but the modiste was in Salisbury visiting her sister and not expected back for another week.

For all the change in her situation and surname, she might as well be a spinster again.

She stared at the bookshelf across the room, noting how her old novels mingled effortlessly with the ones Jasper had inherited from his uncle. If only she knew how to make her and Jasper's hearts and lives fit together so neatly. She could balance ledgers and negotiate contracts but she couldn't win her husband's love or his confidence.

Then one green-leather spine with gold-embossed letters caught her notice. She slipped it out from among the others.

Glenarvon.

She smiled as she traced the shiny title. It had been one of the first books Mrs Hale had secreted for her years ago. The two of them had read it, sneaking off to the garden to discuss the scandalous tome away from Philip's hearing and his disapproval.

Mrs Hale!

She clutched the book to her chest. Speaking to Mrs Hale would mean breaking her promise to Jasper but she had to do it. He was already going back on his vow to honour her and this wasn't how she wanted to live. She needed advice and help and she was sure Mrs Hale would keep her secret. Heaven knew she'd kept some before, even colluding with Jane to create a few. With this being Mrs Hale's second marriage, she must know something about husbands.

* * *

'He's running an illegal gambling hell at night,' Jane blurted out to Mrs Hale as they sat together in the small morning room of Dr Hale's house. Through the wall she heard Dr Hale speaking with a patient, his voice low and steady. Years ago, she'd come here numerous times when Philip had been courting Arabella, his first wife and Dr Hale's daughter.

'A gambling establishment. How exciting!' Mrs Hale drank in the news as she did every other scandal the two of them had ever shared.

'It isn't exciting, it's awful.' Guilt pressed on her as much as anxiety. She'd promised Jasper she wouldn't tell anyone, but he'd also promised to make her his primary concern and he hadn't. 'He's away from me all night and sleeps all morning. I hardly see him except for afternoons and evenings when we, well, you know.'

'I do.' She poured tea in Jane's cup, eyeing her through the steam. 'Is that why you're here?'

'No.' She rose and went to Dr Hale's bookshelf to straighten a few books. She'd rather be here about a possible baby instead of this worry. She turned and took in the familiar room. After Arabella had passed, Jane used to sit here with Dr Hale, trying to help him in a way she hadn't been able to do with Philip. In his grief her brother had retreated into a more severe stoicism than before, while Dr Hale had appeared lost. Later, when Thomas was old enough, Jane used to bring her nephew here to see his grandfather. The visits had helped ease Dr Hale out of his mourning and it had made a great difference to them both. In the cosy sitting room, Jane hoped to garner a little of the comfort she'd been able to offer during that difficult time. 'The gambling hell isn't the worst of it. There's something serious tormenting Jasper, something he won't tell me about, and I think it might be another woman.'

Mrs Hale motioned for Jane to return to her seat at the table. Jane sat across from her and told her about the letter from Savannah and Jasper coming home from the hell in the mornings, troubled but unwilling to discuss it with her. 'I love him and I want this to be a real marriage, but I'm not sure he wants the same.'

Mrs Hale reached across the table and squeezed her hand. 'I think he does and I suspect it's the reason he changed his mind about marrying you. Deep down, he realised you can help him face whatever he's dealing with and you must, or things will never be right between you.'

'But the woman in Savannah?'

'Perhaps she is just a widow he's done business with.'

'And if she's not?'

Mrs Hale let go of her hand and sat back. 'Jane, if there is one thing I've learned after two marriages, it's the need to trust your spouse and to give him the benefit of the doubt. Until you learn otherwise, don't worry yourself into a panic about a woman an ocean away. If you're patient, I'm sure the truth will eventually come out and it will probably be nothing like what you're imagining.'

'It wasn't with Milton.'

'And you must stop allowing your experience with him to guide you in this. Jasper is not his brother and you worrying about what might be, instead of what is, won't help you.'

Jane threw out her arms in frustration. 'I don't even know what is and what isn't. He won't tell me and it's coming between us and I have no idea what to do.'

Mrs Hale picked up her spoon and stirred her tea a moment before she tapped it on the side of the cup and laid it in the saucer. 'I think, deep down, you do know what to do.'

'I don't, it's why I'm here,' she blurted through clenched teeth. This wasn't at all what she'd expected from her old mentor. Jane's outburst didn't rattle Mrs Hale who sat calmly across from her, hands folded in her lap just as she always had when Jane had come to her fuming about one thing or another. Jane rolled her shoulders and calmed herself, not wanting to drive away Mrs Hale like she was driving away Jasper. 'If I did, then I would do it and things wouldn't be as bad as they are.'

'I know you like to take action, to get to the meat of the matter, but Jasper isn't an obstacle to overcome or a problem with a neat solution. If he's holding on to his secrets as you say, he'll fight like a wounded badger if you try to wrest them from him.'

'Are you saying I was wrong to try to force him to talk?'

'Not at all. Sometimes, you have to try something

before you know it won't work. Now it's time to try something else, something only you as his wife can do. You were his closest friend for a very long time, the one person he chose to entrust his secret to and then to wed. You know him better than possibly anyone else and what it will take to reach him and gain his confidence.'

'But—'

Mrs Hale held up one hand to silence her. 'There is nothing to stop you from doing this except your doubt in yourself and your value to him.' She reached over and cupped Jane's face with her hands. 'You're a very strong young lady and, while it hasn't always worked in your favour, it is an advantage and not a weakness, and you must learn to see it as such.'

'How can I when all anyone has ever done is chide me for it?'

Mrs Hale tilted her head at her in amused disbelief. 'And have you ever listened to all those people in other matters, such as purchasing buildings?'

'No.'

'Then why take their word for it this time?'

Because over the years she'd come to realise they were right. She wasn't a strong person, just a stubborn one whose desire to always have her way had killed her parents and now was driving her husband away. Jane took a deep breath and shoved her doubts down deep inside her. She'd always pretended to be strong so others would think she was solid against those who wanted to pull her down and so she might believe it, too. The last few days had shown her how weak she really was. If she dared to speak about it with Mrs Hale, then the woman who held so much faith in her might at last see it, too.

Mrs Hale smoothed a strand of hair off her forehead. 'Trust in yourself, Jane, and in Jasper's concern for you, and I promise all will be well.'

Jane returned from Mrs Hale's, pondering everything she'd told her. She didn't share her friend's belief in her strength or her ability to find a way out of her present troubles. If she could, she would have done it by now, but everything seemed to be growing steadily worse. She shuddered to think how it all might end.

She was not two feet in the door when Johnson approached her. 'Mr Steed is here to see you, Mrs Charton. He's waiting in the sitting room.'

'Thank you.' Jane reluctantly made for the sitting room, in no mood to deal with anyone today. 'Mr Steed, I hope this unexpected visit is good news.'

She needed a little good fortune to lift her spirits.

Mr Steed rose from where he'd been sitting and bowed to her. They'd met before when Jasper had taken her to his office to arrange for her to manage his accounts once they were wed. He was tall with sandy hair and the charm of Jasper, but more sedate in his application of it. 'It's neither good nor bad, Mrs Charton, only necessary. Since Mr Charton has given you power to handle his affairs, I thought you could approve this bank draft. He instructed me to send it at once and there's a ship leaving for America in the morning. He promised to deliver it to me yesterday, but it must have slipped his mind. I'm eager to send this with the captain. It will prevent any unnecessary delay.'

He removed a paper from the fine leather satchel he carried and held out the draft. Jane took it and swallowed hard, determined not to fly into a panic. 'Who is Mrs Robillard and why is Jasper sending her this much money?'

'He's been sending money to her since he first engaged me after coming home. As for why, that is something you will have to discuss with him. He offered me no reason and it isn't my habit to ask. If you'd like, I can wait on the draft and speak to him myself.' He reached for the paper, recognising his mistake in bringing it to her. The pity on his face reminded her of the way the elder Mr and Mrs Charton had looked the morning they'd come to tell her about Milton. It was exactly what she hadn't wanted to experience in marriage, what Jasper had promised her wouldn't happen and yet here it was. What other secrets of his were waiting to rise up and humiliate her? The possibility added to the disquiet surrounding her since leaving Mrs Hale's.

'No, he told me the other day he received a note from Georgia about some unfinished business. This must have something to do with it.' She'd bet her eye teeth it wasn't the sort of commercial interest Jasper had alluded to, but it allowed her to save face with the solicitor. She refused to stand here and have him think her a betrayed wife who'd inadvertently discovered her husband's infidelity. 'I'll sign the draft and speak to Jasper about it later.'

'Of course.'

Jane took the paper to the writing table and signed the document, her fingers tight on the pen to keep it from shaking as she wrote her name. Then she handed it to Mr Steed, who tucked it back in his valise.

'Thank you, Mrs Charton. I hope I haven't inadvertently caused you any distress or concern,' he apologised while Jane escorted him to the front door.

'Of course not.' She smiled brightly, trying to shake off his embarrassment as well as hers. 'Good day, Mr Steed.'

He slipped on his hat and darted down the walk to his waiting carriage.

With as much composure as Jane could manage she returned to the study while Johnson closed the door. She stopped in the centre of the narrow room, fighting back the wave of distress crashing over her.

Jane slumped into the gilded chair by the desk. Maybe this was the real reason he'd been reluctant to marry her. He'd hoped his paramour from Savannah might join him. Except Mrs Robillard was married. No wonder Jasper had changed his mind. Better to wed a free woman in London who could help him with his club then pine for a married one in Savannah. *Except he isn't pining. He's sending her money.*

If he were upstairs sleeping, she would march up there directly and ask Jasper about this mysterious woman. But she didn't know where he'd gone while she'd been out. She would have to wait until he returned to escort her to his parents' house for dinner.

His parents.

It was bad enough she intended to enter their home while lying about Jasper's true occupation and income, but to be forced to play the role of the happy newlywed while she worried about his fidelity was more than she wished to bear. Perhaps she could plead a headache and not go, except it would probably have his sisters flooding in here wondering if she were with child, since she never took ill. There was nothing to do but go and face his family, guilty conscience or not. She'd taken on Jasper's lies when she'd married him and she must endure them and whatever troubles they caused her as she'd sworn to do at the altar. It didn't mean she wouldn't discover the truth, but it wouldn't be tonight. She couldn't hope to maintain any sense of composure if Jasper confirmed her suspicions. She must keep her concerns from everyone, including Jasper, until she could find a moment and a way to face him and discover at last what was going on. It made her feel more alone and isolated than when she'd lived with Philip.

This wasn't the way her marriage was supposed to be.

Chapter Twelve

Jasper sat across from Jane in the coach as it carried them to his parents' house and the dinner party awaiting them. He hadn't seen Jane since their encounter in their bedroom. Even after he'd come home from the jeweller's to dress, she'd been so occupied with Mrs Hodgkin there hadn't been a moment for them to talk. He'd been secretly relieved, in no mood for a fight before they left for his parents' house. When at last he could no longer put off facing her, he'd braced himself and come down from dressing to find her waiting for him in the sitting room. She'd been polite and sweet, peppering him with innocuous questions about his day and allowing him to escort her to the carriage, her small hand on his arm, her copper-coloured evening dress whispering against his legs as they walked. Yet for all her pretence to everything being well, the stiffness of her gait and the shallowness of her smile told him it wasn't and, like him, she was doing her best to hide it.

It was time for him to make amends and bring the light back into her expression.

'I have something for you.' He removed a long, slender velvet box from his coat pocket and held it out to her.

She eyed it and him with suspicion. 'What is it?'

'Open it and see.' He perched on the edge of the squab, eager for the smile his gift would bring to her red lips. He needed her good humour. He didn't have enough of his own.

She pushed back the lid, her eyebrows rising at the gold-and-diamond necklace inside. 'It's stunning.'

Her response wasn't. There were no effusive thanks, no squeal of delight or the throwing of her curving arms around his neck like she'd done before their visit to the theatre. With his gift he'd tried to recapture the joy of their first week together, just as he'd strived to maintain the connection between them this afternoon when he'd kissed her. He hadn't been manipulating her into agreeing to his plan for separate rooms, only searching for the connection which had bound them together over the last few weeks, the one he'd severed with his foolishness. He should have known better than to think he could do it with jewellery.

She lifted out the necklace and the diamonds flashed in the carriage lantern light as she held it out to him. 'Will you put it on me?'

'Of course.'

She turned her back to him and he took both ends of the cool metal and slipped it around her neck. Her perfume encircled him like the gold did her neck, the arch of it tantalising beneath his fingertips. He wanted to press his lips to the tender skin, to make her sigh and tilt her head back to rest on his shoulder, to draw her closer and banish the discomfort between them. He fastened the clasp, then rested his hands on her shoulders. Her skin was soft and warm and as familiar as his own. When he slept in the mornings, he would miss the heat of her beside him and the ease of laying his palm on her firm thigh. The nights would be colder, too, without her in his bed. He thought he'd needed space, but he was fast learning what he needed was her. He was about to admit he'd been a fool to leave her room when the carriage rocked to a halt.

She turned her head, her eyes catching his, the uncertainty in their blue depths as strong as in the pit of his stomach. If he'd never gone to America, if he'd rejected Uncle Peter's vices instead of embracing them, if he'd kept his promise to redeem himself, he'd be worthy of Jane's heart.

Let her help you and make everything right again. He couldn't, not when they were moments away from facing his family.

He removed his hands from her shoulders and she slipped back across the carriage to take her seat and wait for the driver to open the door and hand her down.

Jane held Jasper's arm as they climbed the wide staircase to reach the sitting room and the party waiting for them. The necklace sat heavy around her neck. She wanted Jasper's whole heart and the respect he'd promised her, not expensive gifts. She wasn't as convinced as Mrs Hale of her ability to draw him out, and feared the distance between them would continue to grow until it could never be overcome. One day, she might walk into the Charton home alone the way she had after her failed engagement. She never wanted to face such humiliation again.

Voices and the melodious notes of Lily's piano playing drifted out of the upstairs sitting room, adding a warm cheeriness to the house which could not penetrate her and Jasper. She'd been here a thousand times, but this would be her first as a wife trying to pretend everything with her marriage was well when it wasn't.

They reached the sitting room, and Jasper's sisters surrounded her in a flutter of oohs and ahhs over her new necklace. A week ago Jane would have tossed back her head to display her gift and revel in their admiration. Tonight, she wanted to hide it and herself. She should be grateful he'd thought of her and wanted to make her happy, but it was all on the surface, as false as the sets on the Covent Garden Theatre stage. Beneath the sparkle of the gems were so many questions and troubles she had no idea how to untangle. There'd been no time in the carriage, even during the moment when, with his hands on her shoulders, she'd wanted to reach out to him and ask if he still cherished and cared for her as he'd promised he would.

While Jane spoke with the Charton sisters, Jasper

remained beside her as stiff as a horsehair cushion. He did what was expected of him, greeting his twin brothers with his usual charming smiles and jokes, his clothes impeccable as always, but she caught the tension around his eyes, the subtle avoiding of her questioning glances. It made it difficult for Jane to hold her smile and pretend, like him, everything was splendid.

She believed she was fooling everyone until Mrs Charton approached them, studying them with motherly regard. 'Jasper, Jane, you both look so pale. Tomorrow night you must come with us to Vauxhall Gardens. The distraction will help you both.'

'I think it would be lovely,' Jane lied, adding another to the many already accumulated. Jasper was right, it ate at her like the distance between them did.

'Perhaps another evening, I have some business to attend to,' Jasper refused his mother with an apologetic smile, but it did nothing to ease the tiredness in his eyes. Apparently, she wasn't the only one being worn down by this charade. How he'd managed it for so long while living in his parents' house she couldn't imagine.

'Jasper, come here. Giles wants to talk to you about something called a railway.' Mr Charton drew Jasper away, while Mrs Charton occupied herself with her grandchildren.

Jane was left to the sisters who dragged her to the arrangement of sofas in front of the fireplace, sat her down and peppered her with questions about how she and Jasper were getting on. Jane twisted herself into knots making up the imaginary life she lived with Jasper, the one they should be enjoying instead of this half-marriage.

Camille, Milton's wife, sat across from her, listening intently and saying very little. More than once she caught Jane's eye with a solemnity to make Jane wonder if the woman suspected Jane's unease or if it was lingering discomfort over what had happened between them. For the first time Jane didn't care about the past or Milton or Camille. All she cared about was Jasper and how there seemed to be more than the distance of the room between them.

She watched him while he spoke with his father. He didn't notice her at first, but then his eyes met hers and the regret darkening them made her want to rush to him. Instead, she was forced to remain on the sofa pretending happiness for the benefit of his family. It made her feel more like a trained monkey than a married woman.

When the sisters at last lost interest in discussing Jane's married life, Olivia stood to suggest a new amusement. 'Who'd like to join me in a game of whist?'

A noticeable quiet drifted over the room.

Mr Charton thumped his hand on the table beside him, making a statue of a shepherdess rattle on her porcelain base. 'Not in my house you won't.'

'Risking a pence or two among family isn't going to land anyone in debtors' prison, Father,' Olivia scoffed. 'After all, it's not as if I'm suggesting we establish a gambling den in the sitting room!'

Jane exchanged a wary glance with Jasper, wondering if Olivia suspected them. She didn't believe so. Olivia had always been the most rebellious and outspoken of the three sisters and much more like Jasper than any of the other girls.

Mr Charlton levelled a warning finger at his daughter. 'If you'd seen the many men who've wasted my loans and their livelihoods on cards, you wouldn't think it so funny.'

'Everyone understands your feelings on the matter, Henry,' Mrs Charton gently chided from where she held court near the window, surrounded by her grandchildren. She wore her favourite red-silk gown with a matching turban her daughters called old-fashioned, but which she adored. She was still lithe, despite having borne seven children.

The subject would have been dropped if Milton hadn't decided to step in. 'It's a disgusting habit and, like Father, I'd be ashamed of anyone in this family who ever resorted to such a lowly way of life.'

'Says the man who's proven his talent at sneaking around,' Jasper hissed.

The room went silent—even the grandchildren stopped talking. Across from Jane, Camille lowered her eyes and her cheeks turned bright red.

'I think you've been away too long and forgotten how things are done in this family,' Milton hissed back. Beside him, Alice allowed Jacob a drink from her glass. Jacob started to hand it to Giles when a warning look from Mrs Charton made him hand it back to his sister.

'We can chastise a man for his sins, but once they're done they're finished. Now on to better topics,' Mrs Charton insisted, bringing the matter to a close. But it didn't smooth Jasper or Milton's ruffled feathers, or ease Jane's guilt. The family had accepted her even after the debacle with Milton and here she was, sitting in their midst, as two-faced as Milton.

'Let's play musical chairs instead,' Alice suggested. Chairs scraped over the floor as the siblings and their husbands dragged them into place and Lily struck a chord on the piano to begin the game.

Olivia participated, but appeared more bored than amused. It was clear she and her brewery-owner husband didn't mind small amounts of gambling. Jane wondered if she'd side with her and Jasper if their secret ever came out. She didn't know Olivia well enough to be sure.

While the elder sisters and their husbands laughed and raced around to find open chairs, Milton sulked in the corner with Giles, who rolled his eyes at having been cornered by his complaining elder brother. When he finally managed to slip away and join Jasper and Mr Charton, Milton's wife fawned over her spouse, trying to bring him out of his sulkiness to join the game. When Milton rebuffed her to help himself to the brandy in the corner, his wife remained by the wall, ill at ease among all the laughter.

Jane felt sorry for her. It wasn't an emotion she expected to encounter, but there it was. She had more experience than she cared to admit with a husband pushing her away.

The brewer raced around the chairs behind Olivia who reached the open one first. The activity distracted Jane from noticing Jasper's absence. She had no idea when or where he'd gone. No one else was missing.

Did he leave without me?

She shifted nervously on her feet. She used to read in the papers about husbands sneaking out never to be seen again. There was a ship leaving for America tomorrow. She was about to ask Mrs Charton where Jasper had gone when the rustle of skirts beside her made her turn. Camille approached, as pale as always, but there was a hint of determination in her mouse-like eyes. Jane forced herself not to scurry away from her like some startled elephant.

'Good evening, Jane. I haven't had a chance to speak with you the last two times we've been at events, but I wished to congratulate you on your wedding.'

'Thank you.' Jane did her best to be gracious. She and Camille had never been more than passing acquaintances, her father and mother moving in the same circles as the Rathbones and the Chartons. When they were young, they'd seen one another at birthday parties and teas, but they'd never been close. Other than having stolen Jane's fiancé, Camille had never done or said an ill thing to Jane.

The laughter of the other married siblings rang through the room. It covered the quiet conversation between the ladies, although Jane couldn't help but notice Mrs Charton regarding them before she turned back to her youngest grandson.

'I also want to apologise for what happened,' Camille stated without hesitation.

Jane gaped at Camille. She hadn't expected this. She'd prefer it to be Milton, but she'd take it from the wife.

'I'm quite over it, as you can see.' She would have motioned to Jasper, but he was nowhere to be found. The same awkwardness she'd experienced the first time she'd attended a party after the unexpected elopement, when everyone had cast sympathetic looks her way, draped her again. 'We needn't speak of it.'

'But we must. You see, I didn't mean to hurt you, but Milton and I were so in love we couldn't help ourselves.' Camille said it in such a way Jane knew it wasn't boasting. It stabbed at her because no such driving passion had met her and Jasper's union. It had been a bargain, a negotiation, with little promise of more. 'He also told me you'd already broken with him.'

He would, the lying rat. 'Then why the secrecy and the elopement?'

'My father doesn't share my good opinion of Milton.'

Few did, but Jane didn't want to cast aspersions on the love of Camille's life.

'I would have spoken to you about it sooner, but there's never been a good time. Since we're sure to be together at many gatherings in the future, I don't want any bad blood between us and I'm eager to see Milton and Jasper reconciled, too.'

The woman was a fiancé-stealing saint. 'I'm afraid it isn't up to us.'

She couldn't settle the current tension between her and Jasper, much less work a miracle between the two brothers.

'We can certainly help. If you'll agree to do it, so will I.'

She held out her hand to seal the pact with a shake. Jane stared at the ivory-satin glove covering it before she took it, Camille's honesty and concern melting Jane's grudge, but not her doubts about a reconciliation. It would be even harder to settle things between the brothers if Jasper turned his back on her for good, choosing his American woman over her. Her chest tightened as she imagined the looks and whispering she'd have to endure then.

'I knew I could count on you. You're so clever and quick. I've always admired you because of it.' It wasn't flattery and it left Jane speechless. Milton didn't deserve his kind wife. 'If you ever need someone to discuss things with, I'd be honoured to keep your confidences. I know how difficult it can be in this family.'

'Yes, it can.' Even if Jane wasn't ready to spill her heart to the woman who whispered across the pillow to Milton, it was a comfort to think someone recognised a little of what she was facing, even if they didn't know the true extent. It bolstered her confidence. If Camille could face her after what she and

Milton had done, then Jane could be as courageous when it came to facing Jasper. She didn't care if they were at his parents' house. She wouldn't run away from her fears any more, or try to act as if they didn't exist or as if everything was fine. She'd knowingly gone along with his schemes, allowed him to set the tone for this marriage, afraid if she didn't he would never give her all of himself, but it hadn't worked. It had exhausted her and she couldn't allow it to continue. She'd have a true husband and a real marriage.

'If you'll excuse me, I must find my husband.'

She had no idea where he'd gone, but she knew the Charton house well. She'd spent hours here with Jasper and Milton as a child, going up and down the servants' passage to steal sweets from the cook while doing her best to avoid the dancing lessons Mrs Charton had imposed on her and her older girls. Dancing hadn't interested her and she'd stolen away to find the brothers after the first quadrille. Mrs Charton, seeing the futility of pressing any more lessons on her, had never chased after her or demanded she act like a proper young lady. No one had. She missed the freedom of those old days, especially in regard to Jasper. Her relationship with him had been so simple and straightforward back then without all the complications of secrets, the past and the involvement of her heart.

She headed for Mr Charton's study, remembering how she'd found Jasper there the night of his going-away party. He'd been contemplating the atlas on the stand near the desk, measuring again and again the distance between London and Savannah, the distance between himself and his family, and her. She'd tried to bolster his spirits, realising then how unlikely it was they would ever see each other again. Storms took ships all the time, as did sickness. Yet he had survived it all. He'd come back to her and made her his wife. She wouldn't allow the past or another woman or whatever tormented him do what the entire Atlantic had failed to do—separate them for good.

She peered inside the study, relieved to find him here and not on his way to catch a ship to America. He stood before the fireplace, staring at the portrait of Mrs Charton's siblings from five decades ago. The girls wore the fuller skirts then in fashion, their hair powdered and piled high on their heads. Mrs Charton, her round face fuller but her lively eyes unmistakable, stood holding the hand of her young brother, Patrick, while her elder brother and sister lounged on a nearby *chaise*.

Jane slipped up beside Jasper, the questions about Mrs Robillard and their future together begging to be spoken, but she held back. She was risking being hurt again and for the pain of abandonment to crush her, but she refused to be left alone and forgotten by the one man who'd pledged before their family and friends to cherish her. Mrs Hale was right, she shouldn't doubt herself, but being open with anyone about her fears had never been her strong suit, except with Jasper. It was time to put some faith in herself and her old friend again.

'I had the most interesting conversation with Camille,' she stated, refraining for once from being blunt and jumping right in. She wanted to avoid startling him or setting him on his guard.

This garnered his attention at last. 'Camille?'

She nodded. 'She apologised to me.'

Jasper's eyes widened. 'Wonders never cease.'

'She also wants to help end the trouble between you and Milton.'

Jasper opened and closed his hands where he held them behind his back. 'If she can manage it, then she's quite the miracle worker.'

'I said I'd help her.'

The faint humour in Jasper's eyes faded as he studied the carpet beneath his feet. 'That's very generous of you.'

'I'm not doing it for her, but for you, although I'm not sure I should.' She trembled as she met his eyes. Once she broached the subject, there would be no going back. She would face the truth, no matter the consequences, and live honestly with herself and Jasper at last. 'Who is Mrs Robillard and why are you sending her money?'

Jasper's neck tightened, her question striking him as hard as the news about Mr Robillard's death. Shame welled inside him, fuelled by his family's censure and the widening gulf between him and Jane. He studied her, a thousand excuses and ways to put her off colliding inside him, along with the temptation to answer her questions. He'd tried to keep his past from her, but she'd discovered something of it and, unlike her concern about the hell, he couldn't shrug her off or avoid answering her very direct question. The challenge for him to be honest with her at last tinged her steady gaze, along with numerous unspoken accusations.

He rubbed the back of his neck, for the first time understanding why Mr Robillard had done what he had. The shame of facing his mistakes had left him with little choice. Jasper forced his hand down to his side. No, Mr Robillard had been a coward, taking the easy way out and leaving others to deal with the consequences. Jasper wasn't so cruel or weak. Where Mr Robillard had thrown away all chance to redeem himself, Jasper could reclaim the trust he'd damaged, but in doing so he'd have to show her the darkest parts of himself, the ones even he shied from viewing.

She shifted on her feet and the diamonds around her neck sparkled in the candlelight. They reminded him of her bright eyes the night he'd showed her the hell and her willingness to join with him in all his ventures, good and bad. He'd shown her the basest parts of himself then and she hadn't run from him. It was time to trust she wouldn't again and remove at least one of the obstacles he'd put between them.

He turned to the portrait and his uncle's childish smile. 'Mr Robillard was a plantation owner who used to gamble at the Savannah hell. A week before the yellow fever really took hold, he lost everything at the tables. The next day, he shot himself, leaving behind a widow with three children and no means of support.'

He could feel her ease beside him as she took in what he said. 'So you send her money to help her?'

'It's the least I can do.' He reached out and took hold of the mantel, leaning hard against his hand, hesitant to go on, but he had to. Maybe if she could forgive him he could at last forgive himself. 'I was there the night Mr Robillard lost everything. I was the one who extended him credit, allowing him to continue playing, deeper and deeper until there was nothing left. I'm the one who drove him to ruin and to kill himself.'

She slipped her hand in his free one, squeezing it gently instead of offering him useless condolences or trying to convince him the planter's death wasn't his fault. Her silent patience allowed him to continue.

'After Mr Robillard killed himself, I tried to convince Uncle Patrick to return the plantation to Mrs Robillard, but he wanted to be Lord of the Manor and he wasn't going to let right or wrong get in the way of his dream. It was the first time I realised how cold he really was. Afterwards, I stormed out of his house, ready to be through with him because he wasn't who I wanted to be and it wasn't how I wanted to live. I didn't see him again until a few weeks later when the fever was destroying the town and his maid came to tell me he was ill. I went back to his house to take care of him, expecting to find him more humble and repentant.'

'But he wasn't.'

Jasper shook his head. 'He blamed me for his illness. Said I could have made sure there was food in the house before there was none to be had, paid the nurse and the maid more money to stay, taken care of him the way he'd taken care of me during my illness the year before.'

'And still you stayed to see to him.'

He let go of her hand and tugged off the ruby ring. 'I couldn't let him die like a lonely dog, even if he did it while cursing me for betraying him and everything he'd ever done for me.' He turned the ring between his thumb and forefinger. 'After the quarantine ended, I returned the plantation to Mrs Robillard, but with everyone dead there was no one to work it and the land couldn't support her or her children. By helping her I'm trying to make up for what Uncle Patrick did to them and convince myself I'm nothing like him.'

She cupped his chin and turned his face to hers. 'You are nothing like him.'

'Aren't I?' He pulled away from her and pinched the ring between his fingers, pressing on it so hard he hoped the metal would bend and the stone would shatter. 'All the years I was with Uncle Patrick, I did everything I could to emulate him, wilfully refusing to see what he was or what it made me. Then, when I had the chance to walk away from it, I came home and went right back to being a hell owner.'

'Then give it up, now, tonight.' She laid a settling hand on his shoulder. 'Turn it all over to Mr Bronson and walk away. Stop allowing it to destroy you and us.'

He slid the ring back on his finger as a different fear smothered him. The image of a narrow and dark bedroom stinking with sickness and the thick southern air rose up to blot out Jane, while the weakness of hunger and the uncertainty of survival ripped at his gut once more. 'I can't.'

She plucked her hand off of him. 'What do you mean you can't? If it's tormenting you this much, you must.'

He glanced at the study door, remembering where they were and who might stumble in on him. He dropped his voice and stepped closer to her. 'You don't know what it is like to go without, Jane, to be starving and not be able to buy food, not to be able to escape the death and poverty around you. If I give up the hell and the club fails, we could lose everything.'

'It would never be so dire. We have our families to help us.'

'Not if they find out who I really am.' Chester Stilton's threat echoed in the silence. Uncle Patrick had concealed his real rottenness for years, but it hadn't lasted, and neither had the glamour and gain of the gambling room, or even Jasper's secrets. He touched her cheek, tracing the delicate line of it. 'I won't see you suffer the way I saw so many others suffer in Savannah.'

She covered his hand with hers. 'We're stronger than this, Jasper, strong enough to face anything thrown at us, but only if we do it together. The hell is pulling you away from me and it will continue to do so unless you give it up.'

'If we lose the money from the hell, we'd be poor in months.'

'We can live off my inheritance.'

'I won't ruin you.'

'It's worth the risk if it helps you.' She brushed a few strands of his hair off his forehead. 'Besides, I don't need fancy jewellery. I only need you.'

He stroked the line of her jaw with his thumb. She was offering him a real chance to be a better man and it increased his guilt. He should have confided in her sooner, drawn her closer instead of trying to keep her away. She was an exceptional woman who deserved respect and love.

Love.

He didn't say it, but it was there in his eyes as he gazed at her. He did love her and she loved him, but it wasn't enough. Not even the bonds of family had been able to stop Jasper and Uncle Patrick from falling out, especially when things had turned dire. If he and Jane lost everything, she'd blame him for their misfortune the way Uncle Patrick had blamed him for his. 'Don't you understand? I'm doing this for you.'

Jane lowered her hand and stepped back, a loss of hope to remind him of Mrs Robillard filling her eyes. 'You're choosing the hell and all the lies and troubles it entails over me and our marriage.'

'No, Jane, you're wrong.' He reached for her hand, but she jerked it back.

'I'm not. I've done all I can to establish the club, but in your mind it's already sunk before we've even opened it.'

'I didn't say that. I want out of the hell, but I can't see the men I employ plunged back into poverty, or risk losing my ability to help Mrs Robillard and her children, and I refuse to place our security or our futures in jeopardy.'

'And what future would that be? I've spent most of this evening fooling your family about our livelihood and about us, and you've gone days doing the same to me. You think I don't know you're keeping things about the hell from me, things that are bad enough to make you lose sleep and to ask for separate rooms?'

'I'm doing it to protect you.'

She raised a finger at him. 'Lie to yourself as much as you wish, but I told you the day we were betrothed I didn't want you to conceal things from me, or embarrass me the way Milton did with your secrets and deception, and yet that's all you've done. Do you know what it was like to stand before Mr Steed and sign the draft, not knowing if I was giving him permission to send money to your lover? I don't want to sit around wondering where the next unpleasant surprise will come from or when I'll be humiliated by you again. The Jasper I used to adore never would have done this to me.'

'You're right. He wouldn't have, but that Jasper is gone. He died in Savannah.' At one time, he'd wondered who would appear to destroy her faith in him and in the end it hadn't been anyone but himself. He'd been a fool to think he could return here and redeem himself, and now Jane saw him for the ruined and blighted man he really was. He waited for her to curse him, to rail against him, but she simply stared, as lost today as the morning of her parents' funeral.

He'd comforted her then; he couldn't do it tonight because he was the one making her grieve.

The fast fall of footsteps in the hall punctuated the silence between them before Giles burst into the room. 'Jasper, we need you in the sitting room. It's an emergency.'

Without a word to Jane, Jasper followed Giles out of the room, cursing the interruption. The moment to draw Jane back to him, to find a way out of this mess, had slipped away, taking with it so many things. 'What's happening?'

'Someone Father refused for a loan is here. He's not happy and he won't leave.'

'Why aren't Father's men removing him?'

'Jacob went to fetch them.'

They turned down the hall and made for the sitting room. This wasn't the first time an irate man with a parcel of debts hanging over him had stormed into the house. It had been years and it made Jasper realise Jane was right about his father's lax security. He'd have to make sure it was changed. He wouldn't have his family threatened by anyone.

Then he and Giles turned the corner and Jasper stopped dead on the threshold. Across the sitting room stood Chester Stilton, his bloodshot eyes wider and more frantic than when he'd approached Jasper the other night. His clothes were wrinkled and the aroma of cheap wine hung about him.

'Ah, here's your prodigal son now.' Chester threw out his arms to Jasper, wavering on his feet. 'He can tell you I'm right. He can confirm everything I've told you.'

It was then Jasper noticed the deathly still in the room. The secret he'd feared coming out for so long had been revealed. The evidence was in the faces of his family as they stared at him, especially his father. The disappointment bending his shoulders cut Jasper like a sabre. His mother stared at the rug under her feet, as stunned as the rest of the family by what she'd heard. Everything great and wonderful they'd believed about their son had crumbled and there was nothing Jasper could say or do to defend himself or build back what Chester had torn down.

'He runs a gambling hell in a warehouse near the Thames, enriching himself by ruining honest men, teasing and tempting them with the promise of riches while he plucks them dry,' Chester sneered.

Jasper's father's men, led by Jacob, pushed past him and Giles as they hustled into the room. Chester writhed against them as they grabbed him by the arms, his voice growing higher and more frantic when they dragged him toward the door. 'If you don't believe me, ask his little wife why her husband isn't warming her bed at night. She'll tell you I'm right.'

Jasper turned to discover Jane beside him, her humiliation as palpable as his father's. She didn't come close to him as she had in the study or slip her hand in his and offer her silent support. Instead she moved away and he didn't fault her for it. All she'd ever asked for was his care and friendship, and all he'd done was heap her with scorn and shame and drag her down with him in his family's eyes.

'Get him out of here,' his father commanded his men.

They pulled Chester to the door, bringing him close to Jasper.

'I told you I'd ruin you,' Chester spat out while he continued to fight the men, his feet dragging over the wood when they pulled him into the hallway. Chester's curses faded down the stairs and outside as the men dragged him away. Silence engulfed the room. Not even the coals dared to crackle as Chester's revelation continued to echo off the walls.

'Is it true?' A purple rage tinted his father's face as he fixed on Jasper.

The time for lies was over. It was time for the truth. Deep down in the places he hid from everyone except himself he was glad. 'It is.'

His sisters gasped along with their mother. Only Milton seemed to be enjoying the spectacle, grinning like a covetous player watching the Hazard wheel spin. Jasper ignored him and examined the rest of the family, some of whom, like Lily and Giles, avoided his gaze. Whatever esteem they'd held for him and everything they'd thought or imagined about him had been destroyed, just like he'd torn himself down in Jane's eyes.

'Did you know about this?' his father flung at Jane.

'I did.'

Jasper stepped between his father and Jane, trying to shield her from his mistakes the way he'd failed to do before. 'I made her promise not to tell you. I'm to blame for everything, not her.'

His father's fury whipped back to Jasper. 'How could you? How could you live in this house and deceive us like you did? We loved you, took care of you and all the while you were sneaking behind our backs to betray every value we hold dear.'

Jasper closed his eyes, hearing his uncle's accusations in his father's, except here he deserved them. All the things his father and Jane blamed him for doing, he'd done. He opened his eyes and faced him, ready to confess to everything, even if it destroyed for good their love and concern for him. He refused to hide his real self any longer. 'I didn't come home and do it. I did it in Savannah, too. This is what Uncle Patrick taught me, not the cotton trade. How to lure men into his gambling house and use their weaknesses to enrich myself. He hid it from you and taught me to do it, too.'

His father's jaw slackened and for the first time ever he seemed at a loss for words. His siblings exchanged surprised looks, but his mother's fallen face as she stared at the rug hit Jasper the hardest. Like her son, everything she'd believed about her favourite brother was being ruined. He didn't want to tear his family apart or cause any of them more hurt than he'd already inflicted, but he was done with lying. This was who he was and this was his past, and they must finally see it.

'If we'd known what we were truly sending you

to, we never would have done it,' his mother offered in a soft voice, struggling like the others to take in the news.

'I don't blame you or Uncle Patrick. I blame myself. I could have written to you and come home when he told me his secret, but I didn't. I chose my path in Savannah and I chose it here.' He turned to Jane who nervously spun the bracelet on her arm, as uncertain now as she'd been the morning he'd almost broken their engagement. 'If I could go back and change it all I would. I never wanted to hurt anyone. I only wanted to ensure those I love, especially you, were secure in a way that I wasn't at the end in Savannah and I did it the only way I knew how.'

Jane's fingers stilled on the bracelet, but she said nothing. This wasn't how he'd wanted to reveal his heart to her, but she had to know he loved her. He always had. Maybe it would help her not to regret so many things the way he did. If he could undo it all he would, but it was no longer possible.

Jasper shifted on his feet, eager to leave. He couldn't stay here, not with everyone staring at him as though he were some ugly thing masquerading as a husband and son. He'd violated the beliefs they held sacred and passed himself off as an imposter. It was time for him to go.

Jane stared at the empty doorway to the sitting room, avoiding the accusing and censorious looks of the Charton family. She couldn't face them, especially Milton and the sneer he tossed at her or the disappointment in Mr Charton's eyes. After all their years as friends of her family, everything they'd done for her, she'd rewarded their affection by betraying their trust. She deserved every bit of the shame covering her. Except it wasn't only her own actions garnering their condemnation, but Jasper's, too, and he was no longer here, having left her to face his family alone. He had said he loved her before he'd gone, but it didn't matter if he wasn't willing to remain beside her. Once again someone she loved had left her and she wasn't sure he would ever return.

Unable to stand the silence any longer, she held her head high and walked slowly out of the room. Tears blurred her vision and she hung on tight to the banister to stop from tripping down the stairs. In less than an hour her world had fallen to pieces and she was more alone than the morning the nurse had shooed her from her mother's sickroom.

She reached the bottom of the stairs and crossed the entry hall, wiping her eyes in an attempt to pull herself together in front of Alton, who waited beside the open door. The tears wouldn't stop and no matter how tall she stood, the old butler she used to accept peppermints from continued to watch her with a mixture of pity and disapproval, and it tore at her.

Outside, she wrapped her arms around her against the chill, unwilling to go back inside for her wrap. She approached the carriage with slow steps, hesitant to go home and sit alone while all of her and Jasper's mistakes haunted her. She was tired of being alone and wouldn't do it any more. There was only one place she could go, to the one person who'd never walked away from her, even when she'd done her best to push him away.

Chapter Thirteen

'Jane?' Philip stood behind the butler as Jane stepped through his door, the front of her dress spotted with tears. 'What's wrong?'

'Jasper's gone,' she choked out. 'And everything is a mess.'

Philip opened his arms and she flung herself into them and began to weep into his coat. He rubbed her back while he led her across the foyer and into the sitting room where Laura joined them, offering her embraces along with Philip's. They didn't press her to speak, but waited patiently while she cried until Laura had to excuse herself to see to the children.

Then at last Jane sat back and dried her eyes with Philip's handkerchief and told him what had happened. Philip didn't shake his head in disappointment or greet her confessions with the heartbroken disbelief Mr Charton had offered. He simply listened while she explained about the hell, their fights, her visit to Mrs Hale and Chester Stilton's scene at the Chartons, and how Jasper had left them afterwards.

'He isn't going to come back to me, I'm sure of it. He's going to leave me like so many others have, like I deserve for what I did to Mother and Father.'

Philip frowned, perplexed. 'What did you do?'

'I brought the fever into the house by disobeying them.' Jane hiccupped. 'If I hadn't, they might still be alive.'

Philip shifted on the sofa to face her. 'You don't believe it's your fault they died, do you?'

The dark secret she'd carried for years demanded she remain silent, but she was tired of acting like one person to shield the other wounded one beneath, or pretending like Jasper to be someone she was not. 'I was the one who went to the fair with Jasper and Milton because I wanted to see the elephant, despite Mother telling me not to go. I was the one who brought the fever into the house and gave it to her and Father. I'm the one who caused them to die. I'm sure everything I've had to endure these last few years is a punishment for what I did.'

Tears welled in her eyes again and the years of blame pressing down on her were made worse by tonight and the heartache of losing Jasper.

Philip laid his hands on her shoulders and met her eyes. 'It wasn't you who got them sick. It was Father. He'd been in St Giles to collect a debt, but the man who owed him was suffering with a fever. A number of the people in his building were, but no one had said anything for fear the authorities would send them to the pest house or quarantine their homes. As soon as Father realised how sick the man was, he forgave the debt and left. His charity wasn't enough to stop him from contacting the illness, or giving it to Mother.'

'But my cold?'

'It was an unfortunate coincidence you were sick around the same time.'

Jane stared at the vines in the carpet beneath her feat, stunned by what she was hearing. Her disobedience hadn't killed her parents, it had been something far beyond her control. It didn't seem possible and yet it was. 'I never knew.'

'I never thought to tell you because I didn't realise you blamed yourself for what happened.'

'I never told you or anyone because I was too ashamed, as I was too ashamed to admit the troubles between Jasper and me.'

'Laura and I guessed as much.'

Of course he did, but for the first time it didn't anger her. 'You knew about Jasper's gaming hell, too, didn't you?'

'Yes,' he answered without hesitation or apology. 'I've vetted every man who's ever come to me for a loan, I did doubly so for the one who wanted your hand. I discovered it then.'

'Yet you still let me marry him. Why?'

Philip rested his hands on his knees. 'Do you remember how, after Mother and Father died, you wouldn't leave my side?'

She nodded. 'I was afraid I'd lose you, too.'

'I feared the same thing.'

'You?' She gaped up at him. 'You're never afraid!'

'I am, more than I'm sometimes willing to admit.'

He placed his arm around her and drew her into the crook of his shoulder. 'You were so precious to me. You always have been, since I first saw you wrapped in Mother's white shawl when I was sixteen. When they left us, I was terrified of failing you as a guardian.'

She slipped her arms around her brother's waist and held him tight. 'You've never failed me.'

He hugged her closer. 'Do you remember, in the weeks after the funeral, how Jasper used to come here every day asking you to play with him?'

'I do.'

'One day, he came by when you were asleep on the sofa in my office. When I met him on the portico, he asked again if you could come out. I explained how it might be some time before you'd be ready to play and it would be best if he didn't return until then. Do you know what he said to me?'

'No.' She sat back, amazed. She'd never heard this story.

'He said he knew you were sad and afraid, but he was still going to come every day because he didn't want you to be lonely. He wanted you to know he was here for you and would be until you were ready to meet him again. I admired how, at eight years old, he possessed enough insight into what you were facing to be so persistent, and was grateful he kept coming back until the day you were finally ready to leave my side. It's why I let the two of you get away with half the things you did when you were younger. I was confident he'd watch out for you and keep you safe.'

Tears slipped down Jane's face as she remembered the morning Jasper had come here again and she'd finally been able to meet him in the garden, to smile and play for the first time in weeks.

'He reminded me of our conversation the day you two were betrothed,' Philip continued. 'He told me you were lonely again and needed him, and if I didn't agree to the betrothal, he'd come back every day until I did. I realised then, despite his secret activities, and whatever he was facing from Savannah, together the two of you could handle them all.'

Jane wiped the tears off her face. 'But we haven't.'

'You will.' Philip took her hands in his. 'You'll find a way.'

Jane studied her brother's long fingers entwined with hers, struggling to take in everything he'd said. For all these years she'd been mistaken about so many things, including herself. If she'd had the courage to speak about it sooner, she might have viewed the events of her life, herself and even Jasper differently. She let go of his hands and stared at the large diamond in her ring, turning it back and forth to catch the rainbows inside the stone.

Philip was right, Jasper had always cared for her as she'd cared for him. His refusal to give up the hell hadn't been about choosing it over her, but his desire to look out for her as he'd always done and to see to the welfare of his employees and the widow he felt he'd wronged. Even when they'd faced his family he'd done all he could to protect her, to step between her and them and take the blame for what was happening. Then he'd said he loved her and still walked away. It left her as confused about what to do as the day she'd visited Mrs Hale.

Mrs Hale.

'She was right,' Jane murmured.

'Who was right?'

'Mrs Hale. She said I knew best how to help Jasper and I do. He's the one hurting this time and he needs me to come back for him as often as it takes to make him see he is a good man.' Like Jane, Jasper believed he wasn't worthy of love because of his past. It was time to prove he was wrong.

Jasper climbed up the stairs of the warehouse, his hand shaking as he reached into his pocket to fish out the keys to his office. He stopped in the darkness, not wanting to fumble for the metal like some drunk off his liquor. He pressed his hands against the rough wood of the wall. He'd walked the streets for hours, trying to settle himself before he'd come here, reluctant to face that this was all he had left and all he was. For a while he'd begun to believe he might be more than ruined men, cards and bets. Jane had helped him imagine it, but not even her love had been enough to overcome his past or his flaws. They'd flooded over him like a storm wave and he hadn't been able to stop it.

The memory of his father's disgust when the truth had come out made him screw his eyes shut. The family who'd rushed to embrace him when he'd stepped out of the carriage from Portsmouth, gaunt and stinking of fever, had recoiled from him tonight. It was like the morning he'd set sail for America when he'd believed he'd been banished from everyone he'd ever loved, flung out of the family like some unwanted coat. They'd been right to send him away, to distance themselves from the weakness inside him. It had consumed everything good and wonderful in his life, including Jane.

I should go back to her and try to make things right. He dropped down one step, ready to leave the darkness of the gaming house for the light she offered, then stopped. After the way he'd treated her, he couldn't hope to regain her heart. He'd chosen this over her and didn't deserve her forgiveness or her love.

A strange quiet met him as he trudged down the hallway. The click of chips and the clink of the ball in the Hazard wheel were gone along with the cadence of voices punctuated by laughter. The door to the gambling room stood open.

Jasper stared inside the room in disbelief. It was empty except for Mr Bronson, who sat at a table turning a chip over and over in his fingers. Jasper hadn't seen him this dejected since word had reached him from outside the city of his father's passing. Around him, cards lay scattered on the baize, chips discarded and chairs at haphazard angles to the tables.

'What happened?' Jasper's question broke the silence and halted the steady turning of the chip in Mr Bronson's fingers.

Mr Bronson tossed the chip aside and rose, surveying the empty room. 'Lord Fenton came barging in here with the constable. Demanded we shut down. I challenged him to show me where in the statute it said what we're doing is illegal. When neither his lordship nor the constable could cite the bill, they left. But so did all of our clients. None of them wanted to find himself in gaol or in the newspapers. After the dust up, they aren't likely to return.'

Jasper rested his hands on the back of a chair and leaned hard on his arms. Months of striving to bring this together, to create something for himself, while balancing all of the many lies he'd created to allow it to flourish, had all been ruined. Along with it went the livelihoods of his dealers and footmen and the future support for Mrs Robillard, and especially Jane. He'd come here because he'd believed this was all he had left and even this had been ripped from him.

'I'll open the club as soon as I can and I'll employ the dealers and footmen there. You'll have a place there, too.' He'd already wounded his own family. He wouldn't see others suffer or children starve because of him.

'I can't. These merchants of yours will recognise me from here and they'll avoid me and anything connected with me like the plague. Luckily for you, few people can connect you to this place.'

Jasper dropped into a chair, his belief in the club helping him or anyone else fading. 'They will soon enough.'

Jasper told him what had happened at his parents' house, his voice echoing off the wooden walls and through the empty room. 'In less than one night I've managed to lose everything.'

'You still have your wife and the two of you are clever enough to come out of this some way.'

'She isn't likely to help me, not after what I've done.' He tapped the green baize as he looked around at the messy room.

Mr Bronson hauled himself up, and dropped a wide hand on Jasper's shoulder. 'She didn't look down on me when we met, or scold me for leading you astray. She took me for who I am and didn't judge me for it. Over the last few weeks, I've seen you come here with more enthusiasm for being rid of this place than you ever had for owning it. She helped bring about this change in you. She can help you, if you let her.'

Mr Bronson patted his shoulder, then wandered out of the room, leaving Jasper alone.

Jasper studied the paintings in their gilded frames, his insurance against ruin, but they meant little. It was all money and nothing more, as worthless to his soul as it had been to buying food in Savannah. Jane had been the one thing of value he'd possessed and he'd lost her.

'Jasper?'

Jasper stood and whirled to find Jane standing in the gaming room doorway, as welcome a sight as the ship bobbing in the harbour in Savannah ready to take him to England. 'Jane, what are you doing here?'

'I came to see you. You're my husband and if you think I'm going to allow you to push me out of your life, then you are very much mistaken.' She wound through the tables to reach him, as tenacious as on the afternoon she'd slipped into his bedroom. This was the Jane he remembered and had first fallen in love with, not the wounded one in his parents' house, the one he'd never wanted to hurt. 'It's time for all the guilt and blame to end, for both of us.'

'There is no both of us, just me and what I did.'

'No, for years I believed everything terrible that happened to me was because I deserved it for making my parents sick. It tore me up inside until I was convinced I wasn't worthy of love. I was wrong about it and so are you.'

'I have done bad things.'

'And they end tonight.'

'It doesn't change my past or my breaking my promise to you. You wanted to be cherished and not to be humiliated, and I failed to do both.'

'I forgive you, Jasper. Now it's time to forgive yourself.' She shifted closer to him, her scent pushing aside the stale odour of pipes and wine. She laid her hands on his shoulders, her touch light and powerful all at once. 'I love you, Jasper, I always have and I always will, no matter what.'

He didn't move back or try to silence her. Every lie he'd ever told, each failing he'd endured had been revealed and still Jane wanted him. Nothing, not his own mistakes or anyone's wickedness, had stolen her from him. He'd been searching for evidence of his goodness and it had been here before him all along in her. He encircled her waist with his arms, bringing her as close to his body as she was to his soul. 'I love you, Jane, and I have for years.'

'I know.' She rose up on her toes and pressed her lips to his.

In the circle of her embrace the fear of discovery and ruin he'd carried for so long at last lost their hold over him and nothing remained except the mutual love between them. Nothing could take this away. He was worthy of her and her heart and all the happiness it entailed. The warehouse could be burning down around them and he wouldn't care. The elation inside him was too great. She was peace and he had her.

He broke from her kiss and pressed his forehead to hers. They stood in silence together, their breaths mingling like their hearts. Only one dark spot remained. 'What will we do about our exile from the Charton family?'

'I think it will be a temporary one.' Jane playfully fingered the buttonhole of his coat, beaming brighter than she had at the altar.

'You think so?'

'If they forgave your brother, I'm sure they can forgive you.'

'Even my father?'

'Haven't you realised by now, where his children are concerned, he's all bluster and no bite? Your mother will bring him around. She always does.'

It might be a while before they were invited to dinner again, but with Jane in his arms, he could believe the invitation would eventually come. Until then, he would do all he could to make himself an honest man worthy of their affection and Jane's.

'Perhaps another addition to the Charton clan would help ease the way,' he enticed, nuzzling Jane's neck, her skin as luscious as his first taste of food after the quarantine had ended.

'Are you sure it's wise, given the uncertainty of our income?'

'I don't care. I won't ever put off anything again because I'm concerned or worried.'

She tilted back her head, her eyes wide with her passion for him. 'Then I'm certainly willing to employ such a persuasive a tactic.'

'Then we will start at once.' He pressed his lips to hers and she wrapped her arms around his neck. He had her heart, her life and her future and they were the only things he needed.

Chapter Fourteen

Johnson opened the door and to Jasper's surprise his mother entered. He braced himself, not having expected to see her so soon. In the three days since the notorious dinner party he'd heard from no other Charton, not even Jacob or Giles, who he'd expected to sneak over here in search of details about the hell and Jasper's formerly seedy existence. Instead, it had been Jasper and Jane alone in the house with no visitors, spending every day and even more pleasurable nights together, rebuilding the intimacy they'd almost lost.

Behind him on the stairs, Jane stopped, sliding her hand in his as his mother approached them.

'We must speak.' She marched into the sitting room, expecting them to follow.

Jasper exchanged a wary look with Jane, then they strode into the sitting room together, ready to face whatever his mother had in store for them.

She sat down in a wide bergère chair and motioned

for them to take the facing claw-footed sofa. They sat down together side by side, exchanging sly looks and trying not to smile like naughty children who'd been caught out.

'To what do we owe the pleasure of this visit, Mother?' Jasper asked through a restrained smile.

It was then his mother's stern expression cracked a little about the eyes, and a twitch of amusement lifted one side of her mouth. 'I wish to discuss with you the events of the other night.'

Jasper squeezed Jane's hand tight, humility replacing his humour. 'I'm sorry for what I did. I never meant to hurt anyone, or deceive you, or change your views of Uncle Patrick.'

'Yes, well, that was a shock. But I already knew about the hell.' His mother shifted her shoulders with, if he was not mistaken, a touch of guilt. 'I didn't think your father would find out about it in such a dramatic fashion.'

'You knew?' He and Jane gaped at each other. It wasn't possible.

'Of course I did. I didn't raise seven children, four of whom are boys, and not learn to detect when something suspicious is taking place. It's how I saved most of my china from being broken when you were younger.'

'How did you find out?' His mother wasn't one to frequent questionable establishments.

'After your first month home, when you began to look better, I started questioning your tall tales about where you went at night, so I had Giles and

Jacob follow you to see where you went and learn what was going on.'

'They knew, too?' Jane gasped.

'Yes.' She touched one finger to her chin and peered up at the ceiling. 'Jasper's father and Milton might have been the only ones who didn't know, which surprises me given how poorly everyone in this family holds on to secrets.'

It explained Olivia's boldness about whist at the dinner. 'Mother, I never took you to be so clever.'

'Where do you think you got your talent from?' She settled her wrap around her arm with a sniff of pride.

'Apparently.'

'But I'm here to discuss your future. How soon until your club is ready to be opened?'

'My wife knows best.' Jasper motioned to Jane. 'She's the one who's been managing it.'

'In a day or two if we want,' Jane answered, her pride evident in the quickness of her response and her raised chin.

'Good, then you must open it at once.'

Jasper tapped his boots against the floor. 'Men aren't likely to patronise it if they discover I was the hell owner and I'm sure Chester Stilton has told everyone he knows by now.'

The problem was one of the many things he and Jane had discussed over the last three days, but so far they'd reached no solution. They still owned the building and everything in it, and they had to find a way to make it turn a profit, and employ Mr Bronson, as well as all the old footmen and dealers.

'No one will find out,' his mother proclaimed, quite pleased with herself. 'I met with Mr Rathbone, who spoke to the elder Mr Stilton and explained the risk to his business if you do not maintain your contract with him due to his son's unfortunate outburst. Mr Stilton is sending Chester to the Continent, mostly to escape his creditors since he refuses to pay his boy's debt. The truth about the hell's ownership will go with him. Even if people whisper about it, I think it will help you as much as Mrs Greenwood's couch and china.'

Jasper stared at his mother in disbelief. He'd expected his entire family to shun him, but instead they were doing all they could to help him. 'Is there anything about our lives you aren't aware of?' Jasper laughed.

'Heavens, dear, do you think I sit at home embroidering all day?'

'I'm glad to learn you don't.' He'd have to employ his mother to recruit clients. She was a master of organisation.

'What about Mr Charton?' Jane hazarded, fingering her wedding ring. 'He can't be happy with us.'

'He wasn't, but I brought him around by reminding him of how we forgave Milton and by pointing out if he doesn't forgive and help Jasper, then Jasper might return to gambling.'

'I never would,' Jasper stated with force and his mother nodded.

'I imagined as much, but the threat was enough to convince your father. Your brother might take a little more time, but I imagine as soon as your club is successful and he sees more to gain in being your brother again instead of your rival, things between you will be much better.'

'I hope so.' He and Milton would never be as close as they'd been as children, but that wasn't entirely Jasper's fault. Jasper took Jane's hand again, remembering her desire to help him and Milton reach some reconciliation. If anyone could find a way to make it happen, it was her.

'I never realised your mother was so cunning,' Jane said with a laugh once the door was closed and Mrs Charton was on her way home. 'I wonder if she's aware of the gilded bed upstairs and how long it will be before your sisters barge in here to view it, then go home and demand ones of their own.'

'There isn't another like it.' He slipped his arm around her waist and pulled her close. She pressed her hands to his chest, his heart beating beneath her palms in time to hers. 'It's an original, like you.'

Jane tilted her head back and savoured Jasper lips on hers. She loved him and he loved her, and all their plans for the club and their life together would unfold just as they'd dreamed.

This was exactly how she'd imagined marriage would be.

* * * * *

If you enjoyed this book
make sure you read these linked stories
by Georgie Lee, featuring characters who appear
in THE SECRET MARRIAGE PACT

A DEBT PAID IN MARRIAGE
A TOO CONVENIENT MARRIAGE

And don't miss these other great reads
by the same author:

THE CINDERELLA GOVERNESS
MISS MARIANNE'S DISGRACE
THE CAPTAIN'S FROZEN DREAM

SPECIAL EXCERPT FROM

HARLEQUIN®

HISTORICAL

Desperation forces Georgiana Wickford to propose to her estranged childhood friend. The Earl of Ashenden swore he'd never wed, but the unconventional debutante soon tempts him in ways he never expected!

Read on for a sneak preview of THE DEBUTANTE'S DARING PROPOSAL by Annie Burrows.

Georgiana couldn't really believe that his attitude could still hurt so much. Not after all the times he'd pretended he couldn't even see her, when she'd been standing practically under his nose. She really ought to be immune to his disdain by now.

"Did you have something in particular to ask me," Edmund asked in a bored tone, "or should I take my dog and return to Fontenay Court?"

"You know very well I have something of great importance to ask you," she retorted, finally reaching the end of her tether as she straightened up, "or I wouldn't have sent you that note."

"And are you going to tell me what it is anytime soon?" He pulled his watch from his waistcoat pocket and looked down at it. "Only, I have a great many pressing matters to attend to."

HHEXP0617

She sucked in a deep breath. "I do beg your pardon, my lord," she said, dipping into the best curtsy she could manage with a dog squirming around her ankles and her riding habit still looped over one arm. "Thank you so much for sparing me a few minutes of your valuable time," she added through gritted teeth.

"Not at all." He made one of those graceful, languid gestures with his hand that indicated *noblesse oblige*. "Though I would, of course, appreciate it if you would make it quick."

Make it quick? Make it quick! Four days she'd been waiting for him to show up, four days he'd kept her in an agony of suspense, and now that he was here, he was making it clear he wanted the meeting to be as brief as possible so he could get back to where he belonged. In his stuffy house, with his stuffy servants and his stuffy lifestyle.

Just once, she'd like to shake him out of that horrid, contemptuous, self-satisfied attitude toward the rest of the world. And make him experience a genuine human emotion. No matter what.

"Very well." She'd say what she'd come to say without preamble. Which would at least give her the pleasure of shocking him almost as much as if she really was to throw her boot at him.

"If you must know, I want you to marry me."

Don't miss THE DEBUTANTE'S DARING PROPOSAL by Annie Burrows, available June 2017 wherever Harlequin® Historical books and ebooks are sold.

HARLEQUIN
A Romance FOR EVERY MOOD

SEDUCTION

He kissed her. There was no preamble, no sweet and tentative approach. There was only the heat of his body and the strength of his hands on her arms, holding her as his mouth pressed to hers, hard, hungry. For an instant, she responded. The silk of his tongue, the mingling of breath, the scent of his skin, faintly citrus, filled her. There was pleasure here. Primitive, savage pleasure.

Oh, God, how long since she had felt this?

Never. The truth of that was irrefutable.

Whatever stirrings of passion she had felt in her past, it was a mere prelude to the sensations that drowned her now. She had never been kissed so thoroughly, so savagely. So beautifully.

With only a kiss he had found the part of her she thought she had killed and sliced out with surgical precision. She had been wrong.

Under the press of his lips and the stroke of his tongue she unfurled, the air around them so still it quivered, the storm inside her building until she kissed him back, open-mouthed and hungry. Her fingers twisted in his hair, tugging him down to her as she fed on his strength, his passion, the physical comfort of his hard body and sheltering embrace . . .

Books by Eve Silver

DARK DESIRES

HIS DARK KISS

DARK PRINCE

HIS WICKED SINS

SEDUCED BY A STRANGER

NATURE OF THE BEAST
(with Hannah Howell and Adrienne Basso)

Published by Zebra Books

SEDUCED BY A STRANGER

EVE SILVER

ZEBRA BOOKS
Kensington Publishing Corp.
http://www.kensingtonbooks.com

ZEBRA BOOKS are published by

Kensington Publishing Corp.
119 West 40th Street
New York, NY 10018

ISBN-13: 978-0-8217-8130-2
ISBN-10: 0-8217-8130-8

First Printing: September 2009
10 9 8 7 6 5 4 3 2 1

Printed in the United States of America

This book is for Aida, for so many reasons

Acknowledgments

Many thanks to my editor, John Scognamiglio. To Nancy Frost and Brenda Hammond for the many years of support, friendship, and guidance. To Michelle Rowen, for lunches and laughter when I needed it most. To Ann Christopher, Caroline Linden, Kristi Astor/Kristina Cook, Laura Drewry, Lori Devoti, and Sally MacKenzie for holding my hand through the bleak, frozen winter.

And, as always, to Sheridan, my joy; Dylan, my light; and Henning, my forever love.

Part One

Chapter 1

Marlow, Buckinghamshire, October 1812

At the age of eleven, Catherine Weston was buried alive in a shallow, wet grave.

Two months before that, she had stood in the cemetery beside the ancient stone church, clutching her mother's hand as the tiny coffin containing her brother's remains was lowered into the ground. All four of her infant brothers had been buried this way. Sent to the warmth and light of Heaven, her mother said.

But now, on this miserable, gray October day, as the damp earth weighed impossibly heavy on her chest and forced her to struggle for every breath, Catherine realized her mother had lied. There was no light or warmth. There was only the cold, pungent mud and the choking terror that made her heart beat so hard she was certain it would burst.

She wondered how long it would be until someone missed her. Too long, for though she had been at Browning School for Girls for nearly a month, she had not formed any close friendships. No one would note her absence with any alacrity. She was the only child of two only children, and she had spent the first decade of her life entertaining herself while her parents grieved for their four infant sons and grew distant and tired and old before their time. Solitude was a state she knew best. The constant noise and hubbub at Browning unnerved her. As she lay panting in her grave, she thought with bitter regret that her preference for solitude had come with a terrible price.

The morning had been stormy, the rain pounding, the boom of thunder loud and near. By the afternoon, the downpour abated and as soon as lessons were over, Catherine left the school and sneaked off to gather smooth, cool stones like the ones she and her mother took to her brothers' graves and left there to mark the fact that they had come and gone. In the spring and summer, they left flowers. In the autumn and winter, stones. There was a welcome familiarity to the task.

The large pocket at the front of her pinafore was already heavy with a dozen small rocks when she bent at the edge of a low embankment to pick up one more. Without warning or sound, the earth gave way beneath her feet. One moment she stood on wet ground, the next, she slipped down to the muddy riverbank and sank in the fetid mire as a good chunk of the embankment came sliding down atop her.

And there she was. Buried as her brothers were buried, though they were dead and she was not. Not yet.

Numb, she lay there at an odd incline, her head closer to the surface than her feet. The first thought that came to her mind was that she would die here and her mother would cry a river of tears and her father would have cried if she had been a son, but since she was a daughter he would remain stoically silent. Then all thoughts were swept aside by a roaring, surging panic.

Seized by horror and fear, Catherine tried to scream, but

the weight of the earth did not let her put any force in the sound, and the effort robbed her of what little breath she could summon.

The more she cried and wriggled, the deeper she sank, the muck taking on a sucking, greedy life of its own, pulling her in. Beneath her, the slime parted and oozed to make her grave more secure, cold and dark and so foul that she retched and gagged. Above her, the weight of the fallen embankment pressed down and down, growing heavier by the moment.

She was dying. She knew it and she fought and struggled with all she was because she wanted to live.

Whatever the price, she wanted to live.

Her struggles grew weaker, her movements sluggish, and after a time, she simply lay there, taking shallow little breaths, trapped like a fly in honey.

Luck and happenstance had determined that her right hand was squashed in the space directly before her face, held fast in the posture she had taken as she tumbled, with her hand raised in a futile gesture of protection. Willing herself to hold still and quiet, she wriggled only her fingers, pushing aside the earth before her face, creating a pocket that allowed her to breathe. Then she moved her whole hand at the wrist, sweeping dirt from before her mouth and nose and eyes until finally a tiny opening let the gray of the sky peep through.

The sight of the sky, so welcome and sweet, overwhelmed her. A seedling of hope unfurled. She took a moment then to breathe, just breathe. Or perhaps she took an hour. There was no way to know.

More wriggling and waving of her hand, more inching of her forearm side to side, and the hole grew large enough that she thrust her hand and part of her forearm out of the ground like a dirt-covered branch sticking up toward the heavens.

With careful movements she pushed the earth aside as best she could, large clumps falling on her face, into her eyes and mouth. But the hole grew larger, and it was *that* she held on to, the sight of the ever-expanding edges of the opening and the hope that she could dig her way free.

A sound reached her, faint and distant, a squelching noise like footsteps in mud. It grew louder, then stopped, then started again. Catherine thrust her hand through the hole once more, waggling it to and fro and calling out in a hoarse, dry croak to make what paltry ruckus she could until she was forced to seal her lips against the earth that sprinkled on her face, loosened by her movements.

The footsteps stopped entirely, and Catherine's heart stopped right along with them. Then louder, faster, they pounded toward her. From nowhere a face appeared in place of the patch of gray sky, pale cheeks and dull skin, scraggly yellow ringlets and wide blue eyes.

Catherine blinked against the soil that clung to her lids, and after a moment of hazy desperation, she recognized the face above her. Madeline. The strange, quiet girl from Browning who kept to herself, the girl the others whispered about. She was a little older than Catherine, perhaps three years or four, but her odd nature made her seem younger.

Madeline stood a distance away, her position causing her face to be neatly framed by the margins of the hole. Leaning in a bit, she peered deeper into Catherine's grave, her brow furrowed. Then she reared back as though struck and made a startled sound. "Catherine?"

"Help," Catherine wheezed, the single word all she could summon.

She heard sounds of swishing cloth, and a faint dull thud,

and she realized that Madeline had gotten down on her belly and inched forward to push aside the wet earth at the edges of the hole. A cascade of soil tumbled onto Catherine's face.

"No!" she cried, desperately afraid that these attempts at aid would only serve to bury her completely. They needed adults and more than just Madeline's two hands to dig her free. "Get help!"

Tipping her head to the side, Madeline did nothing, and Catherine ran her dry tongue over dryer lips and struggled to find the breath to explain. But there was no need. Madeline offered an awkward nod.

"I shall return," she said, then squirmed back, straightened, and finally, disappeared.

Catherine longed to call her back. *Do not leave me. I beg of you, do not leave me alone in my grave.* But she knew there was no other way, and Madeline was already gone.

It was a very long while—her despair and terror making time tick away all the more slowly—before Catherine heard the sounds of pounding feet and the shouts of the headmistress and others, and it was even longer until they dug away all the dirt and pulled her free.

She felt arms wrap around her and her body lifted. She cried, racking, dry sobs that faded to nothing, and she was only dimly aware of being bathed and clothed in a nightrail that smelled of soap, and then tucked in her bed. The headmistress made her drink something that was warm and smelled like cloves and milk and her father's brandy.

Much later, she woke from an uneasy doze, her throat raw and dry. There was almost no light, and for a fraught instant she thought she was dead. Buried. Then she recognized the sliver of moonlight that drew a thin line on the floor and the smooth softness of the sheets that covered her, and she realized that she lay in her bed at Browning.

Sounds became recognizable. The beating of her own heart, made loud and strong by her fear. The wind whistling through chinks in the wall. The rattle of the windowpanes. And the huff of steady, soft breathing.

She turned her head. Someone stood at her bedside, cloaked in shadow.

Madeline.

The girl stared at her, eyes glittering with the reflection of what paltry light bled through the darkness. She glided closer, reached out, and laid her palm flat across Catherine's chest, above her heart.

"Tell me," she whispered urgently. "What does it feel like to die?"

Catherine struggled to form a reply. She had not died. She lived. She *lived*. And she was so grateful for that.

Just then, the headmistress came with a candle, the flame dancing and bright against the blackness. Mesmerized, Catherine stared at the orange glow, so beautiful, so warm, and she wondered how to answer her friend, her savior.

What does it feel like to die?

Chapter 2

Cairncroft Abbey, March 1813

The boy made his way through the woods, purposeful and quick, his breath showing white before his lips, for the morning was unseasonably chilly. He knew exactly where he headed, and when he reached the place, he wrapped his strong young arms around the thick trunk and shimmied up, the bark rough beneath his hands. The nest before him held three young birds. They were not newly hatched, but rather almost ready for flight. The sight of them made him smile.

Three. He found their number auspicious.

With care, he eased the nest from the crook of the heavy branch, balancing it with one hand as he clambered back down the tree, using his thighs and his one free hand to guide his descent.

Though the day was winter-cold, the sun shone overhead, peeking through branches and leaves, bright and hot. Like a fire. He liked fires, the sight of the flames, leaping and dancing, the heat, the powerful and unpredictable nature. The destruction left in its wake. In the autumn, he had found a quiet place in the wood and brought a fagot to light the dry sticks. With wonder and awe, he had watched as the flames roared and spread so fast that even had he wished to stop them, he would not have been able.

If his parents knew he was the one who had started the fire that took half the south woods, they had never said. Even if they suspected it, he knew they could not be certain. He was a very good liar, able to hide the truth from almost anyone, except perhaps his cousin Sebastian, who seemed to know things that no one else ever did. But Sebastian did not live with them anymore, and that was for the best.

With the nest carefully held in one hand, and the other arm stretched high where he curled his fingers round an overhead branch, the boy pointed his toes, seeking the ground. At last, they touched and he lowered himself, checking the nest with a sigh of relief. The birds chirped wildly as he turned and walked a brisk pace deeper into the woods.

The foliage grew thicker, blocking the sun, leaving him in cold, dark shadow. It was quiet, save for the clamor of the baby birds. There was no one here. Only him.

Setting the nest on an old, desiccated log, he hunkered down beside it to eye level, staring at the tiny creatures. Their short, high-pitched cries tumbled one against the next.

They were orphaned things. He had poked at the bodies of two adult birds where they had lain near the base of the tree. The nestlings were alone, as his cousin Madeline was alone.

Only . . . *she* was not truly alone, though her parents were dead now as the nestlings' were.

Madeline had family here. She had returned to the abbey, and now there were three, instead of only two as they had been before. He was still not quite certain how he felt about that. Madeline was a strange, quiet thing who glided noiselessly in his shadow, adoring and desperate for any attention he bestowed. At times, he enjoyed that, though he did find it odd, for she was the elder and he the younger by a full three years. Mostly he found her more irritating than anything else.

"Are you afraid?" the boy whispered, reaching out and almost touching one of the birds, only to stop short and draw his hand back as the tiny creature opened its beak and made a piteous sound.

He rose and glanced about. There were twigs aplenty littering the forest floor, and old, brown leaves that smelled like moist rot, piled in a thick, carpeting layer. Picking up a stick, he used it to poke around a bit, until the end clacked against something solid—a rock tucked tight against the log.

Prying loose the rock, then rooting beneath to search for bugs, he caught a fat worm and brought it to the nest. For a moment, he gazed between the single worm and the three open beaks. Then he smiled. Squeezing the squirming, wriggling flesh, he dug deep with his nails and carefully tore the worm into three parts. A shiver of delight wriggled up his spine. He fed a bit into each seeking beak.

"Are you afraid?" he whispered again, reaching down to close his hand around one small, feathered body and lift the bird from its nest.

He stroked his index finger along its head. The creature's heart fluttered violently and it struggled in his grasp. It turned its head toward him, eyes glossy and black, and he wondered if it knew.

Could it sense his intent?

Smiling, he stroked its head once more. A sensation of unutterable power surged, and with a giddy laugh he twisted the nestling's head clear around.

Bright and sharp, the snap echoed through the woods. Or perhaps his joy in the act only served to amplify the sound.

There was no more fluttering heart, no more frightened twitching. There was nothing. Only the still-warm body in his hand. And he *owned* that body. It was his.

The pleasure that bathed him, warm and liquid, nearly sent him to his knees.

He took a slow, deep breath, savoring the moment, enjoying the nuances of scent and touch and sound. He wanted to remember this frozen instant, this feeling. His first time. In the cold, dark forest, he was the master, the king. He was powerful, all-powerful. He claimed this creature's very life.

The remaining two birds began to chirp madly, a crescendo of sound, and he jerked his head to the side, pinning his full attention on them. They peeped louder and faster as he carefully set the little corpse on the log and reached into the nest for the next.

To his right, a twig snapped.

He whirled, fury biting deep. Someone watched him. Someone dared to disturb his play.

There.

He saw a flash of pale hair. Madeline, or someone else?

Following instinct rather than design, determined to protect his secrets, he snatched a stick from the ground. The heft was just right, the end pointed and sharp.

With a snarl he lunged for the shadows.

Night crept in on silent feet. Dark shapes twisted and writhed along the walls, slashed by the flickering tongues of amber and gold cast out by the fire that burned in the hearth. The door to the chamber was cracked open just wide enough for a rat to squirm through, or a sly lad to peer in unnoticed. Curling his fingers around the edge of the door, the boy eased closer and breathed deeply. The fragrance of blood drifted lightly on the current of cold air, a subtle perfume, inviting and mysterious.

Enthralled, he held very still, his body quivering like that of a hound after a scent.

Beside the bed, on a hard, straight chair, sat a woman. His mother. Her back was hunched, her thin shoulders sagging. She sobbed, the sounds grating and harsh, dragging across the boy's senses like a file. At her back—stone-faced and silent—stood her husband, his hands fisted by his sides, for at last he had recognized the futility of his efforts to comfort her. Shadow and light played over the pair, actors in a twisted tableau.

But this scene was part of no fictional play. The participants were real; their torment was real, and the boy found joy in their suffering, pleasure in their pain. The thrill of it danced through him.

After a time, a different sensation invaded, the prickling unease of unseen eyes watching him. From behind came a faint sound, a sigh or a footfall. The rustle of fabric.

Someone there.

Madeline.

Anger surged. *He* was the watcher. *He* was the dweller of darkened doorways and niches.

He turned slowly, narrowed his eyes, and searched for some sign of movement. His heart pounded a hard, steady rhythm as he held his rage in rigid check. The long, empty hallway unfurled like a black ribbon, and the skulking shadows swallowed him whole.

But his cousin was not there. No one was there.

Feeling foolish and liking that not at all, he faced forward once more to peer into the fire-kissed gloom of the bedchamber, careful to make no noise that might alert those inside to his presence. His gaze slid to the bed.

The sheets were a pristine white, the bed frame dark cherry. A boy lay there, his head nestled on a soft pillow, his spun gold hair matted, his skin a paler shade of chalk tinged with gray. His nightshirt flowered crimson where blood seeped through the bandages the housekeeper had wrapped about his limp form hours past when the sun had been a bright ball in the sky.

Ever the interloper, the outcast, the boy at the door leaned in a little, lured by the lovely sight of the blood.

A shiver of delight chased across his skin, raising the fine hairs on his forearms.

The darkness shifted and breathed, a cloud crossing the moon. He glanced at the windows that were set high in the far wall. They were long and narrow as had been the style when this place, Cairncroft Abbey, was built. The cloud passed and cool pale light leaked through the warped panes, past the heavy curtains, but not so far as the dim corners or the recesses of the high ceiling. He liked that, the way the moonlight struggled—and failed—to puncture the suffocating gloom.

The darkness won. It always won.

In the hearth, a log popped, sending a spray of bright sparks dancing through the air. The woman gasped.

Clenching his fists against the urge to push the door fully ajar, to step into the bedchamber where wretched despair played out in perfect melodrama, the boy held his place, apart, separate. Alone.

"I cannot bear it. I cannot," the woman whispered on a dry croak. "Geoffrey"—her voice broke—"Gabriel." She raised her head and turned her face toward the open door, toward *him*, but her eyes were hazy, unfocused. She saw not what was before her.

That was ever the way of things. She never saw *him*.

With a sob, she collapsed forward and buried her face in her hands. Her husband stood at her back, staring straight ahead, until finally, as the sound of her cries burgeoned and grew, he moved to kneel before her. His face was close to hers and he whispered useless words meant to comfort.

Until that moment, the man's broad shoulders had obscured the looking glass that hung above the mantel. Now, his movement left a clear path to the door.

From his place outside the chamber, the boy lifted his gaze and stared into the silvered, dark depths of the mirror. The partially open door was reflected there, and the jamb framing the ghostly oval of his face. His own wide, almond-tipped eyes stared back at him.

'Twas a face identical to that of the cold, motionless boy on the bed.

And the reflection was smiling with dark, secret glee.

Part Two

Chapter 3

Cambridge, England, March 1828

What does it feel like to die?

The question haunted her still. As she lurched to and fro in the swaying coach, Catherine Weston recalled every nuance of the long-ago night when Madeline had climbed onto the bed and stretched out beside her, her mere presence offering solace. She recalled the flare of emotion when the headmistress had come, carrying a single candle with its dancing flame. Catherine had stared at that tiny flickering light, thinking she had never seen anything more beautiful, more comforting.

A few short months later, Madeline's parents were dead, taken by a fever, and Madeline was removed from Browning, never to return. But that night had been the first step on the path to this day.

Within the fetid confines of the hired carriage, Catherine sat in damp discomfort, listening to the wild patter of the rain and staring at the wet stain that darkened the far side of the seat as drop after drop seeped through a crack in the roof and plopped against the velvet in a steady drip. The ancient carriage jerked and jolted, the horses slogging through rivers of mud that overtook the roads and sucked at the wheels. More than once the conveyance lurched to an unwelcome halt, and from her place inside, Catherine heard the coachman's curses and the crack of his whip urging the beasts to pull free.

The sounds were muffled but not completely obscured by the drumming of the storm.

Rage and frustration laced the driver's tone, conjuring less than pleasant memories of another man, his voice taut with fury as he cursed fate. Cursed her.

She curled her fingers, digging the tips of her nails into her palms. That man was dead, but the things he had said and done haunted her still.

Resolutely, she turned her thoughts to nothing at all, locking away the memories and the pain.

Soon, the carriage stopped at a small coaching inn and Catherine went gratefully to a retiring room before making her way to the public dining room where she settled at a small table as close to the fire as possible. She stared into the flames for a long moment, rousing herself when a plate was set before her. She poked at the unpalatable meal—underdone leg of mutton that smelled gamey, and a boiled potato, hot and soft on the outside but hard and uncooked within. Travel weary and bedraggled, she could not deflect the instant of melancholy that touched her, or the thought that her heart was a little like that potato, cold and hard at its core.

Best it stay that way. A soft heart was a certain road to torment.

"'Tis inedible," grumbled a portly man at the adjacent table.

"Inexcusable," groused his companion. "A crime, I tell you, to take good coin for this slop. A heinous crime."

Catherine pressed her lips together, holding back the unsolicited observation that there were things in this life one could label both heinous and criminal. A poorly prepared meal was not one of them.

She sipped her tea, letting the warmth cheer her, grateful for the brief respite from the commingled scents of rot and sweat and old perfume that clung to the walls and seats of the hired carriage. Grateful, too, to sit on a chair that did not sway and jolt.

Almost there, now. And was she not fortunate to have a destination to go to?

From the corner of her eye, she saw the coachman stalk past the door. He had been pacing like that for several minutes, pausing intermittently to stare hard at her as though willing her to hurry.

She finished her tea and set the chipped cup on its mismatched saucer, nostalgia creeping up on her. There had been a time when she had lived in a house with only the finest china, when her tea had been poured from a silver pot. Funny, the things she pined for. Not the china or the silver, but the lemon squares that Cook used to make with such loving care. She wondered what had become of Cook. What had become of all the servants, especially those who had helped her after the fire.

She shivered and again gathered her thoughts, all the more determined to keep the past locked away in its dusty box. That was the only safe place for it to be.

Squaring her shoulders, Catherine took up her reticule and rose from the small table.

Moments later, she climbed into the rank carriage once more. From his ugly glare and muttered complaints,

Catherine thought that the driver might have preferred to remain at the inn and find himself a tankard and a chair, or perhaps leave her there and hie himself back to London. But she had promised him an extra coin at the end of the journey if he brought her to her destination before nightfall. Both foresight and frugality underpinned her promise. The cost of his reward was far less than the cost of overnighting at a coaching inn.

The door slammed shut behind her; the springs creaked and groaned as the driver climbed up. A moment later, the carriage jolted and the horses plodded on.

Time passed, and in the end the downpour stopped, but the sky did not clear. Catherine was unprepared when the carriage made a sharp turn, and she slid across the rain-dampened squabs with a gasp. Bracing one hand on the worn velvet of the seat, she scooted forward and looked out the window to catch her first sight of her destination.

Cairncroft Abbey.

Well, there it was. She knew not what she had expected; she only knew it was not this.

Tipping her head, she contemplated the massive array of limestone and clunch that loomed gray and cold and bleak before her. So many chimneys. They poked up from the steeply pitched tile roof, three on the left, then a single, a double, another single on the far right, dark silhouettes against the suffocating mantle of charcoal cloud. One of the chimneys sent up a thin, whitish curl of weak smoke. No light glimmered in the windows. Instead, they stared, blank and vacant and utterly dark, reflecting the image of the grim sky. Grim as the letter Madeline had written, telling of her desperation and despair.

Please come. I beg of you. Please come.

And what reply could Catherine offer to the girl who had saved her life other than, "I will come."

Her curiosity piqued, she continued to study the place even after the coach rocked to a halt.

"Perhaps the abbey looks better in the sunshine," she muttered, and pushed open the carriage door. She could only hope such was the case, for this dreary dwelling did not bode well for the improvement of Madeline's mood.

Climbing down onto the graveled drive, Catherine looked up at the windows once more. For an instant she thought she saw a flicker of movement, a pale form shimmering, wraithlike, behind the glass, there one moment, gone the next. When she saw nothing more, she dropped her gaze and stepped forward only to stop short, for directly in her path lay a small, dark shape.

Peripherally aware of the coachman muttering and huffing behind her as he fetched her things, she took another step, thinking the shape was a clod of dirt.

She blinked.

Not dirt. A blackbird. It must have hit one of the windows and fallen to the ground.

A dead thing in a dead place.

She stared at the feathered little carcass on the drive with its skinny, twiglike legs stretched toward the sky, and for an instant saw something entirely different, a memory of a human form, rigid and—

"Here you are." The driver's voice drew her attention, scattering her dark memories like smoke. With a grunt, he pulled her trunk down and heaved it to the ground at her feet, then cast a narrow-eyed look first at the uninviting abbey, then at the forest that encroached from the north.

Catherine followed his gaze. The trees grew tightly, one against the next, their limbs twining together as though blocking any unwelcome visitor from entering there. A feeling of unease slunk through her. She shivered and turned away.

"An inhospitable place, bounded by cursed woods on all sides," the driver muttered, and sidled back toward the carriage with a last dubious look toward the door of the abbey. "You certain they're expecting you?"

"They are," Catherine replied. She watched in silence as he clambered up to his perch, the springs creaking beneath his weight. He was leaving her. The realization knifed through her, and she raised her hand in an unintended plea. "Wait—"

"You paid me to bring you, and bring you I did. I've a way to go before dark." He gave a last, nervous glance at the off-putting facade of Cairncroft Abbey. "I'll take that promised reward now, miss."

"Yes, of course." Catherine fetched a precious coin from her reticule and handed it up to him, then stepped back, feeling oddly disconcerted that he did not remain even to see her greeted by a housekeeper or maid.

Taking up the reins in a practiced grip, he released the brake and shouted a command to his horses. The coach groaned and gave a prolonged squeak as it rolled away down the long drive, picking up speed as it went. In time, both conveyance and driver were gone and Catherine was alone.

She turned to face the house once more. Her gaze slid past the dead bird and she froze, taken aback. From this angle, there was something disturbing—unnatural—about the way the wings were spread wide as though still in flight, too contrived, too *posed.*

The bird's yellow-ringed eyes stared up at her, unseeing.

But *something* saw her. Slowly she raised her head. Eerie certainty tickled the fine hairs at her nape and made her skin crawl. She took a short breath, a wash of dismay chilling her. Something watched her with focused intent.

She looked about, first to the windows that showed no light, then to the tangled woods. She was about to turn away when she saw a shadow shifting amongst the thick trunks. It was enough to convince her that there *was* something there in the forest. Perhaps some*one*. She could not say with certainty.

Watched from the window. Watched from the woods. But greeted by no one.

The wind howled down and tunneled into the lee created by the abutting angles of the abbey, twirling and biting, tearing at her cloak and skirt. Wariness dragged forth a shiver that had nothing to do with the chilly clime.

Rubbing her hands along her arms, Catherine faced the abbey once more. Exhaustion, she decided. There was no other explanation for the apprehension that bit at her like a thousand ants. A dead blackbird and shifting shadows were hardly cause for dismay.

She made her way to the heavy wooden front door, but before she could knock, it opened on well-oiled hinges. A woman stood there, her arms folded beneath her ample bosom, her expression utterly blank. She wore a white apron over a dark blue dress, and a white cap on her head. Though her red hair was faded and shot with gray, her face was smooth and unlined. The contradiction left Catherine unable to gauge her age. Perhaps forty, though she might have been a decade older or younger. About her waist was a chain, and a ring of keys hung heavy upon it.

"Come along, Miss Weston," the woman said, her tone flat. "The wind is bitter, and we would both be better off out of it."

For an instant, Catherine did not move, taken unawares

by the housekeeper's tone and words. The woman looked over her shoulder and said something in a quiet voice. After a moment a young man came out, his head bowed, his steps plodding. He hefted Catherine's trunk and carried it off without a word or even a glance in her direction.

"Well?" the housekeeper prodded, leaving Catherine to wonder at her hostility. She was an invited guest, not some vagrant hovering on the doorstep in search of charity. But she made no comment on the oddity of the woman's behavior. Perhaps things were different—less formal—here at Cairncroft Abbey than at other houses. Perhaps there were fewer rules.

The thought of rules and regulations and rigid control made her edgy, and as she stared at the housekeeper who stared back with blatant hostility, Catherine felt her temper spark. So she retreated into the frosty façade that had protected her for so long.

"Are you aware that there is a dead bird on the drive?" she asked, her tone chilly and proper as ever her mother's had been.

"A dead bird," the housekeeper echoed, her posture grown more rigid still.

"Yes. There." With a dip of her chin and an arch of her brows, Catherine indicated the spot and said, "I suspect it hit the window." But that was untrue. She did not suspect that at all now, but rather had the nagging thought that the unfortunate creature had expired by some other, more sinister, means. And that was simply ridiculous, a play of her imagination. Surely it was.

"I'll see to it." The silence stretched and the housekeeper said nothing more, only opened the door wider and waited with obvious impatience. Catherine crossed the last of the space between them and stepped inside, insulted, appalled, and faintly amused by the strange welcome.

The door swung shut behind her, silent save for the final, pronounced thud. Smells drifted to her. Beeswax. A faded overlay of lye soap. Even fainter than that, a hint of tallow.

She found herself in a vast open hall with tiles of cold, gray slate. At the far end was a narrow set of stairs that led to an open archway, beyond which were only shadows and darkness. On one wall was a wide fireplace flanked by two long, stiff-looking couches covered in burgundy velvet. They stood out in harsh contrast to the stark backdrop of pale stone.

"Look up," said the housekeeper.

"I beg your pardon?"

"Look up," she repeated, and Catherine did, staring in amazement at the high, domed ceiling, painted in hues of black and brown and red to depict a scene of the hunt in all its brutal and gory detail. The artist was one of surpassing skill. She almost expected a fat drop of blood to plop on her head.

After a moment, she lowered her gaze and noticed that above the couches the walls were covered with enormous tapestries. They appeared quite old, perhaps hundreds of years, but they were in fine condition, neither frayed nor faded. Each portrayed a scene of war, the one more violent than the next. Both repulsed and lured by the macabre depictions, she walked several paces forward and stared. Moments passed before Catherine turned and saw that the housekeeper watched her with ill-concealed anticipation, waiting for some reaction.

"Well," Catherine said brightly, "the colors are quite rich."

The housekeeper threw back her head and laughed, a harsh sound that echoed through the cavernous space.

"And I suppose that if you cut off a limb you'd say it was fine luck that you still had three attached," the woman observed in a brittle tone.

Catherine made no show of distress, no indication that the housekeeper's words and behavior disturbed her in any way. She had faced barbs and nettles aimed at her by a master. This woman's acrimony barely warranted notice.

She imbued her tone with a shade of hauteur as she asked, "You are the housekeeper, Mrs. . . . ?"

"Bell." The woman's eyes narrowed.

"Mrs. Bell"—Catherine allowed herself a tight smile—"I thank you for this most unique welcome." Her tone hardened. "But my journey has been long and I should like to see my friend now."

The housekeeper opened her mouth, closed it, and pressed her lips tight. She appeared to be engaged in some personal struggle. Then she heaved a sigh and said, "Miss Madeline sleeps poorly, and she is ever agitated during the day. Your being so late has only made it worse. You were expected by midday. She was up and fretting over you with the dawn." She paused. "Given that it is her habit to remain abed past noon, rising at that hour has only added to her distress."

Catherine offered no explanation. She owed none. That was a lesson learned and treasured. No longer did she allow herself to rush into stuttered apologies and desperate, convoluted excuses. That part of her was dead. She had murdered it with careful purpose.

"Then I suggest we attend Miss Madeline to straightaway," she offered crisply.

The housekeeper sniffed, then stalked toward the stairs at the end of the vast hall. Catherine followed. She wondered at the woman's manner. Perhaps it was mere habit.

Mrs. Bell had probably been the housekeeper at the abbey for many years.

They climbed the stairs at the end of the open hall, traversed a dimly lit passage, then took two more flights, the way shadowed and gloomy, for the housekeeper carried neither lamp nor candle. The house was utterly silent. Only the faint shush of their footsteps on the thick carpets disturbed the quiet. A wide passage opened before them. The doors on both sides were shut tight, the atmosphere heavy, the air stale.

"Miss Madeline likes to be private." Mrs. Bell cast a glance over her shoulder. "But she has determined that you are to be roomed in this wing. You will sleep here." She gestured to a door on her right that was slightly ajar, revealing a glimpse of canopied bed. "Do you wish to stop for a moment? Perhaps splash water on your face?"

The kindness of the suggestion made Catherine wary. The housekeeper had been unfailingly rude since her arrival and the sudden concern seemed false. Too, she found it odd that Mrs. Bell had fussed about Madeline's anxious state, yet failed to convey her to her friend with all haste.

"Thank you, no. I should like to see Madeline now." Having stopped at the inn only a few hours past, Catherine felt no immediate need to find a moment's privacy.

"As you please." The housekeeper walked on. At the farthest end of the hallway she stopped before a closed door and rapped sharply. "Miss Madeline?"

There came no reply, but the woman turned the handle and pushed open the paneled door as if an invitation to enter had been issued.

The portal swung inward revealing a deep, cavernous room, quiet and still. An empty church had more noise. There was no light save the embers of a dying fire. Catherine looked past the housekeeper's shoulder into the gloom, able to see only the heavy velvet draperies that were pulled across the windows and the outlines of a table and two chairs.

"Has Catherine come?" A whisper. A plea.

"I am here," she said, making her voice gentle though her inclination was to berate Mrs. Bell, march forward, and drag the velvet curtain from across the window to let in what little light remained of the waning day.

Sidling past the housekeeper, Catherine entered the room and turned toward the bed. Madeline was propped on a mountain of white pillows, her pale hair spread in a bright nimbus. The massive, ornate headboard dwarfed her small frame, and Catherine felt a pang of dismay to see the purple shadows beneath her eyes, the near-translucent quality of her skin, the fretful plucking of her fingers at the coverlet.

The air was flavored with the scent of liniment; she could discern the faint traces of turpentine and perhaps mustard. She was torn between the urge to rush to Madeline's side and the longing to fling open the window and let the wind swirl through the chamber to carry off the stink of sickness and despair.

Madeline's eyes widened as she saw Catherine and in an effort to draw herself to a more upright posture, she wriggled on the pillows like a worm on a hook, twisting this way then that, and in the end, going nowhere. Then she simply flopped back and lay blinking, her exertions turning her cheeks bright crimson in her pale face. Catherine had seen similar coloring in a woman stricken by consumption. She wondered if that was the malady that laid her friend low, for Madeline had not been forthcoming in her letters other than to say she was in ill health.

Stepping close to the bed, Catherine reached down and took Madeline's icy hand between both of her own.

"I am certain Mrs. Bell has been most welcoming,"

Madeline whispered, turning her face toward the open door where Mrs. Bell stood with her hands folded beneath her bosom. In Madeline's gaze, Catherine read both wariness and recrimination, and she knew then that Madeline was aware of exactly how the housekeeper had greeted her. She wondered, too, if the woman was less than kind to Madeline in her time of need.

Mrs. Bell drew a deep breath through her nose and backed from the chamber, leaving Catherine and Madeline alone. Madeline stared at the open doorway for a long while, saying nothing, her eyes burning in her pale face, her lips rolled inward and pressed tight together.

"She does not like me," she offered at last, her gaze darting to Catherine, then back to the empty doorway. "She has never liked me." The assertion made Madeline sound both petulant and very young. "You were the only one, Catherine. They never liked me. Not any of them. You were my only friend."

Catherine offered no demur, for the assertion might well be rooted in truth. The girls at Browning had viewed Madeline askance. Even the teachers had regarded her with wary disdain. She was different, odd, unsettling. She asked troubling questions that had no easy answers.

What does it feel like to die? Time and experience had offered Catherine at least part of the answer.

It felt like pure terror. Icy fear. Desperation and horror that went on and on. Or it felt like escape, freedom, a shedding of pain and suffering. She supposed it depended on the person doing the dying. But that knowledge had come to her with time. She had offered no answers when Madeline had asked so many years ago, for she had had none to give.

Now, she knew far too much of death and dying.

She closed her eyes for a moment, seeking strength. She

would not think of that now, would not allow brutal recollections to claw her. Resolutely, she pictured a little black box, pushed the horror and the memories inside, slammed the lid and turned the key.

Opening her eyes, Catherine glanced about for somewhere to sit. There were books everywhere, stacks of them, covered in dust. They were piled on the floor, on the stiff brocade settee, on the round table in the corner. On the two chairs by the table. And everything was dark. The wood-paneled walls. The floor.

In the end, she eased down on the edge of the bed, rubbing Madeline's hand between her own, trying to warm her icy skin.

"The girls at Browning . . . they feared me. Hated me," Madeline whispered, her gaze darting again to the door.

"Browning was long ago, Madeline." Catherine smoothed Madeline's lank hair back from her brow. "Things that happened so far in the past cannot hurt you now," she lied.

There were voices coming from his cousin's chamber. One was a dreamy whisper, weak and soft. His cousin's voice. But the mellifluous tone of the second speaker arrested Gabriel St. Aubyn in his path. The sound was modulated and pleasing to the ear, the voice of a woman confident of her words, the diction and enunciation clean and crisp. A decisive individual, if her tone was any indication.

Gabriel paused in the shadowed hallway and simply listened as the woman continued to speak, reassuring Madeline and coaxing her into conversation. Something stirred inside him, a mild curiosity that was so foreign and rare it caught him off guard. He was interested in very little of late, save his own personal demons, and *they* had grown frightfully tedious.

'Twas time for a change of venue, a trip to London, even for a short while. There were all manner of distractions and entertainments there.

Stepping forward, he paused in the hallway outside the open door. He had an excellent view of the piles of books, the dark draperies, and the dying fire. But not the woman who spoke once more in that perfectly modulated voice.

He shifted a little and saw her then. First, her boot and the pale blue-gray sweep of her skirt. Another small shift and he saw her hand, her arm, and then the whole of her.

She was not at all what he had expected.

From her voice, he had already formed a picture in his mind. A woman cool and fair, tall and thin, ramrod straight in her bearing. But her appearance did not match the image he had conjured.

Tipping his head a bit to the side, he studied her from his shielded place. If she rose from where she sat at the edge of his cousin's sickbed, she would not be tall and thin and straight. No, not at all. His lips quirked. The top of her head would reach perhaps to his shoulder. In direct opposition to his expectations, she was well curved and in slight disarray, the hem of her skirt a shade darker than the rest, damp and mud splattered. Her hair was coffee brown, pulled back in a simple style. A single long, waving tendril had escaped and slid over her shoulder to curl over her collarbone and along the full curve of her breast.

Interest stirred. He should like to brush that curl from its place. The inclination surprised him.

He recalled then that she was expected. Catherine Weston, his cousin's childhood friend.

She stopped mid-sentence, as though her words were

reined in with a sharp tug. Slowly, she raised her head, and her gaze fixed on the place he stood. Liquid dark eyes, veiled by a thick fringe of lashes that were very long and very straight. Seconds crept past, and her attention did not waver. She knew he was there, watching, though he was certain the shadows cloaked him from view.

"What is it?" Madeline asked, her tone high with fear, her fingers moving restlessly, plumping the coverlet into a lump. She would work herself into a state in a matter of seconds. He knew that from experience.

There was no help for it. He must don the mask of host, bow in greeting to their guest, exchange worthless pleasantries. The opportunity to further observe their visitor was welcome. His cousin's company was not. For that reason only, he would have preferred to step back, feet silent on the thick carpet, and retreat unnoticed. Such cowardice—for that it was in bold truth—would allow his path and Madeline's to continue traveling parallel to each other, never crossing. But if he departed now, his cousin would let the flames of her secret terrors rage. She would raise a hue and cry until her fears were assuaged.

And if he left now, he would not hear the wonderful music of Miss Weston's voice once more.

Gabriel stepped forward, making his presence known. Or, more accurately, allowing Catherine Weston's eyes to confirm what her other senses had already alerted her to. An interloper. A watcher in the shadows.

She stared at him as he paused in the doorway, her expression utterly blank, her features composed. There was no widening of her eyes at his unannounced appearance, no change in her expression, no movement at all, which led to the realization that she, too, wore a mask. He knew his own well enough to recognize such a thing in another.

Madeline was her usual distraught self, in no condition to offer polite introductions, so he took the task upon himself.

"Gabriel St. Aubyn." He offered the words crisply, along with a shallow bow, leaving off the "Sir" and "Baronet" he might have used. Having spent so many years believing the appellations would never be his to claim, he had never become comfortable with them when they finally passed to him.

"Catherine Weston," she replied with her crisp diction, so at odds with her lush, full mouth. Dusky rose lips, forming all those lovely consonants and vowels. Porcelain-pale skin. Brown hair, so dark it appeared black in this poor light. He had the inappropriate urge to thrust his fingers through her neatly pinned hair and set it free to tumble over her shoulders. Such an odd thing. He was not usually so fanciful.

As they watched each other in the dim, quiet room, the silence punctuated by the sound of Madeline's nervous, panting breaths, Gabriel recognized a primitive part of himself uncoiling in a slow, sinuous stretch. He ran the pad of his thumb along the length of his index finger, though he truly wanted to run it along her full lower lip.

The urge stunned him. He was far closer to the edge of control than he had thought, and he rapidly shifted his plans. He had intended to wait until dawn on the morrow to leave for London, but as he held Catherine Weston's calm gaze, he recognized his acute awareness of her, the danger of it, and he thought he ought to leave at once.

Because Miss Weston, with her cool gaze and cultured tone, her wide, lush mouth and carefully cultivated veneer, recognized it as well.

And there was danger in that.

Chapter 4

Sir Gabriel St. Aubyn stayed for tea.

He had no wish to. Catherine discerned his distaste in the rigid set of his jaw and the way he stayed to the far corner of the room, near the open door, after he rang for the maid and instructed that a tray be brought up.

"Frightful weather," Catherine murmured to fill the stilted silence as she fluffed Madeline's pillows and helped her to sit up against them.

Madeline made no reply, but St. Aubyn offered the unusual opinion, "I prefer rain to sun," in a bland, bored tone. He leaned one shoulder against the paneled wall, arms folded across his chest. His pose was casual, but Catherine read leashed tension in the long, lithe lines of his form. A fencer's frame. Not heavy and bulky, but muscled nonetheless.

The silence returned, stifling in its weight. Madeline cast repeated, agitated glances in St. Aubyn's direction, and then quickly looked away if his gaze rested upon her even for an instant. Catherine wondered at the obvious strain between them, wondered, too, if it was perversity that made him inflict his presence on his cousin. She was clearly uncomfortable when he was about.

No, she was more than uncomfortable. She was afraid. Which left Catherine unable to fathom his reasons for remaining. Perhaps he gained pleasure from Madeline's unease. A disturbing possibility.

"Quite a downpour we had earlier," she said, with a glance toward the curtained window, and knew at once that she ought not to have bothered.

St. Aubyn pushed off the wall and turned his attention full upon her. "Shall we venture into the exciting territory of the difference between a drizzle and a mist? Or perhaps between a torrent and a downpour?"

"You dislike the weather as a topic of conversation?" Catherine met his gaze. It would take more than a man's disdain to cow her.

"I dislike conversation without purpose."

"A great majority of conversation has no purpose other than to acquaint the participants with each other in some small measure and perhaps lead to further intimacy as that acquaintance blossoms and grows."

His brows rose. "Intimacy, Miss Weston?" His tone was shaded with multilayered nuance.

Catherine kept her expression neutral, refusing to recoil and look away. Let him imply what he would. He knew perfectly well the intent of her statement.

He offered a spare smile, and then crossed to a small table piled high with books. Leaning down, he blew some of the dust away with three short, sharp puffs. Then he deftly removed the stacks of books to the floor.

"You must let the maid in to clean, Madeline," he chided in a hard tone.

Madeline glanced at him with a quick, frightened shift of her eyes, then resumed her frantic plucking at the coverlet.

"I do not like the servants to poke about my things," she

whispered, her voice so low that Catherine needed to lean in to catch her words. "They watch me and judge me. They wait only for the opportunity to—" She gave a shaky exhalation and said nothing more.

Tension permeated the cousins' exchange. Catherine wondered if Madeline's unease was justified. Time enough to ask her later, when St. Aubyn left them and she was more relaxed. Closing her fingers over Madeline's, Catherine stilled her movements and sent her a reassuring smile, though a tumult of questions danced through her thoughts.

Another stack of books slammed to the floor, and for an instant, Catherine was tempted to laugh at the bizarre nature of the situation. Here she was, ensconced in a dim chamber filled with dusty books and unspoken—but poorly concealed—enmities. Her introduction to Cairncroft Abbey verged on the ridiculous.

"Your trip was pleasant?" St. Aubyn asked, and it took Catherine a moment to understand that his low-voiced query was addressed to her.

"Pointless discourse, sir?"

"Genuine interest," he replied. His tone was polite, but there was an undercurrent of solicitousness, as though he actually cared whether or not the journey had passed in comfort. His attention and consideration disturbed her far more than his thinly veiled disdain had. He seemed able to don the countenance of sincere regard at will. Such a skill was common in the polite world, but St. Aubyn managed it with uncanny talent. Somehow, he imbued his query with sincerity, though he had already made it plain that such dialogue did not interest him in the slightest.

He was either addled, or an excellent actor.

Had she even tuppence to spare, she would bet it on the latter.

"My journey was most pleasant, thank you." If one enjoyed the smell of stale sweat and damp rot and a swaying, jolting ride that brought about a steady wave of nausea. "Most pleasant, indeed."

St. Aubyn dragged the table close to the bed. The pedestal's feet shushed across the carpet.

"You prevaricate well." He leaned in and whispered as he passed her, his arm brushing her side, his breath fanning her cheek, his low-voiced observation telling her that he had intended the query as a means of finding out something about her.

Her heart stuttered.

Yes, she did prevaricate well, but she was not pleased that he had noticed, nor that he was so wily as to have discovered it with such ease. She was even less pleased that the scent of his skin lingered after he passed, faintly citrus. Fresh. Quite lovely.

She pressed her lips tight. There could be no doubt that he had deliberately set out to unnerve her, but she was clever enough not to let him see any sign of his success. Had she not been trained by a master . . . a monster?

She glanced at Madeline to gauge her response to their interplay, but her eyes were closed, her head tipped back on her pillows.

"So you see, Miss Weston," St. Aubyn said, straightening from his task, "you disprove your own assertion and prove mine. Your prevarication prevents all hope of intimacy."

He turned and stalked to a chair in the corner and began removing the stack of books from the seat, saving Catherine from the need to reply. As if there was any appropriate reply to that.

With his attention otherwise occupied, Catherine was free to study him from beneath her lashes. He was neither clean-shaven nor bearded, but rather had a disreputable, dark gold stubble glazing his strong jaw.

His hair was damp, falling in an attractive tumble of thick, messy waves, honey-hued and overlong. The front strands fell to his cheekbones, accentuating their high, curved line; the back strands were longer, the ends curling slightly outward at his nape.

His hair is damp.

A fleeting recollection of the shadow in the woods touched her, and she wondered if it was Gabriel St. Aubyn she had seen upon her arrival at the abbey, if his hair was wet from the rain. If he had stood hidden by the tangle of trunks and limbs and watched her. As she now watched him.

He was beautiful. Alluring.

Distrust flickered and bloomed. In her experience, handsome men were neither pleasant nor good.

He removed a stack of books from a second chair, then dragged both to the table.

"Please," he said, resting his hands on the back of the chair closer to the bed. The tone of his voice made a queer unease flip in her belly. Not a request. An order. Catherine sat, and St. Aubyn settled his long frame in the seat closest to the door, knees splayed in a posture that was anything but proper.

He blocked the only exit.

Her gaze flashed to his. His eyes were liquid topaz with thick, curled lashes, his nose straight and narrow, his mouth a hard, masculine line, the lower lip slightly fuller than the upper. There was a complete lack of expression in his features.

"You must be talented at cards, Sir Gabriel," she murmured. "I suspect you never betray your advantage."

He inclined his head in acknowledgment. "I suspect the same of you, Miss Weston."

"Touché," she allowed with a small smile.

A quick glance at Madeline showed that she yet reclined on her pillows with eyes closed. Catherine doubted she was asleep, and wondered if she simply played at slumber as a means to avoid conversation with her cousin. She pondered an appropriate way to ask him to leave, and stumbled upon none.

A faint rattling announced the arrival of a maid carrying a tray laden with a silver teapot, cups, and a plate of small cakes. The girl paused, stared down at the tabletop, still marked with dust, and hesitated with the tray hovering above the surface.

With a sound of impatience, St. Aubyn took the thing from her and set it down himself. She gave a nervous squeak, bobbed a quick curtsy, and departed in quiet haste. Behind her came a footman with a tea caddy, hot water urn, and a heater. After putting these in place, he followed the maid, closing the door behind him with a soft snick, leaving the room gloomy and silent as it had been a moment past.

A crypt would have more warmth and cheer.

St. Aubyn rose with lithe grace, stalked to the door, and flung it open once more. Startled, Catherine wondered what it was about closed doors that distressed him.

"I dislike the scent of old liniment," he said as he resumed his seat. But she thought that was not the reason he had opened the door. She suspected it was a dislike of the closed door itself. No, not *suspected* . . . she was certain of it.

No longer feigning slumber, Madeline made a mewling sound of distress and wriggled back on the bed, as far from St. Aubyn as she could. Shadows hugged the corners and fell across her face, accentuating angles and hollows until she appeared a ghostly incarnation of herself, with blue eyes burning in a chalk white face.

Her patience frayed, Catherine gestured toward the single candle that battled the gloom, turned to St. Aubyn, and said, "Oh, do light more candles."

He blinked.

"Please," she added as an afterthought. 'Twas a word she despised, but polite conversation could not be had without it. *Ask nicely, my cat. Say please.*

She suppressed a shudder at the memory, reminding herself that *he* was gone. Dead. She was free of him now, and she would never again allow herself to be in a position where she would be forced to plead.

St. Aubyn rose from his seat and did as she bid while Madeline made soft sounds of dismay that were merely noise without form. The tiny, freshly lit flames did little to ease the dimness. They only served to make the dust more apparent and lend the stacks of books a faintly menacing cast.

Taking his seat once more, St. Aubyn leaned forward and warmed the silver pot with hot water, his actions competent and sure. He had done this before, and that in itself amazed Catherine, for it was a hostess's duty to brew the tea, not a host's. But then, Madeline did not appear up to the task, so perhaps St. Aubyn had had some practice. She found it both unsettling and oddly appealing to watch him make his selection from the tea caddy, discard the water from the pot, and pour fresh boiling water over the leaves.

Catherine made several attempts to engage Madeline in conversation, but they only earned her monosyllabic replies and hasty glances. In the end, they sat in stilted silence as the tea steeped . . . five minutes . . . seven . . . an agony of uncomfortable quiet. And all the while, St. Aubyn's gaze was fixed upon her. Catherine suspected that he orchestrated this fraught interlude to elicit her response. Perhaps he wished to see her squirm. He would be disappointed, then. Awkward silence was a mere inconvenience when measured against so many other possible trials.

"Shall I pour, Sir Gabriel?" Catherine offered when the tea was steeped, choosing not to wait for him to make the request, preferring to take control of the situation.

Madeline shifted restlessly, casting nervous glances at her cousin from beneath her lashes.

"Call me Gabriel," he said, his tone cool and bored. But he watched her with a peculiar interest. Not lust. She was familiar enough with that to recognize it. No, it was something else, a puzzled intensity, as though he wanted to study the parts that made up the whole. One side of his mouth lifted in the hint of a smile. "Or St. Aubyn, if you prefer."

She would *prefer* that he leave her alone with Madeline and take his masculine presence elsewhere. He made her uncomfortable. But she said none of that. Instead, she said in an equally cool, even tone, "I shall take that response as an affirmative."

She left off the address altogether and grasped the handle of the pot before he could make his preference known one way or the other. She had neither the patience for nor the interest in whatever game he played.

"By all means, do." St. Aubyn's straight brows rose and his smile edged a little tighter.

She lifted the tea strainer to hold it atop the china cup, then poured and passed out the tea. Madeline's hand trembled as she accepted the saucer, but Catherine was glad to see that she managed to steady it and even raise the cup to her lips for a sip.

"Raspberry tart?" she offered.

St. Aubyn stared at the plate of small cakes and tarts,

revulsion crossing his features so fleetingly that she thought she must have imagined it.

"No, thank you," both he and Madeline murmured, their replies so well timed as to overlap in perfect synchrony.

In the silence that followed, a dull thud sounded against the window, a blow from without, hard enough to rattle the pane. Catherine's head jerked toward the sound.

"Oh, no. Not another," she exclaimed, setting her cup on the table.

"Another?" St. Aubyn inquired, his attention snared.

"There was a blackbird on the drive, its wings spread wide as though frozen in flight," Catherine replied as she rose and crossed to the window to draw the heavy draperies aside and peer down to the drive below. Of course, she could see nothing from this distance. "It must have flown hard against the window and fallen. I wonder if the blow we just heard was another such unfortunate creature."

"No! A bird? A blackbird? Posed in flight?" Madeline's cup rattled in its saucer. Catherine hastened to return to the bedside and take it from her. "Was it dead?"

"Yes. I mentioned it to Mrs. Bell." Catherine could not imagine why a bird would cause such anxiety. Her gaze flashed to St. Aubyn. He sat in his stiff-backed chair exactly as he had a moment past, his teacup held in an easy grasp. There was nothing to make her think he regarded them with anything but meager interest. Yet, something . . . He was too posed, too controlled, his topaz eyes veiled by thick lashes, betraying nothing. It was the very lack of expression that made her wary.

Madeline was breathing hard, her shoulders and chest moving with each inhalation. She stared straight ahead and then her head jerked to the side and she looked to her cousin with wide, horrified eyes.

"Gabriel, why?" she cried, her skin paler than the bleached sheets, her eyes shimmering. "It has been so long. Do not deny—"

"Do you make a formal accusation, cousin?" St. Aubyn cut her off with soft-voiced menace and she fell into abrupt silence, dropping her gaze, panting now in shallow little gasps.

Baffled and dismayed, Catherine watched the interplay, wanting to intervene, uncertain what she could possibly say. She had no understanding of the history and undercurrents between these two, could not be certain precisely what Madeline's implication was.

Did she think St. Aubyn had killed the bird? And what if he had? Though it was not an activity she herself preferred, people hunted all the time. But why leave the thing on the drive?

The air hummed with tension.

"More tea?" Catherine asked as she resumed her seat, her skirt brushing St. Aubyn's knee as she passed.

He studied her for a moment, then set his cup on the tray and rose. His expression did not change, yet Catherine recognized something dark swimming just beneath the surface. It gave her pause.

"No, thank you. I have overstayed my welcome," he murmured, his voice taut. "Please excuse me."

There was something frightening there, something at odds with his controlled manner and golden good looks. He appeared for the moment to be a creature of mystery and shadow, and Catherine watched him with the caution she would afford a predator, half expecting him to burst into a tumult of energy and power.

But her expectations were not met. Instead, he strode from the room without a backward glance, leaving her alone with Madeline. She had wanted exactly this, yet she felt oddly out of sorts as she watched him depart. His presence had been a stimulant, though in all truth, not a pleasant one. She was left wondering why in heaven's name she would regret its loss.

As the faint shush of his footfalls on the carpet faded away, she had the incongruous realization that his hair had dried and lightened during their strange, tense time together. It was not so dark as honey, after all.

Madeline stared at St. Aubyn's now empty chair and shuddered. "I am glad he is gone. We . . ." She shook her head and sighed. "We do not get on well."

An understatement. It was apparent that they loathed each other, could not bear to be in the same room. The question was, why? A mystery Catherine meant to investigate. But now was not the time to force inquiry on Madeline. She would wait for a moment of calm and amiability.

Striving for normalcy, she arranged a choice of small cakes on a plate and attempted to entice Madeline to sample the fare. Her friend looked at her in somber silence, and then shook her head, a tear trickling from the corner of her eye.

"I dare not," she whispered.

"Dare not have a tart?" Catherine asked, instilling the question with cajoling good humor. "Not even one? I thought I recalled a fondness for sweets . . ."

Madeline cast a glance at the open door, and lowered her voice further still. "Poison. They lace my food with poison. Some days it is there, the bitter almond taste so strong on my tongue that it makes me retch. Other days, there is nothing. They only try to keep me guessing, to confuse me and make me question my own perceptions."

A chill crawled across her skin, but not by word or manner

did Catherine betray her shock. Surely such accusation was fueled by fiction rather than fact. What had happened to make Madeline so afraid, so distant from the world, so lost in her own terrible imaginings?

"But I would like more tea," Madeline murmured.

Catherine set the plate on the bed and turned to pour Madeline another cup of tea. Madeline accepted it with thanks, and Catherine lifted the plate once more. Determined to show Madeline that there was nothing to fear, she lifted a tart from the plate, sniffed it and, sensing naught amiss, took a dainty bite.

"No!" Madeline reached out, her hand fluttering weakly, the cup rattling, tea sloshing over the rim onto the saucer.

Catherine took the cup from her and set it aside, then took another bite of the tart. She was not particularly hungry, but she thought perhaps seeing her eat the offered cake might entice Madeline to do the same. She looked so small and frail and weak lying on the wide bed. So afraid.

"It is quite tasty," Catherine said. "There is nothing to fear."

With a sharp cry, Madeline crushed the coverlet in her curled fingers. "Oh, but there is. I tell you, there is."

Her gaze holding Madeline's as she chewed and swallowed, Catherine finished the tart. It tasted of raspberry.

Only after a moment did she wet her lips and frown, wondering if a faint bitter taste of almond did, in fact, linger on her tongue. Resisting the urge to cross to the washstand and rinse her mouth, she silently remonstrated herself for allowing her thoughts to follow this path.

She schooled her features to display none of her concern. No good could come from feeding Madeline's desperate anxieties.

After a brief consideration, she rose and rang for the

maid and once the girl arrived, gave her instructions in clear detail. The maid gazed at her in confusion, but lifted the tea tray and took it off with her as she set out to fill Catherine's request.

Some time later, she returned with a bowl of apples and a knife. These she set on the table, then bobbed a quick curtsy and left the room with only a single quizzical look sent back over her shoulder.

"Come, Madeline," Catherine said, taking up an apple and a knife. Madeline watched her warily. "There can be no threat in this apple. You see me peel and slice it before your eyes, and here"—she popped a bit in her mouth, chewed it and swallowed—"you see there is nothing but apple to be tasted. No almonds." *No poison.* But this last she did not say aloud, for she could not see the benefit of giving voice and power to Madeline's fears.

"You ate the tart," Madeline accused, her voice soft and childlike.

"I did. And you see me hale and hearty before you." She took another bite of apple, then offered a slice to Madeline, who studied her for a long moment, and at last reached out and took the bit of fruit from her hand. She ate that slice, then another and another until the first apple and a second were consumed.

"I am sorry," Madeline whispered, turning her face away. "Sorry that I drew you here to this miserable place, sorry that I am such a poor excuse for a hostess. Tomorrow. Tomorrow will be better. The clouds will ease and my mood will shift." She pressed her lips together. "Tomorrow."

Catherine took such assurance as hopeful, though she could not help but wonder how many bright tomorrows Madeline had waited for, only to have her hopes dashed. Through the years, Catherine had faced her own despair again and again, a rock-strewn path that ended in a dark and tangled wood. Trapped there, she had known the deepest desolation, but somehow, she had spied the dancing flame and followed it back into the light.

Always, the flame gave her comfort.

Her gaze slid to the last embers that glowed in the hearth, then away. "Tell me—"

"I want to sleep," Madeline interjected, forestalling Catherine's questions. "I want so badly to sleep and dream. Sweet dreams, not the nightmares that haunt my rest."

Curiosity swelled.

"Read to me, Catherine." Madeline turned her face away. "A happy tale."

Looking about, Catherine spied the nearest stack of books and selected the one at the very top. She lifted the tome and blew on the cover to dispel the dust from the leather binding, then opened to the first page and began to read. She knew not what she recited, her thoughts swirling with the many questions she had about Cairncroft Abbey and Madeline and St. Aubyn . . . about the nightmares that spilled into Madeline's waking hours. But this was not the moment to ask. No good could come of questioning Madeline at a time when she was disinclined to answer.

Long years of practice at veiling her thoughts kept Catherine's tone even and controlled as she read, the words flowing in a smooth stream. After a time, Madeline's lids drooped again and again, though she fought her exhaustion and roused herself more than once. In the end, her eyes closed and she slept.

Careful to make no noise, Catherine exited the chamber, snuffing candles as she went. Taking up the last one burning to light her way, she walked through inky blackness, the small flame a timid soldier in the face of the fallen night. She glanced about trying to recall exactly which chamber Mrs. Bell had said was to be hers. There were many doors along this corridor.

Sounds filtered through the quiet. A windowpane shaking in the wind. The creak of wood, perhaps a stair or a beam. Unease was a many-legged bug creeping up her spine. She paused and looked about.

"Hello," she called, not really expecting a reply, and none was forthcoming. Still, wariness crept across her skin, raising gooseflesh and setting her pulse racing.

Walking on, she found the chamber that had been assigned to her, recognizable because the door was the only one ajar along the entire corridor. She pushed it fully open and stepped inside. To her surprise, the velvet draperies were pulled back, the window flung wide. A gust of wind swirled through the space, making the flame of her candle plunge this way and that, sending the shadows shifting in a menacing dance. Then the flame guttered, snuffed, leaving her in near-complete darkness, for the moon was obscured by a thick cloud that allowed only a thin gray glow to bleed through the night.

Another gust came, ruffling her skirt and the curling tendrils that had escaped her pins.

A faint shush came from behind her.

The fine hairs at her nape prickled and rose, and her heart slammed hard against her ribs. She spun fast enough that she nearly lost her balance, expecting to see St. Aubyn there, in all his golden and menacing glory.

But she was alone.

Her breath hissed through her teeth as she pressed her open palm to the base of her throat, annoyed with herself. She knew better than to let such things unsettle her. There were true monsters in the night. The wind and shadows did not qualify.

Keeping her pace slow and careful lest she bump against furniture in this unfamiliar place, she moved to the window and pulled it closed, shutting out the cold wind. Then she eased back against the wall, feeling for the bell-pull that would summon a maid to bring a candle and a fagot to light a fire in the grate. Her fingers closed on nothing more than air. She made a slow circuit of the chamber, and her hand brushed against a long, narrow ribbon dangling in the corner. With a sigh of relief, she took hold of it, her thumb pressing on the embroidered surface as she gave a tug. Now there was nothing to do but wait.

Turning, she drifted back toward the window and stood looking out at the empty drive. The cloud cover of the stormy day had carried over into the night, obscuring stars and moon alike. Purple tinged and cool, what little light eked through was just enough that she could discern the grim outline of the encroaching forest, a dark mass that threatened to swallow the abbey whole.

Blackness before her and behind.

Strange, that she was not afraid of the dark. She *had* been before that terrifying day when the embankment came down on her and buried her alive. But not after. After that day, she had come to think that the darkness was the least of all possible threats.

Pity that time and experience had proved her right.

Almost did she turn from the window then and go to sit on the corner of the bed to await the maid, but something stilled her steps, and she stood, rooted in place, aware of some subtle change. The clouds shifted and the moon broke free as a faint sound, rhythmic and even, carried to her through the glass, growing ever louder.

A moment later, a groom led a horse onto the drive and a second man came out the front door to meet him, moving with lithe, easy grace. He was garbed all in black, and the horse was dark as well. Man and beast blended with the shadows, both blowing white puffs of warm breath into the cold night.

She knew it was he. Gabriel St. Aubyn. He was hatless, and his lovely pale hair caught the moonlight that drizzled now through the shifting clouds.

Conflicted, she stood by the window as he spoke with the groom. She wanted to turn away. But more than that, she wanted to watch him. Because he was beautiful. Because he was dangerous. Both elements caught her interest, for vastly different reasons.

Warm candlelight spilled through the room then, making her glance back over her shoulder.

"Miss, I am so sorry," came a mumbled apology from a newly arrived maid. A quick inspection revealed that she was the same girl who had brought both the tea and—later—the bowl of apples to Madeline's chamber. "I should have had the fire started and a lamp lit. Mrs. Bell never said . . ." She shook her head and hurried forward to set her candle on a low table.

So the lack of a fire was no oversight. The housekeeper had orchestrated the paltry discomfort of a chilly, dark room. A gauntlet thrown down. Catherine's lips turned in an ironic smile.

"You are here now. A little moonlight never harmed anyone," she replied as the maid moved to the fireplace with the glowing fagot she carried. Catherine frowned as she watched the girl kneel to her task. "How did you know I needed a fire? I rang, but I could have wanted anything . . ."

"Oh"—the maid glanced back over her shoulder—"did

you ring, miss? I never knew. Probably, I was already on my way. It was the master who bid me see to things. I passed him near the library moments ago. He said he had just come down and that your hearth wanted a fire."

Unease stirred. *Moments ago*. Yet St. Aubyn had left Madeline's chamber some time past. Had he lurked in the hallway, listening to their conversation? Or had he gone off and then returned to stand and watch her? Had her instincts been true when she had turned expecting to see him behind her only to find darkness and shadow?

The possibility was both infinitely disturbing and utterly absurd.

Turning her face to the window once more, Catherine leaned close and gazed out while from behind her came the scraping and scratching of the maid's efforts to light the fire.

Below, on the drive, St. Aubyn mounted the great, black beast, his movements elegant and spare. The horse tossed its head and lifted one massive hoof before clopping it down once more, but St. Aubyn settled it with a practiced hand, leaning forward a bit as he spoke to the animal. Whatever he said, the horse appeared to like the sound of it.

Abruptly, St. Aubyn twisted in the saddle, looking up, his face tipped to her window. She felt the weight and intensity of his gaze. The irony of that did not escape her. A moment ago, he would not have seen her standing here, for the chamber behind her would have been completely dark, making her form in the window only shadow on shadow. But now the maid had come with her candle, leaving Catherine backlit by the glow. Vulnerable to his gaze.

She knew St. Aubyn saw her here, watching him.

He made no overt sign of that, did not incline his head or raise a hand in a farewell wave. But he *did* see her. How confounding that the thought both rattled and pleased her.

Holding her place, she watched him ride away.

"Sir Gabriel takes his leave of the abbey at a late hour," Catherine murmured, turning from the window at last.

"Yes, miss." The kindling had caught under the maid's deft hand and a small blaze already flared to life. The girl stoked it expertly.

Catherine stared at the flames, entranced. She wanted to move closer, to hold her fingers outstretched until the fire danced toward them, but not close enough to singe. She had no desire to court injury. Dragging her gaze away, she smiled at the maid as she rose from the place she knelt.

"I am sorry, miss," the girl said again. "Sorry there was no fire. Of course, the master knows of it, but he'll forget by the time he returns. He's like that. His mind ever on other things. But Mrs. Bell is one who never forgets." Reaching up, she adjusted the skewed mopcap on her limp brown hair. "Please, say nothing to Mrs. Bell. I won't let it happen again. I promise."

"What is your name?"

The girl gnawed at her lower lip, then said, "Susan, miss. Susan Parker."

"There is no reason for me to mention it to Mrs. Bell, Susan." Especially since Catherine suspected that the housekeeper had planned it this way and would take particular glee in Catherine's acknowledgment of any inconvenience.

Susan sagged with relief. Taking up her candle, she held the flame to the wick of the one Catherine had set down after the wind snuffed it. The wick caught and flared. With her free hand, she again fixed her cap and chewed anxiously at her lower lip, then said, "Thank you, miss. Mrs. Corkle—she's the cook—she'll make a supper tray for you and I'll bring it up straightaway."

"That would be lovely. Oh, and do you have a key to this room? There was none in the door."

The maid frowned, and reached for her apron. She had a small ring of keys similar to Mrs. Bell's larger one. Carefully, she toyed with one, then hesitated and reached for another. "Mrs. Bell don't like to come to this wing, so she gave me the keys to all the rooms . . . Is it this one? No . . . this one? One of them's the master key for this wing," she said, and frowned down at the two. "Not this one"—she let the key drop and lifted the first—"this one"—then she dropped it and lifted the other once more to slide it free of the ring as she gave a decisive nod—"this is the one for your door."

Catherine accepted the key and offered her thanks, then waited until the girl was nearly to the door before she spoke again. "Where does Sir Gabriel go at this hour of the night?"

The maid paused but did not turn. "I couldn't say, miss."

A twinge of guilt speared Catherine as she contemplated her next words, but she ignored it and said in a gentle voice, "I could ask Mrs. Bell. I am certain she would enjoy a chat."

The unspoken implication sent the maid spinning back to face her, the candle dish trembling in her hand. Catherine felt low indeed for perpetrating such a foul trick. Of course, she would never report the girl to the housekeeper. And of course, the girl had no way to know that.

"Tell me," Catherine said softly. "Where does he go?" Even as she repeated the question, she could not say why she felt such urgency to know the answer.

Susan made a moan of distress. Her eyes were wide, her brows raised. Catherine noted that the right one was bald in the center, bisected by what appeared to be an old scar.

More lip chewing, and then Susan blurted in a rush, "To

London. He goes to London, miss. He says he likes to travel at night. I heard Mr. Norton, the butler, say once that the way is not safe and is riddled with thieves. Sir Gabriel laughed. I remember it clear as day because the sound of it was off. Harsh and ruthless. Sir Gabriel said he would like to meet a thief on the road, that it would justify any actions, and Mr. Norton went white in the face and said nothing more." Susan dropped her gaze, and Catherine thought that was the end of her story, but then she whispered, "There was a man found dead by the road the following day. People say he was a thief." She shook her head. "'Course, it's all talk. No one hereabouts ever saw the body. It was all just talk."

Catherine stared at her, amazed by such an outpouring of information. She had wanted only to know where St. Aubyn went. She had not expected such panoply of fact and opinion.

"Thank you." She smiled, and felt lower still when the girl did not smile in return, but stared at her with frightened dark eyes, and said bitterly, "Does that buy your silence then, miss?"

"Yes." Catherine wanted to say more, but could summon no appropriate words, and so she held silent as, with a huff of despair, Susan scooted out the door and away.

Interesting that Susan Parker thought her master ruthless. Catherine had heard some similar gossip in London. That Gabriel St. Aubyn had run to ground a thief who had dared to pick his pocket and dragged him to the gaol himself. At the time, she had thought the story exaggeration, but having now met the man, she wondered if the outlandish tale held a kernel of truth.

Later, it was a different girl who brought the supper tray, and Catherine regretted how unkind she had been. But she did not regret the information she had gleaned. In knowledge lay safety. That lesson was hard learned.

She lifted the cover from her supper plate. Roasted beef and cauliflower in cream and a ragout of some sort. The food did not appeal, though it was prettily arranged and aromatic. Catherine left the meal untouched, thinking it was the exhaustion of the journey that stole her appetite and left her with an aching, dizzy head and a dry, tight throat.

But late in the night, when she awoke with a pain in her belly, so hard and sharp that she gasped and pressed her hands tight against the shock of it, she realized she must have eaten something that was off. She recalled the underdone mutton from the coaching inn, and the recollection of that greasy fare was enough to make her moan.

Then the pain twisted even tighter and she recalled Madeline's wild fears of poison and the faint, bitter taste of almond that had flavored the tart. She recalled too the revulsion on Gabriel St. Aubyn's face when she had offered him the plate.

Horror chilled her as she lay panting in her bed, unable to believe that Madeline was right, that someone in this house was trying to kill her, but unable to discount it out of hand in the face of her current suffering.

Mutton or poison.

As Catherine tossed and turned through the endless night, her head swimming, her belly cramping, she was hard-pressed to choose the more likely culprit of the two.

Chapter 5

St. Giles, England, March 1828

Martha Grimsby sat alone in a shabby little room in Church Lane, St. Giles. Her tiny chamber was at the very top of a decrepit three-story building that was so ancient and broken it was forced to lean on the building next door to keep from toppling over. There was a window directly across from where she sat, the glass blackened and cracked, with a board nailed over half of it to keep the rain out.

A piss-poor job it did.

The sleet and rain beat on the glass sending a frigid torrent through the crack at the edge where the board met the window. The night was colder than it ought to have been at this time of year. Martha drew her patched and mended shawl tight around her shoulders and huddled on the soiled bed that was putrefied with old sweat and damp rot. Her single tallow candle burned low, the flame dancing and swaying, painting silhouettes of monsters and gnomes against her wall. Once, in a time long past, she had fancied the shadows as ponies and swans. She knew better now.

With a sigh, she tipped her head back and stared at the

candle-darkened ceiling as she pondered the life that was hers. The instant her thoughts swayed toward the dangerous slope of regret, she dragged them back and forced herself to think of nothing at all. A different girl had grown up in Yorkshire where her father was head groom at a nearby estate. A different girl had been foolish enough to run off to London. A different girl lived this hell on earth.

Not her. She could not think of that rosy-cheeked innocent and imagine it had ever been her. That was a sure path to madness.

Pushing her palms against the mattress, she heaved herself from the bed. She was low on funds and down to the stub of her last candle and a dry crust of bread. She would have to brave the weather and try her luck at finding a willing gent on the nearest streets, close to home. She had little choice, not if she wanted to eat.

The decision made, she moved briskly lest she be tempted to change her mind. She left her sad chamber and went down the flights of creaking, rotted stairs to a narrow corridor at the back of the house. The door there was skewed on its hinges and she had to put her shoulder to it to make it open, then turn and put her shoulder to it again to force it shut.

The wind slapped her, a cold, brutal hand, but the rain had eased to a trickle and she was grateful for that. Head bowed, she made her way to Carrier Street and lounged against a building, glad to see there was only one other girl out, far up the street. Competition on a night like this was unwelcome, for the pickings were slim with people driven indoors by the chill and the damp.

For a long while, no likely candidate arrived. There was a group of drunken laborers who spewed from the alehouse, but they were the type of laborers who never did much work and so had little coin. Martha suspected that what funds they had had were already spent on drink, so she shrank into the shadows and let them pass.

Some time later, the rain stopped altogether and a stocky gent sauntered along. He wasn't a swell. Not by half, for his coat showed shabby at the sleeves with a patch on the elbow, but he looked like he might have a coin or two, so Martha stepped forward with a smile.

Then he turned his face toward her, and she shrank back. He had small eyes, mean eyes, narrowed in contemplation. She knew what sort he was right off.

"Fancy some company?" he asked with an ugly grin, offering the greeting she usually used.

She shivered and backed up a step. She was a smart girl now. She'd learned after a broken bone or two how to be a smart girl. Some men liked it rough, and she had no doubt he was one of 'em.

"Not tonight," she murmured. She spun on her heel and hurried off, skidding and sliding along the wet street, anxious to be away.

Heart racing, she rounded the corner and let one shoulder sag against the wall. He had not followed.

"Hello." The voice came from behind her, low and rich.

With a squeak she jumped and turned, her eyes widening in amazement. A swell stood there, looking at her questioningly. A *real* swell such as one never saw here, for the whores on these streets were not the sort a gentleman would deign to touch. But there was no question. He *was* a gentleman with a fine coat and polished boots and spun gold hair that framed a truly wonderful face.

"Hello," she managed to reply.

"Had a fright?" he asked with a small smile.

She pressed her palm to her chest and nodded. "I have."

For an instant, she felt shy, an odd, overwhelming emotion that she hadn't known in years and years, an emotion she had thought never to know again. Then she summoned her courage and grabbed hold of her opportunity and asked, "Up for some company, sir?"

He studied her in silence, his gaze traveling leisurely from her crown to her toes, and back again. His perusal made her feel both terrible and wonderful. She held her breath, waiting.

Then he smiled, and she thought the sun had come out, though the night was black as Old Mag's rotting toe before they hacked it off.

"You'll do," he said, still smiling. With a twirl of his fingers he offered her a gleaming gold coin. "Come with me."

And like a lamb, Martha followed where he led.

Cairncroft Abbey

A week after her arrival at the abbey, Catherine sat with Madeline on a cold stone bench in the south garden. The sun peeked from between the clouds and the breeze made stray wisps of her hair dance. With her face tipped down, she watched the hem of her dress lift and billow, then settle once more as the gust died. There was little else to watch here at Cairncroft, where time moved at a languid pace.

Madeline's mood had improved with the passing days. Catherine wondered if it was St. Aubyn's absence or her own presence that contributed to the lightening of her friend's spirits. Probably it was some combination of the two, but she did not ask. She had no wish to hamper Madeline's progress or distress her in any way, for Madeline had become almost reasonable. No longer did she turn her face aside when food was brought to her, but instead ate a bite or two, providing that Catherine sampled the fare first and assured her of its palatability.

On Catherine's first morning at Cairncroft, Madeline had refused to eat. With the memory of the previous night's torment—the way her stomach had knotted and cramped, the pain a jagged knife slicing through her—fresh in Catherine's mind, she had been hard-pressed to fault her. In the clear light of day, she had assessed the matter of her nocturnal illness and determined that it was the horrid meal at the coaching inn that had made her unwell rather than the tart she had taken from the tea tray. Nonetheless, that afternoon the sight of a plate of small crumpets and cakes had made her wary. She had thrust aside her qualms, convinced the stomach pains had been mere happenstance, and she had sampled an iced cake, thrilled to detect no hint of almond. Madeline had followed her lead.

But Catherine had avoided the tarts on the tea tray that afternoon and the next, and the following day, Mrs. Corkle left them off entirely.

Madeline had noticed their absence. "My cousin despises raspberry tarts," she had said. "I wonder that Mrs. Corkle does not know it, that she serves them when he is here and leaves them off when he is not."

Her observations made Catherine conjure an image of Gabriel St. Aubyn's expression of revulsion when she had offered him the plate that first day in Madeline's chamber. As though he had known there was something off about those tarts. The memory continued to nag at her like a stone in her boot.

"Are you very bored?" Madeline asked now as a cloud drifted across the sun.

"Not at all," Catherine replied with a smile. She was both surprised by Madeline's perceptiveness—she seemed far too buried in her own misery to notice aught around her—and dismayed that she had lowered her defenses enough to allow Madeline to peek through. "I am very pleased to be here with you, Madeline. These past days have been restful, and your companionship a balm to my soul."

She *was* pleased to be here. She owed Madeline a debt she could never repay and she was grateful to have the opportunity to offer her a kindness, even if it was only the hand of friendship. Besides, the alternatives to Cairncroft Abbey were few, so in effect, Madeline was doing *her* a service.

Madeline made a face. "I know you are pleased to be here, but you are so careful with your words, as though you fear overexciting me. I do wish you would tell me something. Anything." She paused. "What was London like? Certainly more exciting than this." She made a vague gesture toward the looming gray face of the house. "What was your life like *before*?"

For an instant, Catherine could not speak, the question triggering a moment of horror. *Before*. Before her parents died. Before the horrors of the years that followed their loss. Before the fire.

Memories surged in a sickening, swirling tide that grabbed hold of her and threatened to pull her deep. With rigid determination, she gathered the frayed strands of her control.

"My life was . . ." Her life had been a type of death, cold and dark and bleak, and each time she had been raised up with hope, she had been dashed back against the ground. How many times could hope be squashed beneath a heavy, booted heel before it raised up no more?

But Madeline would not wish to know of that. *What was your life like before?*

She did not mean before the fire, she meant *after* . . . in London, before coming here to Cairncroft Abbey.

"My life was busy," Catherine continued in a carefully modulated tone. "My employer, Mrs. Northrop, spent a great deal of time at St. Bartholomew's Hospital ministering to the less fortunate. As her paid companion, I was expected to spend my time there, as well. And she was very involved in the opening of a lodging house for the deserving poor in St. Giles. The hours we did not spend at Bart's, we spent working toward the opening of that house."

"And was that a great success? Were there speeches and crowds and baskets of food handed out, all with much fanfare and glee?" Madeline asked, her eyes sparking with uncharacteristic animation.

Catherine had not the heart to squelch her excitement. The venture—in Mrs. Northrop's opinion—was a wretched failure. More than once after the house had opened, Mrs. Northrop had bemoaned the fact that there were only disreputable creatures in St. Giles and not a single deserving soul in the bunch. But Catherine was a far less rigid judge. She understood that desperation could force one to make all manner of horrific choices.

Had she herself not been poised on the razored edge of just such a sword?

"And do you mean to say you actually went to St. Giles?" Madeline continued.

"I did, almost every day. And I met some lovely women there. Strong women and kind."

"Other women of good works. I recall you mentioned one woman in your letters . . . she runs a school, does she not?" Madeline murmured.

"Yes." Among other pursuits, for in St. Giles, running a school was not something that put food in one's belly or a roof overhead.

"But what terrible wretches you must have seen, as well! Fallen women who are surely bound for Hell."

Catherine cast her a glance through her lashes, and saw that Madeline's pale cheeks were bright with two spots of color, her eyes sparkling and clear. Religious fervor? She had not expected such. But perhaps it was only simple conversation that brought liveliness to her words.

"Is there a Hell that is worse than what those women have endured?" she asked, thinking of the girls who were pale and broken, dying of vile disease, their every word and action laced with clear regret that ever they had been born.

Did their transgressions truly destine them for damnation? If so, then she shared their fate, for her crimes were far worse.

Madeline's brows rose at Catherine's somewhat heretical question. "Do you not believe in Hell?" she whispered, leaning close to peer into Catherine's eyes, her expression intent.

For an instant, Catherine recalled an enormous, bright fire, smelled burning wood and flesh, heard the screams that carried, high and piercing, through the night. She had seen a version of Hell, felt its heat, known the endless despair that surely those wretches thus consigned felt. All the more reason to grab what she could of life, to make what she could of any circumstance.

"I do not know," she temporized. "Perhaps death is all there is."

Madeline recoiled as though struck, and Catherine immediately regretted allowing their conversation to travel this thorny path. She cast about for some other topic to introduce, but Madeline unexpectedly filled the breach.

"Tell me, then, about your time in the hospital," she urged. "You tended to the sick at . . . Bart's, was it? Oh, how awful that must have been." She shuddered. "I had imagined you accompanying Mrs. Northrop on rounds of afternoon visits and walks in Hyde Park. Perhaps a carriage ride or a shopping excursion . . ."

"No." Catherine laughed in a short burst of genuine humor. "*That* would have been awful. I enjoyed working with her at the hospital." She had not liked Mrs. Northrop, with her sour demeanor and ever-woeful predictions, but she *had* liked the way the woman ensured that Catherine's hours were consumed by the needs of the desperately poor and ill. It gave her less time to dwell on her own sorrows, and she preferred that. What value was there in bemoaning the past?

Madeline was silent for a long moment, two faint, vertical lines drawn between her brows. Finally, she whispered, "Did you see many people die in that hospital? Were you there by their bedsides when they breathed their last?"

There was something dark and desperate in her tone.

"No. Never," Catherine lied, determined not to distress Madeline further. *Yes. Far too many times.* And each time, in her mind's eye she had seen different faces, different deaths, ones that would haunt her until she herself went to her grave.

With her chin dipped down, Madeline cast her a sidelong glance, then looked away quickly as her gaze met Catherine's. She bit her lip and plucked at her skirt. "I have seen death. A girl. Killed not far from here."

"Killed? How?"

"I do not know." Madeline shook her head, her expression one of confusion. "My cousin took me away so quickly . . ." A shudder shook her. "He did not want me to see. But I looked back. Like Lot's wife. Only I am not turned to a pillar of salt." She paused, frowned, as though she had lost what she meant to say, then her brow cleared and she continued. "There was blood, so much blood, and I saw that she was cut open . . . or did I only hear that after, from one of the maids?"

Catherine stared at her, appalled. "Madeline, who was the girl who died? A servant? A friend?"

"No . . . no . . . I don't think so. I don't know." Her voice rose in agitation and she began anew to pluck at her skirt. Then she grabbed Catherine's hand and held it tight between both of her own, drawing it to her breast. "I am so very glad you came here. You have done me a service. You will probably never know the magnitude of what you have done for me."

There was such sincerity in her tone that it took Catherine aback. Before she could form a rejoinder, Madeline whispered, "And I think you are safe here, for you are not . . ." She stared into the distance, her expression blank as a marble slab. "Well, I believe he likes to play with a different sort entirely. But have a care . . ." A sigh escaped her and she released Catherine's hand. "Try not to be caught alone or unawares."

Catherine recoiled, the implication of those words knifing through her. Did Madeline refer to the fate of the dead girl and express her concern that there lurked some danger? Her admonition did not make it sound so. Her word choice implied something else. Did Madeline dare to voice aloud St. Aubyn's preferences in female companionship? The first possibility horrified, while the second mortified. But what else could she mean by such an odd observation? The inflection on the word *play* sounded almost . . . sinister, and the warning could be construed as nothing else.

"Madeline, do you—" Catherine hesitated. *Do you believe your cousin killed that girl?* No, of course such fancy was ridiculous. Whatever ill feelings hounded her relationship with Sir Gabriel, Madeline could not mean to imply that he was a murderer.

Rubbing her palms along her upper arms, Catherine mastered her confusion. She knew well that monsters hid behind any façade, but she must not let her own memories color the meanings she heard in the words of others.

Madeline sat unmoving for a moment, and then she whispered, "Do nothing to draw yourself to his attention." She took a shuddering breath. "I cannot say more."

"I see," Catherine murmured, though she did not see at all. But she *did* know that she had no wish for St. Aubyn to turn his attention to her. No wish for any man to notice her in that way. The very thought made a greasy sickness roll in her belly.

She must have made some outward show of her musings, for Madeline made a sound of dismay, and cried, "Oh, I never meant . . . that is . . . well, he is away now, and that is for the best."

For the best, indeed.

Catherine allowed herself to conjure an image of him in her mind's eye, Gabriel St. Aubyn, with his perfect features and thick, pale hair, the breadth of his shoulders, his long fingers holding the cup of tea with such perfect grace. Deceptive grace. She had seen the way lean muscle shifted beneath perfectly tailored cloth. He could have shattered the delicate china with those strong fingers. Crushed it in his fist.

She shuddered, and beside her, Madeline shuddered as well.

"The sun has gone behind a cloud," Madeline observed.

Arranging her expression in a serene smile, Catherine reached over and laid her hand on Madeline's. She thought that even through the gloves she could feel how cold her friend's hands were.

"Come, let us go and have a cup of tea and find a warm fire," she said, and like a child, Madeline rose and did as she was bidden.

St. James's Street, London, March 1828

The position of the moon in the clear night sky left no shadowed niche to cling to. No matter. Gabriel was not here to hide, but rather to be seen by as many as cared to look. He stood on the far side of the street, across and a little down the way from his club, studying the moon in all its bright and pale detail. It made him think of her. Catherine Weston. Of her midnight hair and porcelain skin, and the smooth, cool sound of her voice. He was both surprised and faintly annoyed that his thoughts turned to such whimsy, for his was not a nature inclined to contemplate the poetry found in the curve of a woman's cheek. He was more inclined to the analytical and the focus of the moment.

The focus of *this* moment was the need to walk into White's and pretend interest in gambling and gossip, because that was what gentlemen did. And Gabriel knew the value of doing exactly what was expected. There was no better shield than the mundane.

His gaze dropped and lingered on the club's famous bow window. Several men sat there, backlit by the lamps in the room. They were chatting and laughing, their heads turned subtly so that any who passed could not help but recognize them, but more than that, they wanted to watch those in the street, to judge them, betimes poke fun at them. It was a game of sorts, one Gabriel neither understood nor enjoyed.

Even from this distance, it was not difficult to place names to silhouettes. Bodley and Ashton and Hale, and two others on the opposite side of the table whose faces were in shadow. A few steps closer and he would know their identities, as well. Those steps were difficult to take tonight, for there were other entertainments he would rather seek out. Still, he could not come to London and avoid the club altogether. That would cause talk, speculation, perhaps even a ridiculous wager to be recorded in the betting book that lay open on the table. He preferred not to draw that sort of attention; he preferred to draw no attention at all.

As a matter of course, he was careful to blend into the background, smiling and nodding when others did the same, dragging forth an appropriate quip at an appropriate time. Mimicking his peers had become an easy thing, though in the beginning it had taken some attention and care. Over the years he had become quite adept at appearing to be exactly as they were, to share similar thoughts and emotions. They thought him genial enough, if rather dull, a situation that he found amusing.

He was nothing like them. His thoughts were a twisted maze, what emotions he had a dark, fetid pool.

He was anything but genial. To know it, they had only to ask the companion he had left a mere hour past.

But they would never know of his companion, and so they would never ask.

He was careful about such things. Methodical.

No one ever saw past the mask.

Except he thought that given even a hint of opportunity,

Catherine Weston, with her perceptive gaze and quick tongue, might. And here he was, back to thinking about her. Wondering at the workings of her mind. Pondering the mysteries she hid. He half imagined that spending any length of time with her, catching hold of the chance to search out her secrets, might be worth the risk that she would see him for exactly what he was.

Just then, the front door of the club opened, spilling light across the stairs and cobbles. Two likely fellows sauntered down the steps, Newton and Pratt, a pair of harmless fools. They laughed too loudly and cuffed each other on the shoulder. Pratt's aim was off and his fist glanced across Newton's chest, unbalancing him as he stepped down, his foot sliding on the last stair. He spun, tipped to one side then lurched to the other, swaying and laughing, fighting for balance.

Gabriel moved quickly, thrusting his shoulder forward to bolster Newton as he wove and dipped again, dangerously close to landing on his drink-sodden rump. He had little care if the man sprawled in drunken ignominy, but appearances must be maintained. A gentleman would not fail a friend in need, especially not one who was so clearly foxed.

Of course, Gabriel was no true gentleman. No chivalrous heart beat at his core. But no one knew the man obscured by the veneer he cultivated, and he preferred to keep it that way.

"Careful," he warned as Newton blinked at him blearily.

"Who's that?" Newton demanded, peering up into Gabriel's face. "Ah, St. Aubyn. Impeccable timing. Impeccable." He caught hold of Gabriel's forearm just long enough to steady himself and then straightened and let go, weaving slightly where he stood. "Saw your cousin earlier this evening. Didn't know he was back on English soil."

An interesting tidbit of news.

"Neither did I." Gabriel could feel the eyes of those in the bow window, and he suppressed a smile. He could not have wished for a more perfect circumstance. His presence on the steps would be noticed by all and sundry, but the auspicious timing of Newton and Pratt had saved him the bother of going inside the club. He could wander off with them and all would assume they had gone together to sample a fine brandy or to find a game of chance. Perhaps he would indulge in exactly that for an hour or two, before returning to his other, more interesting pursuits.

Pratt stared at him a moment and then blurted sheepishly, "I must confess . . . I wagered against you, old man."

"Did you?" Gabriel murmured, but asked nothing more. Clearly, he had not escaped the betting book. His name was part of some wager or other, but he could not summon enough interest to inquire what it was. On his last visit to White's, the odds were for Miss L. wearing blue to the Featherstone ball, and against Lord F. marrying Lady B.

"I did. Wagered a nice sum." Pratt bobbed his head up and down. "But I hope I am wrong. 'Twould be a sad thing for her to burn Cairncroft to the ground."

"I beg your pardon?" Gabriel asked, suddenly interested despite himself. "Burn Cairncroft?"

"Surprised you dared leave her there unsupervised." Newton slurred his observation enough that it took Gabriel an instant to understand the words.

He narrowed his eyes and turned his gaze to Pratt, the less inebriated of the two. "Explain." Both men appeared startled by his tone. "If you please," he added, an afterthought.

"Miss Weston. Baron's daughter, though which one"—he pressed his lips together and squinted his eyes as he tried to recall—"Ah, it was the Lord Sunderley," Pratt said.

"Word is, she's visiting Cairncroft. I heard it from my sister, who heard it from Mrs. Foxx, who heard it from Mrs. Northrop herself."

"So she is there, and you are here. In London," Newton supplied helpfully. "Which means there's no one *there* watching her."

Gabriel studied the two, his patience stretched taut. What game were they about? Their words circled around to nothing. "Sunderley died unmarried and without issue. In a fire, as I recall," he said.

"Yes, exactly." Newton beamed up at him, as though he had offered some unique and brilliant insight.

"Terrible thing." Pratt shook his head. "But *he* was not Miss Weston's father. The Right Honorable Lord Sunderley, Aubrey Weston, was. He and his wife died in a carriage accident some years back. *His* daughter is Miss Weston. Miss Catherine Weston."

Gabriel was silent a moment, trying to understand their inebriated logic. "You imply that Miss Weston is somehow responsible for the fire that killed the most *recent* Baron Sunderley?"

"Well, yes . . . She didn't kill her father . . . or perhaps she did . . . can't be certain about any of that." Pratt frowned and muttered under his breath as though trying to work out the logistics of the relationships. His expression brightened. "But she did turn the *next* Sunderley into a torch."

"After Sunderley died, then Sunderley . . . er . . . the *newer* . . . let her stay on. There was some issue of"—Newton lowered his voice—"financial constraint."

"She was left destitute," Pratt offered. "Sunderley was a good sort. Let her remain in her childhood home, somewhere north . . . perhaps Derby or Durham or Lancashire . . ." He waved one hand dismissively. "Then came the fire and circumstances being what they were, there was little doubt that Miss Weston was to blame."

"What circumstances would those be?" Gabriel inquired, tamping down the anger that settled in his gut like a lump of coal. The reaction was odd. Unfamiliar. Unwelcome. What matter was it to him if they gossiped about Catherine Weston? Why did their casual accusation send rage pounding through him? He was never one to succumb to temper. Not in nearly a score of years.

"Well, they were . . . that is . . . she was there when the fire began . . ." Newton shook his head in confusion.

"As was Sunderley and probably a houseful of servants," Gabriel pointed out in clipped tones. "Why blame Miss Weston?"

"Well . . ." Newton looked at Pratt and Pratt looked at Newton, confounded. Then Newton continued as though the question was irrelevant. "Sunderley died. Burned. The servants formed a bucket line but there was no hope. He was trapped. They saw him in the window, begging and writhing, but none could reach him. He lived for two days after that, alternately screaming or passed out cold."

"And they say she stood there, watching, calm as you please," Pratt added. "Some say she smiled as he burned. Some say she smiled the entire two days he screamed."

Not to be outdone, Newton leaned in and spoke in a low, fervent tone. "They say she was not right in the head. There was talk of sending her to a private hospital near York."

That whispered tidbit edged Gabriel's rage up a notch. He knew far too much of such places. The thought of her there—with her hair shorn or plaited and sewn to her head, her nails cut short, her body subject to the tortures they called treatments—made him want to reach out and close his fingers around Newton's throat. Instead, he glanced down, veiling his thoughts, and flicked an imaginary bit of lint from his sleeve.

"Given that she was free to travel to Cairncroft rather than incarcerated or hung by the neck until dead," he observed, "may I assume that the authorities were in disagreement with your suppositions, gentlemen?"

His companions exchanged baffled looks.

"Hadn't thought of it—"

"Couldn't say—"

Pratt shrugged and reached up to sling an arm across Gabriel's shoulders. It took particular concentration not to recoil from the contact.

"I met her once." Newton frowned in recollection. "At Mrs. Northrop's soirée. She said very little. I can't recall . . . fair hair? No, more mousy brown . . . She was utterly forgettable." He shrugged, and let the memory go, uninterested. The topic had already exhausted his attention.

Mousy. The description made Gabriel smile, his earlier anger dulling to a slow simmer. An image of Catherine Weston flashed in his mind's eye, her features composed, her mask perfectly in place.

She was anything but utterly forgettable.

In fact, thoughts of her had haunted him the entire week he had been in London.

And now he knew a great deal about her.

Gabriel was inordinately glad that he had come to his club tonight. Newton and Pratt had been founts of information. Suddenly, he was driven to return to Cairncroft with even greater urgency than he had felt to leave it. London and all its dark lure paled now next to his curiosity about Catherine Weston. He had been right. There was far more to her than the face she presented to the world. Her mask was polished and perfected, her veil secure.

Unless a storm wrenched it free.

He could be that storm.

Carefully disengaging Pratt's arm from across his shoulder, he cast an assessing glance at the window of White's. Several sets of eyes watched their every move. Swallowing his distaste for prolonging his present company, Gabriel smiled and said, "Gentlemen, I have a fine bottle of brandy awaiting us in Berkeley Square. Shall we retire there and sample it?"

But already his thoughts had drifted to Cairncroft and Catherine Weston. He had only to conclude his time with his current companions, then pay a brief visit to the companion who had occupied him earlier in the evening. Once that business was complete, he could be away.

Likely, it would be close to dawn.

Generally, he preferred to travel at night, on horseback. Enclosed coaches and bright sunshine brought back memories he would have preferred to excise with a surgical blade.

But just this once, he found that first light could not come soon enough.

Chapter 6

He returned to the place he had left her. Martha. She had laughed when he asked her name as they had walked through St. Giles, and said that he could call her anything he pleased. But he had wanted her name and so she gave it. Of course, he had known it before he asked, known she was the one, carefully chosen and watched for two days before he approached her. Luck had set her in his path, but if it had not, he would have found her nonetheless because of who she was and what her death would mean.

He used her name now, calling out a singsong greeting as he let himself into the empty warehouse by the river and listened for the faint, frightened whimper that told him she had heard. Dust stirred as he walked briskly to the back of the building, to the room beneath the teetering, rotted stairs. He dragged open the door, paused to turn up the lamp, and savored the sight before him.

She lay on the makeshift table—a plank stretched over two wooden kegs—tracking him with wild, desperate eyes. She was clad only in her thin shift, so much of her skin bare to his touch and the kiss of his blade. Her hands were bound, as were her feet, and the rags he had stuffed in her mouth muffled her cries as he took up his knife and began to play. He would have preferred to let her scream, to free her limbs and let her flail. But London offered little privacy, and so he made do with less than ideal circumstances and the relative seclusion of an empty warehouse, the last in a long row of empty warehouses.

He reveled in her muffled grunts and moans and the tears that tracked down her cheeks.

It was not that he hurt her. Well, not more than a little. It was the fear that built and grew and he could feel it shimmering in the rank air, taste it and smell it. That was the thing he craved. Her terror. The ability to control her and elicit what emotion he wanted.

There were points that she even accepted his comfort. No, not merely accepted it. Begged for it with her eyes. Such was his control over her and in so short a time.

He enjoyed their game as long as he dared in this vacant warehouse filled with the mingled scents of the spices that had once been stored here and the fetid stink of the river.

Time had little meaning. Moments or, perhaps, hours later, he stared down at her with febrile excitement. Sweat beaded his brow and trickled in an itchy line down his back. But he felt . . . right. For the first time in a long time, he felt right.

She was quiet now. No more struggles or frantic mewling pleas lost behind the greasy gag. Emotion—terror, horror, the swell of her panic, or perhaps only the magnitude of her suffering—had overwhelmed her more than once, sending her across the boundary of consciousness. He had been forced to dip a ladleful of water from the bucket on the floor and splash her face to rouse her. The last time, he had left the ladle where it rested and left her in her swoon, for though he had enjoyed every moment of their association, it was time to bring about the grand end.

This encounter had been better than his last. He was more controlled, better prepared for the tide of delight that crashed through him as he worked. And Martha, his partner in this macabre dance, had been more appealing than her predecessor—younger, cleaner, and more worldly wise—which had allowed her to suffer far more before she broke.

He was quite pleased to have been guided to her.

Reaching into his pocket, he withdrew the letter that had detailed Martha Grimsby's name and general whereabouts, written in a lovely, crisp hand. He brought the corner of it to the candle and let the flame catch. A dark swirl of smoke twisted upward and then the paper flared with tongues of orange and gold. He held it as long as he could, finally dropping it to the floor and watching it burn to ash before scattering the remains with the toe of his boot.

Then he turned back to Martha. Sweet, desperate, frightened Martha. She was barely conscious now, her eyes rolled back, her body still save for the occasional twitch or groan.

Stepping close beside her, he stroked her hair back from her damp forehead, and waited until she roused enough to turn her head. She blinked, her eyes hazy and unfocused. Seconds ticked past, and she came around a little more, her brow furrowing, a moan sounding behind the gag.

She saw him then. Truly *saw* him. The connection between them was gossamer as a spider's web and stronger than forged steel. She was his. *His.*

Placing a single, perfect white feather in her hand, he closed her fingers around it, curling his own tight to hers until she grasped the quill and held it. He suspected her hands were numb, for they had been bound for many hours now.

Her vision had cleared and focused, and she stared at his face, her eyes wide, rolling in fright. He caught her hair in his fist and yanked her head back, administering two deep slashes across her throat so that the arteries and veins were cut clean through and the bones of the spine revealed.

The wounds were fatal. He made certain of that this time. It would not do to repeat the debacle of his first foray so many years ago, when he had acted precipitously and, thinking the creature dead, had set to bury her body only to be confronted by a living corpse when she groaned and sat up straight in the grave.

No, this time, he acted with forethought and care.

Copper sweet, the smell of her blood was delicious, tantalizing. He set a wooden tub beneath the table to catch it, but some sprayed in a spurting arc as her heart pulsed and pumped in her breast for nearly a minute in a futile fight until the end. That blood was left to decorate the walls and floor.

He found it lovely.

Memories surged, of long-ago times and long-ago pleasures. A bird. A cat. Child's play.

He simply stood by her side, arms hanging loose, his full attention leveled on her form. He watched. He breathed. He reveled in the joy of this kill.

At length, he roused and touched her wrists, her forearms. Cool, but not stiff. He moved his hand beneath the blood-dampened edge of her shift to the skin above her collarbone where the flesh was warmer, then ran his palms along her arms, her hair. Bending low, he buried his face in the curve of her shoulder and inhaled the fragrances of her skin and her blood. He straightened and stared down at her, memorizing every nuance of her face.

For a time, he stood in quiet contemplation. The air was

perfumed by the metallic flavor of blood, the only sound the quiet huff of his own breathing. This was the time that the beauty of her being belonged to him, solely to him.

His. She was his.

This body was his to control, to touch, to pose. She was subject to his will. The certainty of that filled him with delight. His lips curved in a smile, lazy, satisfied. The intense euphoria of the kill had faded, leaving him relaxed, almost sleepy, affected by a pleased and sated detachment.

From a great distance came a boom of sound, and somewhat later a clatter and shout. Far away. The sounds had no meaning in this place. But at length, he recognized the change in the noise; it became louder, closer, the waking of the wharf, and he roused himself, for there was work to be done, bounty to be gathered.

Reaching down, he opened the lids of the four wide-mouthed ceramic jars he had set on the floor by the table. Then he lifted his knife and turned to his task.

Pinching the cloth of her shift between his thumb and forefinger, he drew it from her skin where the blood made it cling with damp tenacity, and slit the cloth neatly down the middle, baring her torso and abdomen. He stroked the skin, still pliable, but not for long. That was the disappointing thing. They never stayed like this, so perfect, so smooth and warm. Never. A handful of hours and she would be stiff, a handful after that and she would be cold as marble; the heat of her leaked away as the seconds ticked past.

But he would love her still. Even cold and stiff, and after that, soft and wet and rotted in the shallow grave he would prepare for her . . . even then he would love her. Because she was his.

He wanted to linger, to extend each moment so it slid past in slow, silky brilliance. But as he saw the first whisper of dawn's light snake through the crack beneath the door, he acknowledged that his time in London was limited. He could stay away only so long.

Because, in the end, Cairncroft Abbey always called him home.

Cairncroft Abbey, March 1828

Catherine descended to the dining room, her hand gliding along the polished banister as she walked. Madeline, as always, eschewed breakfast; she would keep to her bed until past noon.

It was more than a week since Catherine had come to Cairncroft, and the house was more familiar to her now, though she was not inclined to explore. The place was large enough to get lost in, and she had already been warned that parts were showing their age with crumbling walls and rotting wood.

"How do you do, Miss Weston?"

Startled by the unexpected greeting, Catherine paused in her descent. Mrs. Bell crossed the wide hallway and waited for her at the foot of the stairs, her brow furrowed, her posture tense. She turned the large ring of keys that hung from her apron again and again, the clank of metal on metal loud in the quiet space. They had shared no discourse since the day Catherine had arrived at Cairncroft Abbey. Any contact between them had been limited to a brief look or distant nod. But today, the woman appeared bent on conversation.

Catherine proceeded down the remaining steps and said, "Very well, thank you, Mrs. Bell. And you?"

The housekeeper huffed a breath before mirroring Catherine's reply. "Very well, thank you." She glanced toward the open door of the breakfast room. Sunlight streamed through the portal and danced toward them across the slate floor. "The day is fair and bright."

"So it appears. I have not been outdoors as yet," Catherine offered warily, unable to discern the conversation's purpose. That thought led to recollection of Gabriel St. Aubyn and his disdain of pointless polite discourse. She did not like to think of him, to recall the way his lips shaped words, or the way his amber gold eyes watched her so intently. But for some inexplicable, perverse reason, she had been unable to completely expunge him from her mind, and since his departure, such recollections had occupied far more of her thoughts than she liked.

She focused her attention on Mrs. Bell and continued. "I thought perhaps to take Madeline into the garden."

The housekeeper nodded, but her expression tightened at the mention of Madeline's name. "The south garden has a stone bench overlooking the lake."

"Oh . . ." The lake was a shallow, greenish swamp that smelled like something dead. But perhaps the bench was not very close to the water, and the change of scenery from their usual spot might do Madeline good. "Thank you for the suggestion."

Mrs. Bell pursed her lips. "I am sure this is no concern of mine, Miss Weston," she said, then leaned back a bit and glanced first to her right and then to her left, as though to make certain they were alone. There was a footman standing by the door to the breakfast room, but he was far enough away that he would not overhear if Mrs. Bell kept her voice low. Apparently satisfied, she straightened and blurted in a tense whisper, "I wonder if you are aware of the nature of this place, the dangers you may encounter . . ."

"Dangers?" Catherine kept her voice low as well, but did not bother to hide her incredulity.

"Softly!" Mrs. Bell admonished with a quick glance at the footman who stared straight ahead, his expression blank. "What do you know of the St. Aubyns?"

"Very little. Their affairs are none of mine," Catherine replied carefully. She had expected a verbal assault, either veiled or outright, but Mrs. Bell's dialogue was neither. Catherine was ever wary of the unexpected.

Again the housekeeper glanced about, a quick, darting look. "The St. Aubyns are a family cursed." She held her hand up to stay Catherine's objection. "Oh, say nothing to deny it before you hear the tale. I myself have no belief in curses and such. Nonsense, really. But in this case, it is a word apt and true, for the family has known only ill luck and hardship passed from father to son. They have never flourished. For generations they have been plagued by malady and madness. I can tell you what passed in the time of Sir Gabriel's great-grandfather. First, the youngest son died. Drowned. Then the oldest. And finally, the middle son, leaving the children without parents, without anyone to ensure that they grow straight toward the sun rather than bent and crooked."

"Mrs. Bell," Catherine said, wedging her opposition into the brief silence. "I have no fondness for gossip."

The housekeeper clenched her fists and drew a fortifying breath, and Catherine could clearly see that this conversation caused her discomfort.

"Nor do I. Nor do I. This is not tittle-tattle, Miss Weston," she continued, urgent and low. "There is a history here, do you see? The house . . . it is slowly crumbling about us. The lake is dead. No fish swim there now. And the gardens are filled with nettles, though the groundskeeper tends to everything as best as he can. There is a terrible malady to this place, and to the people who live here. When none of them were in residence, the lake was clear and the woods green and welcoming. The tenants flourished. But no longer. They have returned." She shot a glance over her shoulder. "They have *all* returned, the living and the spirits of the dead, and their curse has returned with them. They are doomed. The St. Aubyns are doomed. Do you see?"

Catherine saw quite well. Mrs. Bell was unhinged.

She drew a slow breath, measuring every possible response to such revelation, and deciding a question was best.

"And why tell me this now?" she asked, making no effort to conceal the suspicion in her tone. Mrs. Bell had originally greeted her with hostility, then set about avoiding her for days. Now she wished to confide the deepest, darkest secrets of the St. Aubyn family. Catherine could not imagine putting her trust in any confidences the woman shared.

But more than that, she knew far too much of rumors and whispers and gossip of all sorts. There was always a story beneath the story, one that might be far different than what was whispered about with vicious titillation. And if one cared to dig deeper, there would be yet another story underlying the others. Layers upon layers. Lies upon lies.

Unbidden, a vicious memory leaped out to bite her. *They whisper about you, you know.* Catherine knew. Mrs. Northrop saying it had not make it any better or worse. *They whisper about you and wonder if you did it. If it was your candle that fell over first . . . if you killed him . . .*

Did it matter whose candle had done the deed? Whose hand had begun the disastrous events? The Right Honorable Lord Sunderley, Jasper Hunt, was dead and buried, and with him, her vile secrets.

But not her culpability. That, Catherine could never bury.

"I tell you this now," Mrs. Bell said, "because you show every indication of remaining here for some time. I thought perhaps you would stay a week. But now the week has passed and you make no preparation to leave, and so it falls upon me to warn you."

She pressed her lips together and wrapped her arms across her apron-swathed belly, as though to hold parts of herself together. Catherine recognized that posture. She had used it herself for months and months after the fire, but her best efforts had failed her. She had not held the jagged bits of herself together. Instead, in the end, she had shattered into a million razored shards.

Then, with no choice left to her, she had picked up all the jagged fragments and forced their poorly fitting edges to approximate in a new self, or rather, a reflection of a self that others could bear.

She had been forced to go on, to live, for she was too much of a coward to take her own life, though she had pondered it more times than she could count. Or perhaps she had been too brave to give up. Either way, the end result was the same. She was here, hiding within herself, behind the person she allowed others to see.

"And I tell you this because I have seen him," Mrs. Bell continued. "He has come back to wreak his vengeance, or perhaps to drive us mad, those of us who let events unfold as they did."

Him? Catherine stared at her in confusion, a horrid thrill of alarm chasing through her. For an instant, she thought Mrs. Bell referred to Sunderley—or his ghost—and then she realized that was impossible. The breath she had not even known she was holding expelled in a rush.

"Whom have you seen?" she asked. "What events do you speak of?"

"I have already said more than I should."

"But you have said nothing useful." *Or coherent.*

Mrs. Bell stepped close, the scents of starched apron and sweat tickling Catherine's nose. The housekeeper lowered her voice even further. "No good thing can come of living in this place. You would be wise to see yourself away from here with all haste."

"You live in this place," Catherine pointed out, fairly certain now that Mrs. Bell had been destined for a career as an actress and instead had been waylaid to her position here.

"Yes, I do live in this place." Mrs. Bell made an ugly sound that might have been a laugh. "And who ever said that any good came from that?"

"Then why do you not leave if Cairncroft is so abhorrent to you?"

"There are ghosts that follow no matter where one runs and hides." The housekeeper's harshly voiced words made Catherine's blood chill. Did she refer to Catherine's secrets, to the ghosts that haunted her? Were they bared for all to see?

No, of course not. The woman spoke of her own regrets and torments.

Distress gave way to curiosity, but she could see no way to question Mrs. Bell without opening herself to similar unwanted query. She was saved from any reply when the housekeeper continued, "Go to the graveyard. Then ask your Madeline about the stone. You'll know the one when you see it." She nodded. "We shall see how tranquil you are then."

With that last, provocative sally, the housekeeper excused herself to see to her duties.

Catherine watched her go, completely baffled by the exchange. She could not fathom what possible outcome Mrs. Bell had anticipated. Her shared secrets had been all intimation without substance, oblique references to ghosts and curses and terrible things. What was Catherine to do with that? Run screaming down the drive in her nightdress?

With a shake of her head and a perplexed sigh, she proceeded to the breakfast room. The footman stood silent and still by the door, not even blinking when she passed. His presence was a familiar thing, for she had spent many years in a home filled with unobtrusive servants. She wondered if he had heard anything of her exchange with Mrs. Bell, despite their caution. It was a distinct possibility, for she was certain that he and the other servants of Cairncroft Abbey saw things . . . *knew* things.

She thought again that she had not done well to alienate the little maid, Susan Parker, that first night, that she would have been better served to cultivate her association to some small degree.

Stepping inside the breakfast room, Catherine was greeted by the tantalizing aromas of breakfast fare that wafted from the covered silver servers on the sideboard. Eggs. Meats. And . . . coffee. Odd. This was the first morning that coffee was offered.

She crossed to the large windows at the far end of the room. The gold brocade draperies were tied back to let the sunlight stream through the clear panes, and the warmth of it on her face was lovely. Mrs. Bell had been right. The day *was* fine and clear,

Idly, she studied the expanse of lawn and the portion of the drive that was visible from this angle, noting that Mrs. Bell was correct in this, as well. The gardens did look rather overgrown and scruffy, though she had seen the occasional worker digging and trimming since her arrival. Perhaps they simply lacked a firm, guiding hand, with Madeline so ill and unable to see to even the most rudimentary duties of the lady of the house. Even the daily menus proved too much for her. She left everything to Mrs. Bell.

Catherine's gaze traveled to the dark and tangled forest that grew at the northern edge of the manicured lawn, threatening to creep forward and swallow whole the abbey and its civilized surroundings. There were woods to the south, as well, though half the trees there were gray and ghostly, burned at some point in the past. She had learned from Madeline that to the southwest of them was Huntingdon and to the east, Thetford, though she was not exactly certain how far either of them lay. Probably too far to walk, though the prospect of an outing was beginning to appeal.

She was about to turn and fetch her breakfast when something at the edge of the woods caught her eye. Did she see a flash of movement there? A glimpse of something pale? A shadow shifting?

Surely not. It was only the housekeeper's talk of ghosts and curses that had conjured an imaginary specter. But as she watched, the shadow moved between the trees and finally, disengaged altogether. In the spill of sunlight, the shadow became a man, dressed in black, tall and broad, fair of hair.

Was it Gabriel St. Aubyn, returned from his journey?

He turned his face to her and she thought he saw her here at the window, that he watched her with intense concentration.

Distance and the angle of the sun made definitive identification impossible. It could be St. Aubyn, or any other blond man. But something in the way he watched the house, watched the window where she stood, made the fine hairs on her forearms prickle and rise.

Wrapping her arms about her waist, she backed away

from the glass. Her heel caught the edge of the rug, and she glanced down, then up once more.

He was gone.

Her gaze darted all along the dark line of the woods, but there truly was no one there. So what had she seen? A fantastical conjuring? An illusion summoned from the depths of her mind by Mrs. Bell's sinister intimations?

Silly, to let her imagination run wild. She was not prone to such behavior. Not since she had outgrown her pinafores.

Gathering herself, she refused to allow unfounded suppositions to surface, certain that it was a restless night's sleep combined with boredom and isolation that sent her mind wandering in the direction of ghostly threat. She turned from the window, crossed to the sideboard, and helped herself to a plate. Eggs. Buttered toast. *That* was a luxury. Mrs. Corkle warmed the bread in the fire until it was golden, then slathered it with butter. The aroma was delicious, and Catherine was thrilled that this invention was included daily with the morning fare.

She chose a seat in the band of sunshine that splashed through the window and set her plate on the table. After fetching a cup of tea, she settled in the chair—a heavy mahogany affair that required the strength of both her hands to draw it from beneath the table. The warmth of the sun bathed her even through the glass panes as she began her meal. She had taken only a few bites when a faint sound from the doorway made her look up.

Her heart slammed against her ribs.

Gabriel St. Aubyn *had* returned. He stood framed in the doorway, dressed in a dark blue coat and white shirt, the cut and quality of which proclaimed his place in the world. The cost of that coat would probably feed a hundred hungry toddlers in St. Giles for a month.

A slurry of thoughts swirled one into the next. Mrs. Bell's oddly verbose behavior earlier undoubtedly had something to do with the baronet's return. His sudden appearance made her certain that she had indeed seen a man step from the woods. *This* man? She thought so. But how had he gone from there to here with such speed? He was not disheveled or out of breath, so he could not have run, and the distance was too great for him to have traversed it at a leisurely pace and arrive here, in the doorway of the breakfast room, so quickly.

"Good morning, Miss Weston," he said, and offered a bland smile, his lips curved in perfect symmetry baring just a hint of white teeth. A welcoming and pleasant expression. She trusted it not at all.

"Good morning, Sir Gabriel." She kept her greeting crisp and brief.

"Gabriel, or St. Aubyn if you prefer," he said, echoing the words and tone he had used the day they took tea in Madeline's chamber.

He crossed to the sideboard and poured himself coffee. So here was the reason for its inclusion this morning. Apparently, Gabriel St. Aubyn preferred coffee to tea.

His eyes met hers as he turned back, the morning light turning them more gold than amber brown, unutterably beautiful. She found his splendor disconcerting; she had no liking for attractive men. No, not so. She had no liking for men in general, least of all a confounding, enigmatic man who treated his own cousin with such shabby disregard. Though she had spent over a week in Madeline's company, subtle prodding had not revealed the reason for the discord between the cousins, and Catherine had not wished to disturb Madeline by escalating gentle query to outright inquisition.

St. Aubyn stared at a spot above her left shoulder, and she glanced up, wondering what it was he studied with such interest. The dust motes dancing in the sunlight?

He set his coffee on the table.

"Your trip was pleasant?" she inquired, and immediately realized she ought not to have bothered.

His brows arched up and she caught a flicker of amusement as he turned away without offering a reply. She supposed that was a reply in itself. He deemed the topic purposeless and, hence, unworthy of discourse. It seemed that St. Aubyn was nothing if not consistent.

Catherine took a bite of toast, chewed, swallowed, tasting nothing, her movements mechanical. She watched from the corner of her eye as he filled a plate.

He moved back to the table, choosing the seat out of direct light, at right angles with hers, too close for her pleasure. The effort of an exchange of small talk with a man who refused to participate was an unappealing prospect. She would have preferred he seat himself at the far end, away from her, and that he read a newspaper while he ate, holding it up to form a wall between them.

On the pretext of eating a meal she no longer desired, she looked down at her plate and sliced a bit of ham.

"Why did you come here?" he asked with neither finesse nor veiled words. He wielded inquiry like a precisely honed blade.

Catherine almost choked, managing to chew and swallow only by dint of will. Gathering herself, she decided to proceed in exactly the tone he set.

"I was invited."

"Yes, of course. But I inquire about your motivations, your thoughts"—he paused, sipped his coffee, then finished in a low tone—"your desires."

His voice touched her like a caress and for the span of a heartbeat she could form no reply. Annoyance surged. At him. At herself. With a sampling of words, he roused a place inside her that she had felt certain was dead.

She would not allow him such power over her.

"My motivation was a letter I received," she said coldly. "It was importunate in nature, desperate, as I am certain you already know. Madeline, a dear friend of my youth, cried out to me in her melancholy and despair. Was I to deny her? To decline her invitation? I am not so cold as that."

"Are you not?" His inquiry slapped her.

But that was his intent. She had no doubt he wished to unsettle her, though she could not begin to imagine his reasons. His gaze slid over her at his leisure, rising to her hair—twisted in a loose knot at her nape—then dropping to her eyes, her nose, her lips, and finally dipping lower.

Did he dare to linger on her breasts?

She felt the heat of her blood in her cheeks, and that startled her. She had not blushed since her early encounters with the new Baron Sunderley after her parents had died.

"We shall work from that premise, then," he continued, his gaze meeting hers. "You are not so cold as to ignore Madeline's pleas. Nor so foolish. I believe you are a woman of intelligence, Miss Weston, one who spies opportunity and leaps upon it like a jaguar upon its prey."

She allowed neither action nor tenor to betray her fury. Her hands did not tremble as she set her cutlery aside.

"Your words are insulting, sir."

"Are they?" He appeared genuinely startled by her accusation. "I meant them to be complimentary. To have the intelligence to exploit one's advantages is a wonderful thing."

She stared at him, both repelled and intrigued to realize that he told nothing but the truth. He *did* mean these insulting observations as praise. How dreadful. All the more so because he was partially correct. Though she had not developed a mercenary nature by choice, there was a part of her that had—by necessity—grown opportunistic, a part that grabbed hold of any prospect with vastly unladylike tenacity and refused to let go. Madeline's letter had been just such a chance.

But these were not truths she would share with him.

Catherine glared at St. Aubyn as he continued his breakfast, his table manners impeccable, his attention now on his meal.

"Excuse me," she said, and pushed her chair back from the table.

He glanced at her, but made no move to rise as common courtesy dictated. "I had not thought you so meek as to flee at the first sign of interesting conversation."

Interesting conversation? She held her serene expression, refusing to be baited. She could not begin to fathom his reasons, but she did not doubt he was bound and determined to elicit a show of temper.

Reaching over, he nudged her plate back toward her. "Finish your breakfast," he said, an instruction, not a request. He did not cajole. She could not imagine him even trying.

After studying him for a moment, she decided a head-on approach was best. "If it is interesting conversation you wish, then perhaps we could discuss why you were watching me from the woods this morning. And how you crossed the vast lawn so quickly, managing to join me without exhibiting any effects of the vigorous activity you must have indulged in to arrive here so precipitously. Do you not find it rather juvenile to slink about?"

He swallowed his food, sipped his coffee, and then settled the cup back in the saucer. His movements were clean and precise. Finally, he looked directly at her. "I was not in the woods this morning, Miss Weston. I enjoyed no activity more vigorous than descending from my chamber on the second floor."

"I saw you at the edge of the woods."

"Did you? You have wonderful visual acuity to recognize me at"—he shot a glance at the window and the distant encroaching trees—"some ten score yards away. Tell me exactly what you saw."

She pondered that a moment, camouflaging her hesitation behind with the overt action of shifting her chair close to the table once more. Exactly what had she seen? A man, or only a man-shaped shadow? A clear view of St. Aubyn, or someone she mistook for him because she expected it to be him?

"I saw a shape shift between the trees. Then it moved into the light and I saw a dark coat and pale hair. A man watching me."

At that, his attention sharpened. There was no explicit sign of that. No tension in his frame or change in his demeanor. But she sensed an alteration and she had learned to trust such instincts.

"Offhand, I can think of at least seven employees of this estate who have blond hair. Perhaps you saw a gardener or a groomsman." He took another sip of coffee. "I have no doubt you saw something, but it was not me."

"As you say." She lifted her fork and poked at the remains of her breakfast, loath to allow him to read her disbelief. A part of her meant to rise and walk away. A part of her was lured to stay. She ate another bite of toast and a sliver of ham, lingering over her tea as St. Aubyn finished his meal, apparently perfectly at ease with the silence.

Only once did he break it, saying, "Have you read *Frankenstein, the Modern Prometheus*?"

Startled by the inquiry, she shook her head. "I have heard of it, but have not had the opportunity to read it."

"You may borrow my copy."

"I . . ." She hesitated, but could think of no reason to decline. "Thank you."

"I look forward to hearing your thoughts." And with that, he returned to his meal, the discussion clearly at end.

But the sincerity of his words did not escape her. *I look forward to hearing your thoughts.* He actually meant it. He was interested in her opinion; a man interested in a woman's opinion, *her* opinion. The novelty of that was startling.

At length, he set aside his napkin and rose.

"Come," he said, and moved to hold her chair. He was too close, too big, too male. She stared at the tips of his boots. Black. Shiny. Speckled with dry dirt in a fine layer, like dust.

If, as he asserted, he had not been outdoors this morning, then someone in his employ had failed to shine the baronet's boots last night.

Was he such a lax employer that he did not notice? She could not imagine such negligence. Not from this man.

"Where do we go?" she asked as she rose.

"Walking." He cast her a sidelong look through his lashes. "The weather is fair, the sun bright."

"It was my understanding that you disdain the weather as a topic of conversation."

His lips curved in private humor. "Only when it is conversation without purpose. I mention the perfection of the day to lure you outdoors. Hence, there is purpose to such conversation."

"Lure me? Like a spider lures the fly?" she murmured.

His smile widened, white teeth, cold eyes. She could read nothing of his true thoughts. "Without a doubt. But which of us is the spider, Miss Weston?"

He offered his arm. Energy crackled between them, the air fairly shimmering with it. Catherine stared at the tailored sleeve of his dark blue coat, and she wanted to tell him to step back, step away. She had no wish to lay her hand there, to touch him. It was too close a contact.

"Are you afraid of me?" he asked.

She examined his expression. There was no humor there, no deviltry or teasing. Not that she had expected such from him. He was neither a gallant nor a rake. In fact, she had never met anyone at all like him.

She wet her lips, floundering for a reply. Yes, she was afraid, of him, of any man who was larger and stronger than she. But she was far more disturbed by her own reaction to him, the confused eddy of attraction and repulsion that made her common sense war with the arousal she felt in his presence. Arousal of both mind and body; he stoked her ire and snared her curiosity, and perhaps even made her want to hit him. He made her want to break down the safe wall she had erected. To press her mouth to his. To reach up and touch her fingers to the softness of his hair. To feel the hardness of his body, defined beneath his tailored coat. But she would do none of those things. She would remain calm and poised, and he would be none the wiser.

"Afraid of you? Without a doubt," she replied, echoing his earlier words.

"Wise of you. You should be."

She inclined her head in acknowledgment of the warning and pondered her options. There was no polite way to decline his less than polite invitation. But that was not the source of her indecision; she was not so very concerned with manners. It was more that he was her host, master of Cairncroft Abbey, and he suffered her presence here at his whim. She could deny him—a dangerous choice, for he might decide then to revoke his acceptance of her in his home—or she could accompany him at his pleasure. It was a small enough task to walk in the sunshine with him for a few moments and pander to whatever whim made him seek out her company. Besides, it would afford her an opportunity to question him about Mrs. Bell's earlier insinuations.

She realized that he found both her hesitation and their dialogue amusing. He allowed her to read it in his smile, genuine now, carving a crease in his cheek and fanning fine lines from the corners of his eyes.

"You find my fear entertaining?" she asked.

"No." His gaze raked her, and were he a different man, she might have imagined the look held interest of a carnal nature. But he was St. Aubyn—cold, controlled—and she decided that any interest sparking in his eyes must surely be analytical. A collector admiring a pinned bug. "But I do find *you* entertaining, Miss Weston. Proper. Restrained. What do you hide?"

Nothing you will ever discover. She made no audible reply. None was necessary.

Then she changed her mind and said, "Interesting that you pose that question, sir. I could ask the same of you. What do you hide"—she paused long enough to lend her next words additional weight—"besides a dislike of closed spaces?"

She had expected a reaction to her observations. A look of startlement, a blink, a gasp. There was none. He merely inclined his head and asked, "What led you to that conclusion?"

"I noticed the first day, in Madeline's chamber. When you stepped into the room, you chose to stand as close to the door as possible. And you never fully closed it behind you. When the footman closed it upon his departure, you immediately remedied the situation. Similarly, this morning. You left the door to the breakfast room ajar. Finally, you rode to London rather than taking a closed carriage."

"And from those small observations you deduced that I dislike closed spaces?" His tone derided her assertion, but somehow, she knew it was true. Whether he admitted it or not, Gabriel St. Aubyn did not like to be caged. A sentiment she shared, though she would not reveal it.

"But we were not speaking of me, Miss Weston." He ran the tip of his finger along the lace trim of her collar, touching only the cloth. Still, it made her shiver as though the contact had been skin to skin. "We were speaking of you and what it is *you* seek to hide."

Stepping back, she lifted her chin a notch and sent him the frostiest look she could summon. "Do you intend your inquisition and intimations to unsettle me, perhaps even to terrify me, sir? To send me running from this place at first opportunity? Do you hate your cousin so much that you begrudge her even the barest human companionship and kindness, a friend by her bedside to ease her suffering?"

"My *inquisition* has nothing to do with her," he said. *And everything to do with you*, he didn't say.

It was the unspoken that made her wary.

He laughed, an unexpected, dark sound of mirth that coiled through her.

"Do you think you know me? That you understand my motivations? You know nothing of me, Miss Weston. Nothing at all." He caught her hand and drew it up even as he lowered his face, his nose grazing the tender skin on the inside of her wrist. She gasped and jerked away, but he held fast. Her heart slammed hard against her ribs.

His head lifted, his gaze met hers. "You do not wear heavy perfumes."

She stared at him dumbstruck, her nerves coiled tight.

"No," she replied on a quick exhale.

"I like the way you smell."

Before she could even begin to formulate a reply to that, he settled her hand in the crook of his arm, holding it there when she again tried to pull away.

"We will walk."

Her choices fanned out like a hand of cards, but when she examined them for variety, they were all identical and equally foul. Escape was not worth her effort.

And so walk they did.

Chapter 7

Outside, in the sunshine, St. Aubyn appeared slightly less threatening. Perhaps it was illusion; his height and breadth filled the confines of the breakfast room, but were rendered less imposing by the vast, blue sky overhead. Catherine thought he was more at ease outdoors, though, in truth, he made no indication of that by action or word. Certainly his expression was as enigmatic as ever.

They skirted the crumbling part of the abbey and walked along a path made dim by an overgrown hedgerow some seven feet high. St. Aubyn offered no conversation as he measured his pace to her comfort, and Catherine was not inclined to mine the depths of her forbearance and search for a topic that might interest him.

Contrary, confounding man.

Casting him only the occasional sidelong glance, she otherwise ignored him, and instead memorized the path they took. Experience had taught her to always know the best route of escape.

Finally, they cleared the maze—she could think of no more apt description for the tangle of paths they traversed, walled on either side by the high, overgrown hedge—and came upon a graveyard. Catherine had no doubt it was the exact place Mrs. Bell had directed her to that very morning. Coincidence was unlikely.

"Did you choose this destination with particular purpose?" she asked.

His eyes glittered, polished amber. "Perhaps I eavesdropped on Mrs. Bell offering her dire warnings and directing you to visit this very spot." He shrugged. "Or perhaps I sent her to speak with you this morning, to set the stage for this encounter. Either way, my actions are suspect."

His logic was infallible, his motivations questionable—a situation he appeared perfectly comfortable with.

She was befuddled as to exactly what he admitted. Had he overheard the housekeeper's remarks or had he sent her to act as messenger? Either choice was distasteful. Either way, he could lie.

And that appeared to be exactly his point.

Which brought her full circle back to nowhere.

"You admit that choosing this graveyard as your destination is no coincidence?" She tugged at her hand where he yet held it securely in the crook of his arm.

"Most assuredly." He did not let her go. His grip was not rough, only firm enough to hold her in place, to exert dominion.

"It appears that I cannot count dishonesty among your flaws." She changed tactics, leaving her hand limp against his arm.

"Is dishonesty a flaw?" he mused. "I rather think the ability to lie well is an asset. Do you lie well, Miss Weston?"

Exasperated, she stared at him. "If I say yes, then I am a liar. If I say no, then I might be a liar. If I say nothing, I lie by omission." She shook her head. "What in heaven's name is your purpose in pursuing such nonsense, sir? I can only wonder at your intent. It appears you seek to cause me distress."

"I have no wish to distress you, Miss Weston. Merely to walk with you." St. Aubyn released his grip then, and she drew her hand away without haste, satisfied that she had won this small skirmish. But not the war. She did not delude herself into imagining that he acquiesced and released her as a concession to anyone but himself.

He stepped away, a blessing, for she found his close proximity disturbing. He had asked her earlier if he frightened her. He did. But it was not because she truly believed he would raise a hand to her in physical brutality. No, his was a subtler form of warfare. It was his manner, his words, his hidden thoughts and—unflinching self-awareness made her admit—his physical self that made her pulse beat a little faster and wariness slide through her veins.

"You asked a question," he continued. "I offered an answer. Then I asked a follow-up question . . . and so on. Is that not what you wanted? Conversation?"

"This is not conversation. It is an exercise in frustration," she muttered.

For an instant, she thought she saw him frown, thought she saw a flicker of hurt in his eyes. Then it was gone and she was certain she deluded herself. A trick of the light.

Turning, she looked about curiously. Behind them was the overgrown hedge that extended to cage the entire graveyard, and before them were two stark and barren trees growing close together, branches twisting and mingling. Sparse tufts of grass dotted the bare brown earth. The sun hit only a single headstone in the far corner of the graveyard, leaving the rest wreathed in shadow. All the headstones—save that solitary one—tilted at precarious inclines, leaving Catherine with the feeling that a simple push with a fingertip would topple them altogether.

"Most of these are very old," she murmured, glancing back at St. Aubyn over her shoulder. He, too, was in the shadows, the hollows beneath his cheeks and the masculine line of his jaw made harder in this light, the dimness darkening his hair to the color of ale. She did not wish to notice these things about him. That path was fraught with danger.

"Yes. Some over two hundred years. Perhaps even more than that. My ancestors, and Madeline's."

She walked between the graves, aware of St. Aubyn's interested regard, a predator studying his dinner. The thought made her shiver.

Some of the stones were marked by dark stains, as though fire had roared through this place and left a trail of soot in its wake. Or perhaps it was the grime of centuries, layered on the cold granite.

"It strikes me that you do nothing without purpose, Sir Gabriel." She turned back to face him. He stood in exactly the place she had left him by the overgrown hedge. "Why did you bring me here?"

"To grant you insight. Some of those buried here died of a similar miasma to what plagues my cousin. Tales passed down from parent to child tell of a ghastly acuity of the senses where even bland food sears the tongue, cloth feels like knives flaying the skin, scents become unbearable. Flowers or aromatic spice or perfume become a torment." He shrugged, a fluid movement, muscle contracting under perfectly tailored cloth. "Some days, Madeline complains of all these things and more. Others, she appears to be in perfect health."

"And did this acuity of the senses kill them?" She made a vague gesture toward the nearest gravestone.

He did not answer her question. Instead he observed, "You are so blunt and forthright, your voice modulated and perfectly cool, lovely even in your irritation." He paused. "I do not misread, do I, Miss Weston? You are irritated with me."

She stared at him, at a loss. Given the events of the morning and the bizarre interchange that had passed as dialogue between them, how could he imagine she was anything but irritated? He made no sense to her at all, and she had no idea how to address that. Such a strange man. Beautiful but troubled. Aloof. Cold. His appearance spoke of summer, his demeanor of winter. Yet somehow, she found him vastly interesting despite his odd ways. That terrified her, that spark of interest. She did not want to know him, spend time with him, feel fascination for him. Not for any man, for her experiences had made her wary. But least of all him. He was too . . . much. Too complicated by far.

"I do not know what it is you want of me," she answered at last.

He turned his face away, and she wished he had not. He was a most difficult man to understand, to read, and she wanted at that moment to see his eyes, to try to know his thoughts.

"I want your company. Only that." And as he said it, she believed him. For some inexplicable reason, Gabriel St. Aubyn wanted to spend time with her. How dreadful.

She answered with unaccustomed honesty, braving much. "I do not want yours."

He laughed, head tipped back, shoulders shaking. A short burst of genuine mirth. The sound danced between the graves, startling her. She had not expected any emotion from him, least of all unfettered humor. For an unguarded instant, he allowed a hint of surprise to reflect in his features and she realized he had not expected it, either.

Then his gaze pinned her and he stepped toward her, all humor fading. "It appears we are at an impasse, Miss Weston, my desires in direct opposition to yours."

There was no question in her mind that this man had little interest in *her* preferences or desires. She thought of the story the maid, Susan, had shared that first night, the implication that he killed a highwayman and left the body by the road. It mattered not if she believed the truth of that. It only mattered that others thought it might be true, for something must have made those who knew him inclined to accept the worst. She thought that perhaps he was ruthless. Or perhaps he only allowed others to believe he was.

A breeze kicked up then, catching her skirt and making it billow.

"Do you think Madeline has succumbed to the same malady as your ancestors?" She steered the conversation to their earlier topic, more comfortable with a discussion of death and malady than any reference to St. Aubyn's desires.

"I do not know for certain that anyone succumbed to anything. Perhaps it was suggestion that laid the seeds of illness. Perhaps it is something particular to the St. Aubyn family"—he paused—"or to this place."

He did not believe that. She knew he only toyed with her, spoke in maddening circles to see what her responses would be. For some inexplicable reason, he found her entertaining. With a shake of her head, she tried a more direct question. "Do you believe she will continue her decline as they did?"

"I think not, but there is no way for me to know for certain. Unless, of course, she dies." He sent her a sardonic look. "That would close the matter."

"You think her mad." Catherine stepped away from the old, cracked headstones, toward the newer one in the corner, the one that caught the sunlight and deflected it back in bright glory. The one that made her think of Mrs. Bell's odd, circuitous revelations, and Madeline's garbled talk of a dead woman drenched in blood.

"I did not say so, though I cannot negate the possibility. I do know there is a vein of madness in our blood." He strode forward only far enough to block her path as she inched toward the grave. "Mad as a hatter, or perfectly sane. She could be either."

She edged to one side and took another step, wondering what it was that he did not wish her to see. Wondering why he had brought her in the first place if he meant to guard his secrets. "Why have you not sent her away? To a madhouse?"

His gaze chilled, winter cold. No, colder than that. Cold and dark like the earth that had buried her when she lay in her grave as a girl of eleven.

"I have seen such places. I know more of them than I care to." His tone was frigid. She felt the touch of it like snow on her skin.

His answer only served to whet her curiosity. Almost did she press him, but in the end she decided that honey was better suited to catching this particular fly.

"And that grave?" She gestured to the lone sunlit stone, abruptly changing the subject in the hope of catching him unprepared. "Who is buried there?"

"No one whom you need concern yourself with."

Of course not.

"Well, Sir Gabriel, I fail to see the purpose of this

interlude. You have given me all manner of suppositions and queries to mull over in the dark of night, but you have given me no detail, no meat to chew on."

She had no idea what image her words conjured for him, but the look he turned on her was disturbing in its intensity.

"The purpose?" he murmured. "To walk in the light."

"But we are standing in the shadows."

The intensity of his gaze made her breath catch. "Sunlight holds . . . memories for me." He spoke utterly without inflection, but she was left with the certainty that those memories were not fond.

She stepped back, immensely aware of him, his height, the breadth of his shoulders, his long, strong fingers. Retreat seemed the wisest option, and she took it, shuffling back. For each inch she ceded, he moved into the breach, stalking her.

Enough. She had granted him what leeway a host deserved. More than what he deserved. She was done with allowing herself to be manipulated so easily.

"Do you seek to frighten me away? Is that your intent?" She held her ground now, retreating no more. "You believe your tour of an ancient graveyard and your stories of some sort of disease or curse will send me running back to London with all haste? Or perhaps your intimations of unseemly interest in my person? Let me assure you, sir, they will not."

"Because you are so very brave?"

"No, of course not. I am not brave at all. I am a coward to the tips of my toes. But I am also pragmatic. My decisions are woven and twined with my past, my admitted cowardice, and my follies. I shall say it, though I do not doubt you know it already. I have nowhere else to go."

The words hung in the graveyard, weighty and stark. St. Aubyn simply stared at her with his usual controlled mask, one she knew was a mirror of her own. Despite the import of the revelations she had shared, she allowed nothing of her true thoughts to leak into either her expression or her tone. St. Aubyn would know only what she permitted him to know. That was the best way to play the game. Lull him into confidence by offering mere snippets of truth.

It would have been an easy thing for him to make inquiries while he was in London. Likely, he already knew the entire unpleasant story, and merely wished to ascertain the honesty of her replies. So she fed him a generous serving of the information that she suspected he already knew, trimmed of fat.

"I am mercenary to the core, as you so politely pointed out earlier," she continued. "Madeline's invitation came at a most opportune time. Mrs. Northrop was put out with me and relieved me of my duties, declining my request for a character. I cannot return to London, for I have no resources, no place to go, no family to speak of. And then there is the question of the rumors that dog me like stink after a garbage scow." She tipped her head back, until she could look in his eyes and read his expression, or rather the lack thereof. He gave her no inkling of his thoughts. "But the most important factor in my decision to stay is Madeline. She is my friend. I owe her my life."

Interest uncoiled in his amber gold gaze.

"Why was Mrs. Northrop put out with you?"

She opened her mouth to reply, then closed it, nonplussed. Of all the questions she had expected him to ask—about her, about Madeline, about the past—he had asked the one that she had not anticipated, the one that had no bearing whatsoever on their current discourse.

Assessing the situation, she contemplated how much to reveal. She had learned that when mixed with truth, falsehoods were swallowed with ease. A measure of truth it would be, then, a stone skipping along the surface of her lies. She had no wish for anyone to look deeper, least of all a perceptive, predatory man with a blatant interest in her secrets.

"Mrs. Northrop was involved in charitable work, and so I was involved, as well. Our time at Bart's passed without difficulty, but when she turned her attention to the newly formed Society for the Care and Reform of Women and Girls, our differences surfaced. She was appalled and outraged when I behaved in a manner most unseemly."

The interest in his gaze sparked and grew.

"Did you?" he murmured. "In what way?"

"I had a"—she hesitated on the word *friendship*, for it implied depth of emotion and shared history, and she did not wish him to know of those, so she said instead—"an acquaintance with a woman she deemed unsuitable. A young woman I knew fleetingly in childhood, now a widow fallen on the hardest of times. She runs a school of sorts in a room in St. Giles." And at night, she whored, because teaching in a stinking, crowded schoolroom in St. Giles did not put a candle on the table or food in one's belly. But Catherine had no intention of telling him that. "We corresponded on occasion. Mrs. Northrop found out and questioned my moral fiber. In her opinion, it was one thing to offer charity to those 'poor unfortunates,' as she called them. Quite another to view them as individuals of value. It marked the end of my employment, and she declined to provide a reference, for she deemed me morally corrupt."

Ah, if Mrs. Northrop had only known the true depth of

her moral corruption. The thought was darkly amusing. "Madeline's invitation came that same day."

He offered a single nod, his attention focused on her face in close scrutiny. "But you would have come to her regardless," he observed softly, the words precise and so true they made her ache. "Even if it had cost you your position, you would have left Mrs. Northrop at Madeline's summons." He reached out and touched the single strand of pearls at her neck—her mother's pearls. Only by dint of will did she manage not to flinch away. "You would have sold an heirloom or something else of value to procure funds, and you would have found a way. You would have come because that is who you are."

She felt violated by the accuracy of his observations. He had spent a handful of moments in her company the day of her arrival and again this morning, yet he was so perceptive that he divined that truth. Or perhaps he merely guessed at it and waited for her to reveal all.

"Yes, I would have come," she acknowledged, a safe enough admission, given that he already knew she had come.

"Because you honor your debts."

She stared at him, unable to fathom how he understood so much about her after such brief acquaintanceship. She did not feel that she could claim such depth of knowledge of him, and that was dangerous. *He* was dangerous.

"What is the debt that you owe my cousin, Miss Weston?"

"She never told you?"

"No. Enlighten me." He bared his teeth in a smile that was neither nice nor comforting.

Catherine raised her chin and told him in the briefest possible terms exactly what had transpired that long-ago day. She left out the heart-pounding terror, the press of the earth on her chest, the certainty she would die. Instead, she used only the most simple and direct of terms to paint a picture of a child in distress and another who ran to summon help. To share more than that with this cold, enigmatic man went beyond her comfort.

"She saved you, and so you rushed to her bedside with the intent to save her." Stepping forward, he laid the backs of his fingers against her cheek. A gentle touch, all the power and dominance of his nature held in rigid constraint. His action was improper, imposing, too intimate for her comfort. She wondered if he was always so controlled, if there was ever a time he let loose the rigid hold he maintained. The mere fact that she devoted thought and curiosity to that left her confused and cautious.

"You cannot save her," he continued, and she wanted to ask why, to demand that he offer explanation for his assertion. But her mouth was dry, her tongue thick, the feel of his fingers on her skin too intimate to be borne.

With a sharp exhalation, she reared back, only there was nowhere for her to go. One of the two gnarled trees was directly at her back. She had trapped herself without realizing it. Her heart fluttered and raced, and she looked about for an avenue of escape.

As though he understood her anxiety, St. Aubyn dropped his hand and took a step away, offering her enough space to let her breathe, but not enough to allow her to bolt. She resented that he could read her emotions when she had no inkling of his. She resented it doubly that he seemed to outmaneuver her at every turn. In truth, she was not even certain of the layout of the game board or what pieces were in play.

"I brought you a gift," he said, abruptly steering the conversation in an entirely unexpected direction.

"A gift? That is very . . ."

"Kind?" he supplied with an ironic smile.

She shook her head. "I was going to say improper. I hardly know you."

"Well"—he slanted her an unreadable glance—"it is a small gift."

Pressing her lips together, she stared at him, waiting.

He reached into his pocket and withdrew an odd tin, oval at the top, long and narrow. The tin was painted red with a gold crest on the front. When he placed it in her hand, she studied it curiously.

"How . . . interesting."

"So polite. But you have no idea what it is."

"No." She shook her head, tracing her index finger over the crest. "What is it?"

"The tin is incidental. It is what lies within that will capture your interest. I saw it my first day in London and bought it out of curiosity after watching its inventor carry out a fascinating demonstration. But by the time I was ready to begin my journey home, I had determined that it could belong to no one but you." He paused, and she knew he was watching her reaction as he said, "It is a fire-making device, Miss Weston."

Her breath left her in a rush and something deep within her chest twisted in a tight knot. A fire-making device.

Dear God. He knew.

He had somehow ferreted out her secrets. How? Her limbs felt heavy, frozen, her thoughts muddy.

. . . by the time I was ready to begin my journey home, I had determined that it could belong to no one but you.

She examined his words for hidden implications and found none. Calm settled over her. She was overreacting. He had been in London. He had heard the gossip. That was all he knew. Nothing more. Not the truth. He determined to give her this device merely to unsettle her, to tell her he had heard about the fire. Of course, everyone knew of it. It was in fact old and tired news.

She was both alarmed and surprised that he had bothered to make inquiries about her. Their initial encounter had left her with the impression that she was almost beneath his notice—a circumstance she would have preferred.

In knowledge lay power, and she had little knowledge of him. The scales were far from balanced.

Careful not to betray her panic, she forced a reply, her tone flat. "How interesting."

"So you have said already," he murmured and stepped closer to take the tin from her hands. She had not brought her gloves down to breakfast, not having anticipated a need for them, and so her skin was bare as his long, beautiful fingers brushed her own. His were hot. Hers felt like ice.

"You see," he said, carefully prying up the lid to reveal the strange contents, "inside each spill—"

"Spill?" she asked, unfamiliar with the term.

"These twists of paper." He slid one free to demonstrate. "Inside the paper is a tiny glass vesicle that contains a drop of vitriol. The paper wrapped about it is primed with chlorate of potash, gum Arabic, and sugar. When you wish to have fire, you use these"—he withdrew a tiny pair of pliers from the tin—"to nip off the end and break the vesicle." He did exactly as he described and Catherine gasped as fire bloomed.

Fire. In a tin.

Her vision narrowed until all she saw, all she knew was

the red tin in his hand with its yellow-gold crest and the fire that danced at the end of the paper twist.

He huffed a breath and the flame snuffed. She wanted to snatch the tin from his hand and snip the end of another match herself with the tiny pliers, to see if indeed each one had this wonderful capacity to burn with spontaneous beauty.

"Why do you give me this?" she whispered, wondering anew exactly how much he had managed to discern of her secrets and how he had ferreted them out.

"Because Mrs. Bell forgot your fire the first night you came to us." He paused. "This tin makes you mistress of your own comfort."

Mistress of her own comfort. His motivations for even considering such a thing were difficult to comprehend. Her head jerked up. He was too close, his dark gold eyes intent upon her. And she knew he lied. His reasons were other than he claimed.

"May I?" he asked in the quietest of tones, but she had no idea what it was he wanted.

Then he moved closer still. Her breath caught, her heart tripped. Her head tipped back and she stared up at him, so close, the scent of his skin purely delicious, beckoning her to lean close and inhale. The intensity of his perusal seared her.

"The first time I saw you, a curl had escaped your pins and lay across your shoulder"—he brushed his fingers along the curve of her collarbone—"here." Slowly, he traced his fingers up the side of her neck to the base of her skull where she had pinned the mass of hair in a loose knot. "May I?" he asked again.

She was beguiled. Every rational thought bid her step away, decline his request, flee this graveyard and not look back. Instead, she nodded, closing her eyes as his warm fingers slid free one of her pins and drew a lock of hair from the knot.

Heat licked at her, and her breath came in sharp, shallow rasps. She opened her eyes to see him before her, head bowed, her hair lying flat on his fingers, his thumb stroking the gently curled end. Feeling as though someone unfamiliar inhabited her skin, she stood there, allowing him to pet her, wariness, perhaps even fear, leaving her light-headed.

But, no, that was a lie.

If she would be honest with no one else, she ought to at least be honest with herself. It was not fear that left her dizzy, but his nearness, the faintly citrus scent of his skin, the way he tipped his head to look at her. She was light-headed because he touched her with his beautiful hands. Because she knew exactly what pleasure a man's touch could bring and it had been so long, so very long.

But more than that, it was because St. Aubyn—Gabriel—was elementally and wholly attractive to her, his cold shell making him intriguing, making her wonder what warmth might lurk beneath the surface. And because sometimes, when he looked at her, he was not cold at all. What sort of lover would such a man be? Would passion free the sinuous beast that prowled just beneath his skin?

If she was afraid of anything in this moment, it was her own unacceptable reaction to him. The breeze made her shiver. Or perhaps it was the way he looked at her as he raised his head.

She was no stranger to a man's lust, nor was she a stranger to her own. But dangerously perceptive and intractable as he was, Gabriel St. Aubyn was the last man on earth she should feel hunger for. Perhaps that was exactly why she did. The knowledge horrified her. She had thought never to feel such a thing, never again to know physical yearning. How could she? What sort of monster did it make her that after all that had passed, she would want a man, *this* man especially, with his cold heart and perfect, chiseled beauty?

If she took a lover, she ought to take a weak man, a man she could control. Not a man such as St. Aubyn, dangerous and enigmatic and rapier sharp.

Tension held her in place, her skin humming from the charge in the air.

"Your hair is very thick," he murmured. For an instant, she did not understand what he meant by such an observation. And then she did. He meant it as a compliment, the way another man might tell a woman she was beautiful.

"I must go." She delved deep for the calm demeanor that was her norm as she pulled her hair from his grasp and deftly twined it back into place. Sidling away, she detoured the tree at her back and the man that faced her, ending up behind a teetering gravestone. She shook out her skirt as an excuse to look away, to gather herself into the woman she habitually let others see.

But not for a moment did she delude herself into believing it was what *he* saw. No, he was too astute to easily accept the image she conveyed. To think otherwise would be a strategic error.

"Take the tin, Miss Weston." He held it out to her. "It was meant for you."

"And here I thought you said you purchased it on a whim," she replied, deliberately misunderstanding his meaning. Still, she accepted the tin, lured despite her better judgment, the metal cool and smooth in her hand.

She moved toward the hedge and the path there, shaking

her head when he stepped forward to escort her. "Do not let me waylay you from your morning's pursuits, Sir Gabriel. I can find my way perfectly well."

She was already at the mouth of the overgrown maze when he replied. "Of that I have no doubt, Miss Weston. It is part of your appeal."

And that, more than any flowery words, was a compliment that warmed her to her core.

Lifting her skirt, she hurried off, confident in the certainty that she would have been far better off if Gabriel St. Aubyn had never imagined she held any appeal at all.

"Miss Weston," he called from behind her. She paused, but did not turn. "Tacking 'Sir' before my name will not create distance anywhere but in your imagination."

Of course, he was correct. And what was she to say to that?

Chapter 8

The way was dim and dark, the stone stairs slick, even on this fine and sunny day. Gabriel carried no lantern, no candle, his feet shaping the familiar path that would pose no challenge even if he closed his eyes and saw nothing at all. As a child, this had been his private place. As a man grown and shaped by the events of his past, he had forced himself to reclaim it. On either side, the stone walls drew close, barely wider than the span of his shoulders, and the stairs turned and twisted as he climbed. There were no windows, which left the air stale and dank, though he had left the iron-girded wooden door at the foot of the stairs open behind him.

He took care not to breathe too deeply, not to think of the narrowness of the passage as he ascended the spiraling stairs that wended to the crumbling tower. Behaviors honed in an eternity of captivity slowed his breathing and moderated his steps. He tolerated no weakness in himself.

Finally, he reached the top, the dark staircase opening into a vast, empty space. He took a deep breath then, letting the air fill his lungs, smelling stone and tallow and mildew.

It made him long for the scent of Catherine's skin, of her

hair. Roses and—he paused, considered, and after a moment it came to him—buttered toast.

No wonder he had wanted to touch his tongue to the place her pulse beat in her neck and lick his way along her vein. The urge had startled him then, as the recollection of it confounded him now. He was not a fanciful man. What was it about her that almost succeeded in making him one?

He had erred in the graveyard. He should not have touched her, stroked the silky length of her hair, conversed with her. It felt too much like a connection. What was he thinking to foster that? To join her at breakfast and encourage discourse? He was not capable of any sort of relationship, least of all one with a woman who would—justifiably—expect some permanent commitment as befitted her station.

That was an impossibility. He would never marry. Never sire an heir. These were inviolable facts.

She was a woman who, despite her current genteel poverty, had been raised to expect all the things he would never offer. Did he imagine he could have her at his whim, on his terms? He did not. He only knew that he wanted her. Naked and panting. Legs wrapped about his waist. Fingers curled, nails digging into his back.

Had he no honor at all left that he entertained such thoughts about her?

No, none at all.

And what was it about her that called to him? He knew better than to try and dissect his attraction into parts of the whole. It was only the sum total that mattered. He wanted her, and in the years since his escape from hell, he had made a habit to take what he wanted. To deny himself nothing in recompense for the time that had been stolen from him, the time where he had been denied everything, even his basic dignity.

Oddly, he rarely wanted anything more than a cloudy day, a good book, a decent meal, and a hot bath. Simple needs. He supposed he had never learned to yearn for anything complicated.

So why did he hesitate? Why did he woo with gentle care what he might have by other means? He had noted the change in her breathing, the darkening of her eyes, the parting of her lips when he was near. He could have her if he pushed just a little. Or perhaps more than a little.

But, somehow, he preferred that she come to him.

The thought drew a dark smile. She was already wary of him, mistrustful, and he suspected his actions this morning had not warmed her to his cause. But he knew no other way to be than the way he was. He was nothing other than the vessel his experiences had shaped, coupled with the efforts he had made to learn what it was that made a man similar to his peers.

Those efforts, though considerable, had yielded paltry results. Shallow results.

Annoyance surged. Enough introspection. He had spent more time on it today than he normally would in a year.

He did not turn and draw the heavy wooden door at the top of the stairs—a twin to the one at the bottom—shut behind him. He had no need to. No one would dare trespass here.

And he had no wish to be confined. Closed doors were for captives, held against their will or desire, not for his home, the place he could roam where he liked.

He crossed to the large mahogany desk by the windows. Taking a leather thong from about his neck, he withdrew the two keys that hung on it from beneath his shirt. He inserted one in the lock of the drawer on the right side of the desk and drew forth a metal box. It, too, was locked.

The second key slid into the lock, and turned with a faint click. Lifting the lid, he stared down at the contents: three leather-bound journals and a packet of letters tied with a string, each addressed to Geoffrey St. Aubyn, Hanham House.

The letters were all sent by his cousin, Sebastian, who had spent his life roaming to all manner of interesting places with his guardian.

Gabriel's hand did not tremble as he lifted the packet. He would not permit it to tremble.

Carefully, he rifled through the corners of the stack with his index finger, then set it aside. The letter he wanted was from an earlier time. He removed a second, smaller packet, these addressed to Gabriel St. Aubyn, Cairncroft Abbey. He slid one letter free of the group, unfolded it, scanned to the bit he wanted and read the words penned there in a neat, childish hand. Sebastian had been so young when he wrote these, and Gabriel even younger.

I have heard talk that a mummy is to be sent home to England to be unwrapped before an audience of physicians. I should like to be there when they do, to see for myself the places they made the cuts in order to remove the lungs, liver, intestine, and stomach. These the ancient Egyptians stored in jars made of stone or ceramic or even wood. If only you could see them, carved and decorated. You would think them wondrous things of fascination, I am sure. I find them mysterious. I wonder at the purpose of such deliberate dissection. I wonder, too, that the heart, they did not take. Gabriel, it would be wonderful if you were here. Perhaps we could even try to make a mummy ourselves using a dead bird or other small creature.

Folding the letter once more, Gabriel slid it back in place, set both bundles in the metal box, locked it, and placed the box in the drawer. He locked that as well, then tucked the keys away beneath his shirt once more.

Sebastian was back on English soil. Gabriel had managed to confirm that much but, so far, his efforts to track his cousin had failed. He had Newton's and Pratt's assertions, and a dozen others, but wherever Sebastian had got to, Gabriel was a step behind.

Memories squirmed and wriggled, but he held them at bay, refusing to set them free. Instead, he crossed to the far wall where tall, narrow panes of leaded glass were set among the stones. They overlooked the path that meandered by the lake. He should have been surprised to see Catherine there. Was he to believe it coincidence that she chose to walk exactly where he looked?

Coincidence or not, there she was.

She walked with Madeline by her side, their arms linked, their heads bowed close together. Slowly, they made their way to a stone bench and settled there, overlooking the lake. The scenery was unlovely, the lake covered in green slime.

For some moments he watched them, then leaned closer to the glass as Catherine drew forth something red and gold, the colors catching the sun. Slowly, she slid the lid free and drew out a single spill, then the tiny pliers. Pleasure warmed him to see his gift in her hands.

Madeline turned on the bench so she was looking full at Catherine.

He could not see either woman's face, could not hear what they said, but as Catherine snipped the tip off the paper spill and watched the fire flare, he had no trouble reading her delight. It was there in every line of her lovely, lush form, and in the faint sound of her laughter that carried up and up until it came to him through the glass.

Closing his eyes, he savored the sound, and for a single shimmering second, he thought that this must be joy.

St. Aubyn's return changed little in Catherine's routine. She attempted to avoid him at breakfast the following day, waking exceptionally early, hoping he would sleep exceptionally late. She was not so fortunate, and ended up in his company for the morning meal. As it turned out, she enjoyed their discussion, though she admitted that only to herself.

The day was gloomy, and Madeline's mood, once she roused at noon, matched the heavy, cloud-laden sky. She was petulant and cranky, but Catherine coaxed her into a game of chess and made certain Madeline won. After that, her mood improved.

It was late in the day when, seeking something to read, Catherine wandered to the library. She had been there only once before, and the way was not easy to retrace. She ended up at the rear of the house, near a narrow, dark staircase—the servants' stairs.

She was lost. There was nothing to do but go back the way she had come. She turned and took but a single step, when the sound of voices drifted up the stairs. One masculine and low, and after a long moment, a higher feminine one, thick with tears.

She recognized the first voice. It was Gabriel St. Aubyn. Again he spoke, his tone firm, the inflection suggesting that he questioned someone. But she could not clearly make out the words.

The only reply he received was a muffled sob.

His business was none of hers, yet curiosity surged and she wondered to whom he spoke and what he did that elicited the woman's tears.

Slowly, she crept down the stairs, placing her foot with care. One step, the next, and another, until she was not careful enough and, beneath her toes, a stair creaked. She froze, aware that what she did was beyond acceptable behavior. She took the servants' stairs to spy on the master of Cairncroft. It was a reckless act, doubly so because she could not imagine that Gabriel St. Aubyn would be pleased to know that anyone spied upon him, least of all a woman whose place in his home was tenuous at best. Almost did she turn back, when the woman gave a sharp cry, cut off as though she slapped a palm across her lips—or someone else did.

A shiver crawled along Catherine's spine.

The next step was silent, and the next, and slowly she made her way down one flight, then a second, where she froze. Though the stairwell was dark, she could see a little of the passage below, for a lit sconce, or perhaps a lamp, threw dancing shadows and flickering light across the form of a woman huddled at the bottom of the stairs. She was dressed all in gray with a white cap on her head, her brown hair tied in a single plait that snaked over her shoulder.

She knelt on the floor, choking back sobs, her body curled forward as though she protected something.

And towering over her was Gabriel St. Aubyn.

Catherine shrank back against the wall, clutched by horror, all manner of terrible possibilities running through her mind. Her own experiences shaped her suspicions. She knew that. Yet she could not imagine this frightening tableau could be anything other than what it appeared: a man misusing his position of power. Her thoughts whirled as she tried to decide how best to proceed, what to do to help this poor girl.

"Please," the maid whispered, the word coiling through Catherine's veins like a poison. How many times had Catherine begged, at times on her knees as this woman was? How many times had she whispered that tearstained plea, to no avail?

Her belly churned, and she drew a shuddering breath.

"Stand up," St. Aubyn said, his tone void of any emotion. He did not touch the maid, did not take even a single step toward her, but the command in his tone was impossible to disobey.

Reaching out to press her palm against the wall, the girl pushed herself to her feet, her head bowed, and Catherine saw then that her other hand was cradled against her belly, the fingers swollen and twisted. She stood there, sobbing and weaving side to side.

Had he done this? Had St. Aubyn hurt her?

Horror congealed in Catherine's gut as she mentally tallied the last of her limited funds. Was there enough to see that this woman received care for her hand, and enough to travel? Enough for her to escape this terrible place?

But then what would Catherine have left for herself?

A confusion of possible outcomes flashed through her mind as she inched down yet another stair, summoning her courage and determination to stand up for this maid as she had never dared stand up for herself. She felt chilled to the bone, her limbs rubbery, her own horrific past colliding with her present.

She was not that terrified girl anymore. She was not.

She recognized that her own experiences were shadowing her ability to judge the situation before her, and she measured her reactions, holding herself back from leaping into the fray before she truly knew what the battle was.

Of course, the maid might have stumbled, hand outstretched, and injured herself. But somehow, Catherine did not think so. Her imagination conjured a horrific scenario of a booted heel hammering on tender flesh, or a brutal hand twisting muscle and bone.

With a shudder, she pressed her palms against the wall and slunk down another stair, intent on speaking up, whatever the personal consequence. A loud scuffling and an angry male voice came from a distant part of the passage, the interruption stilling her movements and interfering with her intent. A moment later, two footmen arrived, and between them swaggered a stocky man dressed in fine clothes, worn at the elbows and knees. A gentleman down on his luck, Catherine suspected.

The maid cried out and shrank back against the wall, her eyes wide with terror.

That terror acted as the catalyst for Catherine's courage. She hurried down the last of the stairs to step forward and speak in her coldest tone. "What is going on here?"

St. Aubyn did not so much as glance her way, though she felt the eyes of everyone else there fix upon her.

"Nothing that concerns you," he said. "Stay, or go. But do not interfere."

His tone was quiet, the words laced with steel.

Ghosts and memories wove a dark spell, making her tremble, making her feel as though she was once more that cowering girl who had no hope, no family, no friends. No way to escape. Horror seized her. She was determined to help this unfortunate maid, to save her from whatever vile thing St. Aubyn meant to visit upon her. But first, she must determine exactly what that was and so she held her place and her silence, her fists clenched by her sides.

He turned toward the maid then and asked, "Is this the man?"

She was crying so hard she could not speak. St. Aubyn stepped toward her and she shrank away. Without thought, Catherine insinuated herself between them, her back to the girl, her entire body shaking as she faced him down. She was dimly aware that the two footmen stood silent, and the man in the faded finery snorted in derision.

St. Aubyn pinned her with a gaze that was barely human, so cold and *knowing* that she felt sick from it.

"Step aside, Miss Weston."

An order.

She held her ground, feeling the weight of his stare and the stares of the maid and the men who stood a short way down the dim passage.

"Please, miss," the maid whispered, and sidled around her to face her fate. "I don't want you to take my trouble as your own."

"Is this the man?" St. Aubyn asked again, his frigid gaze turned to the maid once more.

"Yes," she said, so low that Catherine could barely hear her. Then the girl raised her head and stared down the hallway, fear and loathing glittering in her gaze.

"What? You going to believe her?" the man asked with an ugly laugh. "A lightskirt like her?"

St. Aubyn was before him in three short strides. Without preamble, he took the man's left hand in his and snapped his baby finger. The man cried out, a short, ugly sound that echoed in the narrow hallway, along with the maid's gasp.

Catherine jerked forward, then froze in place, her world

tilting as she tried to make sense of what she had witnessed here.

There was violence in the air. She could taste it, smell it. She looked at St. Aubyn's face and realized it came from him, barely leashed. He *wanted* this man to defend himself. Wanted a reason to unleash the full fury of his rage. He wanted to hurt him.

And in the instant, she finally understood exactly what transpired here. Justice. Or at least, St. Aubyn's definition of it.

The fellow stood rigid, cradling his injured hand, cursing and snarling like the beast he was.

"Be glad I broke only one," St. Aubyn said. "You broke three of hers. Get off my land. Do not return." He bared his teeth in a terrible smile. "Take an unwilling woman again, and I will hear of it. Touch anything of mine again, and I will kill you."

The man's mouth opened and closed, his eyes wide with fear. The two footmen grabbed his elbows and dragged him away down the passage, while the maid slumped against the wall, sobbing wildly.

St. Aubyn turned toward her and stared at her in silence, his expression utterly blank. It was not marked in his features, not expressed by any means, but Catherine could swear that in the face of the maid's tears, he was befuddled. He reached out, paused, drew back, and then finally took the maid's hand at the wrist, not touching her damaged fingers at all as he looked at her injury.

The maid cried all the harder.

"You cannot work in the scullery," he said, letting go his hold.

Her sobs froze, and Catherine's own breath caught.

What would this girl do if he turned her out with her hand broken and battered? How would she survive?

"Until your hand heals, you will—" His lips drew taut and he stared straight ahead, as though pondering what instruction to offer. Then he gave a quick shake of his head and in what could only be described as an exasperated tone, continued, "You will *dust*. Every book in the library. You will take each one down from the shelf and dust it thoroughly."

"There are so many books, sir," the maid said, ending on a hiccupping sob.

"Quite," St. Aubyn replied with a sardonic edge, and the glance he cast her told Catherine that that was exactly the point. "Come along. We will find Mrs. Bell."

He stalked away, tossing over his shoulder, "Not you, Miss Weston. You may return to whatever it was that had you skulking about in the shadows before you stumbled upon our little melodrama. I would in no way wish to inconvenience you." Three steps more, and he stopped, glanced back, and said in a strangely gentle tone, "Come along, Peg."

"Yes, sir." She gave a mighty sniff. "I'm sorry, sir." The maid scurried after him, leaving Catherine alone in the gloom, only now fully realizing that Gabriel St. Aubyn had just played the role of Peg's knight in shining armor.

She recalled the way he had snapped the man's finger, utterly without emotion, seemingly without effort. Judge and executioner.

She supposed that made him more a knight in tarnished armor.

The following morning, Gabriel sipped his coffee and glanced through an outdated copy of the *Times*.

"Oh!" A soft exclamation dusted the silence and he

looked up to see Miss Weston frozen in the doorway of the breakfast room. The hour was early, barely past dawn. No doubt she had timed her arrival with care, intending to finish her meal before he came, and thus avoid him altogether. He found it entertaining to confound her. And *that* confounded him.

"You are an early riser," she observed, stepping inside and crossing to the sideboard. Her voice betrayed no emotion whatsoever, though he suspected she silently cursed him to Hades.

She filled a plate, then joined him, hesitating almost imperceptibly as she selected a seat. Finally she opted for the same one she had chosen the previous day, though she might have moved to the far end of the table and taken a place there.

"It is customary to rise when a lady enters a room," she observed primly.

"Do you chastise me for my appalling manners, Miss Weston?"

She stared at him with cool aplomb. "Someone must."

And that made him laugh, though he had no idea why. The sound startled her. Her brows rose, giving her away before she mastered her responses and turned her attention to her meal.

In truth, the sound startled him, as well. Something about her freed a more primitive part of his nature, a part that was less controlled and rigid.

The silence wove about them like smoke, interrupted only by the nearly absent scrape of silverware on china, the rattle of a cup being set on a saucer, the crinkle of paper as he turned a page of the *Times*.

He thought she must be ruffled by the tension that hummed, vivid and alive, in the air. But she betrayed that not at all. She was cool and poised. Lovely.

He wanted to shake her composure.

Why? Such an uncharacteristic urge.

She had witnessed the episode yesterday by the servants' stairs. For some reason, that made him . . . uncomfortable. He was unaccustomed to anyone gainsaying him. But Catherine Weston had done just that, insinuating herself between him and Peg when she thought the girl was in danger. From him. That, too, made him uncomfortable. That even for a moment, she had thought him capable of brutalizing someone smaller, weaker.

She had seen the violence surge through him, witnessed the cold brutality of his actions. He'd broken the bastard's finger.

As though she sensed the direction of his thoughts, she murmured, "Why did you do it? Break his finger? You might have simply chastised him and sent him on his way."

No, he could not have done that.

Slowly, she raised her gaze to his, a world of knowledge shimmering in her dark, lovely eyes.

"It was less than he deserved." That was explanation enough. But for some reason, he could not let it be, he felt compelled to answer more fully. Peg was a servant girl with no protection, and no way to fight back. "I despise inequity."

"Yes," she said. Only that. Nothing more.

It was enough.

They began to converse, stilted at first, then more easily. Almost comfortably. They discussed philosophy and literature and science.

She was unexpectedly well read, but when he asked her about that, she evaded and danced about the topic, an expert at avoidance. He let it pass. For now.

He had lent her his copy of Mary Shelley's *Frankenstein,* and they spoke of that as well, though she had only read the first bit to date, constrained as she was by her need to care for Madeline.

When she rose and took her leave, he was not pleased to see her go.

The following morning, she came to take her meal a full two hours late. A new tactic, the truce of the previous morning having been destroyed by the passage of time.

He delighted in the complete lack of surprise she evinced at finding him waiting for her, drinking yet another cup of coffee. His third? Fifth? She was composed and controlled, her mask perfectly in place. She presented such a wonderful challenge.

"I trust you slept well," he said.

"Very well, thank you," she replied. Her eyes narrowed as she assessed him, likely wondering why he engaged her in pointless discourse. He wondered that himself. "And you?"

Watching the sway of her hips as she made her way to the sideboard, he murmured an appropriate reply. He kept the *in*appropriate reply to himself, saying nothing of how, with the night a dark cave around him, he had lain between his cool sheets and tossed and dreamed. Of her. Naked. Of her lustrous hair fanning loose about her porcelain-pale shoulders, and her dusky pink lips open to accept him into her mouth. Of her dark eyes, slumberous with need; of her cries, high and loud, as she found her release.

What would she think to know that each night since his return, he had dreamed of her? Restless, wild dreams, sensual and vivid.

He ached to catch her hair in his fist and drag her head back so he could feast on her mouth, her throat, her breasts. He ached to knead the flesh of her sweet, round bottom and watch the pale skin of her buttocks pinken beneath his touch. He wanted to mark her as his.

He wanted her to take her pleasure of him, to lose control for him, to claw and bite and climax for him, again and again. He wanted nothing gentle with her, nothing subject to rigid control.

What was it about her that spoke to him on such a primitive level? He had known many beautiful women. Known many bright women. None had invaded his dreams. But Catherine did.

He tried to dissect her, to understand the allure, but she was something more than the sum of mere parts.

And so they met at breakfast each morning after that. He offered no clue of his private thoughts and lascivious dreams; he only sipped his coffee and watched her sip her tea, and listened to her perfect diction and lovely voice.

And each night, he dreamed. Fierce, dark dreams.

Chapter 9

Susan Parker trudged along the road making practical use of her half-day free from her duties at Cairncroft Abbey. The master had been back from London for more than a week now, and Susan was glad. It seemed Mrs. Bell worked them all harder when he was away, which made no sense, but that was the way of it.

Her thoughts turned to Peg and the gossip that was flying among the servants. What had happened to her the day after Sir Gabriel's return? No one knew for certain and Peg wasn't saying. They only knew that one day, she'd been a scullery maid who'd gone and gotten her hand broke, and in the week since, she had been dusting books.

Susan snorted. Easy work, that. Maybe *she* ought to go and get her hand broke, as well.

The sun was high in the sky, beating down hotter than Susan had a liking for. She wore her heavy cloak over her plain brown dress. When she had set off promptly at noon, the day had been overcast and there had been a nip in the air. The cloak had seemed like a fine idea. The walk to the village had been pleasant, the spring breeze stroking her skin, the birds chirping in the adjacent woods.

Now, with the clouds burned away and the full heat of the day upon her, she saw that the cloak had been a terrible idea. She was hot and sweaty, her hair hanging lank against her forehead, itching where it lay plastered to her skin.

And her toes and the backs of her heels pinched.

That was the whole reason she was on the road at all. She had put her half-day to good use, walking to the village to be measured for new shoes. When that business was done, she had left the shoemaker, turned right around, and begun the trek back to Cairncroft Abbey, for she meant to return in time for supper, and the walk was almost two hours each way.

Her thoughts wandered, revisiting the events of that morning. She'd been tasked to deliver a letter to Miss Weston. She had carried it up on the silver tray, bobbed a curtsy, and mumbled a brief reply when Miss Weston had tried to engage her in conversation. She thought Miss Weston felt bad now for her threats about carrying tales to Mrs. Bell that first night, and her pleasantries were a way of making amends.

Well, Susan was having none of it.

Though she had managed to avoid conversation with Miss Weston since the night she had first arrived, she hadn't been able to avoid tidying the woman's chamber. Duties were duties, after all. She didn't like her. Didn't trust her. What sort of nasty woman wielded threats just to ferret out information?

A smart, nasty woman, that's who.

Susan shook her head, annoyed with herself as she recalled the way she had rambled on about the master and the time they'd found that highwayman dead by the road. What had she been thinking? There was fodder enough to see her dismissed if Miss Weston had had that in her mind.

Shoving a hank of hair off her face, she wiped the back of her hand across her brow as she walked. Truth was . . . she knew Miss Weston wouldn't have ratted her out. Not because she was so very nice, but because she hadn't said anything to anyone about the things Susan had divulged. At least, not that Susan knew of. Besides, she didn't like Mrs. Bell any better than Susan did. And Mrs. Bell seemed to loathe Miss Weston.

Susan knew she'd been duped by the threat, and she'd spilled all in a rambling surge, terrified that if she didn't, she would lose her place. Which made no sense when she thought about it later. She would have been wiser to keep her mouth closed tight if she meant to protect her position. Well, she'd learned a lesson from that. She'd bite her tongue clean through before she would make the same mistake again.

She closed her eyes, recalling again the letter she'd delivered just this morning and Miss Weston's reaction to it. The interesting thing, the bit that made Susan think on it again and again, was the look on Miss Weston's face when she'd flipped the letter over and seen the name of the person what sent it. Whoever it was, Miss Weston clearly had not expected them to write. She'd been gripped by surprise. Her raised brows and open mouth had betrayed her, doubly so because Susan had come to notice that it was not her usual fashion to show any emotion at all.

This letter had caught Miss Weston unawares, and that made Susan curious as a cat.

Maybe one of the other maids would have heard something by the time she got back. Susan was doubtful of that. Miss Weston was a private type, talking about the weather and such to the other girls, but never anything more than that. And though they'd quickly looked through her things a time or two, there hadn't been anything interesting to find. Oh, except the pretty red tin with the gold crest, but Susan had no idea what those twisted papers inside were for. She'd carefully set the tin back where she'd found it, placing it exactly where it had been so Miss Weston wouldn't see it had been touched.

Susan trudged on a bit, the discomfort of the heat and her shoes and the long walk so tedious, made worse by the growing need to piddle.

With a sigh, she paused and peered about. The road had curved, and to her left was a narrow river. The sound of the water rushing over the rocks made the pressing urgency that had plagued her for the past mile even worse. She was close to Cairncroft. Less than another hour to go. But, oh, she did need to piddle. She had thought to wait, but now decided against it.

To her right were the woods, the trees budding and green. There wasn't another soul to be seen, and there was privacy enough to satisfy. Lifting her skirt, she left the road and scooted behind a thick tree trunk, hidden from any who might pass as she did what nature demanded.

There. That was much better. She thought even her pinched feet felt better now that the other discomfort was relieved. Settling her skirt, she then stepped around the tree and was about to resume her walk when she heard the pounding of hooves approaching.

Loath to step directly into the path of a racing horse—hadn't she seen that child trampled before her very eyes five years ago at the Newmarket Fair?—she held her place until horse and rider rounded the bend. She waited there, thinking the rider would simply continue past.

But he did not.

He saw her and reined in the great black beast. It stood,

sides heaving, head tossing, and she watched it warily, for horses frightened her.

The sun was at his back, and she squinted up at him, unable to make out his features. A strange disquiet trickled through her, and she took a step back. He eased the horse forward, one step, two. Clop. Clop. The jingle of the bridle seemed so loud in the quiet.

The movement shifted his relation to the sun, and she saw his face now, her unease evaporating like dew.

"Oh, sir, 'tis you." She pressed her hand to her breast, and gave a nervous laugh. She blinked, unable to fathom why he had stopped to speak with her at all. Other than a directive to her duties, he had never said a conversational word to her. Not a single word.

"Did I give you a fright?" He offered a warm, slow smile. She'd never seen him do that. Not in the three years she'd been at Cairncroft.

"A bit," she admitted shyly, staggered that he bothered to stop and speak with her, that he paid such attention to her.

He studied her at his leisure, his gaze raking her from crown to toes. It left her feeling oddly flustered, like the time Tom the footman had winked at her and tugged on her plait.

"You can't mean to walk in this heat. Let me take you up behind me." Leaning forward, he held out his hand.

She gawped at him, mouth open, thoughts muzzy. He meant to take her up behind him? To have her ride back to Cairncroft with him?

Well, that was something to tell the other girls. Wouldn't they be amazed?

Scrambling forward, she looked up and reached for his hand, the sun in her eyes once more, blinding her.

* * *

Slapping his brown leather gloves against his thigh, Gabriel strode across the slate tiles of the entry hall. Despite his lengthy outing earlier in the afternoon, he was filled with an uncharacteristic restless tension. Because, as happened more and more of late, his thoughts were filled with her—Catherine Weston—and he had no desire to put a halt to where his imagination took him.

"Sir Gabriel." Her voice came to him now, drawing him from his musings. Her words echoed in the vast empty hallway, crisp and precise. She was slightly breathless, as though she had hurried to catch him.

"Catherine," he returned her greeting, pausing to look up, finding her at the top of the stairs, framed by the open arch.

He wondered if she was debating whether to chastise him for his unseemly forwardness, for she had never invited him to use her given name. In the end, she let it pass. It told him much, that acquiescence. Catherine Weston chose her battles with care, and he suspected she had sought him out to fight one of greater import than his unauthorized use of her given name.

She stood on the top step, unmoving. Her dress was the color of smoke, the color of sadness, of mourning. She ought to have looked plain. Instead, the hint of lavender in the gray made her skin gleam like one of the pearls on the strand she wore about her neck.

Waiting and watching, he held his place as she descended the stairs and approached, grace and beauty, each step measured to the last. Perhaps—no, *assuredly*—a true gentleman would have gone to her. The thought amused him.

"If you have a moment, I wish to speak with you about Madeline." She paused, as though waiting for some reaction. He offered none. He merely watched her in silence, letting her have her say. As always, her composure was impeccable, but some small detail of her appearance was left in disarray. Today, as it had been the very first time he saw her, it was a lock of hair that had come free from her twist, curling over her shoulder and along her breast.

"Your cousin is poorly," she said, the mistress of understatement. "I wonder what means have been employed in the past to encourage her from her melancholy."

"Do you?"

A fleeting frown creased her brow. "Do I what?"

"Wonder." He slapped his gloves against his thigh, once. "Or do you obliquely inquire if I have coaxed her and coddled her in the past? If you have a question, ask it outright, Catherine."

She sent him a glance that might have held annoyance. Or disdain. He would prefer the former.

"Have you coaxed and coddled her in the past?"

"I have hired staff to do exactly that."

"Why do you not visit her?" she fired, her expression tranquil once more, her tone sharp as a blade. "Why do you do nothing to help her?"

"I do not visit her because she despises me as I despise her. We mix as well as oil and water." There. Let her mull on that. "And how do you know what I do and do not do to help her? Or what I have done in the past. You do not know me at all, Catherine." He took a step closer, letting the subtle rose scent of her wash over him, letting his action say what his words did not. *We could remedy that. We could know each other as well as you please.*

Only in that moment, with her scent filling him, did he think to regret that his afternoon's activities had left him smelling of horse, with dust on his boots and a splatter of mud on his sleeve.

She did not step away. Not his Catherine. She would not give an inch. Instead, she tipped her head back to glare at him and said, "I do know you, sir. I know that you have a brilliant mind and a cold heart. You have shown me that much of yourself. You answer questions with questions or with answers so oblique they have no value at all. At times, you offer only silence. What else would you like me to know?"

She was so close, he could see the beat of her pulse just beneath the pale skin of her throat.

Clearly, they applied different definitions and nuances to the concept of *knowing*.

He bent his head a little. She froze, the rise and fall of her breasts belying the cool gaze she leveled upon him. He affected her. There was no question of it. But she was poised, icy, her demeanor cultivated and planned to project a very specific impression.

"I did not seek you out to speak of nonsense," she said in her frostiest tone, the sound of her voice only serving to stoke the heat in his loins. "I believe a visit from the doctor is in order. Your cousin has eaten almost nothing in days, and she does not sleep. I fear for her health." She pressed her lips together, contemplating her next words, perhaps debating whether or not to set them free, and then she finished, "I fear for her sanity."

"Ah." And how was he to respond to that? There was nothing to fear. Madeline's sanity had fled years past. And his own, as well. He imagined that if he said so, Catherine's ire would be raised. She might turn and walk away. He was not ready to let her go, and so he settled for the less objectionable observation, "Madeline despises Dr. Graves."

"Then send for someone else."

"There is no one else capable within a day's ride, and the afternoon is nigh over, evening drawing near. Unless you would have her seen by Dr. Jayne. He is close by, but he is a drunk. Last year, he performed an amputation. Quite proud he was, bragging that he'd done it in three minutes flat. Unfortunately, he'd cut off the wrong limb." He let a heartbeat pass for her to digest that, then asked, "Shall I summon him? He could arrive within the hour, unless he is too inebriated to walk."

She stared at him, and he saw a flicker of anger before she composed her expression into one of calm. "Do not make light of this. She needs help. She needs something to steady her nerves."

"She has laudanum."

Catherine shook her head, and the scent of her hair carried to him. A hint of roses. He inhaled, and held it, savoring the moment.

"She has none. I suspect she used what she had some time past. Or perhaps she spilled it. Either way, the bottle is empty." She met his gaze full on, the light hitting her in such a way that the thick, straight veil of her lashes painted faint shadows on her cheeks. "I dislike laudanum. I believe it is a poison," she continued. "At the very least, it does as much harm as good, but in this I feel the choice is clear. She is overset. Frantic. I cannot think what else to do for her."

He heard all she did not say. That Madeline had worsened with his return from London. It was ever so. She did better when he was away. Just as he did better away from her, away from the memories the sight of her stirred and the dark slurry of emotions those memories evoked. He despised those feelings, despised himself for having them.

Because after so many years, he still hated her for what she had done.

Catherine shook her head. "Send for whoever set the splints on Peg's fingers."

"That would be unwise."

"Why? You cannot accuse *him* of incompetence. The splints were perfectly applied."

"Madeline would not like it."

"Oh, you are impossible. Why ever not?"

"Because *I* set the splints on Peg's fingers. Without a doubt, I am the last person Madeline would wish to attend her." He shrugged. "Besides, I have no laudanum."

Nor would he ever. Laudanum. Opium. He would rather suffer the pain of a thousand knives than take something that would steal his rational thoughts.

Her brows lifted and she slanted him a look, as though measuring the truth of his words. "You set Peg's broken hand? How did you learn to do that?"

I read about it. Any book I could find. It was the only way to hold fast to my sanity. I can set a break and—theoretically—apply any number of poultices. I even know the names of every bone in the body. And I am versed in the best way to rotate crops, and the theoretical process of treating a hatband with mercury. I am a veritable fount of information. But he told her none of that.

Instead, he said, "Madeline will not want to see Dr. Graves. She is terrified of him. With just reason." He recalled that Mrs. Bell had last summoned Dr. Graves without Gabriel's knowledge or presence here at Cairncroft. There had been no one to speak for his cousin, except Madeline herself, and that had been a road to certain disaster. "On his last visit, the good doctor applied his lancets with great zeal and bled her enough to fill three saucers.

She was insensate for a day and a night. I almost believed she would not awaken."

A part of me hoped she would not. How perverse that he both hoped his cousin would wither and die, and felt responsible for keeping her alive and well.

The fact that she had been bled—a knife inserted in her flesh to slit her vein—troubled him. He had a particular abhorrence for that specific treatment, and though he bore her no love, he despised the fact that such quackery had been carried out in his home, on his cousin, without his knowledge or permission. It would not happen again.

Catherine was silent a moment, and then, her words echoing his thoughts, she said, "Then we shall have to make certain he does not do so again."

"We? Are we a unit, then, Catherine?" Gabriel challenged her for the pure enjoyment of watching flames spark in her night-dark eyes. He lowered his voice. "A team?"

He had meant only to unsettle her with that proposition, but oddly, it appealed. For a solitary creature, he was illogically drawn to the idea of a pairing with Catherine Weston.

Catherine coaxed a little tea through Madeline's dry, chapped lips, tipping the silver teaspoon so the milky, warm liquid poured through. Madeline swallowed, staring straight ahead. Some of the tea dribbled down the side of her chin and dripped to the pristine white sheets that were pulled up above her breasts.

Earlier in the day, the maid, Susan, had brought an unexpected letter from Mrs. Northrop. But Madeline had required Catherine's full attention, for she had been fretful and plaintive. Catherine was loath to leave her unattended, and so she had not had opportunity to sit down and read the missive as yet. She had had only a moment to hurry to her own chamber, tuck the letter in the front of a book for safekeeping, then return to Madeline's side. There she had remained all day, save for a quick foray downstairs to waylay St. Aubyn when she had spied him from the window late in the afternoon, riding back from an outing.

Thoughts of that encounter were disturbing in the extreme. There had been desire, blatant *lust*, in St. Aubyn's amber gaze, and in response, a disturbing awareness had uncoiled in her belly.

In future, she would be wiser and make a greater effort to avoid him.

Setting aside the tea, she glanced at the window. Dusk was upon them, fingers of red and orange creeping across the sky, heralding the night. She could only hope Dr. Graves would come soon.

"They come through the walls," Madeline whispered, drawing Catherine's attention.

"What comes through the walls, dear? The noise of the servants?"

"No." Madeline turned her face to the side, and Catherine thought that was the end of it, but then she spoke once more, her tone forlorn. "Dark creatures. All manner of horned and hooved things. They crawl through openings in the walls when you are not here. They poke me and prod me. They pinch. You see?" Madeline dragged her arm from beneath the covers and feebly pushed at the sleeve of her nightrail until her forearm was bare. "Do you see?" she asked again.

Catherine stared at the smooth, unmarked skin. There was no bruise, no evidence of a pinch. What to say?

Madeline's gaze locked on hers and for a moment she did not appear lost in madness. She appeared perfectly coherent and lucid. "They are his minions. His army of demons that crawls about and does his bidding."

"Whose army?" But Catherine already suspected Madeline's answer.

"Gabriel's. He wants to punish me."

"Punish you for what?" Catherine asked, her tone hushed.

"For what I did to him." Madeline closed her eyes, and let her head fall back. "For the tales I told."

A chill raised the fine hairs at Catherine's nape. The tales she told. What tales might those be?

As she had done more than once since that day in the garden, Catherine thought of Madeline's garbled story about a dead girl covered in blood.

"What tales?"

Madeline opened her eyes. "It was my fault they sent him away, but what was I to do? I only told what I saw. The terrible things I saw. He killed them. Those tiny, helpless birds. And then—" She broke off and pressed her lips together, her gaze darting to the door.

Catherine stared at her, appalled. "Tell me about the birds, Madeline," she prodded gently, choosing the least probing question to open her inquiry.

But Madeline fell silent then, her breathing rapid and shallow. Catherine lifted the teacup and spoon.

"No more," Madeline murmured, turning her face away from Catherine's attempts to coax the tepid liquid past her lips. "I am so tired. Only let me sleep a little."

"I shall close the drape."

"No. I can sleep better in the light. I told you, at night or in the gloom they come, crawling from the shadows and I am too afraid to even close my eyes. I only lie here and wait for them to become brave enough to take me. They will feed upon me. Gnaw at my bones."

Recognizing the futility of any attempt to convince Madeline that nothing crawled through the walls, Catherine drew near and vowed instead, "I shall not let them. I shall stay right there"—she gestured at a chair beside the window—"and guard you as you sleep."

"Will you?" Madeline asked, her eyes widening, hope sparking. "Will you keep me safe?"

The question twisted in Catherine's heart like a dull blade. She could keep no one safe. She had not even kept herself safe. She had failed to keep—

No. She would not let those thoughts surface to destroy her.

"Of course I shall keep you safe," she lied. She was very good at it now. Lying. Funny, as a child, she had held assiduously to the truth. The one constant in her life. Her honesty. Now she did not even have that.

A soft knock sounded at the door and Catherine crossed to open it.

"I brought the broth, miss, just as you asked," the maid said. "Where would you like it?"

Catherine glanced back over her shoulder. Madeline did not stir. "Set it on the table, please."

The maid did as she was bidden, then left, closing the door softly behind her.

Madeline's chest rose and fell in shallow, huffing breaths. If she was not yet fully asleep, she was on her way to it. Catherine let her be, knowing that Madeline would not be convinced to taste the broth even if she tried to rouse her. And by the time she awoke, the broth would be cold. She would use that as her reason not to eat it. If Catherine summoned a maid to bring a fresh, hot bowl later, Madeline would claim it was too late in the day, or too early, that she was either too tired or too anxious. She was ever ready with an array of excuses.

Her friend's despair gnawed at Catherine, for Madeline had done so well during St. Aubyn's absence. His return had brought this heavy melancholy that did not dissipate, and Catherine was almost tempted to suggest to him that he travel to London once more and leave them in peace.

His mere presence unsettled her almost as much as it did Madeline, but in a far different way. How horrific was it that she had come to anticipate the moments of conversation she had with him? To savor the glances she stole. To drink in the play of light across his features that painted his dark brown lashes gold, and accented the hollows of his cheeks and the clean line of his jaw. To watch his lips form words. To wonder what his mouth would feel like, moving on her own.

What did that say about her nature? She did not want to think on it too carefully.

Leaning her shoulder against the window frame, she folded her arms and stared out, the last of the day giving way to the darkening night, the outline of the moon and the first evening stars winking to life.

What tales had Madeline told, and what tragic consequences had resulted in the burden of guilt she carried?

Catherine wanted to shake her friend awake and demand answers, but she would never do such an unkind thing. She must wait on Madeline's whim for explanations. Impatience would not serve her in this, but she found she could not squelch it. It seemed that when it came to Gabriel St. Aubyn, she was parched for information and insights.

A short time later, a closed carriage rolled slowly up the drive, the cool moonlight illuminating its progress, dancing off the shiny black surface. The doctor had come. She was glad of it.

She watched the carriage for a moment more and then her gaze drifted to the dark line of the woods. Were the trees thicker tonight? More sinister? She made an odd sound between a huff and a laugh, deriding herself for her ridiculous notions.

Then, perhaps conjured by her mood and expectations, a man stepped from the woods. No, not stepped. *Glided.* As though he slid on ice or floated on air. His tall frame was clothed in dark garb, a long coat or a cloak that billowed slightly as the breeze lifted the hem, his head covered by a low crowned hat. He was shadow on shadow, barely there.

Catherine blinked and blinked again, certain that she had summoned a specter simply because she expected one. Her time at Cairncroft Abbey and Madeline's half-formed tales had made her overly imaginative. How many times now had she seen this wraith that lurked at the edge of the wood, then took on the guise of Gabriel St. Aubyn?

In her absurd fancy, she was akin to Madeline with her talk of demons and monsters that crawled out of the walls. Only Catherine's monsters crawled out of the woods.

Then the man removed his hat and turned his face toward her. He was far away. Far enough that she could be certain only of the color of his hair—blond—and the fact that it was either cut short or tied back. From this distance she could not tell with any degree of confidence.

Was it St. Aubyn? Did this game of peek-a-boo in the forest have some purpose?

The carriage rolled closer, distracting her and blocking her view, and after it passed the point where the man had stood, she saw he was there no longer.

Perhaps he never had been.

In that moment, she wondered if Mrs. Bell's whispered warnings had borne fruit, if she was now subject to the same malady that afflicted Madeline, or simply newly prone to illogical imaginings.

At length, the coach rocked to a stop and an older man climbed down, illuminated by the spill of light from the lantern on the side of his conveyance. He was rail thin and very tall, dressed all in black, his pate bald and bare to the elements. She wondered that he did not wear a hat.

He paused there and looked about, and it was then that Catherine noticed a black leather bag in his hand.

Wrapping her arms about herself, Catherine shuddered. The sight of that bag elicited a slew of unpleasant memories, for she knew only too well the instruments of torture it held. After her parents' deaths, Jasper Hunt had come and taken his inherited and rightful place as the new Baron Sunderley. He had taken her home from her, and anything that was entailed. The creditors had taken the rest. It seemed her father had not been particularly good at managing the family fortune. Fortunately for Jasper, he had money of his own, and the title had simply been the jewel in his crown. How kind she had thought him when he let her stay on in the room of her childhood.

He had claimed that he took his responsibilities seriously. All his responsibilities, including her, the destitute daughter of the previous baron. She was family, after all. His distant cousin.

At first, she had only been grateful. Then she had thought she was in love. It was not until much later that she had learned to be afraid. Of him. Of the cadaverous doctor he summoned when he deemed her in need of care. Or discipline.

With a sharp breath, she dragged her thoughts to the

present. She must not allow her own prejudices to hamper Madeline's recovery. She had no reason to think ill of Dr. Graves—who turned now to close the carriage door—no reason to assume he was other than professional and even kind.

Still, she meant to be there every moment that the doctor was with Madeline, just as she had promised. It would take an act of force to make her leave the room, and even then, she would claw and fight against removal. She could only hope it did not come to that.

She was about to turn from the window when St. Aubyn exited the front of the house and strode across the drive. The two men shook hands and spoke. The doctor's pinched expression was clear to her, illuminated by the carriage light, but she could see only a bit of the side of St. Aubyn's face, not enough to gather anything his features might betray.

Of course, in all likelihood, he would betray nothing at all. He never did . . . except earlier that afternoon, when his expression had betrayed his lust. That recollection made her uneasy.

Her gaze slid to the place she had seen the unidentified watcher at the edge of the woods. There was no one there now. But as she had done once before, she made mental measure of the distance, and felt certain that St. Aubyn could not have traversed it in time to be at the front door now, nor could he have crossed the open space unseen.

Which left her with a puzzle.

Angled toward each other, deep in conversation, the two men stood by the carriage for a few moments. Then St. Aubyn nodded at something the doctor said and both turned their faces toward Madeline's window. Of course, it was perfectly reasonable for them to be discussing Madeline. The doctor had come specifically to see her, after all.

Yet Catherine could not help but feel suspicious of exactly what it was they discussed.

The doctor turned away, but St. Aubyn stared up for a moment more. He saw her there. She had no doubt of it. He spoke in reply to the doctor's words, but his gaze remained fixed upon her where she stood framed by the heavy drapery, backlit by the light of the fire and the candle flame that writhed and jumped.

A step to the side and she was shielded by the curtain, unseen from below but able to continue watching the two of them, unobserved. St. Aubyn stared at the place she had stood for a slow count of ten, then he spoke to the doctor once more and together they walked toward the front door.

Turning from the window, Catherine found that Madeline was awake. She had levered herself to a sitting position and her eyes were fever bright.

"Do not let him hurt me," she pleaded, though her tone suggested that she believed nothing could save her from that.

"No, I will let no one hurt you," Catherine reassured her again.

"You will not leave me?"

"Not for a moment."

Masculine voices echoed from the hallway moments later. A knock sounded on the door and Catherine opened it to find that both the doctor and St. Aubyn waited there.

"May we?" St. Aubyn asked.

She drew the door fully open and stepped aside to let them enter. Her nose twitched as Dr. Graves passed. He smelled of sweat and camphor, and she saw that his hands were not clean.

"Here is Dr. Graves," St. Aubyn said, though it was apparent that Madeline knew very well who he was and had no need for this introduction.

Dr. Graves made a short bow, first to Madeline, then to Catherine. He set his black case on the small table beside the bed, and Madeline turned her head to stare at it, her blue eyes shimmering with horror and fear.

The doctor reached out and made to take her wrist in his hand, but she flinched away. He froze with arm outstretched, exchanging a glance with St. Aubyn.

"Will you be so kind as to afford us a little privacy?" the doctor asked. His tone was clipped, his voice rough. Impatience hung on every syllable.

Catherine was not certain if the doctor spoke to her, to St. Aubyn, or to the both of them, but she moved only as far as the foot of the bed while St. Aubyn inclined his head and went to stand by the open door.

Dr. Graves looked at her with a startled expression. "If you please . . ."

"I do not please," Catherine replied. "Madeline has requested my presence. I am a comfort to her. I shall remain exactly where I am."

The doctor blinked and cast a look at St. Aubyn, who was half turned toward them, watching. His expression was as bland as boiled custard, but his eyes glittered with interest. His gaze slid to Catherine's and he raised a straight, tawny brow.

"I must object," the doctor blustered.

"I must insist," St. Aubyn interjected, darkly soft. "Please, proceed, but I will stay here and Miss Weston will stay there and there will be no discussion about it."

The unflinching assertion should have been a comfort. Instead, it sent horror crawling along Catherine's spine. *No discussion.* Of course. St. Aubyn could do almost anything he wished with Madeline, and no one would gainsay him. There was no one to protect her, just as there had been no one to protect Catherine when she was similarly ensconced in a powerful and autocratic man's home. A home that had once been her own.

The similarities were chilling.

Dr. Graves altered his expression then, molding it into a parody of kindness and concern, one that rang purely false. Catherine did not trust him, did not believe the persona he projected, but she made no indication of that by gesture or expression, wary of unsettling Madeline who watched her with frightened eyes.

"Now," said Dr. Graves, putting down the sheet enough that he could grasp Madeline's wrist and hold it. She let him do it, though her muscles were rigid beneath her skin, and her jaw set tense and hard. "Your cousin says you are not eating, and that you sleep poorly. Is that so?"

Madeline said nothing, merely stared straight ahead, small shudders racking her frame.

"She was in fine health for the full week after I arrived," Catherine said, drawing the doctor's attention. Her gaze flicked to St. Aubyn. "Then she began to decline the week after that until she has come to this point."

The doctor frowned. "Does she eat in your presence?"

"She did. But now she does not."

"I see," Dr. Graves said and nodded, as though the information was of great import. Again, he and St. Aubyn exchanged a look. "Well, she must be eating at some time, for she is well fleshed." He reached up and dragged the neck of her nightrail a bit to one side, baring her collarbone. "Her cheeks are not sunken, and her clavicles do not protrude."

Instinctively, Catherine stepped forward as Madeline flinched from the doctor's touch. But she saw the point he made: Madeline was pale and wan, but she did not appear malnourished, for there was some flesh on her bones. Catherine was glad of it.

"She ate well while"—she cast a glance at St. Aubyn—"Sir Gabriel was away."

"Hmm." Dr. Graves turned to his bag and withdrew a black box. Catherine regarded it in distaste. A scarificator. Inside the box were dozens of sharp blades that would cut Madeline's skin and make her bleed. With an involuntary movement, Catherine's hand shifted to her own arm where she yet wore the faint marks of her experience with that particular instrument of torture. Reaching into the bag once more, the doctor removed a shallow glass cup.

"I'll need the fire stoked," he said. "The cup must be warmed to draw out the blood."

Catherine's gaze jerked to Madeline's face. She lay there, eyes closed, lips taut and white. Unable to fathom the benefit of cutting and bleeding her, Catherine stepped forward, intent on arguing with the doctor. To her shock, St. Aubyn was there first.

"No," he said, his tone brooking no argument. His expression was as cool and blank as ever she had seen it, but somehow, though she could see no evidence of it, she sensed his fury.

The doctor glanced up at him, pausing in his preparations. "I beg your pardon?"

"I do not wish you to bleed my cousin. Only give her something to help her sleep."

"She must be bled, Sir Gabriel. If it is the scarificator you object to, I shall use the lancet or the leech."

"You will use none of them. I abhor this ridiculous process, and I will not allow it in my home," St. Aubyn murmured, the very softness of his tone bolstering the words with steel. He did not need to bluster and shout. A whisper from his lips was effective enough. The doctor took a step back.

Catherine wondered if St. Aubyn would simply reach over and snap the man's fingers if he refused to acquiesce. She did not doubt that St. Aubyn would have his way by whatever means necessary. The thought ought to horrify. And, to a degree, it did. But there was comfort, too, in the knowledge that he would stick to his word and not allow the doctor free rein in Madeline's care.

"Why did you summon me if you do not intend to let me treat her?" Dr. Graves asked peevishly.

"I intend to let you treat her. I do not intend to let you bleed her or otherwise perpetrate quackery upon her person."

"Quackery!" Dr. Graves drew himself to his full height, two spots of color burning in his pasty cheeks.

A long moment passed where neither man spoke, and then with a sound that was somewhere between a grunt and an oath, the doctor dropped all he had removed back into the bag. He delved deep to draw out a brown bottle, and set it on the table with a definite thud.

"A few drops in a glass of water or wine is enough," he said through tight lips. "More than that and she may sleep entirely too long. Sleep her life away. I have seen it often enough."

"Thank you," St. Aubyn said. "I shall see you out."

They left without any further conversation, the doctor's posture stiff and unyielding, fury sparking in his gaze.

Catherine watched them go and listened until the sound of their footsteps faded away. Then she stepped close to the bed and brushed Madeline's hair back from her forehead. Her skin was clammy.

"I was afraid." Madeline shuddered. "I hate to be bled. I hate the sight of it dripping into the bowl. I hate the smell of it, like old pennies." She shuddered again. "I thought he would let Dr. Graves do it. He has let him before."

Catherine stared at her a moment, noting that her words conflicted with the story St. Aubyn had offered. According to Madeline, he had let her be bled. But according to what he had said earlier in the day, it was Mrs. Bell who had summoned the doctor while St. Aubyn was away.

Crossing to the washstand, Catherine pondered the contradiction. She poured water into the bowl and carried it to the bed, along with a small towel. She dipped the cloth and wrung it out, then smoothed it across Madeline's brow.

"Are you certain it was Sir Gabriel who allowed the doctor to bleed you on his last visit? It was my understanding that Mrs. Bell summoned him that day."

Madeline only stared at her, a wounded look in her eyes, as though Catherine's questions somehow breached her trust.

After a moment and some consideration, Catherine tried a different tack. "Dr. Graves appears to be a man who is used to taking charge. I suspect he is unaccustomed to being gainsaid."

Madeline continued to stare at her, guileless blue eyes, wide and clear. "He is my cousin's minion. As is the housekeeper and the groundskeeper and the head groom. They watch me. They keep me here against my will. They torment me at every turn." Closing her eyes, she was quiet for a moment, then she said in a whisper, "One day they will kill me. If not by poison then by some other means."

The certainty in her tone made Catherine wary. Not because she necessarily believed such a thing, but because Madeline clearly believed it.

"Madeline, I am here now. I will let no one harm you." She paused, formulating the questions in her mind, wishing to pose them in a way that would do the least harm. At length, she asked, "Why do you think such a thing? Why would your cousin do you harm? What benefit to him?"

"Why would he do me harm?" The words came low and hard, and Madeline panted sharply as though struggling for control. Then one side of her mouth quirked in an unpleasant smirk. "Revenge for what I did to him. And as to the benefit . . . Cairncroft Abbey is entailed and so it is his, but the fortune is not. He has funds only because he is trustee of what is *mine*. My cousin is poor as a church mouse and, though I despise lending voice to such crass truth, I am rich, Catherine. What better reason for murder than greed?" Her tone was calm, matter-of-fact, making her assertions all the more dreadful. Catherine searched for some words of comfort, a way to convince Madeline that surely she was mistaken, but a part of her could not completely discount the possibility that she was not mistaken at all.

Was it only a form of madness talking?

"He only bides his time," Madeline continued, her gaze never wavering, "and waits for the perfect opportunity, one that will paint my death in a believable and credulous light."

Her eyes were clear, her words lucid, and in that moment, Catherine thought Madeline perfectly sane.

Chapter Ten

Alone in her chamber at last, Catherine set her candle on the table. Troubling thoughts gnawed at her. Madeline's assertions. The doctor's visit. The way St. Aubyn had looked at her with something primitive alive in his gaze—unveiled lust. The recollection made her shiver even now. What was she to do with that, and with the answering call she felt singing in her blood? She was not such a fool as to repeat the mistakes of her past, to allow a man, any man, such power over her ever again. Least of all a man who was so shrouded in mystery that she could not hope to see clearly through the fog.

Madeline's accusations against him, her assertions that he would commit murder to gain a fortune, were distressing in the extreme. There were many people who would do exactly that. Kill for money. Kill for pleasure. Kill for revenge.

People killed for any number of reasons. She knew that only too well. But were Madeline's accusations true, or the fancies of a troubled mind?

At the moment, Catherine had no way to know with any confidence. And what sort of creature did it make her that she was attracted to such a man? Fascinated by him?

Seeking to divert her thoughts, she opened the cover of the book where she had secreted Mrs. Northrop's neglected letter. It was the volume of *Frankenstein* that St. Aubyn had lent her. The letter from Mrs. Northrop lay there, innocuous and inoffensive. But only because it was as yet unopened. Catherine had no doubt that the contents would be far from dull, for what purpose could such a venomous woman have in writing to her, other than to cause some sort of distress?

Should she open it now, or wait for morning?

The thought made a short huff of laughter erupt. As if she could find it in herself to wait. Perhaps the contents would provide a necessary diversion and keep her from spending the night tossing and turning and pursuing avenues of contemplation that invariably led back to her enigmatic host.

Lifting the letter, she flipped it over and traced the tip of her index finger along the flowing script of Mrs. Northrop's name and direction, stark against the pale paper. Their acrimonious parting had been accompanied by Mrs. Northrop's insistence that if she never saw Catherine again, it would be a fine thing. She had refused to provide a reference and had only grudgingly provided the last of Catherine's wages. There was no imaginable reason for her to send a correspondence. Which left only an unimaginable one.

With a shudder, Catherine set the letter down, then reached over and drew back the curtains, letting the moonlight come through the panes. She stepped around the small table, unlatched the window, and pushed it open a hair, enough to let the fresh night air kiss her skin. The maids thought her preference for open windows to be exceedingly odd. The bravest one had warned her that outdoor air carried miasma and evil humors that would only make her ill. Catherine disdained the possibility. She could not see how it was perfectly acceptable to walk outdoors, but not acceptable to allow a bit of the outdoors in.

Besides, she had spent enough time as a prisoner in a locked room, working the window latches until her nails tore and her fingers bled. She had never succeeded in getting them open, for they had been painted shut with exactly that purpose in mind.

She cringed away from the memory, and the tumult of other, darker recollections that would tumble free if she let them. The experience had left her with a distinct aversion to closed doors, closed windows, heavy draperies, and stale air—which was why it had made it so easy to recognize the same aversion in Gabriel St. Aubyn. Had she not known the signs so well, she likely would have missed them.

Settling in a chair, she moved the candle so it was away from the draft, then opened the letter from Mrs. Northrop, noticing that a newspaper clipping had been included. She unfolded the single page, revealing script that was clear and precise, if slightly slanted.

Dear Miss Weston,

Our parting was less than convivial, yet I do not have the temperament to carry a grudge.

Only one sentence in, and already a lie. During the term of her employment, Catherine had been subjected to Mrs. Northrop's endless list of grievances against all those who had wronged her since childhood. It was fascinating how often people saw themselves completely in opposition to how others saw them.

For some reason, that thought made an image of Gabriel St. Aubyn fill her mind. Did he see himself as she saw him, cold, aloof, his secrets hidden beneath layers of rigid control? And why did such a man appeal to her so? Perhaps because the only man she had ever believed she loved had been prone to fits of passion and terrifying, deadly rage.

Memories broke over her like a crashing, storm-stirred surf. She wrapped her arms about herself, holding the waves at bay, her determination a dam against the flood. After a moment, she made a conscious effort to relax her shoulders and the rigid muscles of her back, to uncoil her arms and force her attention to the page once more.

I forgive you your impertinence and poor judgment, and as a gesture of goodwill, I write you with news that must surely be of interest. Please do not trouble yourself to reply.

Martha Grimsby is dead. She was murdered.

"Wha—?" Catherine read the sentences a second time and a third, the letters like little black bugs on the page. Martha? Dead?

No. Surely it could not be true. She had seen Martha shortly before she had departed London.

The letter fluttered as her hand trembled, horror sinking its talons bone deep. She felt ill, shaken and clammy, nausea roiling in her belly. What ugly game did Mrs. Northrop play at? Why would she write such a foul thing?

Heart hammering, Catherine reread that line a fourth time, then continued on, searching for some indication that the assertion was a macabre joke.

Martha Grimsby is dead. She was murdered.

There, I have said it outright. The quickest cut is the kindest. Do you not think so? I recall having a rather horrid Affliction of the skin as a child, a vile, weeping Carbuncle. Dr. Marks was quite decisive in his action and his insistence that the lancing be done with all haste and precision. I never forgot that lesson, and consider it one of great value. Hence, I share it with you.

I have taken the clipping from the Times *and included it herein.*

Cordially,
Agnes Northrop

Catherine swallowed convulsively, her throat tight, her chest twisted in a knot. She could not breathe. Could not think. Martha dead. Murdered. Why? How?

It took a moment for her to realize that the low, plaintive moan she heard was coming from her own lips, that she had crumpled the letter into a little ball in her fist. With meticulous care, she smoothed the hated paper flat on the table, her palm stroking the creases until it lay before her like a dried leaf, the edges curled and bent.

She took the newspaper clipping and unfolded it, her hands shaking as though she were struck by a palsy. Almost did she tear the paper, so jerky were her movements. She glanced at the date—March 29, 1828—and the headline—WATERSIDE MURDER. With her vision blurred by tears, she read the whole of it, blinking again and again as the letters swam before her eyes.

Henry Day, Deputy Coroner, opened an inquiry respecting the death of one Martha Grimsby, the woman who was discovered on Friday last, at the London Docks, Wapping, with multiple stabs to her body.

Catherine jerked as though a knife had been stabbed in her own breast. In that moment, she saw Martha as a child, laughing as she and Catherine ran through the garden a lifetime past, when Martha's father had been a groom at Catherine's father's estate.

Closing her eyes against the pain that twisted inside her like a wrung-out rag, Catherine struggled to make sense of this horrific news. Was it not enough that Martha's life had carried her to St. Giles, to poverty and desperation, by day running a school for the local children in a dingy room, at night facing the need to sell her body to survive? Did she have to die like this?

Like *this*?

Feeling as though a hard blow had been struck to the center of her back and all the air driven from her lungs, she opened her eyes and forced herself to read on.

Alfred Barrett, waterside laborer, came upon the place when he went to seek for work. He passed the spot even as George Reese arrived and the two found the deceased, lying on her back in a shallow grave, the soil of which had been washed away in a particularly violent downpour. Both men believe they would not have noticed her there save for the fact that early in the morning, a load of timber was moved unexpectedly, baring the place she lay to passersby. There was no blood, that they could see. Frightened, they did not examine her but instead immediately gave notice to the police. The witnesses saw no footmarks in the mud, nor did they find any weapon.

Dr. J.R. Cuddy, of 73, House-lane, said that he was called to the deceased, and found her dead. Her clothes had been cut away from the torso, and the chest and abdominal cavities opened with a sharp instrument, without precision. On postmortem examination of the body, he found the lungs, liver, stomach, and intestine removed, again, without precision. The heart was untouched. Dr. Cuddy thought these wounds had not been inflicted during life.

Catherine forced herself to inhale against the oppressive weight that bore down on her. The wounds had not been inflicted during life. Martha had suffered so much, but she had not been alive to feel her organs sliced from her body.

That was Catherine's one comfort, that her friend's body had been mutilated only *after* her death. Cold comfort it was.

Tears welled over, trickling down her cheeks, dripping onto the backs of her hands. She stared down at them, aghast, knowing the battle was lost even as she fought to hold back the torrent, to remain composed. Her efforts were to no avail.

Grief swelled beyond the confines she imposed, oozing through cracks in her façade, and for the first time in six long years, Catherine allowed herself to cry. Not only for Martha, but for the child Catherine had borne and never allowed herself to mourn. And for the man she had killed because he had killed her son.

In the dark hallway, Gabriel stood outside Catherine's door. She was crying. The sounds were muffled, as though she struggled to suffocate them into silence. Something inside him shifted and turned, an unpleasant and wholly uncharacteristic instinct of chivalry that insisted he step inside and offer comfort of some sort.

He had no idea how.

What did one offer in the face of another's pain? Here was a lesson he had failed to learn . . . no . . . a lesson he had never been taught. In the place where he had grown from boy to young man, there had been only lessons in survival. Hide behind an emotionless mask. Evade. Lie. Show only what they expected. The level of his suffering had been determined by his ability to guess exactly what they wished to see and hear. If he was right, they left him alone. If he was wrong, there were all manner of tortures and deprivation. He had striven to be right more often than wrong.

The sound of Catherine's sobs confused him. He wanted to comfort her as much as he wanted to avoid the necessity of doing so.

Almost did he turn and walk away. She would never be the wiser, never know he had heard her private sorrow. But some intangible force drew him to stay. His knock went unanswered, and so he went beyond any acceptable boundary of propriety, turned the knob and opened the door, freezing in place at the sight that greeted him.

Catherine sat in a chair by the window, her back hunched, her head resting in her bent arms, supported by a small table. A single candle sent shadows dipping and swaying along the walls. Through the open curtains streamed a cool, pale swath of moonlight that fell across her upper body, leaving the rest of her in shadow. Her shoulders shook as she sobbed, her grief curling her fingers against the tabletop, straining her muscles, carving her in stark, tense lines.

He crossed the room until he stood behind her, his hand outstretched, palm down. He hesitated, not touching, and finally simply rested his hand on her nape.

She jerked and snuffled and raised her head, gasping to see him looming over her. In this moment, she was not beautiful. Her nose was red, her eyes and lips puffy, her cheeks wet with her tears. In this moment, her mask did not slip. It was ripped away, leaving her naked and bare.

In her wide, shimmering eyes, he saw all the unfettered emotions he would never know in himself—grief, horror, desperation, myriad sentiments, vast as the stars—and he was fascinated, both attracted and repelled. He had thought her exactly like him. Damaged. Flawed. Unable to feel.

But she was not. He could see now that she was not.

She was something far more intriguing than that, for she obviously experienced emotion on a deep, visceral level, but somehow managed to control it to an outstanding degree.

In contrast, what little he felt was like a world viewed through sheer fabric. Fear, joy, sadness . . . all were tempered by the walls he erected. He knew such emotions existed. He knew they could be felt, saw the expressions on the faces of others, recognized the situations that summoned specific responses. He analyzed them, but he did not *feel* them, not to any significant degree. His emotions were not buried, not hidden; they had never had the opportunity to evolve. The feelings he saw in others were not part of what he was.

For a long moment, he simply stared down at her, saying nothing, aware that she studied him as he studied her. Reaching out, he touched his thumb to her wet cheek.

Tears. She had shed enough to fill a bucket. He stepped away as she watched him with wary uncertainty, crossed to the washstand and poured a glass of water from the pitcher. Then he took up a folded cloth, wet it, and wrung it out.

Three strides took him back to her side. She was exactly where he had left her, sitting in the stripe of moonlight, her porcelain skin made all the paler by the cool light. He offered her first the cloth—she swiped it over her face and handed it back to him—and then the glass. She drank the water greedily, in thirsty gulps, and set the empty glass on the table with precise, careful movements, as though she feared slamming it down and shattering it into a million shards.

Dropping her hands to her lap, she stared straight ahead, her posture brittle. He thought that the wrong word would shatter *her* into a million shards.

"Catherine," he murmured, reaching down, braceleting her wrist with his fingers. His thumb traced the delicate bumps and dips of her bones, the softness of her skin.

He tightened his grip and drew her to her feet. She allowed this liberty, unresisting, the silence disturbed only by the rustle of her skirt as she rose.

Then, as though waking from a daze, she *did* resist, tugging on her wrist, trying to pull away. He could not say why he did not let her go.

Her head tipped back; her lashes lifted. The moon painted a pale wash on her face, leaving her eyes too dark, too big, shimmering with the tears that had yet to dry. But she did not cry now. She gathered herself, her chin angling up, her posture adjusting as she visibly called forth her inner reserves of strength. Her back arched a little as she strained away, and her arm was stiff and straight against his. Only the quick, hard pulse at her throat betrayed her unease.

Her eyes narrowed, and her features changed from open to guarded. Her mask slid into place. He found he regretted that, though he would not have expected such.

With a last sharp tug, she tried again to pull free.

And this time, he let her go, let her step away, though it went fully against the unfamiliar instinct to draw her close, wrap her in his embrace, and hold her safe from anything that would harm her. Even himself.

Like a slumbering beast, something deep inside him unfurled, a need to claim, to mark, to protect. Primitive. Dark. He understood it not at all. Glancing down, he took refuge in the simple act of lifting the scrap of newspaper from the table, tilting it to the light, and reading the first bit. He saw immediately that he had no need to read it all. He already knew a great deal about Martha Grimsby's murder.

"Is it the murder itself that has you upset, or something more?" He looked up. "The method of it? The organs taken?"

She took a sharp breath.

Ah. His questions only served to distress her more. A tactical error on his part.

He stepped toward her only the single pace that she had stepped away earlier, and when she did not retreat, another pace. They were so close that all that separated them was their clothing and a thin span of night-cooled air. So close that he could feel the graze of her breasts against his chest with each breath she took, feel the trembling in her body as he took her hand in his, drew it down to his side and held it there, shifting them closer still.

Her breathing grew short and rapid. Her head tipped down so she stared straight ahead at his chest rather than his face.

"How do you know there were organs taken? You barely glanced at the page . . . certainly you could not have read it in its entirety." Her voice was roughened by the violence of the sobs that had racked her earlier. He wondered how long she had sat here in the near dark, sobbing her heart out before he had found her.

For a moment, he said nothing, weighing all possible answers, and finally decided on, "This clipping is from a paper days old." He let it flutter to the tabletop once more. "But there is little new information in the more recent reports."

"Oh." She blinked and shook her head mere inches to either side. Then she wet her lips and gave a soft sniffle. "I knew her. The murdered woman. Martha Grimsby. I knew her as a child."

Seconds ticked past. Tipping her head back, she met his gaze, waiting for him to respond, to offer some appropriate rejoinder.

"You feel her loss. You regret it." The words were not enough. He saw it in her eyes. For an instant, the silence roared as he searched . . . and then he came away with the fitting response, the exact words that had been said to him at a time of loss. "My condolences."

She swallowed. Nodded. "Thank you."

Dark lashes swept down, veiling her thoughts. But he knew what they were, read her pain in every tense line of her lush form. He wanted to take her suffering, pull it from her, swallow it into himself where it would not matter anymore.

Her lashes lifted and she looked directly at him, into his eyes. Perhaps even deeper than that.

He wanted to kiss her, to drag her against him and put his lips on hers, to know the hot, sweet taste of her mouth, her tongue.

It was not the right time. Even he, with his shallow grasp of the nuances of emotion, understood that it was the wrong time. But he let instinct guide his hand as he reached out to draw the pins from her hair, letting the thick, heavy waves tumble free over her shoulders and down her back.

There. He liked that, the feel of her silky hair against his palm, the look of her with her hair loose and mussed.

Her eyes and lips were still puffy from her tears, and

he ached to kiss her lids, her mouth, her throat. To lick the salt from her skin. He thought she would not welcome it. But still the urge swelled and grew. He knew nothing of comfort, but he thought that were their positions reversed, were he the one to feel pain, he would crave the succor of her touch. A shocking realization, for he could not recall having such a thought in all his adult life.

Catherine fisted her hands in her skirt and stepped away, suddenly wary. St. Aubyn filled the space, inhabiting it, owning it. Even in the dimness, he was painted in shades of gold and honey and finely brewed ale. Yet the meager light suited him, for he was more akin to shadow than light, regardless of his sun-bright beauty. He was a man who looked nothing like he ought to. If appearance reflected inner self, he would be cast in the smoke and pewter of shadows rather than the gilded gold of sunlight.

That thought was enough to stir fear in her gut, to rouse memories of another man whose appearance had so poorly matched his temperament and secrets. A man who had cost her everything. The worst of it was, she had chosen to trust Jasper Hunt, to love him. In the end, he had broken her, shaped her to obey. By the time she had understood that, it was too late for her. For her baby.

The woman she was now had risen from the ashes of the girl she had been. The woman she was now would not be lulled and tricked by anyone. She was wiser than that. She would force herself to be wiser than that.

"What are you doing here, in my chamber?" she asked, aware even as she did so that the question was belated. She ought to have bid him leave the second he pushed open the door. And now it was too late, because even if he turned and left now, she would still have knowledge of the well-hidden part of him that had been driven to offer his own rather restrained form of comfort—a glass of water for her parched throat, a cool cloth for her fevered brow. He had taken liberties, crossed boundaries, created an intimacy she did not wish to have with him.

"I heard you. From the hallway." His lips curved in a faint, sardonic smile. "We seem to alternate roles skulking about in the shadows, you and I."

There was that. Strangely, his odd attempt at levity eased the ache in her heart just a little.

"Why were you in the hallway? Only Madeline and I are housed in this wing, and I have doubts that you were on your way for a pleasant visit with your cousin."

He watched her for a moment, assessing, measuring. "I was on my way to make certain that Madeline took the laudanum Graves supplied. A night's rest would benefit her."

His solicitous concern for the cousin he freely admitted he despised seemed odd. She studied him, trying to judge his sincerity.

In the meager light of the moon and the single flickering candle, his hair was gilded, his eyes shadowed. But not so shadowed that she did not read the glint of desire that flared in their amber depths as he dropped his gaze to her lips, her breasts.

"I gave her a dose in a glass of Madeira," she said in a rush, startled and appalled by the answering spark of attraction that flickered in her belly, sending hot tendrils snaking through her limbs. No. She dared not feel this. To give a man such power over her once more—

He kissed her. There was no preamble, no sweet and tentative approach. There was only the heat of his body and the strength of his hands on her arms, holding her as his mouth pressed to hers, hard, hungry. For an instant, she responded. The silk of his tongue in her mouth, the mingling of breath, the scent of his skin, faintly citrus, filled her. There was pleasure here. Primitive, savage pleasure.

Oh, God, how long since she had felt this?

Never. The truth of that was irrefutable.

Whatever stirrings of passion she had felt in her past, it was a mere prelude to the sensations that drowned her now. She had never been kissed so thoroughly, so savagely. So beautifully.

With only a kiss he had found the part of her she thought she had killed. She had been wrong. Her passion was not dead, only sleeping.

Under the press of his lips and the stroke of his tongue she unfurled, the air around them so still it quivered, the storm inside her building until she kissed him back, open-mouthed and hungry. Her fingers twisted in his hair, tugging him down to her as she fed on his strength, his passion, the physical comfort of his hard body and sheltering embrace.

He protected what was his. Coldly. Ruthlessly. She had witnessed that with her own eyes. He would protect her if she were his.

And it was that realization that chilled her, drowning the sharp flare of her passion as quickly as it had come.

She would not do this. Would not put herself in this place. Would never again be any man's possession. His property.

With a gasp, she turned her face away and pressed hard against his chest.

"Catherine," he murmured, his voice low and rough, his lips moving against her throat. "I want you."

I want you.

Memories surged. A man's voice, hard with rage. *I want you. Now. On your knees, my cat.*

She felt sick. Dizzy. The room spinning. It was too much. Too many memories. Too many secrets.

Too many losses and regrets.

She worked so hard to hold them at bay, to cage them where they could not harm her anymore. But with a single kiss, Gabriel St. Aubyn freed them, freed the power of her sexual need, and other things. The need for closeness and comfort and human warmth. All things she no longer deserved.

All things she knew better than to imagine that this man, this particular man, could ever want or provide.

The tumult of her passion, too hard, too swift, died as quickly as it had swelled, replaced by a cold knot of dread. What would he do if she refused?

Break her fingers as that man had broken Peg's? No. She could not imagine that of him.

Break her will, then, as Sunderley had tried to do in the end?

The thought made her ill.

With a desperate cry, she ripped herself from Gabriel's embrace and backed away until she felt the cold wall against her back. Pressing her open palms against the wall, she stood there, panting, wishing he would go, just go. Uncertain what she would do if he stayed, if he bid her disrobe, if he ordered her—

Panic swelled, and she battled it with all she was. She would not succumb. She would never again be so weak and helpless.

And then it came to her, the knowledge of how she could deny him that power. She would initiate the interlude, get it over with, on her terms, and she would hold all emotion at bay, make herself safe.

He watched her with an expression that betrayed nothing

of his thoughts. Was he disappointed? Angry? Not even by the faintest flicker of his lashes did he offer insight.

Feeling as though she was not at all herself, as though she were dreaming or had drunk a measure of Madeline's laudanum, she stared past Gabriel's shoulder, straight ahead at the looking glass above the mantel. She saw her reflection there, her expression blank, her face pale.

Gabriel wanted her? Well, she would let him have her. She would let him take her and then it would be over. The anticipation, the heart-pounding lust. The terror that this act of physical joining would dissolve her, dissolve everything she had worked so hard to become.

She could participate in the physical without offering even a bit of her secret self.

She was stronger now, a different woman. Yes. The phoenix risen from the ashes. And she would do this, face this, and come away stronger still. Men did it all the time. Made physical use of a woman they neither knew nor cared about. She suspected many women did that, as well.

There was her answer. She would become one of those women. He would have her body but nothing more. Those were her terms. It was the most she could offer. And she did not dare examine too closely her reasons for even offering this.

Her anticipation had died with the abrupt slice of a guillotine. But neither was there horror of the coming act, and that was an improvement. She had thought never again to face physical intimacy without clammy palms and cold sweat and roiling nausea deep in her gut.

Reaching up behind her neck, she unclasped her mother's pearls and laid them carefully on the polished mahogany of the table. Next, she tunneled her fingers into her hair, taking the few pins he had missed from the thick mass, setting them down side by side like little soldiers in formation. Another pin and another. Heavy hanks of dark hair tumbled down her back to join the ones Gabriel had freed earlier.

He was watching her. She did not look at him, but she could sense his eyes upon her.

She concentrated on each breath, slow and easy, the pattern of inhalation and exhalation relaxing her. She felt as though she was not there, as though some other person inhabited her skin and went through these motions.

The sexual thrill that had electrified her earlier had disappeared, swallowed by the wave of memories that sucked emotion from her, sopping it up like a bone-dry sponge. There was only the rushing of her blood—was it really loud enough that she could hear it?—and the veil that draped her, insulating her from what was to come.

She knew that only a moment past, she had been frenzied with the need for Gabriel to touch her, ached for the feel of his hands and lips on her. That was gone now, buried beneath the defenses she had taken years to build.

The defenses he had almost breached with a single kiss. She had known from the first moment she saw him that he was dangerous to her.

"What are you doing?" Gabriel's voice came as though from a great distance, low, calm. She liked to hear him speak. There was pleasure in that, at least. She wondered if he would talk as he took her, whisper against her ear, cry out in passion. Or if he would be silent. She thought she might not be able to bear the silence, but she could not imagine him as anything but coldly controlled.

"Removing my clothing," she replied, feeling numb and dead and removed, uncertain she could face this any other way. "Isn't that what you want?"

Gabriel crossed the space between them then, and she

forced herself to look in his face. His expression was blank. Distant. He stopped, not touching her at all, and their eyes met.

"No," he said.

She glanced down, opened her fingers. The sound of the last pin dropping to the table was inordinately loud.

"I—"

"No," he said again, cutting her off.

She stared at the row of neatly arranged hairpins, using the tip of her finger to push one into place in the line.

"This is not what I want," he whispered, stepping closer, until she could feel the hard, cold wall at her back and the heat of him before her, until he could lower his face to her hair. She heard him inhale, a long, slow breath, and it made her shudder. Not in fear. Not in revulsion. That realization surprised her, though it was tempered by the fog that had come over her, the ghosts of her past hovering, always hovering.

"If this is not what you want, then what is it you *do* want?" she asked, her voice breaking as the memories twitched in their chains, threatening to overcome her.

He lifted his head, stepped away, his jaw tight, his amber eyes chilled to ice. "Your placid acquiescence is . . . distasteful to me. To have you simply offer yourself—"

Again, she saw his jaw tighten, and she had the sudden, shocking insight that he was enraged, controlling the force of his anger by sheer will.

"You are angry at me," she observed, deflated, a little afraid. How long would his wall hold before the storm tore free?

"I am angry at *him*, at whoever did this to you, made you so—" He made a slashing gesture, clearly frustrated by the turn of events and her response, showing the most emotion she had seen in the time she had known him. "Tell me his name. I will kill him."

I already did. A harsh, choking laugh escaped her.

"Did he force you?" he asked deliberately, cadence and tone icily controlled.

Yes. No. The worst part is . . . no. "Not in the way you mean. My parents were dead, the estate entailed. They left no separate funds for me, and there was no relative, no friend to take me in. A distant cousin I had never met, Jasper Hunt, became the new Baron Sunderley." She swallowed, remembering the first time she had seen him, dark hair arranged in the current style, blue eyes catching the color of the sky. "He was so kind. Handsome. Young. He let me stay on, and with his mother living there as chaperone, who could say anything against his generosity?"

Strange how the words flowed so easily, how she trusted Gabriel to hear them, this cold, hard, enigmatic man. "I was desperately grateful. And he wooed me. Made promises any young girl would believe"—she cast him an assessing glance through her lashes—"especially a desperate young girl with nowhere else to turn. In the secret hours of the night, he came to me . . ."

Her words trailed away, the ease of her confessions suddenly constrained. She could not go on, could not bare herself so fully to his scrutiny. He stayed exactly where he was, unmoving, unblinking. Jasper had wooed her, and she had succumbed. She had believed his promises of marriage and a life together, and when he had begun to choose her clothing, the foods she would eat, the friends she would correspond with, she thought it only the interest of a prospective husband, as smitten with her as she was with him.

"I allowed him liberties. I allowed him to . . ." To do

everything he did. To chasten her. To break her will. To turn her into a pathetic creature wholly under his control.

But she said none of that, only pressed her lips together and shook her head.

Gabriel nodded slowly. She thought he would say nothing at all, that she had shocked him, though the very idea of shocking Gabriel St. Aubyn seemed absurd.

Then he spoke, his tone cool and remote as ever she had heard, but his words, oh, his words reached deep inside her and twisted her in knots. "Some people take joy in breaking others, take pleasure in the pain and humiliation of those in their care."

She gasped, horrified that he saw so much, that he clearly suspected all the things she did not say.

Lifting his hand, he stroked her cheek. "I understand."

Of course, he did not. Could not. What did a man such as Gabriel St. Aubyn understand of being broken . . . shattered?

His stare dropped to her lips, and she saw his naked lust, knew he wanted her still, despite her strange behavior.

He lifted his eyes to hers once more, and when he spoke, his words were a rough whisper. "When we lie together, Catherine—and make no mistake, we *will* lie together—it will be because you want me. Because you are parched and I am water, because you are breathless and I am air. And until then, until you come to me with hunger and need"—he gave a dark smile—"I shall make do with my solitary bed."

With that, he offered a shallow bow and left her there, alone and shaken, both grateful and bereft to see him go.

Chapter 11

Catherine had no idea how long she sat in the chair by the window and stared out at the moon. After a time, she saw Gabriel ride away. She had chased him out into the night.

As soon as the thought formed, she squelched it. No. She would not take responsibility for his choices, his actions, his moods. *He* chose to ride out.

Lucky him.

A part of her wished she could do the same. Ride through the night with the wind slapping her face.

She shook her head. Her thoughts were in turmoil, even as they were wiped clean. She revisited every moment with Gabriel, then she thrust aside any thought of their time together. She did not recognize herself, as though his mere proximity was somehow transforming her, changing her. Freeing her? The thought terrified. She did not want to be free. She wanted to be the woman she had created, controlled, safe behind her walls.

She did not want to remember the wonder of his kiss, the feel of his mouth on hers, the passion that swelled, monstrous and terrifying and beautiful. He frightened her. He soothed her.

She did not want that.

Sleep seemed an impossibility, but she craved the normalcy of routine, and so she rose, removed her clothing, changed to her nightrail. She crossed to the washstand, used her tooth powder, washed her face and hands.

Turning, she spied Mrs. Northrop's letter and the vile clipping she had sent. Rage and pain swelled and she wanted them gone, wanted them never to have been. She wanted to purge the pain of this loss, and all those that had preceded it.

Of course, that could never be. The holes in her heart, her soul, could never fully mend. But she could do *something*. Something symbolic.

Taking up the letter and the clipping, she fetched the tin Gabriel had gifted her with. She had used only a single spill, the morning he had given it to her. She had taken Madeline walking by the lake and showed her the wonder of this marvelous thing. Madeline had recoiled from the flames, but Catherine's joy in the gift had not abated.

The lid pulled open with ease now, and she slowly withdrew a solitary spill and the tiny pliers. Her first attempt failed, for her hands were shaking, her breath too fast. But her second attempt succeeded, the snip of the pliers igniting a small, lovely flame. She stared at it for an instant, feeling the glow reach inside her, warming her, lighting her way. Then she held the flame to the edge of the papers in her hand. A swell of heat. Licking tongues that curled and twined. Hungry.

Almost did she singe her fingers, but at the last, she tossed the tiny glowing remnant into the fire that already burned in the hearth.

"Good-bye, Martha," she whispered. "Rest easy." Easier in death than she had in life.

There were no tears now. She had cried herself dry.

Crossing to the window once more, she took up her silver-backed brush and settled in the chair. There, she stared out at the moon and drew the brush through her hair in long slow strokes.

From the hallway came a sound, the faint clank of metal on metal and the shush of footsteps on the carpet. She paused in what she was doing, listening as the clanking moved along the passage in the direction of Madeline's chamber, the sounds finally fading away.

With her fingers curled around the brush, she sat there a moment more, something gnawing at her, unsettling. And then she knew. The clank of metal on metal. Mrs. Bell carried a large ring of keys that made that exact sound when she walked.

What purpose did the housekeeper have in making a late-night visit to Madeline's chamber?

Catherine set down the brush, rose, and draped a shawl over her shoulders. She left the room, taking her candle to light the way. The hallway was empty now, but at the end, Madeline's door was cracked open and a narrow shard of candlelight bled through into the darkness.

The murmur of voices sounded, one low and firm, the other higher, anxious.

Catherine stepped closer.

"Nnno," Madeline's voice was hazy, confused. "I had—" She broke off and exhaled a long, sighing breath. "Did I not have some? I thought I did."

There came a tapping sound, like a spoon clinking against glass. "Drink it now," Mrs. Bell said. "Your cousin was quite insistent that I dose you with your medicine."

Catherine gasped and hurried forward, pushing open the door to reveal Madeline propped on her pillows, looking sleep rumpled and confused, and Mrs. Bell standing over her with a crystal goblet of wine. The brown bottle of laudanum was open on the bedside table.

Her arrival drew the gazes of both women.

"What exactly are you doing, Mrs. Bell?" she demanded, summoning her frostiest tone.

"Following instructions," Mrs. Bell clipped out in return. "Sir Gabriel bid me see to Miss Madeline's medicine."

Catherine stared at her in confusion, a recollection of her discussion with Gabriel from earlier in the evening leaping to the forefront of her thoughts. She clearly recalled telling him that she had dosed Madeline with laudanum in a glass of Madeira.

But perhaps he had given Mrs. Bell his instruction before he had come to her chamber, before she had told him the task was already complete.

"When did Sir Gabriel give you that directive?" she asked.

Mrs. Bell's eyes narrowed and her expression grew mutinous, her lips compressed, his nostrils pinched. Catherine felt certain it would be a battle of wits to gather what information she could.

Then the housekeeper surprised her, setting the glass down on the table and folding her arms across her belly.

"Perhaps if you tell me the reason you ask then I'll know if I ought to answer," she said.

A fair enough observation. "I ask because I already gave Madeline her medicine earlier this evening." *And I am certain I mentioned that fact to Gabriel.* She did not voice the last bit aloud, wary of what trust she should place in the housekeeper. Catherine vacillated between disbelieving Madeline's outlandish assertions that someone here wished her harm, and believing they were not so outlandish at all. There was something very wrong in this household, and Catherine dared not make a mistake. She had the horrible suspicion that Madeline's life might depend on it. But who posed the danger? Mrs. Bell? Gabriel? Some as yet undisclosed pawn or bishop on the board? How was she to know?

Each time she thought she had her answers, something else happened to make her question all she had already gleaned.

"Did I not tell you so?" Madeline offered in a reedy whisper, as though driven to participate in some small way in this conversation that pertained to her. Her words were a paltry challenge to Mrs. Bell's overwhelming personality.

"Thank you for your solicitude, Mrs. Bell," Catherine said, reaching out to lift the glass of wine from where the housekeeper had placed it on the table, intending to pour out the contents. She had no desire for Madeline to reach for it in a stuporous state and ingest more of the medicine than was safe. "I can only imagine how vast your duties already are. Surely you do not need yet another to add weight to your burdens. I shall take full responsibility for administering Madeline's medicine from here on out."

The housekeeper's lips thinned and she looked positively furious. "I tell you, Sir Gabriel bid me see to her. Only a short time ago I saw him below, and he was very clear in his instruction."

"A short time ago?"

"A matter of moments," Mrs. Bell insisted.

But Catherine knew she was lying. Or perhaps only confused. For she had seen Gabriel ride away at least a half hour past.

"I believe you are mistaken, Mrs. Bell."

The color drained from the woman's cheeks, then rushed back in a crimson flush, but she held her tongue, spun, and stalked from the room. Catherine turned to watch her go.

With a shake of her head, Catherine sniffed at the wine

in her hand, curious to see if the scent would suggest the dosage the housekeeper had doled out. She froze in place. The smell was . . . wrong.

Again she sniffed the glass. There was the sweet scent of the Madeira, and another aroma blending with it. But not the distinctive smell of laudanum that she expected. She had enough experience with the noxious stuff to know there was often a smell of alcohol, perhaps sassafras or cloves, and always the heavy, cloying, distinctive aroma of the laudanum itself.

None of them was present now.

The drink smelled of wine and—she sniffed again—almonds.

The air left her in a rush.

"Madeline," she said, keeping her tone even and smooth as she shifted to face the bed once more. Her friend's eyes were closed, her cheeks pale. At the sound of her name, she roused and turned her head, lifting her lids halfway. "Madeline, did you watch Mrs. Bell pour this wine for you?"

"Wine?" Madeline murmured with a frown. Her lids drifted shut, then opened once more. "Is there wine?"

With a sigh, Catherine realized that Madeline would be no help in solving this mystery. Recollection of laudanum's effects—the dulling lethargy, the weightless floating—came to her, and she knew the state that Madeline was in. The helpless, drugged state.

Carrying the full glass, Catherine crossed to the window, undid the latch, and pushed open the sash. She glanced down to make certain there was no one below, and then she poured the contents of the crystal glass out the window. With a shudder, she pushed it shut and drew the curtains.

Whatever had been mixed with that wine, she suspected it had not been laudanum. What, then? Poison? Did she really believe that? And who was the poisoner? Mrs. Bell? To what purpose?

Her gaze lit on the brown bottle that sat on the bedside table. Quickly, she closed the space, lifted the bottle, removed the lid and sniffed the contents. Cloves, alcohol, and laudanum.

Whatever had been poured into the wine had not come from this bottle. She was certain of it.

But that was her only certainty. Other than that, all she had were questions without answers, for she had no idea if Mrs. Bell had prepared that wine herself or simply brought a glass prepared by another. If Gabriel had misheard when she said she had already given Madeline a dose of her medicine. If he had forgotten, or—horrific as the possibility was—if he had intended to see Madeline receive a second dose, perhaps an amount large enough to kill her. Or had Mrs. Bell fabricated the story altogether, attributing instructions to Gabriel when he had given her none?

She shuddered and went to the washstand where she rinsed the crystal goblet before setting it down. Crossing to the bed, she stayed there for several moments, watching the steady rise and fall of Madeline's chest. Certain that her friend slept, Catherine took the bottle of laudanum and left the room.

It was only later, as she lay in her own bed on the edge of slumber, that her muzzy thoughts revisited the events in Madeline's chamber. She was certain the bottle of laudanum had been open on the table when she had first entered the room to confront Mrs. Bell, but it had been closed when she went to sniff the contents.

Such a small thing to note, but note it she did, though what possible significance there could be to such an observation escaped her. The tendrils of sleep that had begun to wrap around her evaporated like a mist, and she was left restless and troubled, certain that there was something here she had missed.

This one had disappointed him.

Sweat stained his shirt, prickling at the small of his back and under his arms, beading on his forehead and lip.

He had wanted her to moan, to scream against the gag, to thrash as he played. She'd done none of those things. She had only stared at him, eyes blank and glassy, as though she had left her body long before he ended her life. He had broken her before he had truly begun, and that made a cold knot of rage glow in his belly.

Susan Parker had cheated him of the game.

He wanted one who was strong, stubborn. Even brave. The longer they thrashed and moaned and struggled, the better he enjoyed his play. *He* decided when they cried out. *He* decided when they writhed and moaned. *He* decided when the game was done.

But Susan had broken as soon as he slit her dress and peeled it from her shivering form. Where was the fun in that? The challenge? The joy he derived was intricately twined in the knowledge that he controlled them. Their thoughts. Their hopes. One of his favorite parts was when he offered comfort and his chosen victim turned her face to his hand, seeking warmth, seeking succor.

Susan had denied him that. She had denied him the most delicious part.

Her mind had collapsed, and in the end, she had never truly seen him. She was supposed to *see* him, truly see him. They always did in the end. But Susan had not been there anymore; she had gone somewhere else, somewhere he could not reach.

In his rage, he had cut her head clean off. He had shoved his blade deep, sawing back and forth without finesse or delicacy, cutting skin and muscle, artery and vein. He had slashed her windpipe, the white cartilage bright against the river of blood. But his fury had not been assuaged. In the end, he had hacked at her until her head pulled free, slid from his fingers, and hit the floor with a dull thud. Then it had rolled to the side and lain there, glazed eyes staring up at him.

Where was the pleasure in that?

Instead of being the one in control, he had *lost* control, visiting his fury upon her. His arms were completely drenched in blood nearly to the shoulder. The rest of him was splattered with it, dark, glistening splotches.

He licked his lips, tasted her blood on his tongue.

It was then he realized he had forgotten the feather.

Breathing heavily, he stood over the body, rage swelling anew. She had made him forget the feather. Bitch.

He must salvage what he could of this. He must follow his routine. Lifting his knife once more, he plunged it deep and cut open her belly, pulling out loop upon loop of glistening intestine. Ripping it free, he shoved it in the open jar at his feet, then turned his attention to her stomach.

The following morning, Catherine breakfasted alone. She was not certain how she felt about that, for she both missed Gabriel's unique brand of conversation and felt relieved not to have to face him in the aftermath of the kiss they had shared.

Last night, they had both taken their masks off, but

she had been far more naked than he. The thought was unsettling.

A part of her felt certain he absented himself today out of consideration for her, that he offered her a respite from the raw emotions his presence stirred. The larger part of her felt certain that the sole reason she ate alone was because he had business elsewhere, for he had never struck her as an overly empathetic individual. In all likelihood, contemplation of her emotions and her comfort had never entered his mind.

With her meal complete, she rose and took her book to the small yellow sitting room at the front of the house. The light there was wonderful for reading and she was quite enthralled with Dr. Frankenstein's story now, anxious to see where it would take him. And her. In a way, she felt as though she accompanied him on his journey, as though she was the one questing for dangerous knowledge.

The story engrossed and provided a respite from her thoughts. She was restless, tired, for her night had passed in tossing and turning and battling haunting memories. But the fresh light of day had brought renewed determination to bury all the things that had no place in her life now, to lock them away in the box she assigned them, and to build distance between herself and Gabriel St. Aubyn.

That was the only safe option. To let him burrow beneath her defenses was a mistake she would undoubtedly pay for. She felt certain of that.

For a time, she read, immersing herself in the story. Her heart bled for Justine, accused of a murder she did not commit. And though she abhorred his weakness, she understood Victor's hesitance to reveal the reasons Justine could not have killed William, for that would have seen Victor judged insane. There were things in this book that made her shudder, made her feel like weeping, not only for the characters within, but for the parallels to her own secrets.

Had Gabriel known when he gave her this book that the story would reach inside her and pluck at old wounds? Did it do the same for him? Or was it mere entertainment he sought when he read this?

She would know those answers only if she delved into his thoughts. She doubted he would allow such intrusion. Not by her. Not by anyone. And she was not certain if she even wanted to know what tragedies had shaped him, what secrets he held. That could only serve to make her more confused. Better to hold him at a distance, to learn nothing of his secrets and share none of her own. She had already given him far too many glimpses of her private truths.

At length, she rose and crossed to the window, the one that gave her a clear view of the grounds and the distant woods, and a part of the long, graveled drive. Sweeping aside the yellow velvet curtain, she stared out at the world beyond the glass. The sky was overcast, heavy with charcoal-limned clouds, but at brief intervals a bright shaft of sunlight would break through to dance across the grass and trees, then disappear once more.

She heard the sound of hoofbeats before the horse came into view, for her position allowed a glimpse of only the far end of the long drive. She waited, and after a moment, she saw Gabriel, mounted on his great black beast, cantering away from the house.

As she watched, his path crossed that of a carriage that turned into the drive and came toward the abbey. He did not stop, nor did the carriage; they simply passed on the drive, each continuing on their way.

Curiosity stirred. She wondered who came to Cairncroft

that they did not warrant even a brief greeting from the master.

She turned from the window and hurried out of the sitting room, returning to the breakfast room where the window offered a clear view of the section of the drive that was nearer the house. She was just in time to see the gleaming black coach rock to a halt and the door swing open.

A man, tall and broad, stepped down, his face turned away from her. What little she might have seen of his features was obscured by the brim of his hat. A black greatcoat billowed about him as he moved away from the coach, and Catherine felt a stirring of familiarity. Something in the way he walked . . . his height . . . something . . .

He stopped, his posture relaxed, then he turned fully toward her. The face was one she knew well now. Beautiful. Severe.

With a gasp, Catherine shrank into the shadows.

The man was St. Aubyn.

But how? She had seen him only moments past, riding away from the abbey on his great black beast, garbed in tan cord breeches and a dark brown, square-cut riding coat. It was impossible that he could be this man, newly emerged from the carriage, standing on the drive in black greatcoat and hat.

Yet here he was.

Determined to get to the root of this, Catherine lifted her skirt and rushed from the room, tearing along the long, dim hallway in a most unladylike fashion. She was breathing rapidly, her pulse racing as she skidded to a stop on the narrow set of stairs that led to the main entry hall. She paused some five risers from the bottom.

The front door was open, held that way by Mrs. Bell,

and through the portal stepped the man she had seen through the window.

For a moment, her head spun at the impossibility of what she saw. Gabriel, standing in a place he could not possibly be. How? How had she seen him only moments past riding away from Cairncroft, even crossing the path of the carriage, only to have him emerge from within it? What manner of illusion was this?

Mrs. Bell smiled in greeting, even offering her hand, which the newcomer closed in his own black-gloved one and gave a quick squeeze. The oddity of that greeting struck Catherine, as did the bright smile he flashed.

An open, happy smile.

White teeth and crinkles at the corners of his eyes.

It was then she realized the newcomer could not possibly be Gabriel, who never smiled like that and certainly never interacted with the housekeeper in such an easy, friendly manner. No, more than friendly. *Affectionate.*

She saw the differences now. The height and build were similar, the color of his hair, even the angle of his jaw and the slant of his cheeks. But this man had a slight bump at the bridge of his nose, and as he took his hat from his head, she saw that his hair, while thick and honey-hued, was far shorter than Gabriel's and a shade or two darker. Then he turned his face toward her and any doubt she might have harbored evaporated entirely, for his eyes were a clear and vivid green, while Gabriel's were amber gold.

His gaze raked her in a leisurely assessment, his mouth curving in a far different sort of smile than the one he had offered Mrs. Bell, and Catherine understood from that perusal quite a bit about him. This man knew women and liked them very much. He was not the aloof, cold creature that Gabriel was.

Which made him far less intriguing.

"Are you his brother?" Catherine asked, not bothering with niceties, certain he would not be surprised by the question. But *she* was surprised, for in all her time here at Cairncroft, and in all the years she and Madeline had corresponded, she had never heard mention that Gabriel had a brother. Not a word. Not a whisper.

Mrs. Bell gasped and pressed her hand to her mouth, as though the query was horrific in some manner. Catherine might have ignored that reaction except the stranger's eyes narrowed and his expression closed in clear indication that her question crossed some unseen boundary.

"No," he replied, recovering his aplomb so quickly Catherine almost believed she had imagined the telltale signs of caginess. He offered a perfectly executed bow with a flourish. "I am Mr. Sebastian St. Aubyn, the black sheep cousin, the wastrel, the wanderer"—he winked, and added audaciously—"come home for a visit. Haven't I, Mrs. Bell?" He turned to the housekeeper, and to Catherine's utter amazement Mrs. Bell fluttered her lashes like a girl.

Catherine introduced herself, and with the formalities taken care of, she asked, "Where were you wandering, Mr. St. Aubyn?"

"Egypt," he said with a grin, then addressed the housekeeper. "Mrs. Bell, can you offer a starving man some sustenance? In the blue parlor? You know I favor the size and comfort of the chairs in there." He cocked his head to the side. "And Miss Weston, can you offer this lonely soul some company? I shall regale you with stories of my travels and I promise you *will* be entertained."

He shed his greatcoat and offered her his arm.

"I should be delighted to join you," Catherine murmured, curious about more than his travels. She thought he might be persuaded to answer some questions about Gabriel and Madeline and the pall that hung over the abbey. And if not persuaded, tricked.

Taking his arm, she accompanied him to the blue parlor. She could see why he liked it; the size was cozy rather than imposing, the chairs comfortable, the windows opening to a small, walled garden that was pretty if slightly wild.

At first they exchanged small pleasantries. Catherine bit the inside of her cheek to keep from laughing as they discussed the weather at some length. If she had required any further proof that this man was not Gabriel, the turn of their conversation would have provided it beyond a shadow of a doubt.

A maid brought tea and cakes, along with a cold pheasant pie and some fruit.

Sebastian St. Aubyn polished off a healthy portion as they conversed. She noticed that he did not ask after Madeline or Gabriel, and she wondered why, but did not ask. Good manners prevented it, but more than that, she felt that such a line of inquiry would give too much away and perhaps put him on his guard. Better to see where he led the discourse and glean what information she could before formulating her questions and coaxing free what answers she might.

When he was done with his meal, Catherine poured more tea, and said, "Mr. St. Aubyn, I will hold you to your word now. Do tell me about Egypt and your travels."

"There are too many St. Aubyns in this house," he observed. "You must call me Sebastian. I know it is presumptuous on such short acquaintance"—he held up one hand to forestall any argument—"but confusion will otherwise ensue." His lashes lowered and he cast her a sidelong glance. "Besides, I should very much like to hear my name from your lips."

Practiced. Glib. His sultry tone and inappropriate words marked him for a rake. Or perhaps, for a man who wished to be perceived as one.

"Then you must call me Catherine, and we shall both be presumptuous. Now tell me about Egypt."

"Egypt is hot," he said with a laugh, "and full of sand."

"Is it? Only sand? No green river delta? No farms? No cities?" She sipped her tea. "No pyramids or tombs?"

He sent her a sharp look. "You are well read, Catherine. Is it Egypt that fascinates you, or geography in general?"

"I like to read."

His brows rose. "Books on geography rather than the latest penny dreadful?"

"Books on geography and science and philosophy. Even agriculture."

"I suspect there is an interesting reason for that . . ." His voice trailed away into a pregnant pause, and when she made no reply, he leaned back and held both palms forward as he said, "A lady deserves her secrets. I shall not press." But his tone suggested he wanted to do just that.

Pressed or not, the reason for her eclectic self-education was one she would never reveal. There had been months when the books she had read had been her sole link to her sanity, and she had been so grateful for them. They had carried her away from the home that had become her prison.

But she said none of that. Instead, she asked, "Are you recently returned from your travels?"

"Not so recent, but recent enough."

Well, there was an answer that was none at all. Perhaps he was more like his cousin than she had thought.

"Have you come from London today? You must have traveled through the night to be here at such an early hour."

"Not from London, no."

"Then you have been staying in the area? With friends?"

"Something of the sort."

He leaned back in his chair and turned his head fully toward her at the exact moment the sun slid behind a cloud. The light in the room dimmed, casting his features in shadow. The set of his shoulders, the tilt of his head, the dark cloth of his square-cut coat and waistcoat . . . they reminded her of similar shadows painting the man she had seen lurking at the edge of the woods, the one she had mistaken for Gabriel time and again.

Was it Sebastian who prowled and skulked? Did he watch the abbey? For what purpose?

Given the evasive nature of his replies to her questions, she could not discount the possibility. Despite his open, easy manner—or perhaps because of it—there certainly was no reason for her to trust him.

The clouds shifted and the sun broke free once more, shining through the glass panes to refract in a rainbow of color, dispelling the shadows but not the weight of her distrust.

"You chose a lovely day for travel," Catherine observed. "I arrived under the pall of a rainstorm that had me wondering if the coach would become an ark and float away."

"Ah, the incomparable smell of a damp, rotting hired carriage. I know it well," he replied with a small smile.

How had he surmised that she had arrived in a hired carriage? She had never said it.

An accurate guess, or something else? The possibility that Sebastian had been in the area for some time, that he was, in fact, the watcher in the woods—spying on the abbey, spying on *her*—could not be ignored.

In that moment, she was made certain of two things. First, Sebastian's easy, charming manner concealed a different character entirely. Everything was evasion and mild flirtation, but his true nature swam beneath the surface, possibly a dark and dangerous thing. It seemed that Gabriel was not the only St. Aubyn to present a false face. She found she preferred his cool mask to Sebastian's mummery.

Second, Sebastian's words denoted that he knew far more about her than she had willingly shared, far more about her than she knew of him.

"Tell me about the wonderful things you saw in Egypt," she prompted, her tone polite and even, betraying none of her thoughts.

"Wonderful things? I suppose there were some. And dreadful things, as well." He set his cup on the table and shifted forward in his chair, leaning toward her with his forearms on his thighs. "I have been there many times. My most recent travels took me to the tombs of Qurna. There was gold in every tomb. A man could become rich on the treasures buried there."

"Are you such a man?"

He sat back and shrugged. "I must confess that I was tempted. Gold and jewels aplenty beneath a thousand layers of dust. But I suppose I have some principles left. Robbing the dead lacked appeal." Again, he grinned, a practiced, engaging smile. "Now, robbing the living is another matter entirely."

Refusing to be baited, she asked, "What were the tombs like?"

He lifted his cup and saucer once more, and Catherine realized he was always in motion, never still. That in itself was enough to differentiate him from Gabriel, even if there had not been all the other clues. Gabriel was the eye of the storm, motionless, commotionless, but never serene. His was a quivering stillness, like a bowstring drawn taut, while Sebastian was laced with suppressed tension, ever shifting position in a suave, fluid way.

"The tombs," he mused. "Darkness all about, and narrow passages, stale and dank. In some, we were obliged to get down on our knees and crawl, with the bite of sharp stones beneath us and the stink of death heavy in every breath." His smile faded and his gaze grew distant. "The torches flickered and failed for want of air, and my nose and mouth and eyes were filled with grit. And all about . . . I can hardly describe it. Wrapped bodies, ancient and desiccated, stacked one atop the next, and shapes of other things, indistinguishable in the poor light. Statues. Carvings. Things that were half jackal, half man."

Catherine nodded in mute encouragement, drawn in by his tale, imagining the place he described.

"One of the men in our party sought a moment's rest. He sat upon a wooden box, when with a crash of bones and wood, he found himself sinking in a sea of mummies as his weight bore down on centuries of remains. So tenuous was his position that we were forced to wait several moments until the bodies settled and we could haul him out without sacrificing ourselves to the same fate. Imagine"—he gave a short laugh—"drowning in a sea of the ancient dead. For a long while after, I looked over my shoulder, certain that ghosts followed. You have no idea."

Did she not? She had her own ghosts that followed close enough to nip at her heels. "Why would you visit such a place? What is the appeal?"

"I have been visiting such places since I was a child. My guardian, a most unconventional man, had a penchant for travel, and he dragged me along."

His guardian. She wanted to ask about that, to query his exact relationship to Gabriel, to understand the link that made them cousins, but she was not so forward as that.

"Why do I continue to visit?" He paused, rubbed his fingers along his jaw. "Adventure. Knowledge. To be anywhere but here."

She sucked in a breath at his blatant admission. "And yet, you return here and call it home."

"Yes. In the end, Cairncroft always calls us home." There was bitterness in his tone and a sardonic edge. "Do you know," he said, lowering his voice as though to share a confidence, "the Egyptians mummified their dead in preparation for another life." He gave a hard huff of laughter. "We simply bury them and let them rot."

Or let them burn, Catherine thought.

He slanted her a glance beneath his lashes, and she wondered if she had given herself away by expression or action. But, no, he merely wanted to judge her response to his tale as he continued, "One thing I have always found particularly fascinating are the canopic jars and their gruesome contents."

"Gruesome?"

He nodded. "They are jars made of limestone or pottery, or even bronze. They hold the entrails." After a heartbeat, he continued, "The ancient Egyptians cut the organs out and assigned one to each jar. Liver, lungs, stomach, and intestine. Four jars, often decorated with images of their gods."

He was testing her, watching her, determined to see if she would become missish at such vile description. Why? Was this merely a game for his entertainment, or was there a deeper purpose?

"Liver, lungs, stomach, and intestine . . . Not the heart?" she inquired coolly, though her attention was split now between his answers and something in his words that nagged at her, disturbed her.

Again, he laughed. "No, the heart they left intact to be weighed at judgment."

Judgment.

She opened her mouth to ask what the heart was weighed against, but before she could speak a new voice interjected.

"The heart is weighed against a feather."

Catherine gasped and jerked about in her seat. Gabriel stood in the doorway, one shoulder against the frame, arms crossed over his chest. The cut of his brown riding coat accentuated the breadth of his shoulders, and the color reflected in his eyes, lending them a warm brandy glow. His hair was windblown, his gaze intent. Her heart gave a sharp little kick in her breast. Because she was glad to see him, though she ought not to be.

In that instant she realized that despite the cousins' resemblance, for her it was Gabriel who made the air sizzle and crack, made her pulse speed up and her breath come a little faster. Beside him, Sebastian paled.

The realization rankled. Of course she would be attracted to the villain rather than the flirt.

"Gabriel." Sebastian rose from his seat.

"Sebastian." The cousins clasped hands and then broke apart, Sebastian returning to his place on the settee, Gabriel choosing a chair directly to Catherine's right, far too close for her peace of mind. The tip of his boot brushed her hem, and she surreptitiously pulled her skirt away, only to look up and find him watching her. It came to her that he had chosen this proximity with the purpose of warning his cousin off, as though demarcating his territory or ownership. She thrust the thought aside as quickly as it materialized. Surely he did not think of her that way. As *his.*

And what vile malady assailed her that any part of her wanted him to?

"Please, do not let me interrupt," Gabriel said, his lips curved in the barest hint of a smile. It did not reach his eyes. Had she ever seen him smile openly and fully? Had she seen a smile reach his eyes?

Perhaps . . . once or twice. She recalled the day at breakfast when he had first returned from London, she had seen his lips curve enough to carve a crease in his cheek and make tiny lines fan from the corners of his eyes. A rare happenstance. The rest of the time he seemed to mirror the expressions he saw in others, or perhaps he attempted an appropriate response, but never *felt* the emotion he portrayed.

What sort of life had he led to engender such a lack . . . or was it a trick of birth that had made him this way?

She realized that Sebastian was speaking, filling the silence with some unimportant comment. About the weather. Again. Shooting a glance at Gabriel, she found him watching her with the faintest flicker of shared amusement as she murmured a reply.

Quickly returning her attention to Sebastian, she said, "Do continue with your description of your travels."

"Yes, do," Gabriel prompted with a complete lack of inflection. The way the two men had greeted each other was both warm and cool. Was there genuine pleasure in their exchange? She could not say with certainty.

"The Egyptians believe each tomb is sealed with a curse placed there by their ancestors," Sebastian offered, speaking to her, but looking at Gabriel.

"Of course. A curse," Gabriel murmured.

Catherine recalled Mrs. Bell's talk of curses and tragedies, and she wondered if there was some secret the two cousins shared. From the exchange of glances, she thought perhaps there was. "What sort of curse?"

"One that must be nullified with a counter-curse lest the tomb's opener suffer a vile and painful demise," Sebastian replied, his tone overly dramatic, as though he poked fun at himself. Or did he poke fun at her? She was not of a mind to ask him. "They say only a handful of Egyptians know the counter-curse. I cannot claim to have faith in such fribble, but I am a cautious fellow. I made certain never to be at the forefront of the charge into the tombs lest I be afflicted."

Catherine blinked, taken aback at his casual admission of what some might construe as cowardice.

As though he read her thoughts, Sebastian laughed. "Not fear, Catherine. *Caution*. The difference is subtle, but there nonetheless." He slanted an unreadable glance at Gabriel. "Cowardice is not a St. Aubyn trait."

Sebastian used her given name so casually, and she wondered if it was that or the mention of cowardice that had Gabriel stiffening in his seat. The movement was ever so slight and she might have missed it except she was utterly attuned to his presence. His mood. His every breath. The way his lashes swept down to veil his thoughts.

And that made him unutterably dangerous to her.

"Do you believe in curses, Catherine?" Gabriel asked, his tone cool and remote.

Was this the man who had comforted her, kissed her? Yes. Somewhere inside the cold exterior lurked at least a modicum of passion. Perhaps a vast storm of it. She had felt it, shared it. Hadn't she? Or had she only imagined it, a reflection of the tumult he stirred inside her?

"No, I do not." But even as she made her reply, she

wondered if her words were the truth. Had there not been occasions when she believed her own life had been cursed?

The thought had proven anathema to her nature. She had always regarded her ability to overcome whatever horror was visited upon her—to *survive*—as a sort of gift. But at the darkest of times, doubt had crept up on her, whispering to her.

"Perhaps you should," Gabriel said, with an inflection that might have been either humor or derision. Aimed at her? At himself?

Sebastian watched them with blatant interest. He could not have missed the undercurrents in every word they spoke, or the way she subtly shifted her hand away when Gabriel had moved his to brush her own. It was no accident. She did not believe anything Gabriel St. Aubyn did was accidental.

They engaged in innocuous conversation for only a few moments more, when Gabriel abruptly lost patience.

"Enough." He rose and offered Catherine a shallow bow, then turned to his cousin. "We have things to discuss, Sebastian. Join me."

With a dark look, quickly masked, Sebastian rose as well and took his leave, far more politely than his cousin. Gabriel gestured for Sebastian to precede him, and only then did he turn back to Catherine, the light from the window touching half his face, painting his hair and the glint of beard on his jaw in shades of glittering gold, leaving the other half of him in shadow. Reaching out, he stroked the backs of his fingers along her cheek, the touch barely there.

She stared at him, her breath frozen. Then he turned and followed his cousin from the room.

For a long while, she sat alone in the parlor with the

beam of sunlight slanting across her skirt and her thoughts spinning like a child's top. It was only when she glanced up and saw a pottery vase on the pedestal table that she again thought that something about Sebastian's description of the canopic jars nagged at her. Something . . .

And suddenly, it struck her.

Rising, she stood in the center of the room, seeing nothing, her heart pounding, her mouth dry. Recollection of the words from the newspaper clipping that described Martha's body slammed her. Coincidence was an impossibility, but perhaps she was wrong, perhaps—

Closing her eyes, she recalled the horrific article, every word branded in her mind though the actual paper was gone, burned to ash.

Her clothes had been cut away from the torso, and the chest and abdominal cavities opened with a sharp instrument, without precision. On postmortem examination of the body, he found the lungs, liver, stomach, and intestine removed, again, without precision. The heart was untouched.

Her legs trembled and she sank down onto the chair once more. Martha was dead. Four of her organs removed, and the heart left behind, exactly as Sebastian described in his blithe recounting of the canopic jars and their purpose.

Had he shared those stories with a particular purpose in mind?

When exactly had he returned from Egypt? Had he been in London when Martha was killed?

Icy dread touched her. She pressed her fingers to her brow, thinking, thinking. Her suspicions were impossible. Ridiculous.

How many people lived in London? Any one of them could be the killer. Why in Heaven's name did she think there was some significance, some link, between the killer, the organs removed from Martha's body, and Sebastian's recounting of the purpose of the canopic jars?

Her thoughts spun in a cacophony of sound and light, and emerging from the melee was the recollection of Gabriel asking her if it was Martha's death that had her so distressed, or the fact that Martha's organs had been removed. He had known that fact despite only glancing at the article, not reading it in its entirety. She had noted it then, remembered it now.

For some reason, she thought, too, of Madeline's story that day in the garden about a girl found covered in blood.

With a shake of her head, she took a deep breath, counted back the days . . . and realized that although she could not account for Sebastian's whereabouts, she knew from his own admission that Gabriel had been in London in the days before Martha's body was found.

Chapter 12

"On a bright and sunny day"—Sebastian paused long enough to glance at the window—"well, somewhat sunny when the clouds break. Either way, here we sit in the gloom."

"We are not sitting, as yet," Gabriel pointed out, handing him a glass of brandy.

"But we are shrouded in gloom." Sebastian shrugged and settled with lazy insouciance in a high-backed leather and gold chair. "You are nothing if not consistent, cousin."

"It is bright enough," Gabriel said. The sconces were lit and he had dragged the heavy curtain open a hand span. "Besides, I thought you would have had enough of the sun after Egypt. England's clouds must be a welcome change."

"One would think." Sebastian laughed, but there was a brittle edge to the sound. "We make a pair, don't we? Skulking about in the shadows like two creatures of the night."

Gabriel studied him a moment. There was something odd about Sebastian, something hard. A new edge that had not been there the last time Gabriel had seen him, before he left on his latest trip. "Is there a particular reason you are skulking, Sebastian?"

His cousin offered a tight smile, then tossed back half the brandy in his glass.

"I am only restless," he said, and Gabriel knew it for the lie it was. Then Sebastian laughed and winked. "Perhaps your Miss Weston will entertain me."

Anger raised its head and snarled, the emotion so raw and sudden that Gabriel almost let it slide free. He was stunned by the force and speed of his rage.

"Perhaps not," he replied, his tone diamond hard. He turned away and stared into the hearth as the clock on the mantel ticked loud in the quiet. The flames made him think of her, of the light she brought to his world of dim passages and hidden caverns and the darkness of his soul.

He clenched his fist by his side, appalled at his thoughts. He was no romantic fool. Yes, she brought light, but if he let her come too close, she would singe him as surely as any flame.

"Well," Sebastian observed dryly, "you are as charming a conversationalist as ever, cousin." He pushed himself from the chair and half rose. "I believe I *shall* seek out the lovely Miss Weston once more."

"Stay away from her." Gabriel spun to face his cousin, his tone frigid, cold-blooded rage raising its saurian head.

Sebastian sat back down, his expression contemplative, and raised his glass as though in a toast.

"Ah," he mused. "So that is the way of it. I had not imagined that you would ever don the mantle of jealousy, cousin."

"Do not imagine it now," Gabriel replied, his tone even, his mask once more in place.

Jealousy. The notion was absurd. Yet the sight of Sebastian and Catherine sitting in cozy camaraderie in the parlor had reached inside him and clenched like a fist, twisting him up tighter than a Gordian knot. Jealousy. He had never known the like. The emotion was unfamiliar. Unpleasant in the extreme.

Lifting the poker, he prodded the log and watched it spit and pop. He thought of Catherine's night-dark eyes and thick straight lashes, imagined them hooded and lazy with passion. He thought of her lips, forming polite words in conversation. Then he thought of them pressed to his, open and eager. Hungry. As he was hungry.

He wanted her to kiss no other but him, and the fact that he had to leave the choice, the timing, to her was like a blade in his gut. He had wanted her from the start, and grew tired of that wanting. For a patient man, he was remarkably *impatient* when it came to her, edgy and overeager.

"Stay away from her," he said again, and finally turned away from the fire to face his cousin once more.

Sebastian sipped his brandy and studied him with raised brows and overblown surprise.

"Do not tell me you are smitten, Gabriel?" His brows lowered and he continued in a musing tone, "Do you know who she is? What they say about her?"

Gabriel almost laughed. "Do you know who I am? What they say about me?" he answered, faintly mocking.

"Gabriel—"

"No," he said, his tone carrying the rasp of a razor on a strop. "Speak to me of anything but her." He paused, then offered far more than was his habit, only because he *needed* to set the thoughts free and Sebastian was as close to holding his trust as any living being. "She haunts my nights. My days. My every thought." He met his cousin's gaze and made things as plain as he possibly could. "Catherine Weston is mine."

The words echoed in the cavernous room, and in that

moment, he knew them for utter and complete truth. Catherine was his. She only had not recognized it yet.

"Then I shall find another to play my games with," Sebastian said. He leaned forward, his elbows resting on his knees. "Will you marry her?"

The conundrum of that had occurred to him. Would he? The question made Gabriel acutely aware of the differences between himself and a normal man. He knew what the answer ought to be. She was a baron's daughter. Of course she would expect marriage.

Wouldn't she?

And if he did marry her, how was he to keep his secrets then? And how was he to explain that he would never give her a child?

On that topic, he was implacable in his resolve. Never would he doom an innocent babe to the taint of the St. Aubyn line.

"Are you afraid I will sire a pup and any hope you have of a baronetcy will be lost?" Gabriel asked, avoiding a direct answer to his cousin's question because, in truth, he did not have one. "Fear not, cousin. I shall never have a child, and you know my reasons for that. Your right of succession is safe."

"I care little for that," Sebastian said with a wave of his hand.

It was the truth. Gabriel knew it. Sebastian was rich in his own right, and a title would likely only tie him down in a way he would despise. He preferred to move about, to travel. To flee the ghosts of his past rather than face them. Gabriel could understand his actions, even envy them to a degree.

There had been years, endless dark years, when he had dreamed of leaving England and roaming the world as his cousin did.

"What did you learn at Hanham House?" he asked, changing the subject to one far less palatable, but necessary.

"Very little. They were not forthcoming when I asked them to produce him in person. They claimed he was too overwrought for visitors. Suggested I should return another time, perhaps in a matter of weeks. They only brought me a letter that appears to be in his hand, but might have been written days, or even weeks past. There is nothing specific. I have it here if you wish to see for yourself." He dragged the letter from his coat.

Gabriel stared at the thing in revulsion. He did not want to see it or read it or know anything it contained. "Set it there," he said, jutting his chin toward the desk, careful to keep his tone bland as oatmeal.

For though he trusted Sebastian more than most, if he measured that trust evenly against grains of sand, there would be pathetically few on the scale.

"Do you wonder about my cousin?" Madeline asked as they walked in the garden the following afternoon. Catherine had insisted, certain that a bit of fresh air and healthful exercise could only be beneficial. Their pace was sedate, the day fair. They walked the path that curved along the lake. Madeline had chosen it, though Catherine could not say why. The surface was a dark and putrid green, the breeze churning up small waves and carrying the pungent scent of the brackish water.

"Which cousin?" she asked, for there were now two in residence.

"Gabriel." Madeline exhaled in a huff. There was a dark edge to her tone as she said his name. "Sebastian will tell you enough without my help. He finds himself to be a fascinating topic indeed. Besides, I think you are not so interested in him."

Catherine slanted her a sidelong glance, feeling a warm rush of embarrassment at the blunt observation, as though Madeline had somehow peeked into her secret musings. She had been thinking about him. Gabriel. Images came at her, unwanted, unbidden. The touch of his hand on her nape as she sobbed; the small kindnesses he had offered—a cool cloth, a glass of water. Simple things she had not even known she needed until he brought them to her.

The memory of his kiss, hungry, possessive, made her lips tingle even now, and she wondered exactly what Madeline knew that made her raise the topic of her cousin Gabriel.

Nothing. Of course, she knew nothing.

Madeline had been tucked in her bed, cradled in laudanum-induced slumber when Gabriel had come to Catherine's chamber.

"I do wonder about your cousin," she replied at last, linking her arm with Madeline's. "Would you like to talk about him?"

"Not in the slightest." Madeline pressed her lips together and toed at the dirt with the tip of her boot before walking on. "But I shall because there are things you must know, things I must tell you while my mind is my own and I can speak the words I wish to say rather than the ones that trip to the tip of my tongue and fly free whether I will it or nay." She paused and drew a ragged breath. "We both know that I am not always lucid now."

Pity twisted Catherine's heart. The self-portrait painted by Madeline's words was horrifying, all the more so because Madeline was brutally aware of her own decline.

"Tell me whatever you wish," she murmured. "I shall listen."

"Avidly, I am sure," Madeline observed with a dull laugh, and Catherine could not deny it.

"Yes. Avidly." She lowered her head as they walked and stared at the thin, brown grass on either side of the dirt path. A clump of pansies burst from the earth, the color of their petals somewhere between butterscotch and yellow, the centers darker. They made her think of Gabriel's eyes, liquid topaz in the light, amber gold in the shadows.

"Do not romanticize him, Catherine. He is not a good man, or a kind one. Do not paint him in variegated hues of light." Madeline stumbled to a stop, clutched her arm all the tighter, and finished with a harsh cry, "He is a monster."

A handful of black birds that had been pecking at the dirt startled at her cry. Their wings slapped air, the sound like the snap of a rag to shake out the dust. The sight of them reminded Catherine of the night of her arrival and the dead bird on the drive.

She turned her head to find Madeline tracking their flight, her features scrunched tight, as though she battled tears.

A lump clogged her throat as Catherine realized how transparent she was. Even Madeline, with her tenuous grasp on reality, read the yearning that burgeoned in her heart for Gabriel St. Aubyn, a man whose own cousin believed him capable of murder. Her lungs felt tight, each breath a struggle, the weight of her regret heavy on her breast. Once before, she had been blinded by attraction, by gratitude, by the kindness a man showed her that she had believed came from his heart. False kindness. She had paid a horrific price for her folly.

Was she allowing herself to walk the same path once more? Had she learned nothing at all?

No. She was wiser now. Stronger.

Then why did Gabriel's words haunt her in the dark of night and the light of day? Why could she not thrust aside the things he had whispered to her?

Because you are parched and I am water, because you are breathless and I am air, he had said, the images evoked by his words stroking her already sensitized nerves. He believed she would come to need him.

To ache for him.

He was wrong. She must guard herself and make certain that he was wrong.

It was only in a moment of weakness that she had allowed Gabriel to kiss her. There was her excuse. She would not allow it to happen again. She would never permit herself to need him that way. It was a definite path to heartbreak and ruin. She had learned that much, at least.

Beside her, Madeline swayed in place, her eyes closed, her lips pressed tight together. What paltry color had been in her cheeks leached away now until she was white as bone.

"My tale is long, and I tire so easily," she said. "Perhaps it would be best if we return to my chamber"—she looked nervously to the left, the right, and lowered her voice—"though it is likely safer to speak out here. The walls have ears."

Of that, Catherine had no doubt. Mrs. Bell's ears, or the footman's or the cook's. Servants who made themselves invisible, but saw and heard much. But she knew that Madeline spoke of other ears, those belonging to creatures no one but she could see.

They made their way inside, Madeline leaning heavily on Catherine's arm. The trip up the flights of stairs was laborious; Madeline begged for rest again and again. What would take Catherine a matter of minutes to ascend on her own took the two of them the better part of a half hour. At last, they reached Madeline's chamber.

"Shall I summon the maid to help you change?" Catherine asked.

"Will you help me?" Madeline sighed. "I only like Susan. She has gentle hands. But she has gone away."

As Catherine helped Madeline to remove her walking gown and don a fresh nightrail, she was heartened to note that her friend's form was slender but not wasted despite her poor appetite and the minuscule amount of food she ingested in Catherine's presence. Perhaps she nibbled a bit when no one was with her.

"Open the curtains so I might see the sky," Madeline murmured as she settled in her bed.

Catherine did as she requested, then returned to her side and lowered herself to the edge of the bed. A thick ribbon of silence wove about them, interrupted only by the quiet sounds of their breathing. Madeline's eyes were closed, her features relaxed.

After a moment, the chirping of birds carried through the glass panes, and Catherine turned her face to the window, thinking that Madeline had drifted to sleep, that her opportunity to know more about Gabriel was lost for the moment.

"He killed them."

Catherine started at the sound of Madeline's voice, the fine hairs on her arms rising. She bit her tongue against the flood of questions that swelled to her lips like breakers on the shore, agonizingly aware that Madeline would tell her tale at her own pace or not at all. That much she had learned in her time at Cairncroft Abbey. With pounding heart, she waited.

"No, that is not right," Madeline murmured, sounding

perplexed, her eyes remaining closed as she spoke. "He killed only one, lifted it from the nest and twisted its head clear around before he was interrupted. I was there, in the woods, watching though he did not know it. He meant to kill another. I saw it in his face, but there was the snap of a twig. Someone else was there. I heard it, as did he." Her words had taken on a whispery, breathless quality, as though she ran headlong down a hill and could not stop. "He took up a sharp stick and ran through the forest. I could not keep up. He was bigger and faster, and I was hampered by my skirt." She sucked in a sharp breath. Her hand fluttered at her throat. "And then there was so much blood. Everywhere. On his hands. On mine."

"Whose blood was it, Madeline?" Catherine felt the weight of Madeline's story like a great stone on her breast. "Was it yours? Did he hurt you?"

"Me?" Madeline's lids opened wide and she appeared startled by the question. "No." She fell silent, and each second that ticked past made Catherine so anxious for the remainder of the tale that she thought she would jump right out of her skin. But she suspected that Madeline would not be rushed, and to try to press her might well result in no information at all.

Madeline shivered and shifted on the bed and pushed at the covers, writhing to be free of their weight.

"Whose blood was it, Madeline?" Catherine stroked her hand, hoping to ease her distress.

Raising her head, Madeline grew still, her blue eyes wide, her gaze steady and bare.

"She is in the graveyard. Buried under the stone in the corner. No one ever knew her name. There was blood that day, as well. So much blood, and her bodice was split open.

I saw it, though they tried to turn me away. I wanted to go closer. To know."

"To know what?" Catherine tried to make sense of Madeline's ramblings, her thoughts tumbling one against the next. Though the narration was far from clear, Catherine surmised that Madeline described two different occasions, two different deaths.

And that, somehow, Madeline held Gabriel responsible.

Madeline clutched tightly at her wrist, her fingers cold as ice against Catherine's skin.

"I should have told that day." Madeline wet her lips.

Catherine glanced at the pitcher and glass on the washstand. She made to rise and fetch Madeline a drink, but Madeline clung to her like a hawk clinging to its prey, her nails biting tender flesh.

"I should have told them what I saw," Madeline cried, her eyes grown wild now. "But I was afraid they would not believe me. I was only newly come from Browning, my parents so recently dead. I was the outsider. The unwanted burden. I was afraid to tell them what I saw. Do you understand? I was afraid. And then he killed her. *He killed her*."

"Shh, Madeline, shh," Catherine whispered, and Madeline relaxed a little, enough to release her clawlike grasp of Catherine's arm.

"How was I to know they would send him away for good?" she pleaded. "I thought they would send *me* away, and where was I to go? With my father's death, Cairncroft passed to his brother, my uncle, and I became only a guest here in my own home." She sighed. "They never came to love me."

With that admission, Madeline faded, the light in her eyes dulled, the tone of her muscles relaxed. She appeared to sink into the bed, into herself. Even her cheeks grew hollow.

Catherine was at a loss, all the words of comfort she might offer dry and stale on her tongue. She had never known just how closely Madeline's circumstance paralleled her own. Parents and home lost. Dependent on relatives for kindness and charity. But despite her empathy, she was having difficulty believing Madeline's assertions. Only parts of her friend's story made any sense.

Frowning, she tried to follow the tangled threads to some sort of logical conclusion. From what she could patch together, Madeline spoke of two different occasions, perhaps months, or even years apart. One where she had watched someone—presumably Gabriel—kill a bird and then run through the woods with a stick, and ultimate, undefined tragic results.

And a second event, where a girl's body had been found.

Unease crawled through her like a centipede, making her shiver.

That day when she and Gabriel had walked in the graveyard, when he had gifted her with the red and gold tin, he had blocked her path and kept her from seeing the headstone in the corner. Madeline's bewildering account made her suspect that the murdered girl was buried there.

But that knowledge only circled back to more questions. Why had Gabriel kept her from seeing the stone? *Had* he kept her from it? Thinking back on it now, she wondered if she could possibly have misread his actions. Perhaps he had only been intent on holding her attention long enough to offer his gift.

And the girl who was buried there . . . had she been murdered as Madeline intimated, or had she died in some horrific accident? And what did her death have to do with Gabriel, or with Madeline's assertion that she had watched him from the woods while he killed a bird?

None of this made sense, and Catherine had no way to tell if all was fact or all was a fantastical nightmare Madeline had carried forward to her waking hours.

Perhaps the truth was some patchwork of the two.

The place to start was the beginning, and so she picked up that thread of Madeline's ramblings.

"Madeline," she said, taking her friend's hand between her own. "What happened to the birds? Tell me about them."

Turning her head on the pillow, Madeline smiled, serene and calm. "I hear them singing. Such a lovely day. The birds are singing."

They were. Catherine could hear them through the glass of the window. But it appeared she would hear no more of Madeline's tale. Not now.

Whatever brief coherence had touched her friend's mind, it was gone.

Catherine could only wonder when—and if—it would return.

With Madeline fast asleep, Catherine left her for a few moments, intent on retrieving her novel from the sitting room she had visited earlier in the day. Following the maze of stairs down, she came to a sharp corner that she must round to reach the passage that led to the next flight. Voices carried to her, and she hesitated, listening, a feminine voice answered by a masculine; Mrs. Bell and Gabriel engaged in conversation. She could not say what made her remain there, holding her breath, loath to betray her presence.

No, that was not true. She could say exactly what made her do it. She *wanted* to overhear, to listen, unseen. She wanted to glean any information about Gabriel St. Aubyn that she could. Perhaps if she knew enough, she could convince herself he was a villain, convince herself not to long for his touch. His kiss. The feel of his arms tight about her.

Madeline was afraid of him, perhaps even hated him, but given the multitude of things that made Madeline afraid, Catherine could not blindly trust in that. Was he the monster she claimed, or just a man? A strange, enigmatic, arousing man?

He annoyed her, angered her, fascinated her. Beguiled her. And despite it all, he haunted her every thought.

He had comforted her, been a brief calm place in the storm of her grief. Was that enough to make her believe there were depths to him she had not seen? Was it the tiny foundation on which to build the beginnings of . . . something? What? An assignation? An association? What exactly did she want of him? Of herself?

"Will that be all, Mrs. Bell?" Gabriel asked, ruthlessly neutral.

"No, Sir Gabriel. I do not wish to overstep—"

"Then by all means, do not," he interjected.

The housekeeper exhaled noisily, and though Catherine hugged the wall and the shadows and could see them no better than they could see her—which was not at all—she imagined the woman crossing her arms over her belly as she was wont to do, and regarding Gabriel with both wariness and frustration.

"Sir Gabriel," she began again. "I wish to speak with you about Susan."

The silence stretched, and Catherine could imagine the exact expression on his face . . . or rather, lack of expression as he waited for the housekeeper to continue.

"Susan Parker," she clarified, and still he said nothing.

But the name meant something to Catherine. She knew that name. It was—

"She is one of the upstairs maids," Mrs. Bell said, at the exact moment that Catherine recalled precisely who Susan Parker was: the maid she had encountered her very first night here at Cairncroft, the one she had intimidated by implying she would report her to the housekeeper. The episode was not one she was proud of.

"Yes, I am aware of who she is." His assertion surprised Catherine, and then she recalled how he had known Peg's name, and she thought that perhaps he made it his business to know something about each of his staff. She could certainly believe it of him. "What is it you wish to tell me about her?" Gabriel prompted.

"She walked to the shoemaker the day before last to be measured for new shoes. It was her half-day and she left promptly at noon." Catherine heard the clink of Mrs. Bell's key ring, and she thought the housekeeper must have knocked it by accident, or was perhaps worrying it out of nervousness. "Susan never returned."

"Is she due wages?" Gabriel asked, his tone bland. Yet something in his question made Catherine suspect he was more interested in the matter than he wished Mrs. Bell to know.

"No, sir."

"She must have run off."

Mrs. Bell huffed in a breath, loud enough that Catherine could hear it where she stood, far down the corridor and around the corner.

"What if she didn't? What if the same thing happened to her that happened to—"

"Mrs. Bell," Gabriel cut her off, his tone silk and steel.

"We both know that is an impossibility. Let us not raise the issue."

"We do not know—"

"We do." His words, his tone, both absolute in their finality, ended the argument. But again Catherine had the impression that his words masked his true thoughts. "Speak to the other servants. Find out if she had a beau. A sick family member. Any reason that she might have left precipitously."

"And if there is no reason?" Mrs. Bell asked, oddly forlorn.

"There is always a reason, Mrs. Bell. You know that as well as I. Questions always have answers. Puzzles have solutions. It is only that we do not always like the resolutions and explanations we discover, and so we discount them, though they settle the matter quite satisfactorily"—he paused—"even if not pleasantly."

Again, a long moment of silence, and then Mrs. Bell asked in a harsh whisper, "Is that what you call murder? A satisfactory resolution?"

Catherine pressed the back of her hand to her mouth, stifling her gasp, her pulse speeding up like a cart on a hill.

"Our discourse is complete, Mrs. Bell," Gabriel said, his tone calm and even, though Catherine could not imagine how he held his temper in the face of the housekeeper's temerity. "I expect you will keep me apprised of any information that you uncover regarding Susan Parker."

Because he expected information to be uncovered. Catherine was convinced of it. But he did not trust the housekeeper with his suspicions.

Mrs. Bell inhaled sharply, and when she spoke, her voice was tight. "Very well, sir."

A moment later, there came the rapid shush of the housekeeper's footsteps and the swish of her skirt as she moved in the opposite direction. For a slow count of ten, Catherine stayed exactly where she was, motionless as a hare in a field, straining to hear the sounds of Gabriel's retreat. But she heard nothing at all. Not a footstep or breathing or anything to indicate whether he had stayed or gone.

There came a dull thud, like a door closing, or a fist knocked against wood.

Warily, she peeked around the corner. The hallway unfurled before her, the dark walls and blood-red carpet disappearing into dim shadow. Of Gabriel St. Aubyn there was no sign.

"Curiosity can be a dangerous thing." His low voice came from directly behind her right shoulder and she whirled, pressing her palm flat against her chest, her heart twitching and writhing like a landed fish.

"How—" She stumbled away and spun to peer around the wall at the empty hallway where she was certain he had been standing. Of course, the passage was empty. Turning back toward him, she stalked two steps forward, disbelieving. "How did you get there without me seeing you pass?"

He made a hushed laugh, a lush, tantalizing sound she had never before heard him make. It made her shiver. It made her ache.

Deliberately, she took a step back. Equally deliberately, he took a step forward.

Reaching out, he rested his palm against the wall at her back, caging her between wood panel and the length of his body. Her heart slammed against her ribs. Her mouth went dry. He was strong and near, his eyes glittering in the dim light. His gaze dropped to her lips, her breasts, and she stopped breathing entirely.

After a moment, an eternity, his eyes lifted to hers. She gasped at the things she read there: primitive desire, bared and unchained. Bending her knees, she dipped down below his outstretched arm and scooted to the side, away from the threat of him . . . the temptation of him.

He made no move to stop her.

Leaning to the side, he pressed his weight onto his outstretched hand, touching a particular spot on the heavy wooden panel. It swung open to reveal a yawning tunnel, dark as sin.

Grateful for the distraction, she looked away from his face and peered into the gloom, her nose wrinkling at the stale smell and the cobwebs that hung in long, ghostly pale tendrils, broken where he had passed through them.

"You went in there without a candle?" she blurted.

"I did."

"I would not like to." The narrowness of the passage made her shudder.

"Afraid of the dark?" he murmured, too close. He had come up beside her. She wondered that such a tall, powerful man could move with such grace and quiet.

"I am not afraid of the dark," she demurred. "Not since I was a child. It is the confined space I do not like."

As soon as the admission left her lips, she regretted it. What was it about him that made her reveal any part of things better left hidden? She had trained herself to do better than this, but every time he asked a question, she felt driven to answer. She did not want him to know any of her secrets. Not a one. And yet, here she was offering them up without even the slightest consideration, as though a part of her wanted to tell him all. *There* was a sure route to danger.

"I did not like to go in, either," he mused, "for much the same reason."

She blinked, startled that he revealed anything private and personal. It went completely against his nature. She knew enough of him by now to be certain of that. It made his admission something of a gift.

Was it payment in kind? She offered a glimpse of her secret soul, and he did the same? An exchange. A connection. The possibility both thrilled her and made her uneasy.

"Then why did you?" she asked, studying him, noticing a single cobweb woven in the spun gold of his hair. Without thought, she reached up and stroked it away, her fingers lingering at the gently curled ends, so silky and soft.

He stiffened, but did not pull away.

"Because I had no way to know who lurked in this hallway, watching, listening." He offered a tight smile. "I prefer to catch my enemy unawares."

She stared at him, nonplussed, her fingers still twined in his hair. He had known someone was here, listening. How? She was certain she had not made a sound.

"You must have extremely acute senses," she observed, drawing her fingers through his hair.

"Extremely." He looked at her strangely, and it was then she realized what she did: petted and stroked him as though she had a right. Mortified, she pulled her hand away and dropped it to her side.

"You said you like to catch your enemy unawares . . . Am I your enemy?" she whispered.

"The answer to that question resides entirely with you." One corner of his mouth curved in a lazy smile, his eyes darkest amber, his head tipped close, his breath soft on her cheek. "I would prefer that you are not."

Then it was not just his breath on her cheek, but his lips, gliding along her skin to the corner of her mouth. His fingers were warm as they closed on her wrists, and he drew her hands behind his back so she was pulled close against the length of him. Hard muscle beneath perfectly tailored cloth.

She lost her breath, lost her thoughts.

"Why—" She gasped as his tongue traced the edge of her mouth, and turned her face away. Heart pounding, she thought she ought to step away. Run away. But she did not. Instead, she remained exactly where she was. "Why is this tunnel here?" she managed at last.

He shifted his mouth to her ear. "A servants' tunnel. There is a maze of them behind the walls."

With a gentle tug, he drew her closer still, his thighs pressed to hers, and she was drowning in him, the enthralling, faintly citrus scent of his skin, the feel of his body, the way his hands circled her wrists, holding her in place, binding her to him, though he had positioned her so that she was the one whose arms held him close, circling about his lower back.

And why did she not pull away?

Even as he loosed his hold on her wrists and brought one hand to her throat so his thumb stroked her pulse, and the other to her nape, she made no move to break free, but held her arms in an easy loop about his body. Holding him.

Slowly, he tipped his head down, his lips soft on hers, the sweetest caress. She hated him for that, for his gentleness, and for the hard, sharp kick of yearning that even that near-innocent brush of his lips on hers drew from deep inside her.

His mouth was slightly open, his breath warm, mingling with her own, but he did not taste her, did not push his tongue inside her. And she wanted that, ached for it. Oh, how desperately she wanted the taste of him in her mouth.

A whimper tore free, and she arched up, drowning, her lungs and veins and limbs filled only with sharp heat.

Breathless. Hungry.

And then she understood.

. . . because you are breathless and I am air . . .

His mouth played on hers as he *wooed* her, tantalized her, made her breathless so he could be all she craved. She pulsed with the need to press herself tighter against him so that there was no space between them, not even air.

He used only his lips, leaving her imagination to conjure and crave the thrust of his tongue. She wanted him to put his hands on her breasts, and his mouth. His teeth. She wanted him to press her down, here, on the floor, to feel his full weight, heavy and heavenly.

With a nearly chaste kiss he stole her will, her reason, and she had no more breath. He was her air.

She bit his lower lip, lightly, then harder, then soothed the place she had nipped with her tongue.

Abruptly, he pulled away, her name—*Catherine*—no more than a whisper.

No. Do not leave me. She reached for him, her hand pale in the shadows, hovering between them, outstretched.

Chapter 13

"Tell me," Gabriel demanded, holding himself beyond her touch.

Catherine snatched back her hand and pressed it to the hollow of her throat, though she ached with the need to play her fingers across his lips, to stroke his hair, to curl her hands into smooth cloth overlying steely muscle.

She had never yearned, never ached, the way she did in this moment. And he wanted her to say it, to lay herself bare to him, to trust him with full knowledge of her wanting and need.

No, not full knowledge. He had that already. She saw it in the hard glitter of his gaze and the tight line of his jaw. He wanted her *admission*, freely given. He wanted to be water for her thirst, food for her hunger. That night in her chamber he had clearly laid out his terms.

"My bed is down this corridor and up a single flight." His lips curved in a smile dark with promise. "Say it, Catherine. Tell me what you want."

"Please," she breathed, wanting it to be enough. Needing it to be enough. The hated word, offered in supplication.

"No." He frowned and shook his head. "I have no wish to hear you plead. I know it holds dark memories for you."

He knew that? How?

"I am a keen observer," he said, faintly sardonic, answering the questions she had never asked. He caught her hand—the one she had held out to him earlier and now clutched against her throat—and brought her fingers to his lips. His tongue tasted the tips, and then his teeth. She swallowed the moan that begged for escape.

"Say only that you want me. That you hunger." *That I am water and you are parched,* he did not say, but she heard it nonetheless.

"Only that?" she managed with a strangled laugh.

"For now." He stroked the backs of his fingers across her cheek, and she was so sensitized to his touch, so raw, that she had to sink her teeth into her lip to keep from crying out.

Shaking her head from side to side, she backed up a step and then another, poised to flee. He made no move to stop her. Not by expression or action did he alter her course. *Her choice.* With him, it would always be her choice. He had no desire to bend her or break her to his will. She understood that with sudden blinding clarity.

She could give herself to Gabriel without sacrificing who she had become.

Her heart beat, wild and terrible, in her breast. Fear. Lust. Raw, aching need. And then she said it, forced the words through bloodless lips.

"I do. I do want you. I ache for you. I dream of you. I fight it and chain it and lock it behind any boundary I can conjure, and still the wanting steals free." She lowered her head and stared at the tips of his boots, shiny black, catching the paltry light. Her breath came hard and fast, as though she had run for miles. "What have you done to me?"

"Nothing. Not yet. But soon." He yanked her hard against him, his mouth open as he tasted her, his tongue sliding the length of hers, his teeth nipping, gently, then harder, enough to make her gasp. Make her moan. He fed on her, claimed her, his kiss sinking through her to leave fire in its wake.

Lifting her in his arms, he cradled her against his chest, bending his head to nip the skin of her throat. Her breathing was uneven and quick, as was his. He strode along the hallway, then took a flight of stairs with rapid, sure steps, and she clung to him and breathed his scent and buried her face in his neck so she could lick his skin.

He tasted of salt. He tasted like heaven.

Hunger such as she had never known pounded through her.

He kicked open a door, then kicked it shut behind them, and she turned her head to see a massive bed canopied in striped silk, blue on blue, a vast room with rich curtains and a hearth that danced with fire. Something made her notice that—the extravagance of fire in a room no one was expected to use at this hour of the day. The strangeness made her ask, "Why do you keep the hearth burning at this time of the day?"

"I dislike being cold." The words had a sardonic edge. "I keep a fire here and in the library and in any room I expect to spend even a handful of moments." He paused as though grappling with himself and then continued. "I spent too many years shivering, cold to the marrow of my bones."

She sucked in a sharp breath at the naked pain in his tone. Such revelation, from Gabriel? She had no idea how to reply other than to tighten her arms about his neck and kiss his throat, then strain up to reach his mouth and kiss him there.

Delight strummed her senses. The taste of him, like chocolate, like wine, left her dizzy and breathless.

Breaking the kiss, he tossed her in the air. She squealed and landed in a billow of skirt, the mattress dipping as she bounced and bounced again. He dropped down beside her with a laugh, the sound wonderful and startling, a rarity. A gift. She closed her eyes and let it pour over her. Then he kissed her once more, demanding, possessing, and she was lost in a tumult of sensation and need.

Deft fingers worked her gown, her undergarments, yanking aside her half-unbuttoned bodice to bare her breasts. Her nipples hardened in the cool air and she arched, aching, wanting his mouth on her as she had never wanted anything before. His lips closed over her, a gentle swirl of his tongue and then a hard, sucking pull that took her to a place between pain and pleasure. She clenched the covers in her fists and cried out, liquid need pouring through her so powerful and quick she was undone by it, left panting and thrashing.

Tracing his tongue along the dip between her breasts, he freed more buttons, tearing delicate cloth in his haste. His mouth took her other nipple in a sharp tug that made her thrust her hands in his hair to pull him away . . . to drag him closer still. Then he kissed her breast sweetly, his tongue swirling round and round, leaving her wanting—

"Harder," she whispered.

He closed his teeth on her and she felt it clear to her belly, an erotic kick that made her gasp.

Somehow, she found herself naked while he was yet clothed, the situation both embarrassing and arousing, the scrape of his wool coat on her skin and the press of cold metal buttons only serving to layer sensation upon sensation.

She wanted to touch him, to know him, every masculine line and hard angle. She reached for him and he caught her wrists, braceleting them with one hand, stroking the other up her stocking-clad thigh until his palm met bare skin above her garters. He dragged her hands above her head, held them there, and kissed her once more, tongue and teeth, deep. Wet. As he drew back, she followed him, her lips clinging to his.

"Patience, love. We have all the time in the world, and I intend to savor you." To prove his point, he brushed his lips lightly over her own. Not enough. Not nearly enough.

She was not patient. She was greedy and eager.

Through his trousers, the hard length of his arousal pressed against her thigh, powerful, thick, promising to stretch her and fill her. There was nothing subtle or sweet in the way he touched her now, his hands cupping and kneading her breasts, her buttocks. He took. He marked. He drew moans and sighs as he rolled her nipple between his fingers, then dipped his head to suck and bite. She cried out, the pleasure keener than she could bear, her legs scissoring against cool silk.

He rose above her, dragging her hands to the intricately carved headboard, curling her fingers around sections of wood.

"Hold tight to this," he whispered against her ear, "and do not move unless I give you leave." He let a heartbeat pass. "Or I could bind you."

Her breath left her in a rush, the image of that both incredibly erotic and frightening all at once. No. She could not. To trust him with this, to give him leave to do this . . .

she could not. She jerked her hands from the headboard and pushed against his chest.

He let her. She knew that. As his weight lifted and he took it on his outstretched arms, she knew he *let* her push him away.

Then he caught her right wrist and dragged her hand back to the headboard, curling her fingers around the wood once more. Now it was she who let him do this, trembling, panting, wanting him and afraid of what he asked, so many emotions swirling through her she knew not which one swam strongest. He took her other hand, and drew it up the same way, his voice guttural as he repeated his command against her ear.

"Do what I say, Catherine. I will not have him in my bed. Not today, or any other. I will not have you haunted by the dark memories he spawned. There will be only me in your thoughts as I come into your body. Only me there with you." He buried his face in her neck, inhaling against her skin, his weight resting on one hand while the other held hers trapped against the headboard. "Trust me."

She had no reason to. She had *every* reason to.

He would have her no other way. If she denied him, he would leave her here, aching and empty. She knew it with all she was. He would have all or nothing. Of course. Had she not secretly known exactly that all along? Was that not part of what she wanted from him, his perfect, wretched control?

Tightening her grip on the wood, she held fast, and he laughed, a low, sensual slither of sound that wound around her and through her.

"What—" Her question died in a gasp as he kissed his way down her breasts, her belly, clenching his fingers into her thighs to lift her and open her, his tongue tracing the curve of her hip bone, and Gabriel smiled, secretly, darkly pleased.

No one had kissed her here before. The wriggling of her hips and her startled, panting breaths told him that as clearly as if she screamed it aloud, or pushed him away, or leaped from the bed in dismay. No one had kissed her mons or her lovely, swollen folds.

Not yet.

"Do not move," he rasped, imperative. He would have this of her, the taste of her—warm and wet and female—on his tongue. He breathed in the scent of her, aroused to the point of pain.

"Gabriel." A soft, plaintive cry.

He held her hips and dipped his head, his tongue stroking her between the folds of her sex, finding moisture and warmth, salt and heaven. His mouth closed over the hot, sensitive core of her. She jerked as though struck.

"No! You—" Her denial died sharply as he nipped her, then licked her. The sounds she made, the way she thrashed, the fact that she held tight to the headboard because he had asked her to and because she chose to accede to his will, gifting him with her trust—all combined to build his own passion, to feed the flame of it. He licked her again, and when she jerked and gasped, he felt the kick of her pleasure low in his own gut.

He took his time with her, stroking her to the razor's edge, pushing one finger, then two, deep inside her. Tight. She was so tight and wet.

Lost in her, he played and stroked, and she gave herself up to him. His to take as he would.

Soft cries tore from her lips, and her hips rose and fell in a primitive rhythm. Then her whole body went rigid, quivering, frozen in time as her release took her over the edge. The only sounds she made then were a soft catch in her throat, and a series of sighs that could be nothing other than his name.

His name.

A dark smile curved his lips as he raised his head and saw she yet held fast to the bed, her fingers curled so tight her knuckles were white. He crawled up her lush body, kissing her belly, her full, round breasts, her throat, her lips. She made an inarticulate sound and tried to turn away, but he caught her chin in his fingers, a gentle grasp, and kissed her full on the mouth. She tensed, then melted, opening to him with a sensual little moan. He supposed that tasting herself on his tongue was not as horrid as she had expected. In fact, the way she tipped her head and sucked on his tongue, his lips, offering sighs of pleasure, made him certain she had forgotten whatever qualms had assailed her.

This was how he wanted her. Wet and ready and pliable. This was how he wanted their joining. Earthy and messy. Nothing forbidden. Nothing taboo.

She wore only her stockings and as he reared back and looked down at her, he was certain that even one more moment would be a moment too long. Because she was lush and beautiful and there before him, offering herself like a gift.

Her fingers bit into the wooden headboard, and Catherine stared up at Gabriel feeling sultry and sated and aroused all at once. She was fully nude. He was fully clothed. The sensation of being bare and open to him was incredibly erotic.

She had never imagined a man could kiss a woman there. She had never imagined the bliss to be found in that.

"I want—" She broke off, pressed her lips together, wondering how to ask.

"What do you want? Tell me."

"I"—she shook her head, thrust aside her embarrassment—"I want to taste you. Suck you. Feel you hard and hot in my mouth." She did. The thought of it put into words made her yearn all the more.

"Your wish. My command." He moved so that his knees were on either side of her shoulders. Reaching down, he undid his trousers and the long, thick length of his cock sprang free.

Her heart raced. Her belly twisted with lust, and she opened her mouth, taking him inside, and all the while she held her hands where he had placed them, the unenforced captivity only adding an edge to her arousal. She licked the length of him, then sucked him deep. Deeper. And still she did not have the whole of him.

Hot, smooth skin over steel. He impaled her, pumping only deep enough for her comfort and no deeper. She wanted to swallow him, to fill her mouth, her throat with him, and she moaned, arching her back and lifting her head to take more.

With a shaky laugh, he pulled away. "Keep at it, love, and you'll taste more than skin."

Dipping his head, he kissed her, sucking on her lips, nipping them, thrusting his tongue into her mouth to dance with her own as he slid down her body. The rasp of his superfine coat against her naked nipples made her gasp and wriggle.

The heat of his erection pressed against the inside of her thigh. He was so hard, so big, the smooth head stretching her as he pushed at her opening, then withdrew, again and again, a little deeper each time. She gasped, wanting him to press in . . . in . . .

Then he did. Oh, God, he did. A quick, smooth thrust and he was inside her, filling her, joined so close and tight, his pelvis pressed against the most sensitive part of her. She thought he would pump, hard and fast, seek his own pleasure. But that was not Gabriel's way. Instead, he rocked his hips only a little. Just a little. Not enough.

She gasped and writhed, but he whispered—"Still. Be still, Catherine"—and continued that maddening, sensual, gentle rocking that wound her tighter and took her higher. But not high enough.

There was carnality in that, in giving herself over to his will, his desires. His control.

She shuddered.

Catching the back of her knee, he bent her leg and lifted it until her ankle rested on his shoulder, then did the same with the other, dipping his head to kiss her neck, her jaw. She clenched her fists tight to the headboard, beguiled, seduced. She wanted this, wanted him. Liked the places he was taking her.

Then he began a new rhythm, a hot, slick pump and slide, fast and rough enough that it left her mindless, left her gasping. She was lost, her hands tearing free of the place she had willingly fettered them, coming to rest on his shoulders, the cloth of his coat scratchy beneath her palms as she fisted and crushed it. She cried out as he pushed deeper, then withdrew, pleasure driving her, driving him.

One arm was outstretched to take his weight, the other cupped around her buttock, kneading roughly as he moved. He was beautiful, flexing and straining above her. She splayed her hands across his buttocks, pulling him closer still.

For an instant, she wished he were naked, wished it was his warm, smooth skin beneath her palms rather than cloth. And then she lost the thought, lost everything but the sensations he evoked.

Tension wound her like a clock key. And then it broke, she broke, a thousand glittering pieces falling apart and coming together with each pulsing wave that crashed over her. She threw back her head and screamed, the pleasure so hard and tight she was certain she would not survive.

Above her, suddenly rigid, Gabriel made no sound, only pulled from her and found his own release, his seed pumping from him, his head bowed, his long, beautiful hair sliding forward to brush her breasts.

She clung to him, her skin smeared with his seed, her heart pounding.

Slowly, he lowered her legs from his shoulders, turning his head to kiss the inside of first one knee, then the other. Then he smiled at her, a satyr's smile. She could not do other than smile in return.

Rolling to his side, he drew her close, and to her astonishment, he smeared his seed all over her belly with the tips of his fingers, then turned and kissed her on her mouth with leisurely care.

"I—" She glanced down, watching his fingers trace slow swirls, and felt the dark edge of her sadness creep into this moment of joy.

She should tell him that there was no need for him to withdraw and spill his seed outside her body. There as no need for him to fear that she would catch with child. Tears pricked her eyes. She should tell him.

But to say it aloud . . . She never had before. It would make it real.

Of course it was real. She had known it for some time.

Why did she behave so foolishly now? *Tell him.*

"What is it, Catherine?" he asked, his voice low, laced with tension. "Do you know regret already?"

Regret? For lying with him? For experiencing what she had only imagined in the past?

"No. Never." She drew a deep breath, feeling the pull on her lungs that warned her she could inhale no deeper, then she blew out all the air in a rush. "It is only . . . You need not withdraw like that." Her voice broke then, and with it, her composure, and she bit hard on her lip to fight back the tears. Finally, she whispered, "I cannot have a child. Not ever. I cannot—"

His hand stilled. His body tensed. For a long moment, he said nothing, and then, "You cannot have *another* child."

He knew. Somehow, he knew, though she had not told him.

Of course, she should have expected that, perceptive as he was. Perhaps he saw the subtle signs on her body, though she had come away from her pregnancy with few changes save slightly rounder hips and darker nipples, and two fine, silvery lines that marked the skin above her pubis.

Whatever had given her away, he had seen it and guessed the cause.

"No, I cannot." Pain twisted her heart until she thought the organ would break or burst or tear from her breast to lie beating on the floor. Old pain. She had thought she had it caged. She swallowed, wet her lips, dizzy with the speed that her emotions had risen high as a bird, then plummeted like a stone. "How did you know?"

"I did not. Not with any certainty. Until now."

Of course. He had tricked her into revealing all, and he had revealed nothing. Not even his body. He was yet fully clothed.

Had she been the only one to participate here? To feel the things she felt? To feel lo—

No. She would not think that, would not string the letters together to form the word. Not even in her private thoughts. Love was like sand between her fingers, or smoke. Grab hold as tightly as possible, and still it would slip away.

Resting his chin lightly on her crown, he asked, "Where is your baby, Catherine?"

"He died." Liar. He did not die. He was killed. He was murdered. His life was stolen.

She could not share this. Could trust no one with her pain. With the horrible truths that haunted her. Why would she trust him with any of her secrets when he trusted her with nothing? Nothing at all.

He was her lover, not her friend.

She was mad to do this. Mad to lie here. The physicality of their joining was one thing, the deceptive promise of emotional succor quite another. She needed to get away, to flee. She needed—

"Oh, God!" she cried, and tried to leap from the bed, but Gabriel only tightened his grip and turned her so she curled against his body, his arms wrapped tightly around her as horrible, choking sobs tore free. The torrent was shocking and sudden, a brutal wrenching-away of her walls and defenses that she had not expected, certainly not wanted. But she could not seem to make it stop.

On some level, she understood that she cried and ranted, words flowing like a sea of poison, that she struggled in his embrace, that she hit him, pummeling his chest with her closed fists.

That he let her.

In ragged, agonized spurts she cursed fate and men and the brutal world that cast women as lesser beings without rights, without recourse. And he held her and listened, not saying a word.

At length, she sniffed and scrubbed the back of her hand along her cheek, wiping away her tears, then shivered. She was naked still. Without loosing his hold on her, Gabriel shifted to draw the coverlet out from beneath him and drape it over her.

"It seems I cry more when I am around you than I have cried—" Almost did she say *since my son was murdered*, but in the end found she could not. "In a very long while," she said instead, feeling drained and faintly ill.

"And I thank you for that."

"Thank me?" She tipped her head to study his expression. It was as it had always been, calm, cool. "Why do you thank me? Because you see me at my worst?"

"You have no worst. You are who you are, every bit of you, every part of your present and past. You allow yourself to feel, to grieve when you are with me." He stroked her hair back from her face. "Trust is a gift, Catherine. You have given me a gift."

His assertions made her want to cry all over again. And they stole her own words because she knew not what to say. She did not trust him. Not fully. And she certainly did not want to allow such horrific swells of emotion to burst free when she was with him. It only seemed that circumstances arranged for her to behave this way.

The first time he had comforted her as she sobbed out her grief over Martha's murder, he had stumbled upon her. That was happenstance, nothing more.

But today . . . perhaps today it *was* because she trusted him, felt safe with him. At least a little. She had no idea if she would ever trust him enough to tell all.

"What do you know of me?" she asked, certain that he knew all manner of secrets, though not her deepest ones.

"I know you became the ward of Jasper Hunt, Baron Sunderley, when he assumed the title after your father was killed. I know you became his lover, and now I know you bore him a child."

She swallowed and nodded. "He wooed me. Made me such pretty promises. We would be wed, he said. I believed him. In the beginning, I loved him. With the love that a young girl bestows on her first suitor. Innocent, naïve love in a heart and mind that had no understanding of what might follow a first, chaste kiss. He came to my bed in the darkest hours of the night, and I lay there as he did what he would. Always quickly. Never"—she bit her lip, unwilling to compare, but seeing no other way to make it clear to him how she felt—"not like this. Never like this.

"It was not long before he began to change. He did not like the way I wore my hair and had me fix it in a different style. He did not like the gown I wore to supper and had me return to my chamber and don a different one, then said I was too slow and let me have no supper at all. Then he did not like my tone when I spoke. 'Can you not be soft, Catherine?' he would say. 'Can you not be quieter?' And other days it would be 'Can you not speak up? Must you whisper?' As time passed, he began to grow short and sharp with me all the time. Just the sight of me was enough to turn his temper. I pleased him less and less."

"There are those in this world that will not be pleased no matter what we do," Gabriel murmured.

"Yes. I know that now. But I did not know it then. He used to make me beg. 'Say please, my cat.' One night, I did not beg prettily enough. He took up a small wooden box from my table. It was a birthday gift from my grandmother the year she died, a small treasure that had not been sold to pay my father's debts. He used his knife to pry off a bit of the ivory inlay. Then he used the heavy handle of the poker to smash it to dust. I begged, but it only made him angrier. He pried off the next bit and the next, and in the end, he smashed the whole box, bringing the poker down again and again, bidding me reach in and save the damned thing if I wanted it so badly." She fell silent, shuddering as memories toppled against memories like a line of domino bones.

"You sketch for me a skeleton of your life with him," Gabriel said. "I suspect the flesh of it was even worse." There was leashed fury in his tone. She was stunned to hear it. He was normally so calm and even.

"Yes." The word was no more than a breath as she remembered all, remembered that Jasper had broken her, but that, she would tell no one.

For a long while, they only lay on the bed, wrapped around each other, breathing in unison. Then Gabriel asked in his ever-blunt way, "And your child, Catherine?"

Her child. Her baby.

"When I became pregnant, he locked me away and told the servants I was not to be let free and none were to speak to me. I spent the months of my confinement in a single room. The windows were painted shut." She could not help but glance at her hands now, remembering the way she had clawed at the frames until she bled. "The solitude was terrible. I think there is nothing so painful as to be alone, completely and utterly alone."

"Yes," Gabriel agreed, a wealth of meaning in that single word. She wondered that he understood. That he *knew*. She could hear it, feel it in the subtle tension that suddenly laced his frame.

"When were you alone?" she asked, certain that they

shared this, that he had been locked away as she had been locked away, but unable to see the possibility of how.

"This is your time, Catherine," Gabriel replied. "There is time enough for my story."

Was there? Or was he simply avoiding sharing any of his secrets with her?

"Tell me," he urged.

"Why?"

For an instant he looked nonplussed, and tilted his head in contemplation. "Because I wish to know."

He was nothing if not consistent. He wished to know and so he expected an answer. Oddly, despite the tension of the moment and the terrible memories that bit at her, she found a measure of comfort, and perhaps even amusement, at his reply.

"Jasper . . ." She paused, hating to even say his name, hating that he still had that power over her, the power to make any emotion surge in her breast. "Jasper brought a doctor when my pains came, and when it was done, my baby born, the doctor took a"—she swallowed against the horror that swelled at the recollection of the hooked crotchet: cold metal and ripping pain—"he did something inside me, and I sickened after that. I burned with fever. I almost died. I remember him coming again and again, bleeding me, and speaking of scarring to my female parts. He told Jasper I could never again bear a child."

"I will take you to London," Gabriel said. "To Germany. To France. There are doctors there."

She stared at him, not understanding at all. Then it came to her with stunning clarity. "You mean to take me to physicians until you find one that can give me hope?"

"Of course."

"Why?" She shook her head, her confusion absolute. "Because you want a child?"

She could not misread the appalled horror that crossed his features, a fleeting flicker of expression that faded as quickly as it appeared.

"No." Then, "I would take away your pain," he offered gently, as though it was the most obvious thing in the world.

Though it made no sense to her, given that he must surely need an heir, he clearly did not want a child, yet he wanted her to be able to bear one.

"You do understand the contradiction there?" she asked. A moment passed. "I have seen several doctors. Whatever funds I had were spent on them. The answer is always the same. There are no children in my future."

Instead of offering a reply, he leaned close and kissed her lids, her cheek, her mouth. Then he drew the sheets higher over her naked form, rose, and crossed to the bell pull.

"What are you doing?" she asked.

"We need a bath."

A bath. In the middle of the day. The servants would bring the tub and hot water. And they would know. Even if she hid behind the privacy screen, they would know. She was uncomfortable with the thought. It was her nature to be private, even more so now that she had been the object of gossip for so long. She preferred not to draw such notice.

"I have no wish to cause inconvenience," she demurred. "I can make do with the basin and pitcher." She dipped her head toward the washstand.

"No, you cannot." Very deliberately, he tugged the embroidered ribbon to summon a servant. When the maid came, he spoke through the door, giving the order for the tub and hot water to be brought up.

From her place on the bed, she studied him, his broad

shoulders, his now-rumpled coat and waistcoat. The inequity irked her. He was completely clothed.

She rose from the bed and went to him. He only watched her, saying nothing, his eyes narrowed.

"I want to touch you," she said, unable to believe she had made love to a man who had not so much as removed his coat. There had been a certain delicious decadence to that at the time, but it left her a little uncomfortable now.

"Do you?" he murmured.

"May—"

He put his finger to her lips, staying her words.

"Take what you want, Catherine. Take it. I will not have you looking for my permission." He offered the barest smile. "I told you I would not have him in my bed. You are a different woman now than you were then. Whatever he did to you, it is gone. Past. Dead"—she gasped, feeling the blood rush to her cheeks, then drain completely away. Did he know? Did he? But he offered no answer to her secret fears, only kept his finger on her lips, stilling her words—"You want to touch me? To feel my skin beneath your palms?"

She could only nod, wanting that, wanting him, again.

"Then take what you want, love." He dragged her hand to his mouth, pressed a kiss to her palm, then held his arms out, offering her leave to do what she willed.

Sliding her hands beneath his coat, she slanted him a glance through her lashes. Then she clutched the fabric in her fingers and yanked his coat down his arms, leaving him in shirtsleeves and waistcoat.

Something dark crossed his features, and for a moment, she had the strange thought that he would stop her, that he did not wish to disrobe before her. Her gaze raked him. Broad shoulders. Flat belly. Hard contours of muscle apparent even beneath the cloth. What possible reason could he have for refusing her this?

None. He could have none. She was weaving obstacles where none existed.

Next came his waistcoat. Then his cravat of red merino that she slid from beneath the high folded collar of his tucked front shirt. It was only when she went to remove the latter that he caught her wrist, his fingers forming a gentle but firm vise.

"What is it?" she asked. "Has the bath come?" She had not heard a knock.

"No. And when it does, it shall be set in the dressing room. I have no wish to be disturbed, nor to subject you to the servants' scrutiny."

"Thank you," she whispered, touched by his thoughtfulness. "What is it, then?"

His lips tightened, but he said nothing more. Instead, he reached back, caught the collar of his shirt, dragged it over his head, and tossed it to the floor.

Her mouth went dry. He was magnificent. Cool hard planes and angles. Perfect shadows. Supple skin shifted over smooth muscle as he rolled his shoulders, but as her gaze lifted to his face, she read wariness and a guarded watchfulness. Why?

Reaching out, she laid her hand on his chest, stroked along his muscle to his shoulder, his arm, his elbow. There she stopped, her breath catching. Understanding came to her.

He was scarred.

The crooks of his elbows and the front of his forearms bore a multitude of thin white lines, side by side, some overlapping, some of the scars raised and wider, leading her to believe the place had been cut repeatedly.

He had been bled. More than once. More than a hundred

times. Someone had opened his veins again and again and he bore the marks of that on his skin.

Her gaze snapped to his. Not by the flicker of a lash did he betray his thoughts. His expression was calm, reserved, his muscles relaxed. But she sensed the expectancy in him. He waited for what she would say.

And so she said nothing. Not yet. She needed to think on the right words. He had trusted her with this knowledge of him. Exactly as he had said: a gift.

She bent and pressed her mouth to the crook of his elbow, to a raised scar there where she knew the vein lay close to the surface. A faint tremor took him as she kissed him there.

With her fingers resting lightly on his shoulder, she straightened and walked around him to place both palms on his broad back, feeling the play of muscle under smooth skin. He was incredibly beautiful, perfectly formed, his waist lean, his buttocks tight, the curve of his spine a valley between wedges of taut muscle on either side.

She stroked his hair from his nape, a spill of honey gold, wanting to kiss him there. He tensed, then relaxed, the movement so subtle she might have thought she imagined it except . . . She blinked. Frowned. Here, too he was scarred. An odd-shaped mark on the back of his neck was raised and uneven. She had a scar like that, a small one on her knee where she had fallen as a child and the scrape had gone deep and filled with dirt and it had taken a very long while to heal. It had left just such a mark.

But why would he have such a thing on the back of his neck? How would he have injured himself there?

Slowly she finished her circuit, looking her fill, touching him, leaning close to breathe the scent of him, to trace her tongue along the swell of muscle that capped his shoulder, the bulge of his biceps, the raised plane of his chest.

Then she slid his trousers down his thighs, sinking to her knees before him to slide off first one shoe then the other, one trouser leg then the other until he was as naked as she. She sensed he suffered her leisurely ministrations and perusal, but suspected he was not relaxed in this.

And as she peeled away the first of his stockings, his foot resting on her bent knees, what she saw made her certain.

Something terrible had been done to him.

"Who hurt you?" she asked, swallowing the fury that welled in her heart. She knew the marks of a burn well enough, and his feet bore not one such mark, but many.

On her knees before him, she tipped her head back and met his gaze, wanting answers, uncertain exactly what questions to ask. Then from the adjacent dressing room she heard the sound of the tub being prepared, water pouring, a footman's murmur and a maid's reply.

"Your bath awaits," he said, looking down at her, his arms loose by his sides.

She shook her head. "It can wait."

"The water will grow cold."

Leaning forward, she rested her cheek against his thigh. "Then we shall bathe in cold water."

There was a long moment of silence that made her look up, seeking his gaze.

"I do not bathe in cold water. Ever." There was ice in his tone, colder than any winter storm. "And henceforth, neither do you." An order. A pledge. It wasn't about the discomfort of a cold bath. There was something more here.

The fine hairs at her nape rose.

In an easy, fluid motion, he scooped her in his arms and, kicking open the door to the dressing room, carried her through, ending any discussion.

As he sank into the tub with her, sloshing water over the

sides, he kissed her, hard. He made love to her again, there in the bath, and when the water cooled, he carried her to his bed once more, taking his fill of her, and offering her the same in return.

But though her questions were diverted and delayed, they were not forgotten. Later, as they lay together, warm beneath the sheets and coverlet, soft pillows beneath their heads, she asked him again, "Who hurt you?"

Part Three

Chapter 14

Hanham, England, 1814

Gabriel peered out the window of the coach, anxious to know their destination. Mother offered no answer when he asked. Not the first time or the second or the tenth. She only shook her head and tried to make her mouth form a smile, but it was more of a grimace and it never reached her eyes. Her eyes were sad and afraid and she sat on the seat opposite him, not beside him, as though she could not bear to be close to him.

Father had not come for the carriage ride today. He had stood on the drive at Cairncroft, his hands linked at the small of his back, his mouth drawn tight.

Of Geoffrey, there had been no sign.

Gabriel could not find any part of himself that was sad for that. He still bore the scar where Geoffrey had stabbed him, low in the gut, the stick passing clear through. In time, the wound had healed. A miracle, the doctor called it, for Gabriel had been so very sick, feverish and weak. But his parents never called it that. At times, he wondered if they thought it more a curse that he had lived.

He had lost his place as his mother's favorite, lost his welcome in her embrace, and he knew not what he had done to warrant it. She had begun to watch him in a strange way, her expression pinched, her hands always fluttering like two hummingbirds. Somehow, he thought she blamed him for being injured, for becoming ill, for the pain and grief and worry.

Too, she had grown confused since his recovery, calling him by his brother's name and his brother by his name. It was disconcerting to see her behave that way. He felt sorry for her, and he missed the way she used to be. At first, he corrected her each time she erred, but she grew so agitated, so angry, that he soon began to keep to the shadows, to try to blend with the furniture. Better she not notice him at all.

The time since that day in the woods had not been kind to his family. He and Geoffrey could barely stand to be in the same room with each other now. Neither of them had been sent off to school, though at their age, they had expected to be. Gabriel was made to feel that it was somehow his fault, that he had created the tension and dark cloud that hung over the abbey.

Then, last month, they had found the dead girl. Murdered. Lying in a pool of her own blood. No one had known who she was or where she had come from. She was found in a shallow grave, the dirt barely tossed over her, her body mutilated, her chest cut open.

Sebastian had been visiting Cairncroft. It was he who had found her and then Geoffrey and Madeline had followed close behind. Gabriel had only heard the news when he overheard the servants gossiping. The maids had been upset. And Mrs. Bell, the new housekeeper, had sobbed and wailed behind the closed door of her quarters. Gabriel had heard her as he clung to the shadows, listening.

In the end, they had buried the dead girl in a corner of the abbey's ancient graveyard, her marker bare of a name, saying only the date they had found her, for they did not know the dates of her birth or her death, did not know who she was. Or who had killed her.

There were days that Gabriel thought he knew, that memories and images came to him and painted a terrible, terrifying picture. But he thrust those thoughts aside, refusing to believe.

In recent months, the cloud over the abbey had become heavier still, and Gabriel had felt himself a stranger in his home, an outcast in his family. He had slowly begun to lose interest in any of his normal pursuits, while his twin, Geoffrey, gained interest in those same things. Where it had always been Gabriel who was anxious to read, to learn, it was now Geoffrey who professed a love of books. And Geoffrey had begun a strange game, playing into their mother's odd behavior, answering whenever their parents used Gabriel's name.

At first, Gabriel had gone along, answering to Geoffrey's name, believing—as his brother insisted—that it was best to humor their mother who was sad and confused. He likened it to the games they had played as children where they traded places and tricked anyone who was near. In truth, they were identical, able to fool anyone save each other.

Geoffrey laughed at that, and said, "Perhaps we can learn to trick even each other."

Gabriel thought such a thing absurd. How could he be tricked to believe he was other than himself?

Soon the game had turned sour for him, and though he insisted he was Gabriel, not Geoffrey, he was not certain his parents believed him. Certainly his cousin Madeline seemed positive that he was Geoffrey and his brother was Gabriel.

The longer Geoffrey played his tricks, the more Gabriel's sadness and weariness grew, until he was loath to roll from his bed each morning. He stopped answering to any name at all, because no one believed he was who he said he was.

His parents had taken to closeting themselves away, taking first Madeline then Geoffrey into the room for hours at a time. But not Gabriel. Never Gabriel. Not until that day last week when three men in black suits had come to Cairncroft. They had sat with him in the sun-drenched parlor, the windows at their backs, making it hard for him to read their faces. They had asked him all manner of odd questions, one of them making detailed notes in a black, leather-bound book as Gabriel made his replies.

At first, he answered readily. But soon, a cold dread had come upon him, though he could not name a reason for it, and his answers had become terse, his voice betraying his anxiety.

But today things had dawned brighter. Mother had invited him to ride with her in the carriage. Only him. Not Geoffrey. Not Father or Madeline. Only him. She had exchanged a long look with Father and then called Gabriel by his own name, not Geoffrey's.

He knew then that he had done something right, though he had not managed anything right since that horrible day in the woods. The day he had almost died.

The carriage turned now, and stopped. Massive iron gates blocked their path. On either side, extending as far as the eye could see, was a high brick wall. This must be a fine estate indeed to warrant such protection. The gates swung open, and Gabriel could hear a clunking sound from within the small lodge adjacent to the gate.

"Do you suppose there is a mechanism there for opening the gates, Mother? Could we stop? I should like to see it."

But she did not answer. She only stared out the window, her skin stretched taut and thin across the bones of her face.

They went slowly up a long drive with vast squares of open lawn on either side. They were close to the village of Hanham, his mother had told him earlier when he asked. Eager now, he scooted forward on the seat.

"What place is this?"

His mother continued to stare out the window and still did not look at him. "Hanham House," she replied, her voice thick.

He knew that sound, the sound of choked tears, but he knew better than to ask why she was sad. He had stopped asking that question months past. She never answered, only looked at him with eyes that did not see what was before her, but rather something far, far away.

He wished he could change the past. He wished he had never followed Geoffrey into the woods that day, never seen him twist the neck of that baby bird, never run through the woods with his brother pounding at his heels. Never been stabbed with the sharp end of that stick. There were even days that he wished he had never recovered. They had thought he would not. He vaguely remembered endless pain, and the heat of his fever, and doctors coming and going. His mother's sobs. His father kneeling by his bed.

Oft times, he thought they had mourned his passing, and were somehow distressed that he had lived instead.

He wished, too, that they had never found the dead girl in her shallow, leaf-strewn grave. Better if she had been left to rest there quietly. Things had only gone from bad to worse, then.

Once, Madeline had even asked him why he had killed her. Stunned, he had at first made no reply. Then he found his voice and practically snarled at her an order to never say such a thing again. She had run to his father and said he had threatened her, and his father had only looked at him with eyes narrowed and cold. Madeline made certain to leave any room he entered, after that. She was never alone with him again, a situation he had not found overly disappointing.

He had disliked his cousin before. He despised her now.

The carriage rocked to a halt again, and he looked out at a massive house, nearly as large as Cairncroft Abbey. Then he saw it was not one house, but several, built close together.

On the seat across, his mother began to fidget. She played with her collar, her pearls, her hat. She did not meet his gaze, and he felt suddenly afraid. His mother never fidgeted.

The door opened and three men stood all in a row, their faces somber, their hands clasped behind their backs as they stared at him with eyes dark and beady. They were the same men who had come to Cairncroft and asked all those odd, unsettling questions.

"Does your head ache at times? Does your brain feel overheated? Do you suffer seizures or sweats in the night?"

He had only stared at them, befuddled.

"What is your name?"

"Gabriel."

They had looked one at the other with raised brows.

"What is your name?"

"Gabriel St. Aubyn."

"Gabriel? Not Geoffrey?"

He had pressed his lips tight and refused to reply. They had looked to each other and stroked their chins and nodded and muttered about complete delusion and appropriate care.

The sight of them now, standing all in a row like three

black crows, frightened him. Their posture reminded him of his father's that morning, but the look they leveled upon him did not. He thought now that his father had looked at him with pity, but these men seemed to look through him. Beside them was a stocky woman in a black dress, her hair scraped back from her face, her expression austere.

"Step down," his mother whispered as he turned his face toward her. She looked as though she might swoon, her eyes rolling back, her lips and cheeks bloodless, her face chalk white in the shadows of the carriage.

He did not want to step down. He was terribly afraid.

But he was a good son, and he did as he was bidden, stepping out of the dim, hot carriage into the bright sunlight. The breeze caught his hair and ruffled it.

One of the men moved forward and closed his hand around Gabriel's arm, the grip tight. Restraining.

"Mother!" Gabriel cried, his voice rising now, his certainty clear. There was something wrong.

She leaned forward, but did not leave the carriage. Her face was streaked with tears, and her hands clawed so her nails dug into her own forearms through the cloth of her dress.

"Good-bye," she whispered. "Geoffrey"—her voice broke on the name—"be a good little man. Good-bye."

Another man stepped forward and slammed the carriage door as Gabriel stood, stunned and uncomprehending. Only as the carriage rolled away did he come to himself and scream, "Gabriel. I am Gabriel. Not Geoffrey. *I am Gabriel.*"

None of the three men touched him now. Only the nurse swooped forward like a hawk and grabbed hold of both his arms and held him fast as he tried to run. Then she dragged him, kicking and screaming, up the front stairs and through the front door where another woman came and together they wrestled him, one on each side, up a staircase to a long bright hallway, the sun pouring through rows of windows. Finally, they reached a small bedroom and they pushed him inside and slammed the door. He heard the click of the lock and the thud of their footsteps and he was alone with only his terror and his thoughts.

In the weeks that followed, he tried everything to make them listen. He was rational and calm, explaining again and again that he was Gabriel. Not Geoffrey. But they would not listen. So he screamed his name at them each time they called him Geoffrey.

At first, they did nothing other than try to correct him, and the three dark-garbed men came and poked him and prodded him and asked him questions. They asked him to say his name. To write it. To spell it aloud. He found it ridiculous, and in the end lost his patience and told them so.

They did not like that.

That day, the nurses came again and dragged him to a massive, dim room with icy floors and no windows. There, they restrained him in a long, narrow box, with walls like a cage, made of thick bars. His screams for release grew hoarse. In the end he was silent.

Still, he would not answer to his brother's name. Again the three doctors came and asked him all manner of ridiculous questions. Then they took him to a different room and stoked the fire and applied hot irons to his feet to raise blisters. They said that would draw the overabundance of blood from his overheated brain.

"So young to be here," one doctor, newly arrived at Hanham House, observed some months later. "And such complete delusion."

"Please," Gabriel begged, thinking the observation indicated sympathy. "There has been a mistake. I am Gabriel. *Gabriel.* Not Geoffrey. I have done nothing wrong. I swear it. I swear it."

The doctor only shook his head and put him in a device that whirled him round and round until he was dizzy and sick, until dry heaves racked his body because there was nothing left in his belly.

Weeks—or was it months?—passed. A letter came for him from his cousin Sebastian. He leaped upon it like a drowning man on a floating board. Then he saw his brother's name, *Geoffrey St. Aubyn*, and he understood that even Sebastian was in their thrall.

"Whose thrall?" the doctor asked. "Tell me."

"My brother. Maybe my mother. My father. My cousin. I do not know," Gabriel babbled. "I do not know. I only know they have done this to me and I should not be here. I should not be here."

"Cold water baths," the doctor said after he had summoned the nurse once more, and Gabriel was taken to a different room and forced into a different type of box, no wider or longer than a coffin, but with holes in the top and sides.

"Please," he cried. But no one heard. No one listened.

The box was dropped in a vat of icy water again and again. He knew how to swim. There was a lake at Cairncroft Abbey. After the first plunge, the shock and terror of it, he knew better what to expect, and he held his breath as he felt the box drop with him in it. But sometimes, he could hold his breath no longer and the water poured into his nose and mouth and throat, choking him, drowning him.

By the end of it, he wished he could just die. Just close his eyes and never open them again.

"Why are you doing this to me?" he whispered when it

was done and they let him out, barely able to speak, barely able to stand.

"To remedy the disruption of your blood circulation. To improve the circulation to your brain," the doctor said, his tone reasonable and calm. "To cure you."

"Cure me of what?" Gabriel cried, but no one heard him, or if they did, they never answered.

If he struggled too strenuously, they forced opium upon him, or camphor mixed with vinegar.

Weeks bled into months, and months into years.

His one link to the world, to his sanity, were the letters from his cousin Sebastian, written as he traveled the world with his guardian. Gabriel never looked at the name on the direction; it would only make him angry and bitter to see that proof that even Sebastian believed him to be someone other than he was. But he waited for those letters, only hungering for a taste of the world beyond the walls of Hanham House. And he read them over and over, long past the point that he had memorized every word.

A new doctor arrived, Dr. Bradley, who based his treatments on the methods of an American physician, Dr. Rush. Icy baths were replaced by the *relaxation chair*, which offered restraint at both ankles and wrists, and a wooden box that fitted over the patient's head like a shroud.

Gabriel's head.

The first time he was forced onto that chair, he thought he would go well and truly mad.

Dr. Bradley saw Gabriel as a wonderful challenge, and he paid special attention to him. And Dr. Bradley had a fondness for that chair. Gabriel quickly learned that crying and begging and pleading only made it much worse.

Though he could not move, could not see, could not scratch the terrible itch at the tip of his nose, he forced himself to keep silent when they stretched the leather tight across his wrists and fastened the buckles. To bite hard on his tongue when Dr. Bradley took the knife and slit open his vein. To make not a sound as his blood dripped into the bowl.

"Madness," Dr. Bradley expounded to anyone who would listen, "is caused by morbid qualities in the blood." And so he bled Gabriel until he fainted, strapped in the chair, unable to move, his world narrowed to only what his mind could conjure.

"Purgatives," Dr. Bradley pontificated, "are a depleting remedy for the overwhelming state of madness." He would force the patient's mouth open—*Gabriel's mouth*—and if he refused to swallow of his own volition, the doctor used a funnel attached to a long tube to administer his treatments.

Too, Dr. Bradley was a proponent of solitude as punishment. When Gabriel refused to answer to his brother's name, he was locked away in the darkness and the quiet. Too quiet. He hated it there, believed himself truly mad when the only company he had were his memories. Of Cairncroft. Of his childhood, stolen from him now. Of his brother.

Memories of the dead girl, with her chest slit open and parts gone, and her blood staining the ground in a dark, glistening pool. Only, he had not been the one to find her, so how did he know what the others had seen? Was it their description that he conjured? Was it only a horror from his imagination? He had no way to know.

He began to believe he *was* Geoffrey and not Gabriel, that *he* had gone into the woods after Sebastian that day and found the dead girl.

Other days, he knew he was Gabriel. Knew that his brother had *become* him, though he knew not how. Or why.

Those questions gnawed at him like a thousand hungry ants, nipping and biting and squirming beneath his skin.

"How are you today, Gabriel?" Dr. Bradley asked as he strode along the narrow aisle between the tables where the inmates of the house were eating their supper.

"Fine, thank you, Dr. Bradley," Gabriel replied, knowing as soon as the words left his lips that he had erred. He must never answer to his own name. He must answer only to his brother's. Too late.

"To the solitude room," Dr. Bradley said over his shoulder to the nurse. "To ponder his behavior."

By now, Gabriel knew better than to resist. He glanced at the supper he had not yet touched, and knew he would not have any food to eat for some time. Inmates of the solitude room did not warrant dinner.

Hours later, in the damp, frigid darkness, Gabriel curled into a ball, and for the first time since he had arrived at Hanham House, his desperation and fear faded. Suddenly everything became clear.

Nothing mattered.

The questions he had asked so many times needed no answers, because the answers would lead him nowhere. He must look forward, only forward. He must let go of his burning need to understand *why,* and instead think only of how he might escape.

No . . . not just escape. That would only be another sort of hell. He must not just escape. He must regain all he had lost.

To do that, he must become the monster they had judged him to be. In the solitude of his cell, he murdered the boy he had been as surely as if he had plunged a dagger in his breast. And from the rotting corpse of that boy rose a new creature, wily and sly, and coldly focused on revenge.

* * *

"Who are you?" Dr. Bradley asked, his fingers steepled before his face, his brows lowered in contemplation.

"Geoffrey St. Aubyn," Gabriel replied, letting no emotion color his lie. To say his true name aloud would only earn him the doctor's well-intentioned treatments, and he had had enough of those to last him a lifetime.

He had become so adept at lies that he rarely gained any notice at all anymore. All of which made him wary of the reason for this summons by Dr. Bradley, who meted out his attentions only to those patients he deemed in need of reward or punishment. Gut instinct had Gabriel sincerely doubting he was here for reward.

"Did you enjoy your visit with your family, Geoffrey?"

"Very much, thank you." The words tasted like dust on his tongue. The only thing he enjoyed about their visits was the packet of books they invariably brought. He lived for Sebastian's letters, and for those books, devoured them, soaking up knowledge. But the visit itself was always a torment, their faces a reminder of all that had been stolen from him.

Earlier today, they had sat there in a small, windowless room—his mother, his father, his treacherous brother, his cousin Madeline—and stared at him across a bare wooden table. They had done this to him, confined him to this place, to hell on earth. They came now, once every few weeks to visit, and always they brought him a plate of raspberry tarts.

"Your mother was saddened that, yet again, you declined to taste the tarts she brought," Dr. Bradley said, his tone chiding. "Did you mean to cause her distress?"

Yes. I meant to make her tear her hair and beat her breast and truly see what she has done to me. Why, Mother? Why did you leave me in this place, with these people? What wrong did I do to make you hate me so?

"No, I did not mean to cause her distress," Gabriel replied, attempting to color his tone with contrition. That was the one area he was yet lacking. He had trouble summoning genuine emotions other than hate and rage. He knew he had felt other things at one time, in a different life, when he had been free. But no longer. Now, he watched those around him—the nurses, the doctors, the rare visitor—to try and learn from their actions, and he mimicked them to the best of his ability.

"You caused her pain. You will write to her immediately to apologize."

"Of course."

"Why do you not eat the tarts? Your mother goes to some trouble to bring them each time." Dr. Bradley leaned forward, his gaze intent. Gabriel knew that posture, knew the doctor watched for some sign of madness, waited for it, longed for it. He wanted to find something in Gabriel's answer that he could pounce on, cat on mouse.

"I have always preferred lemon to raspberry," Gabriel replied carefully, certain this was a trap, but unable to see exactly how. He made no indication of his anger or frustration, certainly not the fear that flickered in his heart. He did not say that raspberry made his tongue feel numb and thick in his mouth, made him feel that his throat might close entirely and he might die.

"Ah." Dr. Bradley sat back in his chair, his expression jubilant. "I knew it. The madness has returned. It is *Gabriel* who prefers lemon, not you, Geoffrey. Never you. Your mother told me it is raspberry you like." The doctor's eyes gleamed with a zealot's fire and it was all Gabriel could do not to leap across the desk and close his hands about the man's throat and watch his face go blue as he choked.

But he held himself still, kept his expression blank. He must bide his time.

"It is the morbid qualities of your blood, Geoffrey, that create this madness and make you believe you are your brother. But never fear, never fear. Copious bleeding is the answer, the key to your recovery. Tomorrow, we will draw away a full three-fourths of your blood. The disruption to your circulation will be remedied, and your overheated brain will heal."

Gabriel stared across the desk at Dr. Bradley. He knew his face was a mask. He could feel it, his expression cool as marble, for he had practiced and practiced until he had the game down to perfection.

He had come to Hanham House as a boy of thirteen, and now his seventeenth birthday had come and gone—at least, he thought it had. In that time he had endured things no one ever should, and he knew what the outcome would be if he was forced to endure even one more.

If Dr. Bradley did as he wished, if he strapped Gabriel in the chair again as he had so many times before, fed him a purgative and opened his vein and took the amount of blood he described, Gabriel knew for certain he would die.

Unless Dr. Bradley died first.

There were only the two choices.

As he sat and listened to Dr. Bradley extol the virtues of the relaxation chair and bloodletting and applying caustics to a wound at the back of the neck to keep it open and offer discharge for the overheated brain, Gabriel spoke up, a last effort.

"I will not survive it," he said, very polite, very cold.

Dr. Bradley stared at him, jaw open, brows raised. "Do you think you know what is best for you? Do you think yourself so knowledgeable in this?" he sputtered. "I will do as I think best, Geoffrey. Do not doubt it. Resist, and it will go badly for you."

"You will not alter your intent?" Gabriel asked.

"I will not."

"Then events will unfold as you have steered them." Gabriel studied Dr. Bradley's face.

And as Dr. Bradley folded his hands across his round belly and leaned his chair back on two legs, his expression one of bloated self-importance, Gabriel knew he was going to kill this man. In that moment he acknowledged that he had every intention of committing murder. And he thought he might even enjoy it.

He waited for the swell of abhorrence, the conscience that would still his hand. He waited for the certainty that he could not, *would not* do it, no matter the provocation.

But it did not come. In its place was the certainty that he *would.*

If it was a choice between Dr. Bradley's life or his own, he would save his own.

Such was the creature they had made him.

Chapter 15

"You have made exceptional progress, Geoffrey," Dr. Vincent said, his bushy gray brows rising to blend with the heavy thatch of gray hair that fell over his forehead.

"Thank you," Gabriel replied, offering no evidence of the repulsion he felt at being addressed by his brother's name. He had trained himself never to betray emotion, had become quite adept at it, in fact. It was too dangerous here, where even a smile could be read as a sign of an excitable state. In truth, he thought he no longer felt emotion, not the way normal people did.

Hanham House had changed him, molded him, forged a new being from the creature he had been.

He read things in the faces of others and he had vague recollections of understanding their emotions, but he did not feel such things himself. Not anymore. His world was viewed through a haze, a fog. One that both insulated and caged.

"My recovery is a testament to your skill, sir," he said, blandly.

Dr. Vincent was new, only one year at Hanham House, a replacement for Dr. Bradley, who had tripped late one night and tumbled to his death, his body twisted and broken at the foot of the stairs. None of the inmates of Hanham House had shed a tear at his loss. And none had been blamed for the tragedy. How could they be? After all, they had been locked in their rooms each night, and no one had the key save the doctors and nurses.

And if one young nurse, horribly scarred by smallpox, was smitten with a certain handsome inmate of the house, and if she visited his room on occasion and stayed for some time, creating the perfect opportunity for him to steal her key . . . well, no one remarked upon it.

Dr. Bradley had not been a well-liked man.

By contrast, Dr. Vincent was. He had brought his own mores and methods with him to Hanham House. No more icy baths. No more restraining chair. Even bloodletting was kept to a minimum. Patients were only restrained if they presented a genuine physical risk to themselves or others.

"You see," Dr. Vincent said to the small group of gentlemen—visitors who had come from other asylums to study his methods—as they walked together across the vast grounds of Hanham House. The manicured grass was springy beneath their feet. "Intractable though my predecessors deemed him, Geoffrey here is an excellent representation of the efficacy of my treatments. He is proof that dignity and respect are essential parts of the daily regime. Along with fresh air"—he made an encompassing gesture at the surrounding manicured lawns and gardens—"and soothing scenery. We encourage horticultural pursuits here, and attendance at services in the chapel. Our patients are kept busy. Idleness breeds illness, after all. The benefits of activity—both bodily exercise and mental recreation—along with dignity are stressed, gentlemen. Dignity, I say."

Murmurs followed this statement, and Gabriel only

walked quietly by Dr. Vincent's side, his expression carefully blank, his gait measured.

"Why, just yesterday, Geoffrey's mother fell upon me after her visit, prostrate with gratitude. She said that in his early years here, Geoffrey barely acknowledged their presence when they came. But now, he shows great interest in his brother, Gabriel, discussing his time at school, his teachers, his friends, hanging on every bit of information. And yesterday he ate a raspberry tart." He glanced at Gabriel. "For some reason, your mother found that exceptionally encouraging, Geoffrey."

"They have always been my favorite," he replied. "It was kind of her to bring them." His tongue had begun to tingle not ten minutes after he ate the vile thing, and his throat had felt tight enough that he wondered if all his plotting and planning was for naught and he would asphyxiate there on the spot. But finally, the tingling and numbness had abated, and his breath had come freely once more.

The easing of his brother's ever-vigilant expression had been his reward. He had lulled Geoffrey into trust. It had only taken him the better part of a year.

"So she said. She fondly recalled you gorging yourself on them as a boy. She is immensely encouraged by your progress." Dr. Vincent clapped him on the back. It was all Gabriel could do not to turn on him with a snarl and tell him to keep his distance, to keep his hands to himself. Instead, he offered a bland smile and said nothing at all and merely strolled in the garden with the flock of black-clad crows beside him.

"Excellent. Excellent. And your brother will visit again next month?"

"So he has said, much to my pleasure," Gabriel replied, his lips shaping a parody of a smile as he contemplated that visit and the ones that would follow, each a stepping stone on his path to vengeance. "Very much to my pleasure."

In the months that followed, Geoffrey came often, always solicitous and kind, but when no one watched, his lips would curve in an ugly sneer and his eyes would glitter with malice. Gabriel pretended not see it, not to know what his brother was. A villain. No one would think to look for such a creature, for no one would imagine such a one existed. Certainly, he had not. His own brother had orchestrated his imprisonment at Hanham House and usurped his place at Cairncroft Abbey. For Gabriel was the elder by three minutes, the heir, and Geoffrey had become him now, in manner and name.

Was that the reason for all of this, then? For money and the title? Had Geoffrey switched places with him so he would be the one to inherit all?

How had he summoned such a convoluted plan? When it had been orchestrated they had been little more than children, Geoffrey and Gabriel twelve, Madeline nearly fifteen, and Sebastian a year older than she. Had one of them helped him? He could not fathom it. Madeline, so silly and weepy and wan. Sebastian, away for such lengthy periods of time. Neither seemed a viable choice.

Which left only Geoffrey, alone, to spawn his poisonous plot.

But then, Geoffrey had ever been more cunning and wily. He had been the brilliant one. He had been the one to think up every plot and plan that had landed them in trouble in their childhood.

And always, it had been Gabriel who took the blame. He

recollected that now. He had had so many endless days and nights to recollect that.

Still, it made no sense to him. Other than the abbey, which was entailed, there were funds enough for both of them, separately allotted.

Was it greed, a need to possess all, that had driven Geoffrey to this end?

Gabriel had no answers, but he did have a plan. Each time his brother visited he aped his mannerisms and tone and posture, a matter that Geoffrey found amusing. Every few weeks, one of the nurses trimmed the residents' hair. Gabriel always begged her to cut his just like his brother's. Geoffrey found that amusing as well, and Dr. Vincent took it as encouraging, saying, "Imitation is a form of flattery. I am gratified to see you holding your brother in such esteem."

"Hello, Geoffrey," Geoffrey would say each time he came, and laugh as though delighted to see him. But Gabriel knew the darkness that lurked in his heart, the enjoyment of his predicament, for what was he to do other than call his brother by *his* name.

"Hello, Gabriel," he would reply, his tone even. It was a confusing and vicious thing that twisted his thoughts and left him sick with rage. And each time Geoffrey came, Gabriel begged for books. His brother twisted even that into a game for his private amusement, arriving with tomes on agriculture or geography or some other topic he considered dry as dust, believing that he perpetrated a subtle torture in those deeds.

"I suppose you would prefer a novel," Geoffrey said with a malicious laugh as he handed over two weighty books written in French.

As a boy, Gabriel had preferred tales of adventure to texts and treatises. But he was a different person now. Hanham

House had forged a new person out of flame and suffering. This new Gabriel—the one known here as Geoffrey, forged in icy baths and hot irons, isolation and blood and pain—was grateful for any knowledge, any diversion that filled the empty hours and the empty spaces in his mind. In fact, he had come to crave educational texts more than imaginative ones. Dr. Vincent even allowed him to borrow from his own personal library of anatomy and medicine.

"Thank you, Gabriel. You are most kind." He held his brother's gaze as he accepted the books, letting him see none of the rage and hate. Only a blank mask. "Will you come again soon?"

Geoffrey leaned close, his eyes narrowed, his expression hawkish. "They've done it, haven't they? They've broken you to heel. You believe you're Geoffrey now? Do you believe it?"

Gabriel held his gaze and forced his brows together, offering a carefully crafted look of puzzlement. "What do you mean? I *am* Geoffrey."

Throwing back his head, Geoffrey laughed. "Wonderful. Perfectly wonderful."

Gabriel stole a knife from the dining room. He had spent a great deal of time on planning exactly how he might accomplish that feat, for to be caught at it would be disastrous. Ironically, in the end, it was pure luck that saw him succeed.

A new inmate—Mr. Winston—came one day, an older man who was genial one moment and rabid the next, then almost childlike as he sang to himself in a language Gabriel did not understand. At supper one evening the new arrival went into a rage, throwing his plate and his cutlery and upending a chair.

"Grab him," cried Dr. Vincent, who had been passing between the long tables, stopping now and again to greet a patient. The nurses hurried forward.

Gabriel dipped his head and watched as a fork went spinning across the floor between Nurse Little's feet as she reached to grab hold of Mr. Winston's arm. He flapped and screamed and landed a hard crack to her jaw. With a cry, she jerked back and the pandemonium continued.

Snapping and biting and thrashing, Mr. Winston evaded all attempts at restraint. Gabriel glanced about to see if any eyes had wandered from the frantic tableau, for at his feet lay Mr. Winston's knife where it had been tossed, the blade catching the lamplight, singing a siren's song.

Almost did Gabriel reach down and snatch it up. But at the last moment, he hesitated, certain that any gift came with a price. Again, he glanced about and found that Dr. Vincent's gaze lit on him, then slid away, watching all the patients lest they, too, become deranged of a sudden.

Deciding against bending forward and reaching for the knife, Gabriel turned his attention to his plate even as he nudged at Mr. Winston's knife with the tip of his shoe. He pushed it, a little at a time, until it was fully beneath the table. Then he pressed his feet together and slowly, slowly eased his right foot up his left calf, the knife hilt caught between them, slowly rolling higher and higher.

His breath stopped as it almost slipped free. Then he managed to right the handle and slide the thing a little higher, mid-calf. Almost there.

After what felt like a thousand years, he had it to his knee. Reaching down, he closed his fist around the handle and secreted the knife up his left sleeve.

The blade, dull though it was, was essential to his plan.

Because he had a scar, low on his left side, while his

brother did not. They were twins. Identical in every respect. For the first six years of his life, his parents had made Geoffrey wear a thick, braided leather band around his left ankle, tied too tightly to ever remove. It was the only way anyone could tell them apart. It would not do for them to have even a single differentiating marker now. Certainly not a scar on one that was absent from the other. Not if his plan was to succeed.

Precisely how long he had been incarcerated at Hanham House, Gabriel could not say. Years. He knew that much, though he could not recall the exact date he had come here. Nor did he know the exact date it was today. His only marker of time were the dates noted at the tops of Sebastian's letters, and those were often months old by the time they reached him. Too, he had Geoffrey's visits to mark the passage of time. Otherwise, the sameness of the days blended one into the next.

Then, one day in spring, perhaps April or May, Geoffrey came to Hanham House unexpectedly. Gabriel sat on a bench outdoors near the grotto, a raised circle of stone surrounded by lush vegetation. It was a cloudy day. He preferred such weather to full sun and heat—sunshine always reminded him of the day his mother had left him here, not even bothering to step down from the coach as she consigned him to hell.

He sat now under the charcoal sky, reading a text on medicine that Dr. Vincent had lent him, when he heard the sound of muted conversation drawing ever closer.

Looking up, he saw his brother and Dr. Vincent approaching. Two things struck him immediately. Geoffrey was not expected. And Dr. Vincent had himself acted as guide rather than sending one of the nurses. Neither point boded well.

Whatever news his brother brought, it was not good.

He rose as the two approached, and said, “Brother, how good to see you.”

“And you.” Geoffrey drew closer, his gaze intent. He reached out as though to lay a hand on Gabriel’s arm, and then shot a quick glance at Dr. Vincent. Finally, he dropped his hand to his side once more.

Well played, Gabriel thought. Geoffrey had added just the right touch of fear to his expression. Just enough that he clearly conveyed his concern that the news he brought might unhinge his brother and send him into a dangerous fit.

He had no idea that he had just given Gabriel a gift.

As children, Geoffrey had always won at chess. But in the years since then, Gabriel had become a much more adept player. He could only hope his skill was now such that he could outmaneuver his brother.

“I am afraid I have tragic news,” Geoffrey said. “Dr. Vincent has accompanied me in the event you are overcome and require assistance.”

The breeze stilled, as though the weather itself waited for Geoffrey’s pronouncement.

“Our parents are dead.”

Ah. Oddly, he felt no surprise, almost as though a part of him had anticipated the words.

What to say? Gabriel’s gaze flicked to Dr. Vincent as he searched for the appropriate response, the one that would not mark him as mad.

“How?” he asked, injecting as much volume into the inquiry as he thought practical, hoping it would serve to indicate shock and grief.

“Father fell from his best hunter. Broke his neck.

Mother pined for three weeks, and then succumbed to a broken heart."

Gabriel froze as, to his shock, genuine emotion surged. Rage. Regret. He had been cheated. His opportunity to show them, to make them see who he truly was, to make them acknowledge what they had done. To make them love him . . . gone. It was gone. They were dead.

He would never have the opportunity to face them.

The sun broke through the clouds at that moment, bathing him in light. He flinched, ducked his head, acutely aware of his brother standing by his side, watching him. And Dr. Vincent, as well. He must play this with care. Everything depended on it now.

Whatever Dr. Vincent saw in his face, it must have satisfied, for he patted Gabriel's arm, and murmured, "My condolences."

For a second, Gabriel could not think of the correct rejoinder, so he merely nodded in acknowledgment. It was enough. The tension in Dr. Vincent's expression eased.

But the tension in Gabriel's gut only twisted tighter. With his parents dead, his brother was his legal guardian. Geoffrey, who masqueraded as Gabriel, as *him*, was now his legal guardian. Without Geoffrey's agreement, Gabriel could never leave Hanham House. Never. Not by walking free. No. All his planning and plotting . . . it *must* be today. His chance. His one chance. He knew with complete certainty he would never have another.

After today, his brother would not return.

He had come to deliver this news in person only to glean some sort of vile satisfaction in watching as he tossed the last shovelful of dirt to bury Gabriel alive.

Gabriel kept his breaths slow and even, though his heart

raced and his thoughts whirled. He was not ready. He had not expected that today would be the day.

"Will you walk with me, brother?" Gabriel asked, turning to Geoffrey, offering no glimpse of his true thoughts in either tone or manner. "Will you tell me of their last days. Happy things, if you please."

Geoffrey shot a glance at Dr. Vincent. He could not easily decline such a pretty request. "Of course," he replied.

With a few more murmured words of condolence, Dr. Vincent took his leave.

Gabriel thought of his bedroom and the loose board beneath his bed and the knife he had hidden there in preparation for this day. All for naught. He could not go there and retrieve it with none the wiser. Geoffrey would leave and his opportunity would be lost.

He would need to find another way.

"How sad that you never got to say good-bye," Geoffrey said, his look sly and dark.

"Yes," Gabriel agreed, and searched for a question, any question that might do to fill the silence and hold Geoffrey here a little longer. "How is Madeline?" he asked, though he could not have cared less for the answer.

Geoffrey laughed. "Devastated."

His answer was so short and succinct that for a moment, Gabriel wondered if he recognized the ploy. And then he realized he had asked the wrong question. He must ask about Geoffrey; there was no topic his brother enjoyed more than a dialogue about himself. And so he posed question after question, about Geoffrey's friends and his time in London and the gambling hells he frequented, using the opportunity to divert and delay, while at the same time prying out the last bits of knowledge he could.

They walked side by side, separated by a span of two or

three feet, separated by an immeasurable volume of knowledge and trickery.

Along the way, Gabriel found a stick, long and thick, the end rather dull. He lifted it and offered it to Geoffrey, who regarded him quizzically for a moment and then took it. And they walked on.

Moments later, he found a second stick, far more suited to his needs. This one, he kept for himself. They walked, Geoffrey talking, Gabriel listening, memorizing every word, their sticks touching the ground with each step.

"Just like when we were children." Geoffrey laughed.

"Yes. Just like when we were children." *Except today, I will not be the one left stabbed and bleeding. Today will have a different end.* "We were so happy then, so imaginative in our . . . games."

Geoffrey stopped and turned to him, his brow furrowed. "Can it be that you do not remember? That you recall nothing of that day . . ."

"I recall many happy days," Gabriel replied. "Which day do you speak of?"

"Only happy days?" Geoffrey asked, clearly perplexed. "What an odd thing. They have truly cured you here"—he turned and kept walking—"or truly driven you mad," he finished under his breath.

Gabriel pretended not to hear, only measured his steps to his brother's, waiting. Waiting.

At length, they reached a lovely garden far into the estate, surrounded on all sides by a tall hedge of dogwood. It was an isolated place, one Gabriel had steered them to with care, allowing his brother to think he chose their way, then subtly guiding him.

"What is the date today?" Gabriel asked, falling back behind his brother, dragging the stick he carried hard against a large boulder that had a series of small bushes with tiny white flowers circling its base.

"The fifteenth of March," Geoffrey replied, tossing his own stick aside and kicking impatiently at a clod of dirt. He was bored. Ready to leave.

A moment more. Just a moment. Gabriel dragged the tip of the stick back again along the boulder, and again, faster.

"Must you do that?" Geoffrey snapped.

"Only March?" Gabriel asked, ignoring his brother's show of temper. He made a disbelieving laugh, stunned in truth. "I had thought it May already." Then he paused and wondered at the irony. "The fifteenth, you say? The ides of March," he murmured.

"What did you say?" Geoffrey turned to him, and his eyes widened, his hands raised in defense as Gabriel moved.

Gabriel closed his hands about his brother's throat. With his thumbs, he pressed hard on either side of his windpipe. Geoffrey's fingers clawed his wrists, and he tugged and pulled, but to no avail. For Geoffrey lived the soft life of a dissolute heir, while Gabriel spent his endless hours of solitude pulling his weight up with his fingers curled around the lip of his door frame or doing push-ups, shadow boxing or running in place, anything to stave off desperation and madness.

Thumbs digging in hard, Gabriel waited, and after a time—seconds? Minutes?—Geoffrey's eyes rolled back in his head until the whites showed and his lids flickered, and then he slumped, his breath lost, his body dropping like a stone.

Not dead. That was never Gabriel's plan. He had no intention of killing him. Death was too easy. To go sweetly into that eternal slumber was not what he wished for his brother. No. He would not be his brother's murderer, would not add that dark deed to any others he had gathered. He only wanted turnabout. Fair play.

As he stared at his brother's slumped form, he offered silent thanks to Dr. Vincent and the many books he had shared. Texts on anatomy and medicine and philosophy. They had all played a role in the formulation of his plan.

Geoffrey's lids fluttered, and Gabriel knelt at his side.

There was little time.

Deftly, he stripped his brother bare, no mean feat given that every so often he moaned and thrashed and fought against Gabriel's grasp. Each time Geoffrey began to rouse, Gabriel pressed on the arteries in his throat once more until he mumbled and became disoriented, his lids fluttering down. And if he did not precisely fall unconscious each time, he became pliant enough for Gabriel to do what he must.

Gabriel shucked his own clothing and made quick work of redressing himself and then his brother in their exchanged wardrobe.

He was breathing heavily, his heart pounding, his palms slick with sweat. He had dreamed this moment so many times, planned it in all its minutiae. But now that it was here, nothing was going precisely according to his plan; he had to improvise and alter his course every step of the way.

"What? What?" Geoffrey moaned, and Gabriel pressed at his throat once more, hoping against hope that it was not one time too many, that his brother would not die of this.

He so desperately wanted him to live.

Closing his hand around a small rock, he threaded the fingers of his other hand through his brother's hair, yanked his head up, and used the stone to rub hard at the back of his neck. Hard enough to open a wound in the place of the scar on the back of his own, a reminder of the wound Dr.

Bradley had made there, then kept open with caustics for weeks on end. To let his brain breathe, Dr. Bradley had said. Well, if it was true, then Geoffrey's brain was breathing quite nicely now.

He positioned the rock beneath his brother's head and quickly smeared the blood to mask the marks of his fingers. He hoped it would appear that Geoffrey had opened the wound when he fell.

There was nothing Gabriel could do to mimic the marks on his forearms, the ones they had made when they bled him, the terrible scars that grew one on the next. Geoffrey had two very faint ones on his right arm, the remnants of being bled when a fever had taken him as a child. Gabriel prayed they would suffice should anyone care to search for them, for in no way did they match the extent and number of his own. But he had no way to change that, and so he wasted no further thought on it.

Time was ticking away. He could hear the clock in his mind. Faster. He must work faster.

Geoffrey moaned and turned his head, becoming more lucid by the second.

Scrabbling on his hands and knees, Gabriel snatched the stick he'd found earlier. The end had been pointed to start with, all the more so now that he'd dragged it across the stone.

It was the matter of his scar, the damned scar his brother had marked him with. He would not be believed if that scar was missing on his brother.

Pushing to his feet, he took an instant to feel for the top of Geoffrey's hipbone. It offered him a point of reference and he slid off it four finger's-widths up. Then he slapped his palm across his brother's mouth, both holding him down and muffling the scream he knew would come.

He brought the point of the stick down with a quick, brutal thrust, piercing cloth and skin.

Geoffrey arched and twitched, rousing completely now from his stuporous state, reacting to the pain and shock of his wound.

The wood stuck up toward the sky, vibrating.

"Welcome to hell," Gabriel whispered. He grabbed Geoffrey's hands and pressed them to the stick, close to the wound, enough to cover them in blood. "Do not pull it out. You will die."

With that warning, he bounded to his feet and ran full tilt for the house, screaming for help.

"My brother," he cried at the top of his lungs, gasping for breath between words. "Help. I need help."

They came rushing from the house. Nurse Little, Nurse Bates, Nurse Holby, and a half dozen others, and there, Dr. Vincent and Dr. Spade.

"In that direction." Gabriel waved toward the garden where he had left Geoffrey bleeding on the grass. He bent forward, resting his hand on his thigh, gasping and heaving, forcing the words out between breaths. "Our parents' deaths . . . too much for him . . . tried to . . . kill . . . himself."

"Dear God," Dr. Vincent gasped. "I was afraid of such a thing."

And then they were running toward the distant garden.

Gabriel silently gave thanks for Dr. Vincent's obsession with healthful exercise as a means of recovery, and his own efforts in that regard, as well. Used to a variety of physical exercises that were part of his prescribed regime, he was not nearly so breathless as he appeared.

He followed them at a slower pace, playing his part, the distraught brother hovering and waving his hands helplessly.

Geoffrey was on his side when they came upon him, both hands grasped tight about the stick, his whole body trembling.

"Now then, Geoffrey. Now then, what have you done to yourself?" Dr. Vincent asked, falling to his knees on the ground.

Gabriel had a momentary shock to see the doctor's face then, white and drawn with dismay. Dr. Vincent actually *cared* about him, he realized then. It came at him like a blow, taking his breath. A good thing, because at exactly that moment, Geoffrey rolled and cried, "I am Gabriel. *He* is Geoffrey. Do you not see it?"

All eyes turned to him then, and whatever they saw in his face must have convinced them of the lie. He thought perhaps there was shock and horror there, a momentary tearing away of his carefully cultivated mask. Enough to convince them that he was his brother and his brother was he.

"He does not know his own name," Nurse Little said sadly as Dr. Vincent caught Geoffrey's hands and hauled them away from the stick that yet protruded from his belly.

"What have you done? What have you done, Geoffrey?" Dr. Vincent said softly, shaking his head.

Geoffrey let out a strangled cry. "I am Gabriel. *Gabriel.*" His voice grew shrill. He rolled on the grass, flecks of spittle flying from his lips as he cried the name again and again. Then his gaze locked on Gabriel and he snarled, "You have done this to me, you sodding bastard. You!"

"Hold him!" Dr. Vincent cried, and others came forward, reaching, confining. "He'll injure himself. Mind your hands lest he bite."

Gabriel stepped back as a nurse came with a canvas stretcher. Snarling and thrashing, then crying out in pain, Geoffrey fought them. But they held him. Strong hands.

Implacable minds. And he was weak with loss of blood and pain. They held him as they had held Gabriel that long-ago day.

He felt neither pity nor remorse.

"Take him inside," Dr. Vincent ordered. "Steady, Geoffrey. Steady now."

They hurried into the house, Goeffrey's enraged howls following him like a tail. Gabriel came close behind, wringing his hands as he recalled his mother used to do in times of distress. A perfect touch, he thought.

As they passed indoors, he drew close to the stretcher and said, "Do not die, brother. There is so much that awaits you here. You must live to experience it fully. You must."

Dr. Vincent clapped him on the shoulder and muttered reassuring words. "He is not bleeding so very much. We must hope he did not puncture any viscera. My preliminary examination suggests he stabbed muscle and skin, but not colon. A good thing, that."

Then one of the nurses patted Gabriel on the forearm, and he let her, though inside, he recoiled at the touch. She murmured words of encouragement and hope, and led him to a small parlor at the front of the house, one he knew was reserved for visitors who were considering damning their relatives to this place. She promised to return once they knew something of Geoffrey's condition.

He did not want to wait. He wanted to fling open the doors and run as fast and as far as he could. But he only thanked her, his mask firmly in place, revealing none of the nervous energy that coursed through his veins. Only an hour more, perhaps two. He must only wait for the news that Geoffrey would live. And then he would be away. He would be free. It would not do for him to flee through the doors now, with his brother injured. They would think it odd. He was certain of that.

Instead, he paced, and after a time, peered through the open door to determine who was about. There was no one in the passage and so he hurried from the room and took the stairs and corridors on a path familiar and known. He went to his bedroom and collected Sebastian's letters. He had saved them all these years. They had been his link to sanity for a very long while, and he would not leave them here. Could not leave them here.

Then he returned to the room at the front of the house. Pulling aside the curtains, he looked out at the gathering clouds, charcoal edged and heavy. Sunlight had marked the day he came here; clouds marked the day he would leave. Beautiful, heavy gray clouds.

Less than an hour later, Dr. Vincent came to him, his hair standing on end, lines bracketing either side of his mouth.

"I am terribly sorry to say your brother has relapsed in a most horrific way. The news of your parents' deaths has driven him beyond his ability to bear. The circulation to his brain is clearly disrupted. He will need extensive treatment." He drew a deep breath and squared his shoulders as though in preparation for the task ahead.

"But he is alive," Gabriel said.

"Yes. Yes. The wound was not so serious as it appeared. Not very deep. I suspect it was the presence of previous scar tissue there that slowed his thrust. I have every confidence that he will recover. Physically, that is."

"I cannot tell you how pleased I am to hear it," Gabriel said. "May I see him?"

"Of course. Of course. I will take you there now. But . . ." Dr. Vincent's voice trailed away.

"Go on," Gabriel urged.

"But I think perhaps it might be best if you not visit him for a time. Until his state is more balanced. You understand?"

"I do." *I had not intended to visit him, ever.* "Only let me see him for a moment now."

They made their way to a small room with a narrow wooden table. Geoffrey lay upon it, a white bandage stretched around his torso. He was mumbling to himself, his eyes hazy and unfocused. Gabriel had no doubt they had fed him opium. For the pain, or perhaps to make him docile.

He glanced at Dr. Vincent and then stepped closer, leaning down so his lips were directly beside his brother's ear. "Have no fear, Geoffrey. I vow on my life that I will do everything for you, exactly as you would do, and have always done, for me."

The he covered his face as though overcome by emotion and backed from the room to the sound of Geoffrey's screams.

He arrived at Cairncroft Abbey, a stranger in his own home. He knew things from Geoffrey's endless talk. The cook was Mrs. Corkle, a new arrival. The housekeeper was Mrs. Bell, who had been at Cairncroft all those years ago. Geoffrey had clearly found it amusing that she despised both him and Madeline, and favored Sebastian, who visited on any occasion he was on English soil. Gabriel was glad of the housekeeper's sentiment. It would make his own distance and reserve less noticeable.

The rest would come eventually. The basics of agriculture and accounting and the business of running an estate, Gabriel felt relatively confident of, for he had gleaned knowledge by reading the books Geoffrey had brought to him over the years. His brother had meant those boring tomes as a cruel joke. Gabriel felt certain he had never dreamed they would be welcomed.

As he stood on the drive looking up at the darkened windows, the door flew open and his cousin Madeline came tearing down the stairs, her blond hair tumbling in loose ringlets, her blue eyes sparkling. In that moment, she was pretty. He had never thought her so before, but as she looked at him, her face alight as though he was the sun and moon, he was struck by the realization that she adored him.

No. Not him. Geoffrey.

She adored the imposter who had stood in his shoes these many years. How many? He could not say. He thought he might be nineteen or twenty years old, but he was not certain.

Madeline came to him now and put her hands in his, and held them as she said, "Gabriel, welcome home."

She stared into his face, tipped her head to the side, and slowly her smile faded. The breeze ruffled her hair.

"Gabriel?"

"Yes, cousin. I have come home."

Her brow creased. Then she gasped and fell back a step, tearing her hands from his grasp to press them against her breast.

"Gabriel?" she whispered again.

"Yes," he said, suddenly certain that she *knew*. He was not the cousin who had lived here with her all these years. He was not the man she had expected to greet here on the drive beneath the blanket of cloud.

"Glad to see me, cousin?" he asked.

She was panting now, quick shallow breaths, and her face was chalk white.

"Did you kill him?" she whispered.

No, I only buried him alive in the very grave he dug for me. "Shall we go indoors?" he asked and offered his arm.

Madeline's eyes narrowed and her jaw tightened. He could read her expression as nothing other than hate. With a cry, she whirled and ran, up the steps, through the door, her cries trailing behind.

"Well, there's a homecoming," he said, and smiled. He was free. At last, he was free.

Part Four

Chapter 16

Cairncroft Abbey, England, April 1828

Catherine sat in the middle of Gabriel's massive bed, her arms wrapped around her bent knees. She wore only Gabriel's shirt, for warmth. He lay on his side, facing her, his fingers curled possessively about her ankle, his words hovering, ghostly, between them though his story was done.

He had not told her everything. She knew that with certainty. At times, he had paused in the telling and stared at her, seeming to look far into the distance. Perhaps into the past.

"This is more than I have ever told another living soul," he said, and the look he gave her was indecipherable, cool and remote, completely at odds with the baring of his soul and the secrets he had entrusted to her.

But perhaps that was the point. Perhaps he feared her reaction and held himself remote. Protected.

She would do the same.

"I know." She did. He was not a man to bestow his trust easily. Yet he bestowed an enormous measure of it on her.

"Do you think me a monster? A madman?" He stroked his

fingers up her calf and down again, then closed them about her ankle once more. "A murderer?" he continued.

She thought he waited for her to flinch away, to cringe in disgust or horror.

"Are you?" she asked.

"To the former, I would say 'perhaps.' To the latter"—he shifted, dropped his gaze—"I should think you would like to hear me say 'no.'"

He kept himself still, utterly motionless, and she chose her words with care. "Am I to understand that you neither deny nor accept the appellations of madman and monster, but hesitate to refute"—she chewed her lower lip, faltering, and finally finished on a whisper—"hesitate to deny the last?"

His lashes lowered, lifted, his amber gaze pinning her, and his fingers tightened around her ankle as though he wanted to hold her there in his bed regardless of her possible reaction to his coming revelation. Foolish man. She would not flee no matter what he said. His crimes could be no worse than her own.

"Dr. Bradley meant to do it. To drain away my blood nearly unto death. There was no reasoning with him, though I tried. I meant to simply twist his neck and kill him"—another look through his lashes, measuring her expression. She only watched him and waited, certain that if she betrayed any emotion at all, it would not be she who fled this bed, but he—"But in the end, I tried reason instead. But Bradley would not be reasoned with. He pulled his whistle to his lips, the dreadful whistle that would summon the nurses and other doctors, and I stepped forward. To intimidate? Certainly. To push him? I believe so. But I shall never know with certainty. He backed away and tumbled to his death all of his own volition."

He shrugged then, a lazy roll of muscle under smooth

skin. "I could not bear the death he planned for me, strapped in that chair with the wooden box over my head, and the knives slicing me until I bled and bled and closed my eyes and floated away with no fight whatsoever." He made a soft, mocking laugh. "I went to Hanham House like a lamb to the slaughter. I refused to die the same way."

"Yes," she said, and reached down to close her fingers around his where they yet curved about her ankle, holding him where he held her.

His gaze jerked up, glittering and bare.

And then he was on her, a surge of power and grace, tumbling her back in the sheets so he was pressed against her, hot skin and hard muscle. Thigh to thigh, tousled golden hair falling forward to brush her cheeks as he pressed his mouth to hers.

His fingers slid into her hair, holding her, cradling her, his body a solid weight against her, his mouth seeking, hungry.

Sinew and muscle and hot skin. She let her hands roam down his wide back to the firm swell of his buttocks, and she opened to him, kissed him as fiercely as he kissed her. Taking. Giving. A melding of tongues and breath and soft, desperate sounds of need.

He took her roughly, plunging deep inside her, and there was pleasure in that, bone-deep, soul-searing pleasure that made her moan and writhe. He kissed her neck and closed his teeth on her, then closed his lips on hers, stealing her breath, her thoughts, her heart.

There was a wildness in this, a primitive dominion, and with his hands on her buttocks and hers on his, she climaxed with brutal suddenness, and he was there with her, crying out as she cried out, harsh masculine sounds that only pushed her higher. The world dropped away, and she was left breathless and shaking, held together only by his arms about her and his lips against her ear, whispering her name like a prayer.

The following night, they supped with Sebastian, and even Madeline came to the dining room, though she mostly sat silent, poking at her meal, watching both her cousins with wide, wary eyes.

She was put out with Catherine.

"You left me alone for so long," she had complained when Catherine had returned to her late in the afternoon. Then she had looked at Catherine suspiciously. "Where were you all day yesterday and today?"

"I went to fetch my book and . . . became distracted," Catherine had replied, her words in no way easing Madeline's petulant mood.

"I was forced to ring for a maid. And she did not read to me. When I asked for you, she said you were with my cousin, that he said you were not to be disturbed." Madeline had lifted a book and flung it across the room. "You are not to go to him again! You are not!"

She crossed her arms on her chest and thrust out her lip and spent the next three hours staring sullenly at the wall.

But when a maid had come to request their presence at supper with both Gabriel and Sebastian, Madeline had shocked Catherine by agreeing to join them.

So here they were, the four of them seated at the large dining room table, Madeline silent and pale, Sebastian gregarious and chatty.

And Gabriel. He said little, only watched Catherine with eyes hot and dark, and she felt his heated look like a caress.

She tried to keep her own gaze on her plate, fearing that if she looked at him, she would betray herself with a blatantly adoring gaze that would scream to him and anyone else that she was well and truly smitten with him.

Heaven help her.

"Do not tell me he had you read *Frankenstein*." Sebastian laughed as she raised the topic of the novel Gabriel had lent her. "That book is a monster in itself, a patched together panoply of letters and journals and notes. It is reminiscent of those nesting lacquered boxes I brought home for you from China"—he turned to Madeline, who picked at her meal with listless interest, her eyes dull, dark shadows in the hollows beneath them—"You remember, Madeline, the smaller inside the larger?"

"Yes," Madeline whispered, but said nothing more.

Sebastian ignored her lack of enthusiasm and turned back to Gabriel and Catherine as he continued. "You see the similarity. There is Victor's story neatly put inside Walton's letters, and the monster's story inside Victor's." He laughed. "What a dizzying, stitched-together thing it is. Truths inside truths, and lies inside truths. And"—he laughed again—"you see what I mean."

Lies inside truths. From beneath her lashes, Catherine cut a sidelong glance at Gabriel. He watched her, amber-gold eyes reflecting the candlelight.

She wondered what lies he hid inside the truths he told her. What truths he hid with lies. And if it even mattered. He had shared so much of himself with her, yet she wondered if there was still more. She was a master at this game, her skills honed at the edge of a blade held to her throat.

Would she ever know the whole of his story, would she understand all that had made *him* a master, as well?

He had shared so much with her, and yet she sensed there was so much she did not know.

You have a lifetime to come to know him. The thought shocked and frightened her. There had been no discussion of lifetimes. Only a span of a day and a night, a handful of stolen moments.

"And you, Gabriel? What holds such fascination for you in that book?"

He smiled, a feral baring of teeth, and when he answered, his gaze slid away to light on Madeline, before returning to Catherine.

"The monster escapes," he said blandly.

Madeline's fork clattered against her plate.

Yes, of course, there was that. The monster escaped. No wonder he enjoyed the story. She wanted to go to him and wrap him in her arms and tell him he was not the monster, but he would not welcome such action. This was neither the time nor the place.

Across from her, Madeline shuddered, but said nothing. Silence shrouded them, the only sound the clock ticking on the mantel.

"You have been to China?" Catherine asked brightly after some moments, turning her attention back to Sebastian as the turbot in lobster sauce was served.

"There, and many other places. I traveled with my guardian from the time I was a lad of ten. It was a most unusual education. I used to write of all the wonderful things I saw. Do you recall, Gabriel? One letter for you and one for—" He stopped abruptly and coughed, then lifted his glass and took a sip of wine.

Catherine waited, but he said nothing more, and Gabriel uncharacteristically stepped into the breach. "I recall those letters, Sebastian. They were my . . . window to a world I was not part of."

She noted the hesitation, and knew its cause. But did Sebastian? Did Madeline?

Secrets wrapped in secrets.

What must Gabriel's life have been like, trapped, a prisoner cut off from the world with only his cousin's letters providing a glimpse of freedom?

She understood what it meant to be trapped, but her own incarceration had not even included letters. Only a barred window and a man who did as he willed with her.

The fragrance of the meal painted the air, aromatic and lush, but the memories tainted her appetite.

Madeline sat with her hands below the table, staring at the plate before her.

"Madeline, the turbot is lovely. Try it," Catherine coaxed, forcing herself to sample a bit from her own plate.

With her lower lips caught between her teeth, Madeline only looked at her and shook her head. Aware of the two men watching them in puzzled silence, Catherine heaved a sigh. Almost did she exchange her plate for Madeline's, just to prove the safety of the food, the absence of poison. But that would not suffice. Madeline would still cry poison and still refuse to eat.

She had had quite enough. Her patience was at an end.

Shooting Gabriel a look, daring him to say a single thing, she rose and took Madeline's plate, switching it for his and his for Madeline's.

Everyone stared at her, stunned and appalled, and she did not care a whit.

"Now, eat," she said, and sat and sampled her meal once more as though it was the most natural thing in the world to shuffle plates in the middle of supper.

"What—" Sebastian asked.

"Do not ask," she interrupted, her tone forbidding him to say another word.

An odd choked sound came from the head of the table, but when she turned to him, she found Gabriel's face was composed and cool. Except . . . the corners of his mouth quirked ever so slightly.

Catching her gaze, he raised his brows and said, "It will make no difference."

Catherine narrowed her eyes at him, willing him to be silent.

"You have traveled extensively, Sebastian," she said brightly. "But the first day I met you . . . you said Cairncroft always calls you home."

The tines of Madeline's fork scraped on her plate, and Catherine glanced at her to see that she stared at Sebastian with a twisted, pained expression.

"It does call to me," Sebastian said, exchanging a look with Gabriel.

There was an odd current in the air now, an expectancy, a humming tension.

"Sebastian is my heir." Gabriel said the words negligently, as though the matter was of little import. But of course, it was.

Sharp claws of dismay gouged her as his words penetrated on a level he could not have intended, a reminder of exactly why what they had shared could never be more than an interlude.

His heir.

Gabriel would need an heir, a *son*. Not his cousin. Gabriel would marry. He would have a wife and child, perhaps more than one. Burning agony twisted a knot in her heart. What had she imagined? That she would live here at

Cairncroft indefinitely, taking care of Madeline by day, making love with Gabriel at night?

The absurdity of that sliced her with a jagged blade.

Her place here was temporary, as was her place in his life. How had she allowed herself to imagine otherwise, even for a moment?

Gabriel watched her, and she thought there was a trace of concern in his gaze. It was impossible to know with him. He gave so little away. He opened his mouth as though to speak, when a commotion came from the hallway and Mrs. Bell burst into the dining room, her hair wild about her face, her eyes red-rimmed, her face pale as alabaster.

Both Gabriel and Sebastian came to their feet, Sebastian's expression wary, Gabriel's icy.

"They found her. Two boys from the village skulking where they had no business being. They found her." Mrs. Bell breathed heavily, her open palm pressed to her chest, her shoulders heaving. "Susan Parker. They found her."

Time stretched like taffy pulled from a pot.

"She is dead. Murdered," Mrs. Bell whispered.

Horror congealed in Catherine's throat, making her feel as though she would retch and gag. Susan Parker. Dead. Murdered. How?

It was only when Mrs. Bell turned her face toward her that Catherine realized she had asked the question aloud.

"Her throat was slit"—the housekeeper's voice broke on the last word and she made a visible effort to rein in her emotion before she continued—"just like . . . that other girl, so many years ago." The words were horrific but there was something else. Something in Mrs. Bell's tone snared Catherine's interest. The hesitation in her words. Almost as though she had been about to say something other than what she had.

"Only this was worse," Mrs. Bell continued. "Ever so much worse. Her head was hacked clean off. Her head . . ." She sank down to her knees with a moan, her eyes rolling back, her limbs trembling.

Sebastian went to her and squatted down by her side, taking her hand in his and murmuring words of comfort, but Gabriel stood frozen, a statue of ice gilded by firelight. His expression was so hard and cold that Catherine thought even the slightest tap would shatter him.

"It is like before. Exactly like before. She had been cut open and her . . . they're . . . missing . . . parts of her . . ." Mrs. Bell's voice faded away.

Missing parts of her . . .

Catherine stiffened, her skin prickling, the hairs at the nape rising. *Martha.*

"You were in London." Madeline hurled the words at Gabriel like knives, then she turned her gaze on Sebastian. "And you. And now you are both here and Susan is dead. *Dead.*"

All eyes turned to her, the air crackling.

Then Madeline rose with the grace of a queen, twitching her skirt to the side as she passed Sebastian, as though she would not suffer the cloth to touch him.

"A moment, if you please." Gabriel's voice halted her, and she looked back over her shoulder. His gaze never left Madeline's face as he continued. "Why do you mention London, Madeline? What is the relevance?"

For an endless moment, Madeline made no reply. Then she whispered, "You know. The murdered woman in the newspaper. Killed, as Susan was killed. As the girl buried in the graveyard was killed." She turned her face to Catherine, eyes shimmering, features twisted in a mask of despair. Her voice rose. "Explain it, Sebastian. Explain it, if you can." Turning, she fled.

The air rang with her accusation, with all she had said and all she had not.

And Mrs. Bell huddled on the floor shaking her head from side to side, moaning as she buried her face in her hands.

Catherine stood by the window in Madeline's chamber and stared out, the stars winking in the velvet sky, the outline of the encroaching woods dark and formidable in the distance. Gabriel and Sebastian had gone from Cairncroft. Though they had not shared their destination with her, she suspected they went to the place that Susan Parker had been found. Mrs. Bell said it was a shallow grave dug in the same place that the body of that nameless girl had been discovered so many years ago.

An eerie and chilling happenstance; Catherine had long ago learned not to trust such coincidence. It was as though the killer meant for Susan to be discovered, meant to leave her body as a horrific clue in some macabre scavenger hunt. She shivered now to think of it.

When she had said as much to Gabriel, catching his arm as he walked past her, feeling an urgency to tell him her thoughts, he had stared at her for a long moment.

"Or perhaps he never meant to be discovered," he had replied. "The grave is not along a road or well-worn path, but instead deep in the woods. Perhaps he only meant her to be in a place he found familiar, one he could visit again and again."

Catherine had felt en inexplicable horror clutch at her. "Why would he visit her again and again? Why?"

But Gabriel had offered no reply. His expression

shuttered, he had glanced at Sebastian, the current between the two cousins crackling in the cool evening air as something Catherine could not grasp passed between them. There was something dark and terrifying in Gabriel's eyes, something awful and knowing.

Could he suspect his cousin of these horrific crimes? Could he?

She had not been afforded the opportunity to ask. He had reached out and grazed the backs of his knuckles along her cheek, his gaze intent, his jaw hard, and then he and Sebastian were away, riding into the night. But in the wake of Madeline's accusatory words, Catherine could not help but recall her strange thoughts that first day Sebastian had come to Cairncroft, her ponderings about whether or not he had been in London when Martha Grimsby was killed. Nor could she discount his self-avowed fascination with the canopic jars and the removal of organs in preparation for burial.

Madeline had certainly made her suspicions clear. She thought one—or perhaps both—of her cousins was involved in these monstrous deeds. Was Catherine a fool to discount the possibility?

The thoughts that came to her now were horrific. Chilling.

Closing her fingers in the thick cloth of the draperies, she drew them across the window and turned to Madeline to help her prepare for bed. She wondered how either of them would be able to sleep this night.

"Why did he take Susan?" Madeline asked, forlorn. "I preferred her to any other. Surely he knew that. She had soft hands. Susan had soft hands." She wrung her own hands together, and sighed and moaned, sinking down on the edge of a chair.

Catherine went to her and stroked her hair, her own sadness welling in her heart.

"I knew she was gone," Madeline said, looking up at Catherine. "But I did not want to believe it. Why would he take her, of all those he could choose? Why did he not take another? I do not like it that he took Susan."

Catherine had no idea how to reply. She did not like it that he took *anyone*.

She shook her head, faintly repulsed by Madeline's behavior. Then she reminded herself that her friend was not well, that she likely had no idea what she said. Clearly she was overset by the maid's death. She vaguely recalled that Madeline had mentioned Susan before, had expressed a preference for her, perhaps even a fondness.

There was the explanation, then. It was shock and grief that had Madeline rambling so.

"Open the drapes. I must see the sky," Madeline said after Catherine had helped her change into the nightrail and brushed her hair and tucked her into bed.

Moving to the window, she did as Madeline asked.

"Stay until I fall asleep," Madeline pleaded, childlike and small.

"Yes, of course. Close your eyes now, and sleep," Catherine replied, wondering if any of them would sleep this night, or if vivid images of blood and murder would haunt their rest. "Would you like laudanum?" she asked, thinking to fetch it from her chamber.

"No. Not tonight. It makes me afraid. I feel as though I am floating away from my body and may never return." Madeline shuddered.

Catherine only nodded and turned back to the window, staring out at the dark, endless night, wondering where Gabriel was, and what horrors he would find.

* * *

Standing at the edge of the woods with the overhead branches blocking the moonlight and the blackest shadows swallowing his form, he stared up at Madeline's window. Flickering light silhouetted a woman behind the glass panes, the pale oval of her face framed by the spill of her dark hair.

He had not expected to see her there, so clear that as he stretched out his hand, his blade showing silver even in the darkness of the forest, he almost imagined the tip would just touch her.

Yet there she was. Catherine. She made him think of the night sky and the moon.

She made him think of blood and pain. Long for them.

He had not planned to take the maid. That he had done so without forethought was unusual. Normally, he chose his dance partners with care. But there she had stood, alone on the road, innocent and impossibly young, squinting against the sun. The lure had been too much to resist. But the maid had been a mere morsel, a taste.

Catherine would be a banquet. He felt certain of that. She had killed a man. Burned him to a charred lump. So the gossipmongers said, and though he often placed little weight in rumors, this once, he thought they might be true.

What had she felt when she killed him? What had she thought? What would she think when she realized he was here for her? A killer come to claim a killer.

Boxes within boxes, like the ones Madeline had stacked and unstacked as a child.

He had everything ready. The jars. The perfect white feather. He had taken such care choosing the right one for her. He wanted not a spot of color or dirt to mar its perfection. Catherine would be a masterpiece. He would stroke her and pluck the strings of her torment, make music of her muffled cries and pleas.

Ever since he had first learned of the scales and the feather and the belief in another life, one that came after death, he had known what he was meant to be. The judge. The executioner. He had been so young, then. So naïve.

But he had practiced and he had learned. He was so much more adept now.

The first time he had acted, there had been comfort and a soft voice talking to him afterward, promising him he had made the right choice. He had only to trust in her. To do as she bid, and he would become stronger. Braver. Her guidance would help him find joy.

And it did. Oh, it did.

He took those who caught his eye, and he controlled them. For those endless perfect moments, he controlled his precious chosen one, controlled her breath, her sobs, her life, her death.

He was the master. All powerful.

For those moments he owned his chosen partner. As he would soon own Catherine Weston.

Tipping his head back, he watched the window. Watched her pull the pins from her hair, shake her head, and let the loose curls tumble free. Watched as she ran her fingers through the lustrous length.

Soon. Soon, he would take those strands in his fist and yank her hair back and she would taste his kiss. The only kiss he would offer: honed steel on soft flesh.

Her blood blooming like a rose.

She smelled of roses. She would bloom in death, for him, at his will and command.

He had been forced to wait, to show patience. *Patience.*

He was not good at that. Not after all the years of forced patience. But the time was near now. He could feel the anticipation racing through his veins, making his skin tingle and his muscles clench.

A soft huff of laughter escaped him.

He was more than ready for her. More than ready.

Chapter 17

Catherine slept and dreamed of fire, always fire, dancing and writhing, the heat coming upon her like a blow, filling her nose and throat. She was woken by the pounding of her own heart. At least, she assumed that was what had done it, for the house around her was silent. She did not even hear birds beyond the window, though the first fingers of dawn crept through the narrow crack between the curtains.

Sitting up in her bed, she tried to clear the cobwebs from her thoughts, and for a moment, could not recall what day it was or the reason for the unease that nibbled at her with sharp rat teeth. In the end, the fog cleared and she knew exactly the cause, harsh memories rubbing her like lye soap.

A girl was dead. No, not just one. At least three that she knew of—Martha and Susan and the nameless girl buried in the graveyard—and perhaps even more. She felt certain there were more, though she had no proof. But what was the common thread that tied the victims together?

Susan Parker and the nameless girl buried in the graveyard were connected to Cairncroft. But what of Martha? She had no link to Cairncroft save the tenuous one through her friendship with Catherine.

Climbing from her bed, Catherine prepared for the day, her limbs heavy, as though weighted by stones, a result, no doubt, of a restless sleep. Yet her mood was not as somber as it might have been, for the prospect of seeing Gabriel was like a candle in the darkness. Her ablutions complete, she pushed the last of her pins into her hair and went down to the breakfast room.

Gabriel was not there.

It was more than disappointment she felt. The unease that had nibbled at her earlier burgeoned into a stronger distress, though she had no solid reason for that. She felt as though she waited for something, a great shadowy beast that would prowl from the corner, unexpected. With a shake of her head, she pushed aside such fancy and went to the sideboard where the covered servers held eggs and toast and pickled salmon.

The morning fare held no appeal. She took only a cup of tea and when that was done she paused by the open door and asked the footman, "Have Sir Gabriel and Mr. St. Aubyn returned?"

"They did, miss. Late last night. But they rode off again early this morning. The sun had not yet risen when they went."

"Is there any news?" she asked.

The footman shook his head, his expression somber. "No, miss."

Having exhausted that resource, she was left at odds, worry clouding her thoughts. She went to the blue parlor and paced, then sat, then rose and paced again, trying not to think of Susan and Martha, then trying to think of them as they had been when they were alive. They deserved that, at least. Someone to remember them.

At noon, she roused Madeline from slumber and tried

to coax her to dress, to eat, to venture outdoors for a walk. Catherine's efforts met with failure and in the end she settled in to read to Madeline for a bit, then to simply sit by her and listen to her broken ramblings for the remainder of the time.

It was not until late afternoon that Gabriel returned, and Catherine knew that only because she caught a glimpse of him quite by accident.

She had fled Madeline's company for a few stolen moments outdoors, desperate for air and activity and a short break away from her despondent friend. Madeline only lay in her bed and twisted the sheets in her fingers, then untwisted them, again and again, saying little. She made monosyllablic responses to Catherine's attempts at conversation, and those only grudgingly.

Catherine thought that she must escape that stale, closed room or she would go mad. She ought to feel guilty for that, she supposed. But in truth, she could not.

Once outdoors, she chose to take the path that she and Gabriel had walked that first morning, the twisted maze to the graveyard. The sun was high, casting the path half in light, half in shadow as the tall hedge blocked its rays. She walked to the graveyard, acknowledging the silent hope that she would find Gabriel there, waiting for her.

Of course, he was not.

Turning, she retraced her steps and was just leaving the mouth of the maze between the high walls of hedge on either side when she saw him. His back was toward her, his strides quick and sure. Her heart gladdened, her steps lightened. Almost did she cry his name. Then something—she could not say what—stilled her tongue.

Perhaps it was his purposeful tread away from any place he might have hoped to find her. He did not go to the parlor, or her chamber or even Madeline's. He went to the crumbling ruin at the side of the abbey, a place he could be certain she was not.

And that struck her as odd. Not that she bloated her own importance, but that it seemed very strange that he did not seek her out.

Catherine could not say what made her follow him, only that curiosity got the best of common sense. She was adept at creeping about. Her childhood had made her that way. All the times her parents had sunk into the dark depths of mourning, she had tiptoed about the house, never seen, never heard. Now she called upon those skills and followed Gabriel, driven to do so, unable to understand why.

He went to a part of the abbey she had never explored. It was dank and crumbling, parts of the stone chipped away. At the bottom of a listing tower, he pushed open an old, iron-girded door, the wood stained by time. Stepping through, he disappeared within, leaving the door half ajar behind him. She waited and watched, careful to remain concealed lest he look out one of the narrow windows above and spy her here spying on him.

She could not help but acknowledge how ridiculous her behavior was. She clung to a large bush and peeked through its thick foliage and stared at the crumbling stones for a very long while.

What was she thinking?

For a moment, she considered turning and going back the way she had come, leaving Gabriel to his privacy and secrets. The day was fading. Madeline would be anxious if she woke from her nap and found Catherine gone. Susan Parker's murder had had a terrible effect on her mood.

But something made her stay. Curiosity, yes. And something more. She felt compelled to remain here, as though this was her sole hope for answers. So she stayed where she was, waiting, though for what, she was not certain.

Finally, the door opened once more and Gabriel emerged looking grim and drawn. Something in his expression chilled her. He looked . . . tired. But it was more than that. He appeared tense, anxious.

His gaze slid past the place she hid, but did not linger, and she was certain he did not see her there for he strode off the way he had come earlier. She watched him until he disappeared.

Still, she held her place. When moments passed and he did not return, she ran to the door and tried it, expecting it to be locked, startled to find it was not.

With a quick glance about, she slipped inside and drew the door closed behind her. It moved on well-oiled hinges without a sound.

A narrow stone staircase rose before her, and as she placed her foot on the first step, she wondered again why she did this. What did she think to find?

What did she *hope* to find?

Answers evaded her. She only knew that she must climb these steps, must discover what awaited her above.

She was so tired of secrets. His. Hers. She wanted trust between them.

Why?

There could not be love without trust. The thought sneaked up on her, like a fox pouncing on a hare. She was left feeling just as shocked and startled and afraid.

Love.

Dear God, did she think she loved him? Loved Gabriel St. Aubyn?

A shudder took her and she dropped her head, dizzy with the answer that slapped her. Yes, she did. She loved him. She had been so foolish as to fall in love with him. Where were her boundaries, her walls, her guards? They had failed her.

She slid her foot from the step, freezing in place, suddenly certain that she could not go up and steal his secrets like a thief. She refused. It was a betrayal of the worst sort, and his secrets were of no value to her if he did not share them willingly.

She loved him.

And so she would not betray him. She would find him and ask him what he hid in this moldering tower, and trust that he would tell her. And if he did not . . . Well, she would have to hope that in time, he would.

Spinning away, she barely had time to find her balance before arms closed around her, strong and tight. She struggled, shoving and kicking, the sound erupting from her more squeak than scream. Fear coiled about her heart, serpentine, tight.

"Catherine!"

She gasped. It was Gabriel. He had caught her out. But still, the fear eased.

"You frightened me," she accused, her heart yet pounding, her breath coming in sharp rasps.

"If you sneak about in dark places, you must expect to be frightened."

There was that.

Despite his cool tone, his arms about her were warm and sheltering. He kissed her forehead, then her mouth, forgiving her trespass before she even asked.

"I did not go up," she said in a rush, needing for him to know that, to know she had not betrayed him. "I took only one step, but turned back."

His arms tightened around her, and he whispered, "Why?"

"It felt like the worst sort of betrayal, a breach of your privacy. I thought that if I lo—" She bit off the word before it could fly free and reared back to look into his beautiful, cold, beloved face. "I thought that if I have any . . . respect for you, I ought not to trespass."

The side of his mouth quirked. "But you wanted to."

"Yes."

"Well, come along, love." He took her hand and led the way, confident in each step though the staircase was gloomy and dim. He had walked this path many times, she realized.

The stone stairs were slick beneath her feet, and she clung tightly to Gabriel's hand as they climbed up and up.

"The walls feel very close," she said, reaching out to trail her hand along the stones as she passed.

"They *are* very close." He did not sound particularly concerned, though she knew he did not like confined places any better than she.

"You have been this way often." Her words echoed back at her. He said nothing, and she thought he must view this as one of those pointless conversations he abhorred. She supposed it was, but she preferred to hear something, even if it was only the sound of her own voice.

Then he said, "It was my secret place when I was a child," and she realized he had only delayed, likely weighing the decision of whether or not to share that information. She was more pleased that he had than the situation warranted, as though any bit of knowledge about him eased her hunger.

Finally, they came to the top of the stairs and a large space with stone walls and a stone floor and a hearth to her left. Across the far wall were high, narrow windows set in the stone, and before them a desk and a tall, leather-backed chair. Before the hearth was a rug. And that was all. There was not another stick of furniture to be seen.

Gabriel drew her hand to his lips and pressed a kiss to her palm. Then he left her and crossed to the large mahogany desk, rounding it so he stood with his back to the windows. With the position of the light, she could not clearly see his face or his expression.

Reaching up, he drew a necklace from beneath his shirt. She stepped closer and saw that it was a leather thong bearing two keys. He had not worn it the other day when they had made love, or perhaps she had only not noticed it then. One key, he separated from the other and unlocked a drawer in the desk. He withdrew a metal box and set it down, then unlocked that as well, pushing back the lid so it hit the polished wooden desktop with a thud.

Then he placed the keys beside it and crossed to the hearth, where he took up a flint box and set about making a fire. Catherine watched him warily, uncertain what his intention was.

"Go ahead," he said, glancing at her before turning his attention back to his task.

Slowly, she made her way to the desk. She peered into the box and saw the cover of a leather-bound journal and some letters.

"What are these?" she asked.

"My secrets." He was watching her very carefully now. "And the secrets of others."

Her heart gave a hard thud in her breast. He offered her these things? Nothing could be so easy. Why would he bring her here and show her this now? Why?

He *trusted* her with this? So it appeared. Yet she had difficulty in trusting his trust.

Such a tangled web.

She reached out and rested her fingers on the string that tied the packet of letters. Then she looked up at him once more.

"You mean for me to read them?"

"Yes."

He held her gaze for a long, measured moment, then turned back to his efforts to start a fire. At length, it was done and he rose to stand facing her, but so far away. She had yet to summon the courage to take the packet from the box, let alone unfold the letters and discover their dark truths.

She shivered, suddenly chilled.

"Look your fill, Catherine. And when you are done, burn them. Burn everything. It is past time." He crossed to her then and put his palms against her cheeks, tipping her face to his, her mouth to his. He kissed her. There was nothing tentative or gentle about it. His mouth was hard and hungry, his tongue a hot slide of velvet in her mouth, his teeth nipping at her. Sharp. Deliberate. His breath mingling with hers.

His body was hard and warm and solid against her, and for an instant she lost her breath, lost her thoughts, lost all will to delve into his secrets. For an instant, she wanted to draw him to the thick rug before the hearth and make love with him there and simply burn everything without ever looking at the words written within. She was not certain now that she wanted to know.

He pulled back, ran the pad of his thumb along her lower lip, his eyes reflecting the light of the fire.

"Why?" she whispered.

"Catherine." He studied her for a long moment, and then offered a dry smile. "You have woken my dead heart, the heart I stabbed and believed I had sliced from my breast years ago at Hanham House. I love you," he said, his tone smooth and even and cool as it always was, but the words, oh, the words, the gift of them, made her heart soar. "I have loved you since the first moment I heard your voice. Since I sensed your pain and recognized your strength." He pressed his lips to hers, swift and firm. "Only one who has suffered can understand depth of suffering in another."

And she knew not if he spoke of his suffering or hers. Or perhaps both. Two pieces of broken pottery, brought together at the jagged edge, made whole, though imperfect still.

He loved her. He would not say it unless he meant it with every breath and every fiber of his being. He was not a man to say anything lightly.

Her heart danced in a rough, jagged rhythm. Her breath whooshed from her lungs as though a blow had been struck. It had. His words were like a physical thrust, stabbing as deep as they could go, filling her, lifting her, offering her the impossible.

He loved her and so he gifted her with his trust, opening his metal box, but more than that, opening his heart. She could only begin to imagine what that cost him.

Wanting to offer her own vows, her own baring of heart and soul, she parted her lips, intending to speak, but no words came out, only the soft huff of her breath. *Say it. Say it.* But she did not. She only stared at him and wished she were so brave.

As though he knew her thoughts, he said, "Tell me when you are ready, Catherine. I can wait. You have no idea how long I can wait."

But she did. She knew how long he had waited to be free, how long he had waited for his vengeance. He would wait that long for her. She knew it.

"Read them. And then burn them," he said. "I shall await you in my chamber."

Turning, he headed for the stairs, leaving her alone with

only the hiss and the pop of the fire for company, leaving her with his secrets open and bare on the table. Trusting her with them.

"Wait," she cried, and tore after him, pausing at the top of the narrow staircase, seeing the shadowy shape of him below her. He paused, but did not turn, only stood on the stair with his back to her. She needed to tell him she loved him. She needed to set the words free.

But when she made to speak, something entirely different came out instead.

"I killed him," she said, feeling both heavy and light. "Jasper Hunt. I was lying on the pallet where I had birthed my child. Two days had passed, perhaps three. I do not know. I was ill. Feverish. He came to that room. I heard the rasp of the key." She shuddered, forced herself to go on, the words coming faster now, in a hushed frantic rush. "He pushed the door open. The baby, *my* baby began to wail. Jasper staggered in. I could smell the stale stink of liquor on him. 'Make it quiet,' he ordered, and I tried. I tried. But the baby would not quiet. Jasper came to stand beside me, and he reached down, tore my child from my grasp, and put his hand over the baby's mouth. 'Quiet,' he cried. And again, 'Quiet.' I tried to take the child from him. I begged. I pleaded. I clawed at his wrist and his fingers, but he only kicked me away." Her voice grew hoarse. "He held his hand there, and in the end, my son was quiet."

She swallowed the sob that choked her, forced herself to go on. Below her, on the stair, Gabriel was preternaturally still.

"He fell upon me, tried to . . . to . . . *take* me, but he was so far into his cups that he only fell asleep, his weight crushing me so I could not breathe. I pushed at him and struggled, and finally, he rolled enough that I could wriggle free.

But when he rolled, he knocked the candle and the flames began to dance. They licked at the rug, the curtains, the bedsheets . . ."

"And you took your child and you left Jasper Hunt there, in your bed, to burn," Gabriel finished, his tone flat.

She put her palm across her mouth, and took a jagged, raspy breath.

"I did." She forced the admission through lips that felt frozen. "I watched from the lawn, holding my dead baby tucked inside my dress, still warm against my breast. The flames leaped and danced and burned my childhood home to the ground, and Jasper danced in the window. He screamed and screamed then, and for two days after. A part of me was sorry when he died. I wanted him to live forever, just like that." Her body trembled, though she could not say if it was horror for her own story and the memories and the pain, or the relief of finally setting it free that made her shake. "So you see, I killed him."

"I know," Gabriel said, and finally looked back at her, his face pale in the darkness, his eyes burning, fierce. He came up the stairs to her then and pulled her close and held her, just held her, for what seemed a very long time. "I have known all along, my brave love."

Then he stepped back and held her gaze long enough that she understood what he told her. She could have said anything, and it would not have mattered. He loved her. *Her.* For all she was, and all she was not.

And now it was her turn to discover what was in that metal box, to know his secrets and accept or reject him.

He loved her enough that he even gave her that.

Offering a faint smile, he turned away once more and descended the stairs, disappearing round the bend.

Absolution, just like that.

If only she could truly forgive herself so easily. Not for Jasper's death—he had made his own ugly choices—but for the death of her child.

It was only after she stood there for some moments, wrestling her emotions under control, living and reliving the past few moments, that she understood Gabriel's smile.

He knew more than what she had admitted aloud. He knew she loved him. The very act of trusting him with her secrets had told him so. And he expected that she would love him still, no matter what the letters and journals revealed.

Catherine lit a taper in the fire and touched it to the candle on the desk. The room was dim, but there was light enough to read by. She settled in the high-backed leather chair. Carefully she withdrew the packets of letters from the metal box, and saw that there were three leather-bound journals, as well.

She started first with the letters addressed to Gabriel St. Aubyn, Cairncroft Abbey. Tipping them to the light, she read Sebastian's descriptions of his travels. One letter stood out from the others, the words eerie and disconcerting. Tracing her finger over the page, she read them twice.

I have heard talk that a mummy is to be sent home to England to be unwrapped before an audience of physicians. I should like to be there when they do, to see for myself the places they made the cuts in order to remove the lungs, liver, intestine, and stomach. These the ancient Egyptians stored in jars made of stone or ceramic or even wood. If only you could see them, carved and decorated. You would think them wondrous things of fascination, I am sure. I find them mysterious. I wonder at the purpose of such deliberate dissection. I wonder, too, that the heart, they did not take. Gabriel, it would be wonderful if you were here. Perhaps we could even try to make a mummy ourselves using a dead bird or other small creature.

The description was evocative. She could not help but think of Martha Grimsby and the clipping she had read, so thoughtfully provided by Mrs. Northrop. Again, she recalled the suspicions she had felt after meeting Sebastian for the first time, her curiosity about whether he had been in London at the time of Martha's death. From the dates on these letters and the things written therein, she knew he had been at Cairncroft Abbey at approximately the same time that the dead girl buried in the unmarked grave had been found. In fact, she thought she recalled someone—Madeline? Gabriel?—had mentioned that Sebastian had been the one to find her.

Was there significance in that? She could not bear to think so, but the possibility nagged at her.

Carefully, she set that letter aside, and then took up the packet addressed to Geoffrey St. Aubyn, Hanham House. She had no question of how Gabriel had come to have these letters in his possession. Gabriel had been incarcerated in a madhouse, and now, his brother was there in his stead. Or was his brother dead now?

Gabriel had never said, she realized, and it had not occurred to her to ask.

She read letter after letter, and at length, she set the whole pile aside and put her palm on the small of her back as she arched and stretched.

Idly, she reached for the first of the three leather-bound journals and flipped it open to the first page. Childish drawings greeted her. Tipping her head, she studied the first one. It appeared to be a cat pouncing on a mouse. She flipped to the next page and the next and each one depicted a predator taking its prey.

A memory touched her, of drawings in a similar style. She had seen them before, but could not think where. Flipping pages faster now, she gave only cursory scrutiny to each. By the end of the journal, the look of the sketches changed. Matured. And the drawings became increasingly more gruesome.

Sliding the next journal along the desktop, she flipped it open. A drawing of a flower, and on the next page more flowers, and on the next, a tree. Again, she felt an odd sense of having seen these before. Turning another page, she froze, gasped, horror clogging her throat. The drawing was some sort of animal—a cat? A fox?—lying in a pool of blood. She wanted to think otherwise, wanted to imagine her vision betrayed her. But, no, though the drawing was crude, it could be mistaken for nothing else.

She turned the pages faster, her breath coming quick and harsh, and a soft cry escaped her as she came to the very last sketch. Four jars. And below them on the page something that looked like the beef liver she had watched Cook prepare as a child.

She was panting now. Closing her eyes, she willed her breathing to slow. To whom did these journals belong? Three boys had lived at Cairncroft Abbey—Gabriel, Geoffrey, and Sebastian—and one of them had grown to be a monster. These journals documented that. Or perhaps, one of them had been a monster all along.

Or was it someone else? A servant? A villager?

A shiver crawled up her spine.

Not Gabriel. She trusted *that* truth.

Slamming the cover shut, she laid her palm flat atop it.

She did not want to know everything contained herein. She certainly did not want to look at the next book. Breathing in a jagged rhythm, she sat there and stared at the fire.

Burn them. Burn everything.

Scooping up the journals and the letters, she hurried to the hearth. There was a thick oval carpet there covering the stone floor. She knelt on it, feeding letter after letter to the flames, and finally, opening the journals and laying them face down on the fire, watching the orange and red tongues curl and dance.

Beautiful, cleansing fire.

Chapter 18

Catherine went first to Madeline's chamber, though her heart bid her go to Gabriel's. But Madeline had been alone too long and she would work herself into a frenzy. Better to soothe her first, then slip away. She wanted nothing weighing on her, no other thoughts in her mind when she went to Gabriel's arms, to his bed.

Her feet were heavy on the stairs, and her lids pricked, though she did not weep, did not even understand why she wanted to. She felt as though there was something clear as day before her eyes—something frightening and dangerous—and she was not seeing it.

The passage that led to her chamber and Madeline's was dark. The doors on all sides were closed tight. She paused a moment in her own room, taking only enough time to splash water on her face and hands, locking her door behind her and slipping the key in her pocket. The hallway seemed to stretch before her interminably, and she found herself reluctant to return to Madeline's closed and quiet bedroom, to the dim light and the smell of liniment.

But she must. Only a little longer and she could be with

Gabriel, touch him, hold him, tell him all the things in her heart.

The passage seemed very long and very quiet and she quickened her pace, feeling a strange, inexplicable urgency. Madeline's door was partly open, and she pressed her palm flat against it and pushed on the wood until it swung inward. Her gaze slid to the bed, and she froze, for Madeline was not there.

"Where did you go for so long?" came the petulant query, and she turned to find Madeline sitting in the chair before the fire surrounded by stacks and stacks of books. It seemed that every book she had stored in her bedroom for so long had been moved close to the fire to form a series of towers like the turrets of a castle.

And in their midst sat Madeline.

"I went walking. I had a need for some air," Catherine replied, startled to realize that her friend had not only left her bed, but had dressed in a walking gown and combed and pinned her hair. "You look very well, Madeline," she said.

"Thank you." Madeline thrust her lower lip out in a pout and closed the book that lay open on her lap. "I waited and waited and when you never came, I was forced to rise and ring for the maid. Peg was the one they sent. I do not like her. She is awkward and rough, her fingers tied up in splints." She tipped her head to the side. "You should have been here to help me. You are my friend, as I have always been yours. You have no one but me."

The words were harsh. Unkind. And no longer true.

She had Gabriel, but she thought it would not be wise to say so.

"Well," Madeline said in the face of her silence. "Things change." Her words carried a hard edge of anger.

Uncertain of Madeline's mood, Catherine offered,

"Would you like to go outdoors? Perhaps a walk by the lake?"

Madeline glanced at her from beneath her lashes. "Not yet, but soon." Her gaze slid to the open door. "Would you close it, please, Catherine? And lock it, as well?" She lowered her voice. "It is Mrs. Bell. She has come three times to bring me food and drink." She nodded at the small table by the window, where a covered plate sat. "Smell it," she said. "Go ahead."

With a frown, Catherine did as she bid, lifting the cover and leaning down to sniff the array of cold meat and cheese and bread. There . . . she *did* smell it. Almonds.

Dropping the cover on the plate with a clatter, she spun to face Madeline, horror congealing in her breast. Were all Madeline's fears and terrors true? Was the housekeeper trying to poison her?

"Madeline—" she began, only to have her friend cut her off.

"Not now," Madeline whispered, glancing frantically about. "Did I not tell you the walls have ears? Please, close and lock the door."

Seeing no other way to ease her dismay, Catherine did as Madeline asked, pushing the door shut and turning the key in the lock. There was an unpleasant finality to that, as though she entombed the two of them in this dim, dark space. She did not like to be trapped in this room with the door closed and locked and the windows shut tight.

"Give the key here," Madeline said. "Oh, please, Catherine, let me have it. I will only feel safe if I have it in my hand."

Catherine knew that feeling quite well, yet she was loath to part with the key, to give someone else, even a friend, control over her in that way. She wanted to be able to open the door at her will, not at Madeline's whim. She hesitated, and then laid the key atop the high bureau next to the door. When she looked to Madeline once more, she was startled to see that she was smiling, a tight, ugly smile that Catherine could not understand.

The firelight danced across her features, painting her skin and hair with gold, coloring her smile as red lips and white teeth, small as a child's. For a moment, she did not appear at all herself, but rather a doll painted to look like Madeline.

It was then that Catherine heard the sounds, low but quite distinct, footsteps echoing, not in the hallway but behind the walls. She spun, startled, her gaze flicking to the door, then to the far wall across from the bed, then back to Madeline once more.

"Do you hear it?" Madeline asked, her lips stiff. She turned her face to the wall, then away. "He is come for me."

"No." Catherine crossed to her and knelt before her, taking Madeline's hand between her own. "It is only an ancient servants' tunnel in the wall. I have seen it myself. There are no monsters, no creatures that come for you."

"I never said a monster had come for me." Madeline laughed then, the sound like fragile china fallen from a table to shatter against a hard floor. "I said that *he* has come. At last. I have waited so long. It was no mean feat to grease their palms and see him free. And then he could not come right away. He had business in London to see to first. But he is here now. He is here."

Catherine only looked at her, uncomprehending. But there was something . . . something she felt certain she ought to know. "Do you speak of Sebastian?" she asked, though a part of her knew already that Madeline did not.

Madeline closed her hand tight around Catherine's,

squeezing until bone rubbed on bone. She leaned in, bringing their faces close.

"Do you think you are sly? And wise and wily?" she whispered. "I am smarter than all of you, dear girl. I always have been. Smarter and more sly than my aunt and uncle, or the headmistress or the teachers at Browning. Certainly wiser and more wily than any of the other girls." She paused and shook her head. "When I heard what you had done, that you had killed a man, your own guardian, I thought you would do. I thought we could be true friends. That you would understand. But you have proven a disappointment, Catherine. That you have."

Yanking her hands free, Catherine fell back, the impetus sending her sprawling. "What do you mean?" But she *knew*. In that second, she recalled exactly why the journals had seemed so familiar, the drawing style was something she had seen before. They were Madeline's pictures. *Madeline's*. She recalled her sketches and paintings from Browning, and the way Miss Chalmers, the drawing teacher, had frowned and shaken her head and taken Madeline's work to show the headmistress again and again.

Madeline was the killer? How was that possible? She had been here, at Cairncroft with Catherine when Martha was killed, and here in this very chamber when Susan was murdered.

Again came the footfalls from behind the wall and then a scraping and dragging sound as the portal swung wide. She jerked her head toward the sound, her thoughts as twisted and tangled as a knot of string.

A man stood there with a candle, and behind him yawned a great, black hole. Catherine blinked against the light, and she saw long honey-gold hair and eyes of liquid topaz and chiseled features painted in light and shadow by the small flickering flame.

"Gabriel," she cried and scrambled to her feet, her heart pounding, her mouth dry. She rushed to him and skidded to a stop only inches away, never so glad to see anyone as she was to see him. From the corner of her eye, she saw Madeline rise and cross to the door, but she thought it did not matter now. If she fled, Gabriel would catch her.

Taking deep, shaking breaths, Catherine trembled with the horror of what she had only just come to know.

"The journals. They were Madeline's. I remember now." She held his gaze, cold and flat, and a chill started deep inside her, though she could not say why. Words tumbled free, faster, more urgent. "She used to draw sketches just like that when we were at school. Terrible pictures that made the other girls cry. She said she only drew the world as she saw it—"

"—for the spider *does* eat the fly, and the ants the dead worm. The fox eats the mouse." Madeline cut her off as she stepped close behind her. Catherine jerked to the side, feeling hemmed in and trapped. "I have always wanted to know what it feels like to die. But no one would tell me. Not until the day I saw my cousin kill the bird in the woods. And then I knew. We were destined to be together, to share our fascination. I was meant to see what he did that day. I shared my thoughts with him. My ideas. And he took them and used them as thread to embroider his tapestry, ever more intriguing and complex."

Catherine could not bear to look at her. The thoughts Madeline shared were horrific in and of themselves, but to look into her guileless blue eyes as she spoke of such things was too terrible. She jerked her gaze to Gabriel's face, a thick lump choking her throat. He did not reach for her or touch her or close his fingers upon hers. Instead, he only looked at her with his head tipped to the side.

"Are you afraid?" he asked, and smiled.

Her blood turned to ice in her veins.

His voice was wrong. His eyes were wrong. She saw that clearly now. It was as though Gabriel had shed his skin and someone else entirely had stepped inside to wear it like a suit.

"Geoffrey," Catherine whispered, horror congealing in her gut like cold blood pudding.

"Geoffrey," Madeline mimicked her, and stepped forward to press a kiss to his cheek. "Aren't you astute?"

Catherine backed away another step, and Geoffrey followed her, two strides for her one.

"How did you get away from Hanham House?"

"He told you about Hanham House? How unexpected." He shrugged, a sharp, angry movement. "Gabriel's precious Dr. Vincent left recently. The doctors there now know their *business* well and care to keep their income more than anything else." His eyes grew colder still. "In all the years I have been there, no one has come to visit, save Madeline. And when she paid them to set me free, she said they had only to continue to charge my brother for my care and he would pay, none the wiser. That way, they got twice the coin for none of the work."

He stepped closer still and lifted a lock of Catherine's hair from where it had come loose to lie along her shoulder. Then he leaned in and pressed her hair to his nose, breathing deeply.

With a gasp, she turned her face away and yanked her hair from his grasp, horrified to have him stand so close and touch her at all, even her hair.

"She is not for you, dear."

"She *is*." He snarled. "You promised."

"There is no time. We must be away." Madeline patted his arm and gave a brittle laugh. "We shall find you another. Did I not guide you to Martha? Was she not a lovely treat? This one must be sacrificed to the fire. We discussed it. You recall. It is the only way."

The words penetrated her numbed thoughts and Catherine stumbled back until she was pressed against the wall. *Martha*. Madeline had told this monster where to find Martha. And Catherine had given her the direction. She had written to Madeline about her friend, told her Martha's name and that she ran a school in St. Giles. It would have been an easy matter to make inquiries with that. Dear God. She had handed Martha to a killer.

No, not *a* killer. A pair of killers. Monsters.

Her chest heaved and her palms were slick with sweat. She felt sick, bile crawling up her throat.

And the smell of smoke stung her nostrils.

She looked about and realized that the smell was carrying from the tunnel. The smell of smoke and fire.

Edging to the side, she tried to reach the bureau to retrieve the key that would open the door and see her flee this chamber and whatever horrors they planned. Geoffrey watched her with a hawkish gaze, but made no move to stop her. Frantic, she fell against the bureau and reached up for the key, disappointment lodging in her gut like a lump of coal.

It was not there. Of course. Madeline had taken it.

Her gaze flashed to the open panel of the servants' tunnel, but Geoffrey blocked her way.

With remarkable strength for a woman who claimed to be an invalid, Madeline yanked the coverlet from her bed and dragged it across the floor, tossing one end into the crackling hearth and leaving the other to trail over the piles of books. She was no more ill than Catherine. It had all been a dupe.

"What of the laudanum, the poison?" Catherine asked, hoping against hope that if she kept them talking long enough, Gabriel would come searching for her. Would he know to look here, or would he go only to the ruined tower to search for her?

Madeline slanted her a glance. "Oil of bitter almonds, cooked to make certain it was harmless. I had to make sure that you found no allies here, trusted no one. Making you suspect Mrs. Bell was the easiest way."

"And the night Mrs. Bell came to give you the extra dose of laudanum? The night she said Gabriel instructed her to do so?"

"Geoffrey looks exactly like his brother. Even you were fooled for a moment, just now." She looked to Geoffrey, who stood with arms folded across his chest, blocking Catherine's path to the open door of the tunnel. "This place will go up like a tinderbox. I shall enjoy watching it burn. Did you set the other wings alight?"

"Yes. As you say, the place should go up like a tinderbox," Geoffrey replied, the sound of his voice making Catherine shiver.

"Now here is a question," Madeline said, whirling to face her. "Will you scream for him as you burn? Or will you leap from the window to your death?"

Smoke began to fill the room now as more and more of the books caught the flames that snaked and writhed from the hearth to lick at the carpet and the edge of the curtains.

"What of the servants?" Catherine cried. "They will be killed."

"I care naught for them." Madeline shrugged. "But

probably, most will get free. You are the only one who will stay here to burn."

Catherine screamed then, long and loud. They only looked at her as she drew breath to scream again.

"Go ahead," Madeline said, weaving her fingers with Geoffrey's as she smiled gently at Catherine and nodded her head. "You and I are the only ones housed in this wing. Go ahead and scream. No one will hear you." She laughed. "Tell me now how you will stay with me and keep the monsters at bay, how you will let none harm me. You fool. You would have done better to think of how to keep them from coming for *you*."

"Don't do this." Catherine looked about desperately, seeing no way to escape, her eyes and nose and throat stinging from the gathering smoke. "Do not."

But they disappeared into the yawning black tunnel and pulled the portal shut. Catherine turned to the door and closed her hand on the doorknob, twisting and yanking in desperation. Locked tight. And Madeline had taken the key.

Panic surged. She snatched a towel from the washstand and held it over her mouth and nose as she flew to the portal they had closed behind them. She ran her hands along the wood, but whatever trick would open it evaded her.

The fire roared and the smoke churned and she thought that Madeline was right.

She could scream, but no one would hear her.

Geoffrey led the way through the narrow, dark passage, the single candle he held sending out fingers of light to touch the shadows. He could hear Madeline close behind him, breathing fast.

He wanted to turn and strike her.

She had cheated him. Anger churned in his gut, a simmering rage. Catherine was to be his. He wanted her. Wanted to lead her through the steps of his dance. She would be his most satisfying partner, one who fulfilled him. One who could assuage his need, soothe the burn that coursed through his veins. Because she was strong. Because she was brave.

And because his brother loved her.

It would be excruciatingly sweet to take her from him.

But Madeline said no. There was no time. Did he dare go against her? Somehow, over the years, they had become intertwined in a way that made them equal, but not. He was the stronger, the more deadly. But she was cunning and wily. It was always Madeline who helped him hone and channel his urges, helped him created a lovely finesse in his work.

She had even helped him kill during the years he was at Hanham House, utilizing an isolated shed deep in the grounds, bringing him three victims and disposing of them when he was done. Those encounters had been exercises in planning and timing such as no other. But Madeline was ever so good at planning.

Perhaps that was why the episode with Susan Parker had devolved so quickly. Because Madeline was not there to guide him, to calm the power of his need. Susan had been an aberration, an unplanned kill. Not since the first had he been alone like that.

Oh, Madeline had not been there when he killed Martha. Not in person. But they had discussed it at length, and so she was there in his thoughts, in his heart, in the surge of electricity that thrilled his blood. Her voice was there in his mind, guiding him.

He stopped dead, and turned to face her. She was so close at his back that she bumped against him.

"Geoffrey, we must hurry. Do you not smell it? The smoke?"

He did. But he could not squelch the growing urgency to go back, to fetch Catherine.

"I want her," he said. "In the confusion of the fire, we can bring her away." They could do it. And he could slake his urges upon her. The thought made him shiver, made his hand stray to his blade, his fingers playing over the hilt.

Pushing Madeline aside, he paced back the way they had come, the tunnel dark and narrow around them.

Madeline caught his arm and tried to make him stop, but he would not. *Could* not. He shook her off with a snarl. Catherine was the jewel in his brother's heart. There was no surer way to strike him than to take her. Savor her. Cut her and make her bleed.

Aside from the sheer delight of taking her life, she would serve a second purpose. One of vengeance. He owed Gabriel for all the years at Hanham House.

Behind him, Madeline coughed. The sound made his own chest feel heavy and scratchy, and he too began to hack, his nose and eyes stinging.

"Geoffrey, the smoke rises from below," Madeline cried, clutching at his arm once more. "Where did you set the second fire?"

He paused, looked about. She was right. The air was thick, the smoke curling about their heads and shoulders.

"The library," he said, and realized that he had made a poor choice. The tunnel from the library joined with this one.

Madeline turned to and fro, agitated, and Geoffrey froze, undecided now. Press on? Retreat? What to do?

"We will go back," she said, then coughed long and hard into her hand. "Quickly now."

Good. This was what he wanted. They would go back

and fetch Catherine and bring her with them, find another way to flee the burning abbey. Yes, this was good.

He caught Madeline's hand and they hurried on, the smoke growing thicker, the air warmer.

They came to the portal, and Geoffrey thrust it open. Smoke billowed out toward them, a heavy yellowish-brown cloud. A sickly tongue of flame reached through the open door and curled along the ceiling.

"Geoffrey?" Madeline's voice was tentative, wary, her fingers curling tight with his.

They could see nothing beyond the door, the fire that Madeline had started earlier creating a thick, greasy barrier. Of Catherine, there was no sign.

Was she dead?

"No!" He would not be cheated of his prize. Geoffrey surged forward, dragging Madeline with him. The smoke seemed to recede before them, sucked back through the open portal into the chamber beyond.

"Geoffrey—" Madeline cried as a ball of fire erupted toward them. Bright. Hot.

So hot.

"Catherine!" Gabriel flung open the heavy, iron-girded door and tore up the stone stairs. The metal strongbox was open on the desk, the letters and journals gone, the fire almost dead in the hearth. But Catherine was not here.

Which meant she was somewhere in the house.

He knew not what malady took him then, but it was a twisted, monstrous thing that robbed him of reason and broke out cold sweat on his skin.

Catherine was in the house, and it was burning.

With a roar, he ran down the stairs, half sliding on the

smooth, worn stone, then burst through the door and ran, legs pumping, chest heaving. He could see the flames, great, grotesque flames, ravenously swallowing anything that was not metal or stone.

The servants were running, panicked, across the lawns. Some were organizing to bring water from the lake. Wooden buckets of water passed from hand to hand. A mosquito against a behemoth. A part of him was cool and calm, rational enough to recognize that he must stop and organize them and cull a few from the line to help him search.

But the greater part was filled with hot, swelling terror that rivaled the flames themselves, burning him to ash, eating him alive.

Where? Where would she be?

Madeline's chamber or her own were the most likely places. His gaze slid to that wing. It was alive, a writhing, twisting creature of orange and red and unbearable heat, belching great towers of black smoke into the darkening sky.

On instinct, he ran full tilt for the garden door. It was the closest. His best hope. If he could only reach her. He would save her. He would drag her from the greedy fire and—

Panting, he reached the door, grabbed for it, and cried out as the handle seared his skin. He tried a second time and a third, even tearing off his coat to wrap it about his hand, but the door would not open. Locked or melted.

From above him came a loud, whooshing roar and the sound of glass shattering. Shards rained down on him, a hailstorm of sparks and ash and glass. He stumbled back, his gaze jerking frantically along the windows on the lower level, searching for one, just one, where fire did not dance behind the panes.

There. At the end.

He ran, vaulting a line of shrubs. He bent his elbow to slam it hard against the glass.

"Gabriel!" A woman's voice, but he could not stop. Could not wait. He had to reach her. Reach Catherine. She would burn. She would die.

And he could not lose her. Could not face a life without her.

He would survive anything but that.

"Gabriel!" Again, the cry. Louder, more frantic, and he turned and saw her, running toward him, her face streaked with soot, her hair falling about her shoulders, her dress mottled with black-rimmed holes where sparks must have landed and singed the cloth.

The blood rushed from his head until he was dizzy and swaying, barely able to trust what his eyes beheld. Catherine, there before him.

His throat too tight to speak, he surged forward and caught her against him, brutal in his handling, too far into the terrible miasma that overcame him to understand what he said or did. He only held her and buried his face in the curve of her shoulder, and led the two of them in a stumbling dance away from the fire and the danger.

Terrible sounds surrounded them, like an animal crying out in pain, and it was only when she caught his hair and yanked it hard enough to draw his head back and when she pressed her mouth to his and swallowed the din, only then did he realize the sounds came from him.

He was crying, great choking sobs that tore him in two, because he was so grateful, so damned grateful.

"Catherine," he whispered, and kissed her with all he was, with passion and dominion. She was his. *His.* And she was safe, here in his arms. He kissed her as though there was no one else there, as though he was buried inside her, as though they were not here on the vast lawn with the fire at their back, its monstrous roar filling their senses.

He kissed her as though he was a drowning man and she was air.

"I could not save you." His chest rose and fell with harsh, gasping breaths. "I could not see how to save you."

"I found a way to save myself," she said and kissed him, then kissed him again.

"How?"

"Susan Parker saved me."

He thought then that she was as addled as he. "Susan Parker is dead."

"I know, and I am sorry for it. I shall be sorry for the rest of my days. But she saved me. The first night I came to Cairncroft, she accidentally gave me a master key for any room in this wing. I had it in my pocket. It set me free."

Her words made no sense to him and he did not care. She was here in his arms, and she was alive.

"I thought I had lost you. I thought you were gone," he said. "I thought—"

Then he only kissed her again because she knew what he had thought.

She eased away and drew a deep breath, cradling his face in her hands before continuing in the tone he recalled from the very first time he heard her speak, her enunciation clean and crisp, her dusky pink lips forming consonants and vowels with perfect elocution. "What sort of wife would I be if I deserted you in your time of need?"

The reflection of the raging flames turned her skin to gold and her hair to copper. In all his wretched life, he had never dared dream that he might find love. That he might find peace from the demons of his past. How was he to know they would come twined together, one and the same?

"What sort of . . . wife, indeed," he murmured.

"Gabriel St. Aubyn, will you marry me?"

"Tell me you love me," he said.

"I love you."

"Then, yes, Catherine Weston, I will marry you."

Leaning close, he kissed her, and she clung to him and kissed him back and he could taste smoke and ash and love on her lips. He thought it the sweetest flavor he had ever known.

Epilogue

Gabriel sat across from the window, the draperies pulled back to reveal distant mountains. The Alps. He and Catherine had been traveling for nearly a year now, yet he felt more than ever before in his life that he had a home.

His fingers closed around the letter from Sebastian that had arrived that morning. His cousin had offered to stay and oversee the rebuilding of Cairncroft after that terrible night. Gabriel had accepted his offer. He could not bear to be there. Perhaps never again.

The servants had all escaped the fire. None were hurt. He was grateful for that. But his twin had not been so fortunate, nor had his cousin Madeline. They had succumbed to the smoke, their charred bodies found clinging to each other in the remnants of the tunnels. He had yet to fully accept how he felt about that—both grief and relief, and a bit of guilt for both.

Sunlight streamed through the panes to paint a swath across Catherine's bowed form. She was on her knees, head bowed, the dark curtain of her hair falling forward to hide her face. Her feet were wrapped in two pairs of his stockings. She said they kept her warmer than her own.

The rest of her was wrapped in his shirt. He could not see how that kept her warm at all, for it gaped and allowed him wondrous glimpses of skin. Now, a bare shoulder, then a rosy-tipped breast, then the sweet curve of her collarbone as she dipped and bent and moved her hands.

A cold wind swirled through the open window, and Gabriel sipped his coffee, thinking that this weather was coffee weather. The chill in the air made the flavor better, richer, more wondrous on his tongue.

She had done this, awakened in him the understanding of the difference between simply drinking his coffee, and *enjoying* it.

Catherine made a sound of dismay as the wind caught the edge of the map she had smoothed out before her on the floor. She lunged for the corner and slapped her palm flat, offering him a truly magnificent view of her round, unclad backside, the tail of his shirt sliding over porcelain-pale skin.

His fingers twitched.

She turned her head and looked at him, her eyes coffee dark, framed in thick brown lashes, very long, very straight. And he thought she saw through him, clear to his tarnished soul.

No, not thought it. *Knew* it.

And she loved him despite what she saw.

She smiled at him, and his breath caught.

"Catherine?"

"Mmm?" She crawled across the floor toward him, prowling on all fours, sinuous and graceful.

"I love you, Catherine St. Aubyn."

"Yes. You do." Lifting her head, she tossed a heavy curl off her forehead and smiled up at him. She crawled up his body, pausing to press a kiss to his chest, then climbing to his lips.

Opening her mouth on his, she kissed him and then rocked back on her heels as he made to draw her close.

She wrinkled her nose and laughed. "You taste like coffee."

He loved the sound of her voice, cool and cultured and controlled. Except when he made love to her. Then she was anything but controlled.

Offering her the cup, he said, "Have a sip. Then we'll both taste like coffee. A perfect match."

"We are already that." But she leaned in, took a sip as he tipped the cup to her lips. She held it a moment without swallowing, then lowered her head to his lap and took him in her mouth.

He hissed and rocked his hips toward her, the warmth of her mouth and the coffee just shy of too hot, thrilling and luscious and more than decadent. She teased him until he had no desire to be teased any more, and with a chest-deep growl he rolled her beneath him on the thick carpet and made love to her there in the bright strip of sunlight that fell across them both.

Later, much later, he asked, "Where do we go next, Catherine? Italy? Spain?"—he paused, willing to do even this if it would please her—"Home?"

She glanced at the map she had been poring over earlier. The wind had caught it and blown it into the corner. Then she looked back at him and rested her open palm on his cheek, her eyes shimmering with all the love in her soul.

"Home, Gabriel?" She pressed her lips to his. "I am with you, and so I am home."